MW00929145

Death

By A

Dark Horse

Enjoy the Adventure!

[signature]

DEATH
BY A
DARK HORSE

SUSAN SCHREYER

WHITEHORSE MOUNTAIN PRESS

OTHER BOOKS BY SUSAN SCHREYER

Death by a Dark Horse

Levels of Deception

An Error in Judgment

BushWhacked

Shooting to Kill

"Death By A Dark Horse"

Copyright © 2010 by Susan Schreyer
®Susan Schreyer
www.susanschreyer.com

First Edition 2010

All rights reserved, including the right of reproduction in whole or
part in any format. No part may be reproduced without prior
written permission, except in the case of brief quotations embodied
in critical articles or reviews.

This book is a work of fiction. Characters, incidents, and dialog are
drawn from the author's imagination. Any resemblance to actual
persons or events is coincidental, except in instances where
permission has been granted.

Cover design by Tracy Hayes
www.pastiche-studios.com
Cover photograph by Susan Schreyer

FOR

EDDIE

Acknowledgments

Writing may be a solo endeavor, but turning a raw manuscript into a polished book is not. I have many people to thank for their contributions to turning my humble effort into a book I am proud of. These are but some of the individuals from whom I have drawn inspiration, knowledge and encouragement.

Lisa Stowe, a talented writer and editor, supplied the first round of edits and the first round of encouragement. She remains a valued friend and resource.

Judy Morrison, my co-president of the Puget Sound Chapter of Sisters in Crime, also provided valuable insights and encouragement.

The brilliant editing of Chris Roerden taught me much, as did the equally brilliant Mary Buckham.

Lisa Harris and Jessica Miller, long suffering critique partners both, and true fans of both Thea and Blackie deserve many thanks for all they have done.

Likewise, Larry Karp and Jane Isenberg and the other members of my Puget Sound Chapter of SinC have my eternal gratitude, along with the members of O-Pen.

And where would I be without the Guppy Chapter of Sisters in Crime? You have all taught me more than you can ever know, and provided the kind of support every writer deserves to have. I am forever in the debt of each and every one of you.

Last, but never least, I thank my husband Jeff and our two children Arianne and Ford. I may never have had the nerve to begin if not for you.

Love you all,

Susan

Chapter One

It shouldn't be hard to find an eleven-hundred-pound horse -- particularly when looking in the places I normally find my sixteen-two hand, dark bay, Hanoverian gelding. The pinto in Blackie's usual paddock at Copper Creek Equestrian Center was not my Blackie. Neither were any of the other blue, green, or plaid-blanketed chestnuts, bays, or grays. In each white-railed turn-out along the south edge of the huge equestrian center's acreage in Snohomish, Washington, a scant hour north of Seattle, contented horses had their noses deep in their breakfast hay.

In contrast, I was fast losing my calm. "Contented" wasn't even orbiting nearby.

I pushed back the cuff of my parka and consulted my watch. Eight twenty-three. Not an unusual time for me to want to school my dressage horse, even on a Sunday. Blackie should still be in his stall at this hour. But I'd just come from the barn he lived in. The stall had been cleaned, re-bedded, and water buckets filled, and he clearly wasn't there.

I rubbed at the same headache I'd gone to bed with last night, which had stuck around to greet me this morning.

Dammit, why is it so impossible for those guys to tell you when they change the schedule? In all fairness, Eric, the barn manager, and Miguel, his assistant, always did. It was Jorge, Miguel's nineteen-year-old son who frequently forgot to relay information. *And dammit, this time you're not going to smile and tell him it's okay.*

I turned away from the paddocks and scanned the big outdoor arena. Two lessons were in progress. In the round-pen a woman I knew well enough to chat with was free-lungeing her Quarter Horse gelding, or having problems catching him. Her rigid shoulders and tightfisted grip on the lead rope dangling at her side made me think it was the later. Closer, a teenager I recognized as being part of Blackie's "fan club" led a school horse toward the Lesson Barn. The animal didn't seem dirty, but you'd have thought he was caked with mud by the way the girl kept side-stepping when he got too close. I set off at a quick walk. She must have seen my horse. Today, more than ever, I needed the sanity and perspective I gained from my daily rides, as well as the simple, warm contact with Blackie. I'd have come here last night if it hadn't been nearly midnight by the time I'd gotten home. What started out as a formal dinner-date with my boyfriend Jonathan and his parents had turned into a disaster.

"Hey, excuse me!" I'd forgotten her name. "Have you seen Blackie?"

The teenager took an extra step before she stopped and turned wide eyes in my direction. She blinked a couple of times, then her expression cleared and she smiled.

"Oh, you're Blackie's mom, aren't you? Terry..?"

"Thea," I corrected. "Thea Campbell."

"Duh. Right. Thea. Nope. Haven't seen him. He's not in his stall. I checked, 'cuz I've got a carrot for him." Her horse's ears pricked at the word "carrot," but he seemed otherwise uninspired. "He's around here somewhere. Miguel or Eric must have moved him. But," her brow scrunched. "I saw Jorge and he said you wouldn't be here today."

Now *that* was peculiar. I shrugged it off and thanked her. She dragged at her horse's lead, and the animal allowed his stubby neck to be stretched as far as it was ever likely to go before he gave in and plodded along after her, his metal shoes scuffing rather than clopping on the asphalt path.

I set off to check the other paddocks on the west side of the property. The route I chose took me past the Copper Creek office where a bright yellow Kawasaki Ninja 650R motorcycle was parked near the door. It looked like my younger sister Juliet was here. Odd. She's the office manager for Delores Salatini, the stable's owner, but she only works on Sundays when there's a horse show. During the week she schedules lessons for the equestrian center's school program and deals with the many people who board their horses here in addition to her office-type duties. A small spike of conscience caused me to do a quick rummage through my mental files. Had I forgotten to do something for Copper Creek, my biggest client? I ticked through the accounting jobs I was contracted for. No, I was okay. Perhaps Juliet was catching up on something that didn't involve me. I'd double check after I found Blackie and rode.

A chilly gust of April wind blew my parka open and chased the warmth away from my body. Without slacking my step, I worked to close it, but the zipper wouldn't catch. I struggled with it as I cut across the gravel parking lot, crowded, even this early, with the cars of students and people like me who needed their daily fix of horse-contact.

Half way to the west-side paddocks the slow crunching of car tires on gravel caused me to step to my right. A black Nissan Z eased alongside, and the smooth whisper of the passenger-side window lowering caught my attention.

"Hey, BC! Thea!"

I bent slightly to see the driver through the open window. Greg Marshall. I should have known. Although I'm an accountant, no one else calls me BC -- Bean Counter. How original. He hadn't called me that last night, but then he hadn't been sober, either. I didn't want to talk to him right now. I wanted to find my horse. I wanted to forget last night. If I could forget both him and Jonathan that would be okay, too.

"Hi, Greg." I kept walking.

He kept pace with his car. "Hang on a sec."

My shoulders sagged. I stopped and looked in the window again.

He appeared very Abercrombie & Fitch casual this morning, instead of the GQ businessman of last night. He flashed his ever-handy thousand-watt smile. I flashed a forty-watt one back. Then my gaze dropped to the passenger seat of his spotless Z. It overflowed with red roses. Hastily, I returned my attention to my jacket's balky zipper, hoping I'd jumped to the wrong conclusion. The relentless pain in my head tightened up a notch. He needed to run along now.

"Beautiful day," he said.

I turned the urge to roll my eyes into a glance at the cloud layer. "About time for some rain, though." Okay, enough of this. The pointed look I meant to toss at him got sidetracked by the roses again. He laughed softly and I felt myself flush.

"Don't worry." The teasing smile was still there. "They're for Valerie."

Thank God. "They're stunning. She'll love them."

He held my gaze for a fraction of a moment. The intensity of his smile flickered, like a kid waiting for a much anticipated event, but who didn't want to act overexcited and uncool. "They're, um, to go with this." He leaned across the passenger seat and I caught the spicy scent of his expensive cologne through the open window. From the glove compartment he produced a small, light-blue box tied with a white satin ribbon.

A Tiffany & Company box.

"Oh. Nice."

Jonathan, my boyfriend, had given me one like it last Valentine's Day. I'd been sick with apprehension until I discovered the tasteful pearl earrings instead of a diamond ring I would have handed right back. I doubted Greg's box held earrings of any kind. He's a financial planner, so I expected the box held an investment -- the kind Valerie would wear on her left hand. Why was he showing all this to me?

Greg's smile turned apologetic. "Listen, about last night...." His words glued me to his gaze. "I'm kicking myself for my behavior. All the traveling and meetings wore me out. I wasn't keeping track of the number of beers I'd had. Forgive me?"

Kicking himself? He could have chosen better words. Well, fine. "Don't worry about it. I've had to fight off worse." I aligned my zipper again and yanked. No luck. Was he really afraid I'd taken his sloppily executed, unasked-for kiss as a serious invitation? Idiot. I started walking, again, but the car rolled along beside me. I stopped. What now? I slid a look at him.

"Hey...." He hung his head, and half pouted. Despite knowing the remorse was fake I couldn't hold down a tiny chuckle, and shook my head when it snuck out. He should have known better than to worry. I knew my five-foot-two-inch self was no competition for Valerie. Leggy and graceful, she was the personification of the elegant dressage rider. Women either envied or hated her. Men fell over each other to get next to her. And that's before taking into consideration her net worth.

"Thanks," he said, giving me a you're-a-pal wink. "I'm going to drive around back and surprise Valerie. I expect she's parked in her usual spot."

That would be the spot behind the New Barn, where her horse was stabled. Where no one was supposed to park -- including her. He wouldn't mention last night's blunder, would he? That'd just make my morning.

My head throbbed.

Now, not only did I have to find my horse, I had to avoid Valerie just in case he was dumb enough to say something. He was egotistical enough to twist things and brag that I'd been the one to make a pass at him.

"See you later." He lifted a hand in a casual salute. "Oh, the top half of your zipper-pull is up by your collar."

I shifted my focus. Huh. No wonder it wasn't working.

I wiggled my fingers good-bye and watched his car disappear around the corner of the Big Barn before continuing my trek to the paddocks. I hoped Valerie was at her gym instead of here at Copper Creek. Even if Greg kept his mouth shut I had good reason to avoid her. She never missed an opportunity to fire some salvo at me designed to point out her superiority.

I was perfectly aware of her superiority.

She was my age, twenty-nine, and had been long-listed for the last Olympic Dressage Team. It would surprise no one if on the next go-round she made the short-list. She had a long career ahead of her. Goody for her. Showing held no appeal for me, despite my famous uncle. Sure, I was several levels below her and I'd catch up eventually, but my goal was to be the best dressage rider I could. I had a fabulously talented horse I loved, and wanted only to do right by him. She could keep her competitions.

I dismissed Valerie from my thoughts. I had other, more important issues in my life. And, arriving at the west paddocks, eyes squinting against the pounding in my head, I could see I also had a long search ahead of me.

Blackie wasn't in any of these paddocks either.

When I got my hands on Jorge I was going to wring his neck. I turned around and strode back toward the Big Barn, gravel flying out from under the heels of my boots.

Ten minutes later I stood in the doorway of the last of the three barns, having checked the occupants of every stall. I had located neither Jorge nor Blackie. Jorge could be on break in the house, but Blackie....

It shouldn't be this hard to find an eleven-hundred-pound horse.

Chapter Two

I fought to hold back the knife edge of panic, ignored the numerous, pointed suggestions to walk, and hurried to the Copper Creek office. I was sure to find a reasonable explanation for my inability to locate my horse in the form of the equestrian center's owner, Delores Salatini, who was always in the office in the mornings regardless of the day of the week. My sister Juliet was there, too -- I'd seen her motorcycle. It was conceivable she would be able to help since she made it her business to know what everyone was doing all the time.

I nearly lost my grip on the office door's knob when I pulled it open, and didn't quite manage to get it closed behind me before I hauled myself to a stop inside the office. Delores sat at her old wooden teacher's desk, coffee mug raised halfway to her lips, and phone pressed against an ear.

"We seem to have a problem," she said into the handset, eyebrows hovering above her reading glasses. "I'll call you back." She hung up the phone, not once taking her eyes off me.

It took me a second to get words out. I was uncharacteristically out of breath for a short jog. "Where's Blackie? I can't find Blackie."

She leaned forward slightly, frowning. "Blackie?"

"Yes, Blackie. I can't find him. I've checked every barn, every stall, and every paddock." I steadied my breathing and glanced around the office. "Where's Juliet? I thought she'd be here since her bike is. Where's Eric? I haven't seen him this morning -- or Miguel."

Delores pushed away from her desk and grabbed her old down vest off the back of her chair. "It's Eric's day off. He does get them, you know. Miguel's on break. He's in charge of the barns today."

I spun to go. "He must be at the house."

"Wait for me." She hustled around her desk, pulling the vest over her flannel shirt.

We lost no time crossing the parking lot to the two-story white house where the staff -- except for Eric, Copper Creek's barn manager -- lived. Maria, Miguel's wife, answered our knock, purse over her arm, dressed for church. She greeted us with her customary warmth, but her smile vanished. She pressed a hand to her heart.

"There is something wrong, no?" she asked in heavily accented English.

Delores's chin jerked an affirmative. "I need to talk to Miguel --"

I edged forward, next to Delores. "I can't find my horse."

Maria's eyes grew twice their normal size. Her gaze darted from me to Delores. "Come in, come in!" She hustled through the tidy living room ahead of us. The staccato click of her heels on the hardwood floor punctuated her words. "¡Miguel! ¡Miguel! ¡Delores y Thea están aquí! ¡Miguel!"

I followed Delores into the living room, but she didn't sit. She stood with her shoulders drawn up, hands jammed into her vest pockets, mouth and eyes narrowed to mere slits. I'd never seen her look like this. Any hope I had that Miguel would be of help sank.

The big, mustachioed man emerged, yawning and rumpled, from the direction of the first floor bedroom. "¿Que *pasó?*" He didn't appear to notice Delores or me.

"Miguel, I can't find Blackie." My breath shook around the words, surprising me.

He turned toward us, a flush turning his normally dark complexion ruddy as he shoved his shirt tails into his pants. "You checked the paddocks?"

Unable to voice a word, I nodded. Oh God, I'd read Delores right. He didn't know where Blackie was.

"Yes, of course she did." Despite her severe expression, Delores's reply was no more brusque than usual.

All traces of sleep were gone from Miguel's expression. "I did not do his barn this morning. Jorge did. I will ask him." He dashed up the stairs, surprisingly agile for a man of his age and girth.

There was a pounding on an upstairs door then a conversation in breakneck, agitated Spanish that I couldn't follow. One pair of heavy footsteps crossed the floor and thudded a brisk beat down the stairs. Miguel returned to the living room, his bandito moustache in a fierce downward slant, and a deep furrow between his eyebrows. Before he could open his mouth Jorge's footsteps clattered down the stairs. He arrived with his boots mostly on, buttoning his jeans. His gaze flitted between Delores and me.

"Tell them." Miguel, arms folded high across his barrel chest, jerked his head at us.

Jorge licked his lips and swallowed. Maria echoed her husband's stance, but the accusing glare she aimed at her son had the edge only a mother is capable of honing. Jorge shrank under his parents' scrutiny, then forced his shoulders down and focused his worried gaze on me.

"Last night, about ten, when I was checking the barns I saw you drive off in a truck and horse trailer with Blackie. He had his head out the window and whinnied at me."

My arms dropped to my sides. I stared.

He hurried on. "At least I thought it was you, Thea. I figured someone forgot to tell me you were coming."

"No." I swallowed most of the word and it came out overly soft. This went beyond his usual goof-up. He should have known better than to let an unexpected rig go unchallenged. Even I knew it was one of Eric's rules. "I didn't take Blackie anywhere. Besides, I don't own a truck and trailer. You know that."

Maria's short, round frame vibrated with fury and her temper blew with a single exhale. "You men! You have let Thea's horse be stolen! The best horse in the barn, the one every professional horseman has wanted to buy, her Blackie who she loves with all her heart, and you let a thief drive off with him! I am ashamed to know you." Her eyes flashed from son to startled husband.

"But Mom—"

"None of your excuses. None! I am done with them."

Miguel opened his mouth to speak but, wisely, closed it again as she snapped a look at him.

"I must miss church because of your carelessness. How can I go to church when my husband and son cannot be trusted out of my sight? If you know what is good for you, you will ask the good Lord to forgive you. I wash my hair of you both!"

Miguel shifted uncomfortably and Jorge studied his boots. Maria's struggles with English usually drew teasing from her son. Not this time.

Then Jorge looked up and snapped his fingers. "The truck and trailer -- I can tell you what they looked like." His eager gaze swept all of us, and a thread of hope dragged me up from complete despair.

"Don't keep us waiting," Delores said.

He drew a quick breath. "The truck was new, a Ford F350, super-duty dually, silver, with a four-door crew cab."

At least he remembered the vehicle. But, everybody in Snohomish drives a truck. Half of them are gray, or grayish.

"I didn't get the license plate," he added, dejected. A beat later he brightened. "The trailer was a Sundowner goose-neck, same color as the truck, three-horse, with a camper in the front."

Hope surged. An expensive rig -- and familiar sounding. Delores's eyes narrowed and she shook her head once, but she was silent. Maybe I was wrong. Despair made a comeback.

"Well, that very tiny news could be helpful," Maria said, and sniffed disparagingly.

"I really screwed up, didn't I?" Jorge said, and pressed both hands to his head. "I should have stopped a rig I didn't recognize."

"We'll discuss that later." Delores tapped an index finger against her lips. "Did you see who was driving?"

"No. The truck was pulling around the corner of the Big Barn when I saw it so I just had a quick look at the rig."

Blackie was truly gone. I pulled in a shaky breath trying to control the tears. Nearly eleven hours -- he could be in California by now, or who knew where.

"I'm sorry, Thea. I --" Jorge's voice caught.

Delores put a hand on my shoulder.

"Did you let Valerie think you changed your mind about selling Blackie?"

I could only gape at her. Delores knew I'd never sell him.

"The rig Jorge described matches hers," she said.

I walked two steps and dropped into a chair. "No. Valerie? No. I never...." My words trailed away into disbelief. That didn't make any sense. I looked, again, at Delores. She nodded. I closed my dry mouth and straightened. Crap. Valerie offered to buy Blackie several times and for increasingly exorbitant amounts of money, although I'd made it clear he was not for sale at any price. But Valerie never believed me. To her, everything had a price.

I imagined the self-satisfied look on her face when she waltzed off with my horse in her trailer, and my initial anguish rebounded into rage. Not only could I handle this, but I would make that self-centered, miserable excuse for a human-being sorry she was ever born. Cold, clear purpose had me on my feet and in motion.

"Thea!" Delores barked.

"I'm going to Valerie's." I shot over my shoulder. "That bitch stole my horse!"

"Thea!" Delores's roar stopped me, and I turned to challenge her. She tossed her keys at me and I snatched them out of the air in a one-handed catch. "Take my truck and trailer. Jorge, help her hook up and go with her. I'll call the police and report the theft."

I ran across the parking lot to Delores's dark green Dodge Ram 3500, Jorge on my heels.

Damn. This was unbelievable, just plain effing unbelievable. How could she? Bitch.

Fifteen minutes later I stomped on the clutch and tried again to downshift without grinding the truck's gears. No success. The gnashing of metal on metal as the stick shift jerked and vibrated under my hand pissed me off even more.

"Goddammit." I tried to force it.

"Do you want me to drive, Thea?" Jorge's offer was his third.

"No." I found the gear and accelerated carefully.

I knew exactly where Valerie lived and where to look for my horse, having been there twice before over the past year. At the end of the summer she'd hosted an auction for the Puget Sound Sporthorse Breeders' Association, and on another occasion invited the local dressage club there to hold a special meeting.

"At least let me drive back. If we find Blackie at Valerie's your driving will sour him on getting in a trailer for the rest of his life."

I shot him a scowl. He was right, of course, but considering my frame of mind, he was lucky I didn't drop him off at the side of the road and tell him to walk home. A small portion of my mind, a fragment that still retained some semblance of reason, reminded me that it was Valerie I was angry with and not Jorge. I needed to keep my head if I was going to make sure she paid for this. The very first thing I'd do was call the police, if they weren't already there from Delores's phone call. Then, when they hauled Valerie away in handcuffs I'd load up Blackie and take him home. Then I'd get an attorney and sue her ass.

We approached the turn on to OK Mill Road and I eased the truck into second gear to negotiate the turn. The gears ground, again, and the truck bucked despite my efforts to finesse the clutch. Jorge slouched in his seat and covered his face with his hands. I dismissed his silent critique, turning my attention back to self-involved Valerie. Could she really be so stupid as to steal my horse? Arrogance was normal for her, but she'd made quite a leap from conceit to criminal, and in one greedy move destroyed her chances to ride in the Olympics.

I downshifted to negotiate the curve where OK Mill became Carpenter Road, flinching as the gears ground -- again. Thankfully, we were almost there. Just a little farther up this twisty, gear-shifting excuse for a road before we arrived at Valerie's and rescued Blackie.

The steep, sharp curve ahead required another downshift. I shoved the clutch to the floor, found second gear, and eased my foot onto the accelerator. Success. My shoulders dropped and I exhaled at the exact moment a silver sedan hurtled around the blind curve, straddling the centerline. I jumped on the brake and twisted the wheel, heading for the nonexistent shoulder. Too late, I remembered the clutch. The truck stalled, lurching to a stop. I braced for the impact. The car missed us by inches.

I exhaled in a rush, too surprised and relieved to cuss out the other driver. Jorge managed for me.

"Shit! Bitch!" He spun against his shoulder harness trying to get a look at the other car. "How did Valerie know we were coming? That was her BMW."

"It wasn't Valerie." I shoved the clutch in, pushed the stick into neutral, and turned the key in the ignition. The engine roared back to life. The image of the other driver was seared into my retina. I'd been unable to blink. "Just looked like Valerie's car. I saw the driver. It was a man. He might have been able to see the damn road if he'd taken off the damn sunglasses."

I put the truck back into gear and it bucked as I let the clutch out. Yeah, well, my knees were still shaking. Jorge was silent, but he wasn't slouching in his seat anymore, and he'd taken off his own sunglasses.

In less than a mile I turned the truck and trailer onto Valerie's asphalt driveway, managed to keep the gears from grinding, and carefully plied the turns up the wooded hillside. A quarter mile later we emerged onto the edge of a twenty-two-acre manicured meadow, made more impressive by its contrast with the wild forest we'd just driven through. The house, a huge old Victorian-type farmhouse, painted yellow and trimmed in white and blue gingerbread, was positioned perfectly to grab one's attention regardless of the availability of a view. And on a clear day the view of the Cascade Mountains to the east was spectacular.

"Wow," Jorge said, then slid me a nervous glance.

"Get over it," I muttered between clenched teeth.

The only vehicle in sight was Valerie's BMW parked in front of the house. Good. She was home, and I was right -- her's hadn't been the car I'd nearly flattened. A single-minded calm settled over me. I was so going to nail her.

I didn't drive to the house, but turned onto a secondary, gravel driveway and steered Delores's rig to the barn -- a miniature version of the house -- around in back. I wanted to be able to load my horse without wasting time. And I needed to make sure Blackie was there before I knocked on Valerie's door.

For the first time since leaving Copper Creek, I had a moment of gut-wrenching doubt. What if Blackie wasn't there? How was I going to find him? Even sitting, my legs lost strength and I gripped the wheel tighter to keep my hands from shaking.

But as we rounded the old Victorian I saw my dark bay horse out in one of the large pastures, happily munching rich grass. He lifted his head and whinnied loudly before returning to graze. I swung my arm to point, nearly punching Jorge in the face with my exuberance.

"There he is. Thank God. I hope he's all right." Then, with the same speed the elation had swept me when seeing my horse, anger blew in full force. "Dammit, I could rip her a new one. What the hell does she think she's doing?

Jorge rolled wide eyes at me, and was silent.

I slammed the truck to a stop, jumped out, and ran up to the house. I hammered on the back door.

No one answered. She had to be hiding.

"I've come to take my horse back," I yelled. "I suggest you get your sorry ass out here and explain why I shouldn't call the police."

Still no answer. I stalked back to the truck and grabbed my cell phone.

"I'm calling the cops," I shouted at the house.

"Delores already --" Jorge clamped his lips together.

"I'm calling again," I said.

Jorge nodded, his large, unblinking brown eyes reminding me of a horse ready to bolt.

Blackie ambled to the white rail fence near the truck and watched me with ears pricked in friendly interest. I jogged to where he stood. He stretched his head and neck toward me, and I took his big dark face between my hands, kissed his velvet nose, then rubbed the large splotch of white on his forehead.

"Are you okay, buddy? We're going home. I won't let anyone drive off with you again. I'm so sorry." I kissed his nose once more, and gave him a cursory nose-to-toes examination, checking for any obvious signs of injury. He looked okay. I stroked his neck.

"Come on, Blackie. Gate. Let's go home." He heaved a sigh

and moved off in the direction of the barn. The gate to this pasture was on the other side of it.

I grabbed a halter and lead rope out of the truck, and dialed 9-1-1. As I walked I explained the situation to the operator and gave her Valerie's address.

"Has the horse been injured or abused in any way?" she asked.

"Not that I can tell right now, but I haven't had a chance to thoroughly check him." I reached the gate, my attention divided between managing the latch and the phone call. "I'm - -" I stopped. Something was wrong. Where was Blackie?

The wind shifted, blowing my hair across my eyes. With my hands otherwise occupied, I turned my face into the breeze to clear my vision and inhaled a stench so dense it had weight.

A thousand spiders crawled up my spine.

Chapter Three

Then I saw her. I exhaled over and over without inhaling. My feet would not obey my brain's demand to flee. My throat seized and the rush of blood in my ears obliterated every sound except a thin, high pitched wail. It came from me.

"Ma'am? Ma'am? Hello? Are you still there?"

I forced the wail into words. "I ... Oh, God, she's dead!" Then I gagged on my next breath.

"Who's dead, ma'am?"

Valerie. It had to be Valerie sprawled a few feet away. Every detail of her body and clothing stood out as though magnified. One half of her once-beautiful face was crushed, her skin sickly gray, wax-like. Blood matted her blond hair. Blue eyes, surrounded by black, mascaraed lashes stared, vacant. Her jaw was slack and oddly bent. Flies crawled with jerky little movements over the gaping wound, the surface of her eyes and, with wings suddenly buzzing, darted in and out of her open mouth, pausing on lips that were pink only where lipstick remained.

My stomach heaved and I fought to keep my breakfast from exiting with my words. "It's Valerie ... oh my God, it's Valerie."

"Valerie who, ma'am?"

"Parsons. Valerie Parsons." My hand jerked, banging the phone against my ear. I heaved again and frantically swallowed down bile.

"Did you take her pulse? Do you want to try to rouse her? Do CPR?"

I shook my head to each question unable to look away. "No!" The word was half shouted, half begged. "She's ... she's got blood, and flies ... her head ... oh, dear God, the smell."

"I have an ambulance and patrol car in route. Don't touch anything and don't leave the scene." The calm in the operator's voice was finally reaching me. I clung to her instructions. "Is anyone with you?"

"Yes." I tried to steady my voice to match hers.

"Okay," she continued, "do you have somewhere safe you can go to, like your vehicle?"

"Yes."

"All right now, stay calm. I'll remain on the line with you until the police arrive. Go to your vehicle and wait. They're on their way."

Wasting no time, I spun, collided with a live body, and screamed. My brain registered "Jorge" as he leapt away from me. His gaze, however, never moved from the place past my shoulder where Valerie lay.

"Ma'am?" It was the operator's firm voice. "Are you --?"

"Fine, I'm fine -- my friend -- I ran into him. I'm okay."

"Are you certain there's not a problem with him?"

"Yes, yes, I'm sure." I was gaining some control now that my back was to Valerie's body. "It's okay. I'm okay. We're going to the truck now."

Jorge tripped over himself as he continued to back away. I lunged and grabbed his arm to steady him. He clutched at mine. His earlier, confident macho attitude had vanished.

"What -- was -- is --?"

"Yes," I said. "Don't look, Jorge. Don't look!" I pushed him toward the truck.

He obeyed my command with alacrity, and dragged me

with him, speaking rapidly in English punctuated with Spanish. The operator spoke to me at the same time, and I couldn't figure out what either one said. We reached the truck and I gave up trying to listen.

"Ma'am?" I said into the phone. "Talk to my friend, please, he's kind of upset."

I handed the phone to Jorge, dropped the truck's tailgate, and hoisted myself up. The cold metal bit through my riding pants. Muscles from my thighs to my shoulders clenched in response. A chill breeze blew through my short hair and around my neck. I turned my collar up, and pulled the jacket tighter around me. It didn't help.

Jorge hopped up next to me, still on the phone, but I wasn't listening. The situation was too surreal. If anyone had suggested to me five minutes ago that Valerie might be dead I'd have laughed. I snuck a look in the direction of her body. My shoulders eased down when I couldn't see her from where I sat.

Blackie turned from where he had stopped and went back to grazing. Thank God he seemed undisturbed. Then an awful, unwelcomed thought worked its way front and center.

Could my gentle, kind horse have done this awful thing?

No. How could I even consider such a question? Yet that's exactly what it looked like.

I watched him graze, silently begging him to be innocent. As if sensing my distress, he raised his head and, with his ears pricked at me, whinnied softly. A lump grew in my throat. Of course he hadn't killed her.

I knew why Valerie wanted my horse. Even at the tender age of seven my sixteen-and-a-half hand Hanoverian gelding finds the rigors of dressage easy. He applies himself to his job with cheerful cooperation. His disposition makes him a joy to work with, and he loves any and all human company. He would not have hurt her. In fact, anyone who makes eye contact with him is his new best friend. On the rare occasion when someone chooses to ignore him he follows their every move with those big, intelligent, brown eyes until he breaks through their indifference. The memory of his successful use of that tactic pulled me into a calmer frame of mind. He's sweet and handsome, and if he were a man I'd date him. Heck, I trust him enough to marry him.

Blackie already had his own groupies among the young teenagers who rode at Copper Creek. During training sessions we often had an audience, and my incorrigible showoff always put in extra effort for any noises of appreciation. Actual dressage shows, however, are not something I'm particularly inclined to do, and Valerie fired that spit-ball at me every chance she got.

According to her, I did not deserve a horse like Blackie. I should, in her opinion, admit my massive shortcomings and sell him to her. But Blackie was not for sale. Not to anyone. At least her constant pressure was no longer a worry.

The wail of sirens announced the arrival of the first Snohomish County Sheriff's car. Relief welled up, mixed with a good dose of anxiety. This ordeal was not over.

The approaching noise and sudden appearance of flashing lights from the white and green Crown Victoria sent Blackie, in true equine fashion, fleeing to the far end of the pasture. Jorge handed my cell phone back to me as a brown-uniformed deputy swung out of his patrol car and walked purposefully toward us, one hand resting on his utility belt near his holstered gun. I pointed in the direction of Valerie's body without speaking or getting off the truck's tailgate. The deputy nodded sharply and told us to stay put. Someone would talk to us soon. I shivered.

The ambulance lumbered into view not thirty seconds later, with its own impressive display of flashing strobes and pulsing noise. The deputy waved an arm directing them to a spot close to the barn. Before the ambulance crew finished unloading their gurney, another vehicle roared around the side of the house, brakes rasping a squeal as it stopped. Eric's car. Both doors flew open. Delores popped from the driver's side and jogged toward us. Eric, Delores's barn manager, followed at a quick walk.

"I called right after I hung up from the 9-1-1 operator," Jorge said, heading off my question.

I could have hugged him. And I thought he'd spent all those "anytime minutes" on my phone with the operator. I sat up a little straighter. *Time to get a grip, Thea.*

"You look like hell, missy," Delores said.

I drew a breath, but was unable to speak. Cripes. I was going to cry.

Delores looked away, casting a critical eye on Jorge. "You don't look much better. I see you found Blackie."

"Yeah, among other things," Jorge said.

Delores shook her head and strode off toward the barn and the deputy, with an extremely worried-looking Eric on her heels.

"I see she found Mr. Tall-dark-and-got-no-time-for-my-buds," Jorge said, watching Eric's back.

"Jorge!" His snippy tone surprised my voice into use. Everyone liked Eric. I thought they were friends, despite Eric being his boss and a good ten years older.

Two more Snohomish County Sheriff's cars arrived, diverting my attention. Vehicles now clogged the once spacious area around the barn. How was I going to get the truck and trailer turned around? Delores could manage it. Or Eric. Jorge could probably do a better job of it than I could. I wanted to take Blackie and leave. Now. Did we have to wait to be dismissed? I glanced at Jorge. He was hunched over, elbows on his knees and swinging his feet while he watched the official activity. Damn. Even he knew we were going to have to wait. And we were probably going to have to give statements to someone. Double damn. I huddled deeper into my jacket, shivering again, and desperate for a distraction. Jorge's earlier comment about Eric was preferable to thinking about Valerie's body.

"What's with the attitude?" I asked, teeth chattering. "I

thought you and Eric were friends."

"We are. Sorry. I should be glad he's got himself a lady, right? Guess I'm just jealous. Your sister's too old for me anyway, but she's mighty fine."

My eyes widened and I snorted. Wishful thinking, kid. Yeah, Juliet was a "major babe," and at twenty-three, too old for Jorge, who'd just turned nineteen. I wondered who .... "Who's Eric dating?"

Jorge turned his attention from the police cars and leaned slightly away from me as his eyebrows shot up. "Juliet. You mean you didn't know?"

"Juliet? My sister, Juliet?" Not possible. It was like trying to picture Mr. Darcy with Lucy Ricardo. Cripes. I was looking for a distraction, not another problem. What was going on here? I always knew who my little sister was dating. She regaled me with each new hunky guy's sterling qualities. She'd said nothing about Eric.

"Yeah. You know any others? It amazes me a hot woman like her would be interested in a boy scout like Eric. Didn't the last guy she was going with climb the outside of the Space Needle? Man, extreme to the max."

I stared at Jorge, speechless for half a moment. "The idiot got arrested before he went twenty feet."

"Well, still ...." Jorge shrugged and swung a leg.

Never mind Juliet and her heretofore poor choices in men. Even though Eric was a "boy scout" there wasn't a woman on the planet who didn't know what my sister saw in him. But Eric -- what was he thinking?

I turned my unseeing gaze to the police cars. Juliet was not making me happy right now. She'd just added secret-keeping to her recent spate of unreliability. I'd called her to come pick me up after last night's disastrous date with my now-likely-ex-boyfriend, but she never showed.

I'd sat in a popular tavern in downtown Seattle for an hour, which was where I'd run into Greg. He'd never paid much attention to me in the past, and really wasn't that obnoxious until right before I'd left. I hadn't expected the kiss. But now I couldn't help feeling sorry for him. When he heard about Valerie he was going to feel exponentially worse about last night's indiscretion.

This was insane. Every train of thought was leading me back to Valerie.

"I need to get statements from both of you." An officer with aviator sunglasses and shaved head startled me out of my brooding. He stood with his feet well apart, and chest thrown out, holding a large notebook against one hip and his fist on the other. He looked from me to Jorge, lips compressed into a frown. "Which one of you found the body?"

"I did." The body, not Valerie or Miss Parsons. Two words reduced her to the status of road kill. Just how many bodies did baldy see on a daily basis? Didn't he feel any compassion at all?

"Well," he said, flipping open his notebook, "let's start with you. Let's have your driver's license."

I retrieved my purse from the front seat of the truck and fumbled through my wallet for my license. I handed it to his royal highness, and waited while he copied the information. He took Jorge's when he was done with mine, then slid a couple of clipboards out from under the notebook and shoved them at us.

"Write what happened," he said, and left to join his buddies.

I tried the pen that came with my clipboard, scribbled with it to get some ink to flow, then rifled through my purse for one that worked. Then I settled in and wrote diligently, but when I got to the part where I'd entered the pasture I caught my breath and stopped writing. I hadn't picked up on this detail earlier -- this important detail. Too important to skim over. The chain securing the gate to the fence post was fastened all wrong. The chain that held the gate closed was the loose type. Many other people use the same simple set up. It loops around the fence post and the upright on the gate, attaching to itself with a snap. This is impossible for a horse to unfasten, but easy for a human. I had unsnapped it, gone through, then slid the chain so I could secure the gate from the inside of the pasture. It was habit -- a routine everyone does to make sure no horses escape out the gate. Valerie would have done the same. She could not have been the last one to close the gate.

Blackie had not killed Valerie.

The sound of shod hoof steps on gravel drew my attention. The ambulance crew scattered giving more than adequate room for Delores to pass with Blackie. The men kept watch as she led him into the barn.

This wasn't good. People were already jumping to conclusions. I hopped off the tailgate and, clipboard in hand, jogged toward the deputies.

"Excuse me," I said, approaching the bald deputy. He lounged against his car, arms crossed over his chest, watching what was going on in the vicinity of "the body." He rocked upright and hooked his thumbs on his utility belt.

"Yeah?"

"The gate -- the chain was fastened on the outside when I got here."

"So?"

"So, I think Valerie would have fastened it on the inside when she went into the pasture."

His chin lowered as he pulled off his sunglasses and squinted at me. "What's your question?"

"I think it's important. I don't think --"

"Just put what happened in your statement. Not what you think happened."

"It's important I let someone know --"

"Write exactly what you remember." He put his glasses back on and returned to leaning on his car.

I lifted my chin. "Okay," I said, but he ignored me. I could prove Blackie wasn't responsible for Valerie's death, but he obviously wasn't the right person to talk to. Never mind the fact I could save them all a lot of trouble.

I stalked back to the truck and again hoisted my butt onto the icy cold tailgate. Jorge, finished with his paperwork, wandered around, hands in his pockets, kicking at an occasional piece of gravel. I applied myself to writing every detail of my account and was still at it when the truck was jostled. I looked up. Eric, his complexion an unhealthy shade of green, had parked his butt against the fender and was rubbing his eyes with the thumb and index finger of one hand.

"Delores put Blackie in a stall," he said, obviously confident I was listening. "He's too curious about all the people."

That was tactful of him. "We need to take Blackie home." He didn't answer. I cleared my throat. "Eric," I said louder. "We need to take Blackie home. Okay?"

He nodded, without looking at me. Was he just responding to the sound of my voice?

"As soon as I'm done with my statement, let's load him up and take him home. Eric, are you listening?"

"Yeah, I heard you." He rubbed his hands over his face then crossed his arms and stared at the ground.

I gritted my teeth and took a breath. *No, forget it. Finish your statement, it's more important. You won't be able to leave until it's done anyway.*

I went back to my task, but Jorge's fiddling with the trailer hitch, the lights, and the condition of the paint on the trailer was distracting. I climbed into the truck's cab to complete my lengthy narrative.

Once done, I sought out the deputy and handed him the clipboard. He skimmed it and grunted.

"I'll need you both to come down to the station and sign your statements when we've got them ready. Looks like an accident. That horse of hers nailed her pretty good." He shook his head in disgust. "Dangerous animals like him ought to be put down." He patted his holstered gun for emphasis.

"No!" This guy couldn't be serious. He was acting like he

wanted to shoot Blackie on the spot. "First of all, he's my horse, and secondly, I'll have you know he would never hurt anyone. Read what I wrote before you jump to conclusions, for God's sake."

I had his undivided attention. He reached for his notebook.

"Your horse, huh? Maybe you didn't notice, but he's the only animal in the field. That kind of narrows the list of suspects."

"If you'd read my statement, you'd realize how wrong you are." I swung toward Eric and Jorge. "Eric ...." My voice shook.

My friends strode over. Eric put a hand on my shoulder.

"Blackie never would have hurt her on purpose. He's a nice horse, very gentle."

Jorge nodded, and held the deputy's gaze when he looked at him.

"Not so gentle this time," the officer scoffed and hooked a thumb on his gun belt.

"No, you're wrong." I set my jaw. Maybe if I said it enough I'd convince him to listen.

"Look lady, uh, Miss Campbell --"

"No, you look. You have no evidence to accuse my horse of this."

Eric increased the pressure of his hand on my shoulder. I pulled away.

"Seems to me there's plenty of evidence lying a few yards over that way." The deputy whipped off his sunglasses and pointed them toward Valerie's body.

"You're jumping to conclusions."

"Not much jumping needs to be done to solve this one." His lip turned up in a sneer.

"You haven't even bothered to investigate. You're assuming."

"Thea --" Eric started.

I ignored him. The deputy needed convincing. "It's so easy

to blame my horse because he happens to be here. That'd sure save you a lot of paperwork, wouldn't it?" The officer's face glowed red. I wasn't done. "Even I noticed the way the gate was latched, and I told you about it. If you had any brains you'd realize --"

"That you could be making it up?" His eyes narrowed.

"You're accusing me of lying?" I nearly choked on the words.

"What's going on here?" Delores popped into the midst of our discussion.

"I think this young woman needs to come down to the station with me."

"You're Marty, aren't you?" she said to the officer. He nodded. "Now you just sit still for a minute."

His eyes widened as she turned to me. But I jumped in before she could utter a word.

"He thinks Blackie is responsible for Valerie's death." I glared at this sorry-excuse-for-a-deputy-Marty-person.

"And I think you need to come down to the station." Marty glared back.

"Fine," I snarled.

"What on earth for?" Delores asked. "You're only going to get more upset. Marty, she needs to go home. She's had a bad shock. You've got everyone's statements, you know where they live, there's nothing that can't wait until tomorrow." She took Marty's arm, patting it in a little-old-lady fashion, and steered him away from me. Looking over her shoulder, she caught Eric's eye and jerked her head toward the truck. Eric's hand closed around my upper arm, but I stood fast.

Marty jerked his arm out of Delores's grasp, leaned toward me, and jabbed a finger at my face. "We have laws about dangerous animals in this county, and the law is they don't live long after they've attacked a human. It's the responsible thing to do. You might want to think about that. Tomorrow morning. Sheriff's office. Both of you." He jabbed at Jorge, too.

I rose on my toes, sputtering, but Eric's grip tightened on my arm and he half carried me toward the truck. Marty's lip curled.

"You believe me, don't you, Eric? Jorge?" I asked when Eric finally let me go. Their support was more important right now than the humiliation of being dragged around like a puppy. "Blackie didn't kill her. They can't shoot him."

A squeal of tires silenced me and stopped Eric's answer. A black Nissan Z slid to a stop, spraying gravel. Greg catapulted out the door and barreled toward the deputies.

"Hey, what the hell's going on here?"

Two deputies stopped him, taking him by the arms, their voices too low for me to hear what they said.

"No!" Greg struggled to get past them, but they stopped him. "No!" He leaned toward the place where the ambulance crew was now working. "Valerie, no!"

His knees buckled and both deputies shifted, supporting him this time. They steered him toward one of the patrol cars. Delores, Eric, Jorge and I watched in silence. I glanced at Eric. His mouth was set in a thin line, his face pasty pale. Greg's keening sobs turned the chill morning air to ice.

"Eric," Delores said. He didn't respond, but continued to stare. "Eric!"

His dark eyes shifted to her.

"Take Thea and Jorge home. It's best if you all leave."

"But Blackie --" I began.

"Don't you worry, I'll take care of him."

"Don't let them hurt him. You heard that deputy."

"Don't worry," she repeated, cocking her head and firing a narrow look at me. "Go on, all three of you. I'll catch up with you later. Get out of here. Now."

Chapter Four

I had no choice but to trust my very capable friend. Eric, in his uncharacteristic mood, all but shoved Jorge and me into his car, demanded my cell phone, and made a quick call I paid no attention to. I had more important things to do -- like figure out how to save my horse.

On the short trip to my house I tested and rejected a thousand plans. *Hide him. Where? Run away. Impractical. A lawyer. Where do you find a lawyer to represent a horse? Delores will have ideas. So will Uncle Henry -- and you can depend on him and Aunt Vi. They're right here in town, not ten minutes away, like Delores. They'll help you figure out what to do next. Blackie didn't kill Valerie.*

The car slowed to a stop and Eric turned off the engine, distracting me from my tactical planning. We were in front of my old, Craftsman style cottage, and behind Juliet's motorcycle, angle-parked at the curb. Eric's call had been to my sister. The front door of my house opened and Juliet stepped onto my porch. Her sober expression contrasted with the layers of brightly colored tops she wore. She chewed her bottom lip as she watched me approach.

"You okay?" she asked as we put our arms around each other. The breeze lifted her long, golden-brown curls, and a few fragrant strands dropped across my face.

"Yeah." I hugged her tightly.

She released me, gave Jorge a quick hug, then moved to Eric. Her stiletto heeled boots put her close to his six-foot-plus height. His arms slid around her and one hand gathered her hair in a tight fist as he pressed her, hard, against him. His eyes shut and the hair by Juliet's ear stirred with his breath before he placed a soft kiss on her forehead. I'd never seen Eric so emotional.

I headed into the house, away from the awkwardness of the moment. The smell of freshly brewed coffee beckoned me to the kitchen.

"Eric and I just got back from breakfast when Jorge called Delores," Juliet said as we all settled at the big kitchen table with our coffee. "Miguel told me Valerie took Blackie and now she's dead. What happened? How'd she die?"

My shoulders tightened. "I don't know, but I can tell you one thing for sure. Blackie didn't kill her like that idiot deputy thinks."

Juliet's gray eyes widened. She started to speak, but stopped. Her hands dropped to her lap.

Eric looked quickly at Juliet. "It's possible he kicked out of excitement when she turned him loose, and got her by accident." He reached for her hands.

"Do you really think that's what happened?" Juliet almost whispered her question -- to Eric.

"No, of course not," I snapped.

"I don't know." Eric leaned back in his chair, closing his eyes. He let out a long breath before he continued. "Blackie usually hangs around the gate when you turn him out. That's your doing, Thea." He opened his eyes a slit and gave me a wry smile. "Blackie thinks everyone's his friend. I can't see him deliberately going after anyone."

"I'm sure Blackie didn't touch her," I said, unmoved by his attempt to soften his opinion. "Besides, I noticed something odd."

"Besides her being dead?" Jorge asked.

"I'm serious. Blackie didn't kill her, accidentally or otherwise. I'm sure of it. The gate was secured with the same chain and snap set-up as Copper Creek and Uncle Henry have. It was fastened on the outside of the fence, not the inside. Valerie would have fastened it on the inside if she was the last to close the gate."

"Not necessarily," Eric said. "Although I'll admit it would be easier."

"Oh, come on, Eric. If you were turning a horse out in a paddock would you take the trouble --"

"Did you tell the police?" Juliet asked.

"Yes, of course I did. He just told me to put it in my report." I took a big swig of coffee.

"I think the deputy just wanted to blame it on Blackie," Jorge said and drained his mug. "It's convenient."

At least Jorge backed me up. My arms relaxed a little. "I have to find a way to prove Blackie didn't kill Valerie. Otherwise they'll put him down." The silence pulled my attention up from the table top. Everyone looked as if they were holding their breath waiting for me to blow. I was under control. I wasn't crying or yelling. I was simply determined. I changed the subject. "Greg drove up right before we left Valerie's place."

"Oh no." Juliet grasped Eric's hand tightly in both of hers. "What happened?"

"It was awful. He was so upset. Two of the deputies tried to help him."

Juliet's lip trembled and she slid a quick look at Eric.

"I talked to him at Copper Creek earlier today before I knew Blackie was missing," I said. "He had flowers and a little Tiffany's box for Valerie."

Juliet jumped to her feet, grabbed the coffee pot and topped off everyone's mugs. She sniffed, but her hair hid her face from my view. I shook my head. Okay, it was sad, but it wasn't like Juliet to react like this. I poured a bit of creamer into my coffee and stirred it slowly. A cup of coffee in a crisis—the Northwest version of the British cup-of-tea-in-a-crisis. In fact, if we were across town in Aunt Vi and Uncle Henry's kitchen we would be drinking tea. Although they moved here to Snohomish when I was a kid, they maintained their English traditions. I guess we weren't so terribly removed from our roots -- just put our own spin on it.

"Anybody want lunch?" Juliet asked.

Eric's expression looked as sour as mine felt. Jorge was uncharacteristically unenthusiastic. Juliet sat.

A bit of sunshine found its way through the kitchen windows for a moment, and the white cabinet glowed crisp against the light blue walls. It was good to be home, and a relief to find Blackie, but the knot in my stomach would stay until I found a way to clear my horse.

Around the table, everyone had retreated into their own thoughts. For diversion, I opened Aunt Vi's copy of *Fine Gardening Magazine* I'd borrowed last week and counted the times the letter "e" appeared in the "Letter from the Editor" column.

The crash of my front door rocketing open sent my blood pressure spiking. Eric and Jorge leapt to their feet, chairs tipping wildly. Juliet jerked around to face the living room and froze, wide-eyed.

"Sorry!" Came Delores's raspy voice. "Where are you people?" The front door slammed shut.

Cripes. I let go of the lungful of air I'd hung on to for dear life.

"Kitchen," Juliet called, rolling her eyes and slumping back against her chair.

Eric and Jorge dropped into their chairs. Jorge groaned with relief.

"Oh good, coffee." Delores made for the coffee pot as she strode in.

"Is Blackie okay?" I tried not to insult her by sounding anxious. Her brief frown told me I hadn't quite pulled it off.

"Yes, he's fine." She took a mug out of the cabinet and poured what was left of the coffee into it. "What's for lunch? I'm getting a little wonky."

"I'll make some sandwiches." Juliet was on her feet and moving efficiently between the pantry and the fridge. I couldn't help but notice the liberal use she was making of the groceries I'd just bought. But she seemed glad for something to do, and at least wasn't packing them up to take home with her like she often did.

"Did you take Blackie back to Copper Creek?" I asked.

"No, the deputies decided it wouldn't be a good idea."

My heart stopped. "You didn't leave him there --"

"Settle down." Her steady look made me cringe. Of course she'd take care of my horse. "I took him over to your uncle's place. The deputies seemed to think that Henry might be able to handle him." She snorted a laugh.

I didn't have to ask whose idea that had been.

"Uncle Henry and Aunt Vi … you told them … are they …?"

"Upset? Of course. They'll be fine, though."

My heart made an effort to resume beating, but it was worried.

"Delores," Jorge said, "Thea noticed something interesting about the gate."

"Really?" She looked at me across the top of her coffee mug. "And you think it means Blackie didn't kill Valerie?"

"Yes, exactly. That was what I was trying to explain to that deputy."

A corner of her mouth twitched, and she took a swallow of coffee. I took the opportunity to explain what I believed the position of the latch on the gate meant. The explanation Marty wouldn't give me a chance to tell him.

Juliet brought the sandwiches to the table. Jorge eyed them and reached for one before she had a chance to set the plate down.

"Marty's not such a bad guy," Delores said, and raised an

eyebrow at me. She picked up half a ham and cheese and took a bite. "Excellent rye bread. Purdy's bakery?"

"Uh huh." I frowned.

"So you decided Valerie was murdered?"

"I guess it would have to be murder," I said, almost apologetic. Why couldn't this be easy? Find Blackie, take him home, and live happily ever after. I looked around the table. I don't think I was the only one who had failed to make the leap from "Blackie couldn't have done it" to "murder." Jorge had stopped chewing, a deep crease was between Eric's eyebrows, and Juliet was gnawing on her lip.

"Couldn't it have been that someone was with her, saw the accident happen and went to get help?" Delores's suggestion was possible, but not very.

"No." I sat up straighter. "Let's assume it was an accident like you said, why didn't the person stay there and call from the house or the barn? Why leave? Someone killed her."

Delores took a swallow of coffee and looked around the table. "If that's the case, who would want to kill her? I'm sure none of us will miss her, but I can't imagine anyone wanting to do her in because she was an annoying snob." She took a bite of her sandwich, and chewed for a moment. Her gaze settled on me. "Unless she did something unforgivable."

"You think *I* killed her because she took my horse? How can you suggest such a thing?" I leaned toward her. "I didn't even know Blackie was missing until this morning. You know that." My index finger rapped the table punctuating each of my last three words. "Besides, Jorge was with me when I found her." I sat back, crossing my arms.

"I know." Delores put her mug down with a thump. "I don't think you'd hurt a fly, much less kill Valerie. What I'm saying is, if the sheriff decides she was murdered they're going to be looking at you pretty closely. You had plenty of reason to be angry with her, and they may think it's motive enough to arrest you. If I were you, I'd be reaching for the phone and giving that lawyer boyfriend of yours a call."

I combed my fingers through my hair. Twice. "I, uh, I kind of broke up with him last night. Sort of."

"Already? Holy mackerel, girl." She reached for another half sandwich.

What did she mean "already"? Was there a relationship expiration date I hadn't gotten to yet? "It's been a long time coming and last night was...not good." I glared at Juliet to remind her she let me down, but it was Eric who blushed. "Calling him wouldn't be a good idea."

"What happened?" Delores asked. "I thought you were meeting his parents in Seattle at some fancy restaurant."

"We had a disagreement."

"Must have been some disagreement," my oh-so-helpful little sister commented. "You were practically in tears when you phoned, but you wouldn't tell me anything. Just, 'drop what you're doing and come get me.'" She dropped her chin and stared at me.

I now knew why she hadn't come when she knew how upset I'd been, but I didn't ask because of how intently Eric was studying his coffee cup. I tried for evasive. "He embarrassed me."

"How bad could that have been?" Delores asked, finishing her ham and cheese.

"Bad enough that I don't feel comfortable calling him right now."

"I see." A little smile curved her lips and her eyebrows made tiny jerks up and down.

"No, you don't." I didn't know what it was she thought she saw, but now I felt compelled to explain my hasty departure from the Georgian Restaurant, Jonathan's parents and Jonathan. "If you must know, he got down on his knees with this God-awful monster of a ring and proposed. In front of everyone. The whole restaurant. He never even mentioned marriage before last night. I tried to make him stop, but he wouldn't listen. Then his father announced to everyone in earshot that I was a 'foolish young woman.' His mother yelled at his father to sit down, and I accidentally knocked over my chair and a couple of water glasses." I looked around at the faces of my so-called friends. Eric tried hard to look concerned, Jorge grinned, and Juliet ... I could have smacked that highly-entertained, open-mouthed, bug-eyed look right off her face. "I *had* to leave." I raised my chin and shook back my bangs. "I went to McMurphy's Tavern and ran into Greg." A ripple of glances passed around the table. "What? It's a perfectly respectable place. No smoking, well lit, everybody I know goes there. In fact, Greg's got a condo in the neighborhood and ... jeez, you guys! He *told* me his condo was a couple blocks away. I didn't see it. He was with Sarah Fuller -- you know her, Delores, she takes lessons --"

"I know who she is. I thought he was dating Valerie." Delores said.

"Sarah just picked him up at the airport. He was at a meeting in Chicago the last couple of days so there was probably some business he needed to talk to her about, since she works for him." I sniffed. People could be so dense. "Anyway, Juliet was *supposed* to pick me up," I shot her a skinny-eyed look, "but Paul Hudson came instead -- "

"Paul picked you up?" Delores's interruption and inflection showed genuine surprise. She gave Juliet an incomprehensible look.

"I was busy," Juliet said. A tiny, ate-the-canary smile settled on her lips.

Eric crossed his arms and slouched in his chair.

"Yes," I said to Delores, after a frown at Juliet. "He's Uncle Henry's new tenant."

"I know who Paul is." Delores scowled. "He's my nephew."

"Your nephew?"

"Yes."

There were little bobble-headed nods from the other well-informed individuals in the room. Jorge added a smirk as he finished his roast beef on rye. He was such a smart-ass sometimes.

"I didn't know."

"Really?"

"What?" I beseeched the ceiling. "How would I know?"

"He didn't mention it?" Delores asked.

"Why would he mention it to me? I just met him, and briefly, I might add, in Uncle Henry's driveway yesterday afternoon."

Juliet covered her eyes with a hand and turned away. Delores glanced at her.

What was the big deal? Was I supposed to know who *all* of Delores's relatives were? She had hundreds of them. Italian Catholics, most of them. Just say "no" to birth control.

"I'd have thought he'd say something," Delores said. "If he picked you up downtown and took you home then you spent a good hour in his car."

"He didn't take me home." I sighed at the ceiling. "He dropped me at the Snohomish airport where I left my car. Jonathan insisted on flying his plane to Boeing Field and his parents' driver picked us up. Anyway, I was kind of upset and didn't feel much like having an actual conversation last night."

"Oh, *tell* me you didn't cry." Juliet half laughed.

"Oh, *give* me some credit. I just gave him a brief run down of what happened so he wouldn't wonder why he was being so inconvenienced, thanks to you." It was her fault I'd subjected him to forty minutes of whiny monologue.

Delores snorted.

"What?" I drummed my nails on the table. "I called Juliet to come get me and she bailed. And how the hell am I supposed to know who all your thousands of relatives are?"

Delores shrugged. No one else commented. Or looked at me. Eric broke the uncomfortable silence.

"Since Blackie won't be at Copper Creek, how about I take some hay and grain over to Henry? Thea paid for it already anyway."

"Fine." Delores pushed her chair back and stood --

everyone's signal it was time to go. "Where's your car, Thea?"

"I'll bring it over," Eric said. "Sorry. I forgot it was still at Copper Creek."

I dug my keys out of my pocket, handed them to him, then followed everyone out the door.

"Are you angry with me?" I asked Delores as the others pulled away from the curb.

"No, Thea, I'm not angry with you." She smiled at me and patted my arm. "Things aren't going quite the way I expected, that's all."

"What do you mean?"

"Nothing you need to worry about." She patted my arm again. All this patting made me think she was worried. "Why don't you go check on your horse when your car comes back? Henry and Vi want to see you. It would make them feel better if you would stop by and explain what happened."

"I will."

"Come get your equipment tomorrow. I expect you'll be keeping Blackie at the farm until November. Might as well. You'd be moving him there next month anyway."

Every spring I take Blackie to my aunt and uncle's. It's so much more convenient for Uncle Henry to do our dressage training at his farm. Blackie also enjoys the big pastures and companionship with Duke, Uncle Henry's horse. Then, in late fall, when it's dark early and begins to rain in earnest, I move Blackie back to Copper Creek. Uncle Henry's arena doesn't have a roof.

"I'm sorry for jumping on you in there." Delores gestured toward my house with a sideways nod.

"That's okay. It's been tough on everyone this morning." I started to turn away and a thought tugged at me. "Where did you find Blackie's halter? The leather one, not the nylon one I took from the truck." I remembered seeing it somewhere at Valerie's, but so much had gone on I couldn't be sure.

"It was on the ground outside the gate," she said.

"Hmm...."

"'Hmm' what?"

"I'm trying to imagine what would cause Valerie to drop the halter on the ground and go back into the paddock."

"Maybe she went in to toss him some hay," Delores said.

"With all that grass? You're right, though. It'd be like her to do that -- would have been like her." Valerie was past tense now.

"Wait a minute. That can't be right. When I put him in the stall I looked for hay so he'd have something to do. There wasn't any. What about the water tank -- where's that? Maybe she went back in to fill it."

"Next to the gate, I think. She could have filled it easily from outside the pasture."

She looked at me and frowned. "Looks like support for your tell-tale-gate theory. What about last night? You said you ran into Greg. Was Valerie with him?"

"No." I thought I'd mentioned Valerie's absence from McMurphy's. "I guess she was busy stealing my horse." Even I could hear how harsh that sounded. I bit my lip.

"Humph." She patted my shoulder once more. "Let me know if you need help lining up an attorney."

"I appreciate your looking out for me, but after we prove Blackie didn't kill Valerie there'll be no reason for anyone to involve me."

"I hope you're right."

I watched her drive off in her big truck and empty trailer, then wandered back toward the house. I hoped I was right, too.

As soon as Eric brought my car back I would go see Aunt Vi and Uncle Henry. They needed to hear, from me, all that happened this morning. This couldn't possibly get any more personal for them. Blackie was one of the last horses they bred at their farm. Valerie had been one of Uncle Henry's most successful students. She would have followed in his Olympic footsteps.

The wind gusted. I hunched my shoulders against it, but it

seemed to whistle right through me. I felt small and desperate as I hurried back into the comfort of my house.

Chapter Five

I still struggled with the words to use to convince Uncle Henry a horse he raised didn't kill his best student as I pulled into the gravel driveway. I drove past the two-story, steep-roofed brick house where my aunt and uncle lived, and parked by the arena next to the barn. Distractions were plentiful and I shamelessly took refuge in them. The rose garden looked recently tended. Daffodils were blooming. Other spring flowers would be doing so soon, if the profusion of green shoots was any indication. Large pots and empty window boxes sat on the back porch, lined up, clean, and ready for planting. By the time the first of May rolled around there would be enough flowers to make any Brit think she'd walked straight into an English country garden. I sighed thinking of all the work they did. I knew they hired help from time to time, but still, I wished Aunt Vi had called me to help with all this prep work.

Aunt Vi and Uncle Henry are my mother's aunt and uncle. Aunt Vi's older sister, my grandmother, lives in Seattle in a retirement community. She said life in the country was boring, and refused to move into the apartment Aunt Vi and Uncle Henry remodeled for her from their detached garage -- the one they now rented to Paul.

Uncle Henry was in the arena riding his old gelding Iron Duke. I wanted to watch, but I went first to the paddock to see Blackie. He was busy sampling the rich grass and gave me a loud half whinny as a cursory acknowledgment. I ducked through the fence and went to him, inspecting him closely, running my hands over his soft mahogany coat and down each black leg. Delores and Uncle Henry had undoubtedly done the same, but it was reassuring for me to do it. Satisfied nothing was amiss, I ruffled his mane, left him alone to graze, and went back to the arena. I made myself comfortable on my car's warm hood and allowed myself to be swept up watching a master at work.

Uncle Henry is a dressage trainer and former Olympian. He competed for Great Britain in two Olympic games: Tokyo in nineteen sixty-four and again in Mexico in nineteen sixty-eight, winning a silver and a bronze. He won two World Championships, as well as countless other international honors before retiring and moving here, to Snohomish, to breed horses and teach. Six years ago he sold the last of his brood mares and limited himself to teaching.

The farm's arena is the standard twenty-meter by sixty-meter dressage size, enclosed by a low white fence, and marked at specific intervals with letters. These are used in dressage tests to indicate where each movement starts and stops, and are useful when one is training to help with accuracy. Oddly, the letters are not arranged in alphabetical order. Even Uncle Henry hasn't been able to explain to me why that is, but they're the same wherever you go in the world. I recalled overhearing Uncle Henry's reassuring words to Valerie before she was to leave for her first international competition. He told her the familiarity of the arena, no matter where she was, would give her a boost of confidence. He was right. I watched the tape. She entered the arena with her chin up, shoulders squared, and the focused eyes of a competitor in "the zone."

Uncle Henry guided Duke through a series of schooling

exercises I'd seen him do before, so I knew the movements he would execute and at which letters. As I settled in to watch, the sun managed to find a hole in the clouds and illuminated horse and rider for a few moments with spotlight brilliance. Duke's chestnut coat gleamed like polished copper, and the white of his legs accentuated his powerful, elastic strides. His hooves beat a steady, muffled rhythm on the sand, and from time to time he blew great, long, relaxed snorts through his big nostrils. The strength and grace of this horse, who I knew to be over twenty years old, held me mesmerized just as he did every time I watched Uncle Henry ride him.

They cantered a half-pass, an oblique sideways movement, with practiced ease across the diagonal of the arena and executed a text-book flying change at A, the mid-point of the short side. Uncle Henry sat straight in the saddle, a commanding, silver-haired presence. His aids were visible only as eloquently expressed answers from Duke.

Performing a quarter pirouette at E, they continued across the arena changing direction, but not canter lead. The flying change came after the ten-meter counter-canter circle at C. I could have wept. I longed for that level of skill. Every stride seemed effortless, every movement a consensus of two minds. They transitioned smoothly to walk and Uncle Henry let Duke stretch his neck after a few strides and patted him. He smiled at me and lifted a hand in greeting.

"I'll meet you in the house. We're done here."

I nodded and my insides did a twist. Great, I still didn't know what I was going to say to them. Sliding off my car, I went to the house.

Aunt Vi was busy in the big country kitchen, pinching a fluted edge on a pie -- strawberry and rhubarb, if I wasn't mistaken. She greeted me, wiped her hands on a tea towel, and folded me in a brief but comforting hug.

"How are you holding up?" she asked, then scrutinized me at arms' length.

"Fine," I replied. I inhaled the warm air laden with the

aromas of cinnamon, vanilla, and yeasty dough, mixed with Aunt Vi's floral perfume. Not just pie, but cinnamon rolls, too. I loved her cinnamon rolls. The tension in my shoulders eased. A little. "What about you and Uncle Henry? How are you doing?"

"Oh, you know your uncle -- stiff upper lip and all that. But yes, the news upset him. We talked for a bit after Delores left. Then he went to the barn. He's been there ever since, doing chores and now riding." She shook her head. "I expect he'll give Hans a ring in a little while and let him know."

Hans Boermer, a friend and former student of Uncle Henry's -- and the current king of American dressage -- worked with Valerie and her horse Nachtfeder every winter from November to March in Wellington, Florida.

Aunt Vi hadn't said a word about how she felt.

"They had high hopes for Valerie and Nachtfeder, didn't they?" I knew the answer to my question, but I asked to be polite.

"Yes, I suppose they did. But the real tragedy is she lost her life at such a young age, and so violently." She contemplated me for a moment while she rubbed a bit of flour on her rolling pin. "I know you two girls never got on -- no, don't apologize. Valerie was who she was, and it was her nature to try and grab the spotlight all the time --"

"And buy people," I said, emboldened by Aunt Vi's honesty.

But the momentary silence telegraphed her anger with me. "Yes, you're right. She did that. And I sincerely hope, young lady, that you don't think we accepted all those lavish gifts."

I tried to keep a neutral expression on my face, but my gaze dragged through the doorway to the dining room where a stunning, crystal Lalique horse held a prominent place in the china cabinet. Aunt Vi's cheeks flushed. Now I'd done it.

"Don't give me your uppity face."

Guilt smacked me hard. "No! I --"

"We exchanged Christmas presents. Only. You're well aware of that. The one thing Henry would accept without a quibble was that crystal horse. Valerie's determination and talent in the show ring impressed us, not her money. As a competitor she was top notch --"

That hit a raw nerve. "Yes, I'm well aware I could never measure up."

My aunt wiped her hands on the tea towel, pursed her lips and looked away. When she turned back to me the anger was gone from her expression. "You know, love, Henry and I have talked about this and I can tell you it never bothered him when you gave up showing. Why I've said to him, many times, he doesn't need to experience the thrill of competition through you. He agrees with me wholeheartedly. It's enough for him that you enjoy riding."

"I know," I said, sheepish. I sat at the kitchen table. This was going worse than I imagined -- thanks to me.

"I mean that sincerely. You're an excellent rider, too, and you've done a wonderful job with Blackie. Henry often says that the true test of training is what happens every day in the schooling arena, and not how lucky you get in the show ring."

"I know."

"Of course, if you should ever want to show, you know Henry would be there for you. You're better than you think you are. And don't go supposing Henry hasn't made his share of blunders -- so have every one of those judges you'd ride for. They don't expect you to be perfect, you know. And most of them are quite human."

"I know."

"Without Valerie now, I expect Henry will have a little more time on his hands, just in case you want to do more, that is."

"Thanks." My smile felt brittle. "He's always been available for me, and I appreciate it."

This was worse than uncomfortable. Aunt Vi knew why I didn't show. Why couldn't people just leave it alone? Why was it so damned important? I was tired of justifying myself on this particular issue -- especially since it was an issue Valerie had always picked at with such delight. I needed to shift the focus and I blurted the first thing that came to mind.

"I saw Greg this morning. He drove in to Valerie's after the ambulance and deputies --" I choked on the rest of the sentence, horrified at the topic I'd chosen. For the first time I had tears in my eyes. Neither one of us spoke. Then Aunt Vi cleared her throat and dabbed at the corner of her eyes with a hankie she'd pulled from her sleeve.

"I never met Greg. He's quite a charmer, I'm told."

I nodded.

"So." Her hankie covered a discreet sniffle, before she tucked the bit of lace away. "Last night everything turned out all right? I mean Paul didn't have any trouble finding you?" She tossed a ball of dough on the floured board. Another pie was in the offing.

"No. No problem." I cleared my throat, too.

"Lovely of him to drive all the way down there. Henry can't see as well at night as he used to, you know. He doesn't fancy driving after dark if he can help it."

"Uh huh." What luck. We'd managed to hop right to another topic I wasn't too thrilled with at the moment.

"Paul's a nice young man. Good looking and smart, too." She made a quick, angled pass over the dough ball with the rolling pin.

"Uh huh."

"He's been a lot of help around here this week since he moved in." She rolled the dough in a different direction.

I nodded.

The kettle whistled and Aunt Vi wiped her hands before pouring some of the hot water into the teapot to warm it. She dumped it out, spooned in some loose tea, poured in more water, and covered it with a cozy to let it steep.

"So I take it your dinner with Jonathan and his parents didn't go awfully well." She took three cups and saucers from the cabinet and set them on the kitchen table.

"You could say that. He asked me to marry him in the middle of the restaurant after dinner, with his parents and everyone else as an audience."

"Oh my." She stopped arranging cups and saucers and trained her attention on me.

"Yeah, well, he caught me by surprise. I was under a different impression."

"What impression was that, love?"

"I didn't think he cared for me any longer."

Aunt Vi watched me intently, saying nothing. I swallowed and waved a hand through the air to disperse her concern.

"Oh well, you know how he's always finding fault with me. I figured our relationship had run its course. Obviously, he had a different opinion. I didn't handle the situation very well."

"Now Thea, I'm sure you're being too hard on yourself."

I had the impression her reference took in more than the way I'd handled Jonathan's proposal. My adversarial relationship with Valerie was in there, too, and a lot of other things I typically beat myself up over. I drew little designs on the smooth table top with a finger as I answered her — mostly so I didn't have to see her expression while I pretended we were still talking about Jonathan.

"Aunt Vi, I literally ran out of the restaurant."

"Ohhh. Have you talked to Jonathan yet today?" The rolling pin made a soft rattle and a little whoosh. I glanced up. Aunt Vi's attention was back on the dough.

"No."

"I think you might want to do that."

Uncle Henry came through the kitchen door. "Do what?" He hung his jacket on a peg.

Aunt Vi left her dough-rolling to pour tea. "Talk to Jonathan. He asked her to marry him last night."

He cocked his head at me. "Did he now? So ...."

"So nothing. I overreacted and left without giving him an

answer."

"Ah, that's why Paul --"

"Yes," I said, a little sharper than I intended. "But it was *Juliet* I called to come and get me."

I poured milk into my tea and stirred it, spilling some into the saucer. Uncle Henry watched me before fixing his own tea. "Was there a problem with Paul?"

"No."

"Oh?"

"He picked me up and dropped me off at my car. That's all. Nothing happened. He was perfectly fine. I'm just upset with Juliet for putting everyone out. By the way, why didn't you tell me Paul was Delores's nephew?"

"I thought you knew, dear," Aunt Vi said. She put the strawberry-rhubarb pie in the oven.

"No, I didn't. Though everyone else seems to have been told." I winced at how whiny I sounded.

"He used to come out here in the summers from Minneapolis when he was a teenager and clean stalls at Copper Creek." Aunt Vi said with extreme patience. "I suppose you were too interested in the horses to notice him."

That explained exactly nothing. I grunted a response. Whatever.

Aunt Vi and Uncle Henry exchanged a look, and we sat in silence drinking tea while the pie baked. My shoulders sagged. I wanted to curl up on the big overstuffed sofa in the living room, but I was too tired to move. At least I had Blackie back.

"I notice the tractor is working again, Henry," Aunt Vi said.

"It's limping along. I had to order parts for it again."

"You can get parts for that old thing?"

I half listened to their discussion. I wanted to tell them Blackie didn't kill Valerie. It was important. I debated the best way to broach my murder theory. Maybe it would be best to return to my concerns from last night's dinner. I botched it, big-time. Obviously, I needed advice.

I had wanted to run, screaming, from Jonathan, and had done almost exactly that. How was I going to save face with him? My own mother was going to be more than willing to hand me an itemized list of how completely I'd screwed up and disappointed her. By Mother's standards Jonathan was quite a catch. Blond haired and handsome, a successful attorney in his father's law firm, secure future. Even Jonathan made it clear I was lucky to have him.

When Mother found out I was dating an attorney, she began to drop hints. Visions of tiny lawyers and accountants danced through her head, along with four thousand square feet of house in any upscale Seattle suburb. Let not forget matching BMWs. If I wanted any peace I'd better not broadcast last night's disaster. Ha! Now that Juliet and Aunt Vi knew, I could kiss that idea goodbye. Fortunately, Mother and Dad lived near San Francisco and it would take at least until this evening before the news reached them. But, judging from the lack of opinions being tossed in my direction by Juliet, Aunt Vi, and Delores, a lot of talking was going on behind my back. It wasn't like us to keep our mouths shut and let others make their own mistakes. Everyone had to have a hand in it. Their lack of spirited advice made me edgy.

"I don't know, Henry. If we can get some more use out of it—"

"Depends on the cost to repair it this time. Might be worth finding a used model in good shape. Paul can't spend all his time tinkering with it, you know."

Paul. I'd met him for what I swear was the first time yesterday. Met. Right. Now that's stretching a definition. Jonathan and I conducted a rather loud discussion in the middle of Uncle Henry's driveway. When Jonathan drove out in a high-handed snit, I'd made an obscene gesture at his back that turned into a feeble wave as I saw him look into his rear view mirror.

"Hubby having problems keeping the little woman in

line?"

I'd spun to confront the speaker, mortified not only because my silent opinion had been witnessed, but because the nature of our confrontation so obvious. And there he was, standing by the old tractor, dressed in jeans and t-shirt so worn they looked like they'd lost their will to live, wiping his hands on a rag, a sardonic grin on his face. I thought he was the tractor repair guy.

And I thought he had a hell-of-a-nerve.

"Not that it's any of your flippin' business, but he's *not* my husband."

"My mistake." That damn grin was still there.

"Damn right it's your mistake. And another thing — I'm *nobody's* 'little woman' and *nobody* keeps me in line."

"I can see that." Still grinning.

I could have come back with something to put him in his place if I hadn't been so flustered. It wasn't his undeniable masculinity that threw me off stride (I know plenty of good looking men), or that he'd witnessed my rudeness. It was those eyes. Those blue eyes. They cut right through my crap. The unwavering look told me he knew how much of the fight with Jonathan was my fault. I felt a complete fool. Then, later that evening, when *he* arrived at McMurphy's instead of Juliet embarrassment rendered me incoherent. Juliet would have died laughing.

"Tell me what happened this morning, dear," Aunt Vi said. "It might make you feel better if you don't keep it all inside. Delores said it was quite a shock."

Aunt Vi just handed me the answer to how I could tell them Blackie had no part in Valerie's death.

I sipped my barely warm tea and set the cup carefully on its saucer. "Blackie didn't kill Valerie. I know it, and I'm sure I can prove it. Someone murdered her and is trying to make it look like Blackie kicked her. I need help protecting him until I can convince the sheriff."

Aunt Vi clasped both hands over her mouth. Uncle Henry

drew up, taller, in his chair, his gaze fixed on me.

I reached a hand across the table toward him and plunged on, attempting to soften my raw statement. "I can't imagine someone hating her enough to want to kill her. It's possible it was an accident and someone is frightened. The thing is, though, I don't understand why she would steal my horse and take him to her place. That's plain stupid. But I'm convinced Blackie didn't kill her. He never would have kicked her. I need to prove it. If I can't they'll put him down."

"I'm surprised at you, Thea." Uncle Henry's tone had a hard edge I rarely heard from him. "You, of all people should know any horse is capable of causing severe injury to a person."

"But --"

"Including Blackie. Furthermore, you have no proof she stole your horse. None. It is completely contrary to what she wanted. She worked hard for years for a chance to be selected for the U.S. Team, and she would not have risked her dream by stealing Blackie. I can't and I won't believe it. It simply makes no sense."

His eyes held mine in a silent reprimand. I closed my dry mouth and swallowed. With his mouth still set in an angry line, he turned his attention to his tea cup and nudged the handle with his index finger until it lined up precisely parallel to the edge of the table.

He'd missed my point completely. Blackie's life was at stake. I raised my chin and laid my hand on the table. "I don't care who took him. It's not important any more. What's important is that Blackie not be blamed for something he didn't do. They'll kill him if they think he's at fault. Uncle Henry, please. I need to know what to do."

"You're losing sight of what's important. Valerie's reputation --"

My imploring hand turned into a fist. I barely restrained my impulse to pound the table. "Valerie's dead. What's important is Blackie didn't kill her."

"Stop it, both of you! Not one bit of this makes any sense!" Aunt Vi's voice, now that she'd found it, was half an octave higher than normal. "Henry, you will stop trying to shoulder the responsibility for all of this. You've been blaming yourself all day and I've had enough. And you, young lady, could show a little more compassion and a little more sense. Neither one of you has given one thought to what this means. I must say it frightens me to even consider that the poor girl was murdered. And the thought of you involved in the ... oh, I can't bear it!" My aunt sprang to her feet, took her cup to the sink, dumped out the contents, then refilled it from the teapot on the kitchen table.

Alarmed at the degree of her anxiety, I half rose from my chair and knocked my cup over. Milky tea spread across the table and dripped onto my leg. I grabbed a handful of napkins from the nearby holder and rushed to sop it up. Aunt Vi didn't seem to notice.

"What if the murderer is looking for you? What if he thinks you know more than you do and you're a threat to him?" She sat and set her tea cup, rattling, in its saucer. She took my free hand in both of hers, arresting my attempt to clean up the spill.

I perched on the edge of my chair, my mind struggling for something coherent to say. She was coming at this from a completely different angle than Uncle Henry and me. Anything I said was going to be wrong.

"Now, Vi --" my uncle started.

"I'll make another pot of tea." She jumped up, snatched the kettle from the range top, and filled it from the tap.

"Vi!"

"Henry, have some sense," she snapped. "There's nothing that can be done for that poor girl now, and your niece may be in danger. That was Thea's horse in that pasture. You don't think he got there on his own, do you? The murderer put him there."

You made a huge mistake burdening them with your theories,

Thea. You should have asked them to help you protect Blackie and left it at that. What were you thinking?

"We don't know with any certainty how Blackie got there or what happened," Uncle Henry said, his words clipped. "It could have been an accident like the police think. They'll figure out what happened. Speculation won't help and will just get you more upset."

My aunt's lips pressed together until they were white. Her bosom heaved twice before she spoke. "Better upset than sticking my head in the sand, Henry. I don't believe we should be so naïve as to let our guard down. Thea could be in grave danger. Valerie is already gone, and the circumstances are anything but clear. We can't allow anything to happen to our niece." Little bright pink spots glowed on her cheeks.

Uncle Henry's expression made a quick change from anger to distress.

"Well, um, why don't we have Thea stay here with us?" Relief washed across his face as the bright pink spots began to fade from Aunt Vi's complexion and her mouth regained its usual appearance.

"That's more like it," she said. Then she went to the sink, got a handful of paper towels and gave them to me. "You go into the bathroom. Take those pants off and rinse the tea out with cold water -- from the back -- before that stain sets. Put them in the wash right away when you get home."

I swallowed. "Yes, ma'am." And did what I was told.

In the bathroom, I stripped and rinsed, not listening to the murmur of my aunt and uncle's conversation that reached me through the closed door. At least neither sounded angry anymore, but I still felt guilty. They never got mad at each other.

I squeezed what water I could out of my pants and pulled them back on. I wanted nothing more than to go home -- okay, and dry clothes, too -- and stay there. But I had to come back. I opened the door in time to catch my aunt's question to my uncle.

"What are we going to do? This isn't going the way we planned."

I stopped.

"There's nothing we *can* do. Remember, we weren't going to be involved past this point, anyway."

Chapter Six

I stopped breathing and backed silently into the bathroom. What were they talking about? Please, please, not about what happened today.

Don't be a fool, Thea. Aunt Vi and Uncle Henry would never do anything to hurt anyone. This is something entirely different. Get a grip.

I flushed the toilet and opened the bathroom door with as much noise as I could manage, and clomped down the hall to the kitchen. They were still at the table. I said a hurried good-bye and assured them I'd be back soon.

By the time I got home I'd replayed my entire conversation with them a hundred times. Valerie's death truly shocked and upset them. What I'd overheard was something entirely different -- something that had nothing to do with me and was none of my business. So there was no point in bringing it up. Ever.

But the fact remained I was the cause of the arguing between the three of us. I'd never witnessed them raise their voices at each other, much less at me, and as I tossed my things in an overnight bag I vowed to make it up to them.

A gear in my memory caught when I returned to my aunt and uncle's and saw Paul's car, a gray Honda, parked nose out by the apartment. The car I'd nearly collided with on Carpenter Road this morning looked just like it. So it was a Honda, not a BMW as Jorge thought. I eyed Paul's car as I parked my own, but couldn't be sure if it was that shade of gray.

The driver's face was etched in my mind forever, though, and it wasn't Paul's.

I had no interest in Paul, not really. Besides, even if I had the tiniest bit his refusal to chat on the drive home last night would have squashed it. My face heated up with the memory. How I wished I'd sat quietly and watched the scenery go by. But could I do that? No, not me. I took advantage of having a captive, silent audience and unburdened myself. Yup. It was the old strangers-on-a-bus thing, except I hadn't bothered to consider that I'd see him again. I couldn't have done a better imitation of the landlord's pain-in-the-ass niece if it'd been my goal. After listening to me whine for more than half an hour he probably went home and took a fistful of Advil.

My car knocked as I turned off the ignition, helpfully announcing my arrival. Dammitallanyway. I didn't want him to know I was here. He probably heard my stupid car and looked out the window. I grabbed my overnight bag as I got out, slammed the door, and hightailed it for the house.

Getting sidetracked again, Thea. Pull yourself together. If you aren't careful you'll say something else you'll regret.

I took a steadying breath, resolving to stay away from the topics of Jonathan's proposal and Valerie's death. The sheriff would find out soon, somehow, she'd been murdered and Blackie would be safe. No way could anyone think I had killed that horse thief, as Delores had speculated, and no way could Aunt Vi's worries be real. I slowed my pace. I refused to be concerned about Paul's supposed opinion of me. That was simply finding distraction in the inconsequential. I swept it all under my rug of composure, forgave myself for my lapse, opened the back door and walked confidently into the kitchen.

And smack into Aunt Vi's narration of the latest news to the inconsequential Paul.

He leaned against the counter, looking way too much at home, as Aunt Vi chopped carrots and chatted. I stopped dead in the doorway, and she glanced up from her prep work. He took advantage of her diverted attention and reached for a carrot. She slapped his hand.

"If you don't stop eating those, there'll be no vegetables to go with the roast."

He grinned. Her head cocked a warning at him before she smiled at me.

"That didn't take you long, love. I was just telling Paul what happened earlier."

"Tough day," he said. The look he flicked my way lasted long enough to make me simultaneously uncomfortable and peeved.

"You could say. It's not every day you get your horse stolen, and find him in the same pasture with a body." I flushed and looked away. So much for censoring my mouth. What was it about this guy that made me spew out whatever was on my mind?

"I understand the police think Blackie delivered the fatal blow."

My attention snapped back to him, but he was watching Aunt Vi's progress with the carrots again. She had a choke hold on the knife handle and cut each carrot with surgical precision. This conversation needed to end. He needed to leave.

"So they informed me, but I don't believe it."

Aunt Vi's lips pursed.

There you go again, Thea, letting your favorite opinion fly out of your mouth. And instead of letting him know he'd be hearing no sorrow for Valerie from you so he'd leave, you upset your aunt. Again.

Yes, I knew he knew Valerie, and I was using that knowledge. My memory was jarred last night. He wore the same blue plaid shirt when he picked me up as he had on earlier in the week. Although I hadn't known who he was at the time, I recalled clearly how Valerie cozied up to him in front of the Copper Creek office. She'd walked her fingers up his bicep to his shoulder and back down in that way of hers that should have made him smile or blush. He'd done neither.

Last night at McMurphy's he and Greg acted like they knew each other, too. But, they didn't appear to be on friendly terms -- addressing each other by last name in tones that could have been mistaken for warning growls if they were dogs. And the body language! Each man had made such an obvious effort to take up as much space as possible while simultaneously appearing casual that I'd almost laughed. Had Paul come between Greg and Valerie? That could account for the animosity. But if Valerie's death disturbed Paul he hid it well.

"I expect the autopsy will shed some light on it," Paul said, and deftly snatched another carrot before my aunt could react. She scowled at him and he chuckled.

"What a pretty jumper you have on," Aunt Vi said, changing the subject faster than a horse can get dirty after a bath. "That shade of green brings out the color of your eyes."

I dropped my gaze to my modest chest. Aunt Vi had given the sweater to me for Christmas three years ago. She was well acquainted with it. I looked up and caught Paul's ice blue gaze. A corner of his mouth turned up slightly.

"Yeah, it does. I didn't notice last night how green your eyes are." The other corner of his mouth curved, completing the grin. My cheeks burned.

"Uh, thanks," I said, and fled to the guest room.

Why did she do that? I felt I'd been trotted out for inspection. And he was having dinner with us? Maybe I could tell them I had a dinner appointment with a client and get out of here.

I fussed around in the guest room for a long while. As I hoped, Paul wasn't in the kitchen when I came back through, but neither was Aunt Vi. I grumbled, debating whether I should track her down for a little chat. Instead, I put on my jacket and went outdoors. I wanted to see Blackie. I needed my friend.

He was still in the field with Duke. I could borrow Uncle Henry's saddle if I wanted to ride, but I was drained. Blackie saw me climb through the fence and whinnied. He walked over, ears up and neck low, then butted me gently with his head when he reached me. I laughed and rubbed his forehead. He blinked, long and slow, then blew forcefully through his nostrils, spraying me with little droplets of moisture.

"Thanks a lot." I wiped my sleeve across my face, then took his muzzle in my hands and kissed his velvet nose.

He rested his chin on my shoulder for a moment. Sighing deeply, he curved his neck around and pulled me against his chest. The gesture was touchingly human. I murmured little endearments to him, gave him a hug, and scratched his withers, which is what he really wanted. His silky neck was warm against my cheek, and I inhaled the unique, comforting smell of horse. What would I do without my dear friend? I leaned against his solid shoulder as my throat tightened. A tear stung, and I dabbed at a corner of my eye with the back of my hand, trying to think of something else. But non-emotional subjects seemed hard to find. I settled on mentally reviewing the clients I needed to get in touch with in the morning.

When Blackie was satisfied with his back scratch he meandered away and resumed grazing. Chill seeped in where the warmth of his body had been. I went back to the pasture fence, parked my butt against the middle rail and watched him do what horses do best -- eat.

The crunch of gravel announced someone's approach. I turned my head expecting to see Uncle Henry. It was Paul. He was on the other side of the fence a few feet away, feet planted in a wide stance, hands slid into his pockets. Irritation at the disruption of my solitude turned my mood sullen. I folded my arms and returned to watching the horses.

"Vi asked me to tell you dinner will be ready in about ten minutes," he said.

"Oh. Thanks." Great. I'm trying to avoid the guy who made me upset Aunt Vi again and she sends him looking for me.

After a silence lasting the same amount of time it took for Blackie to investigate and eat five different clumps of grass, Paul said, "He's not black."

"No," I said, without looking away from the munching horses. "He's bay."

Two more patches of grass disappeared into Blackie's mouth. Paul didn't leave.

"Why do you call him Blackie?"

"His registered name is 'The Black Queen's Bishop.'" I offered no further explanation. Out of the corner of my eye I saw Paul nod.

"'The eternal problem child of chess,'" he said.

His knowledge of this obscure reference surprised me, but I said nothing.

He continued after a slight pause. "Reuben Fine coined that phrase, if I'm not mistaken."

Blackie inspected and rejected a patch of grass that looked good to me. I don't know why horses get so picky some times and not others. The fence jiggled slightly. Paul leaned against both forearms, now resting casually on the top rail. One foot braced on the bottom rail.

"So is he? Is Blackie a 'problem child'?"

"He was." I held down a sigh. He wasn't leaving anytime soon.

Paul's making an effort to be civil. Be an adult, Thea, it won't kill you to be polite.

I took a breath. "There were complications at birth and numerous health issues before he was even a year old. I spent many long hours here taking care of him when I should have been studying." Memories played before my mind's eye. "Uncle Henry named him. He's an avid chess player and thought the name appropriate. It just got shortened to Blackie. Nothing else seemed quite right."

A smile took control as I remembered how silly we thought it was to call a mostly brown horse Blackie. We enjoyed the absurdity of it. I made no comment to Paul, though. I would not share my personal memories with an outsider, despite having unloaded on him last night. That was different. Completely different.

I glanced at Paul, about to cross my arms again, but the small gold hoop that glinted in his earlobe distracted me. I hadn't noticed that before.

"You don't seem the type to wear an earring." I felt myself blush. I hadn't intended to say that aloud, not that it made any difference. It was a good bet he already thought me rude.

He touched it, as though he had forgotten it was there, and chuckled.

"I wear it to remind myself that it is possible, once in a great while, that I can be wrong about something." His gaze caught mine before making a hasty shift toward the horses.

"Wouldn't it be easier to tie a string around you finger, or write yourself a note and stick it on the refrigerator?"

"Quite possibly. But this," he indicated the earring, "wasn't exactly my choice."

I knew an open-ended comment when I heard one. "Obviously, there's a story here."

With one hand, he combed his fingers through his hair, smiled to himself and shook his head once. "A couple of years ago I had a class of undergrads for a summer course in field work. There are a couple of locations in Montana where we go to teach proper field procedure for fossil recovery. Hopefully, the students start to develop an eye for what to look for and where to look. This particular group was, without a doubt, the most inept bunch I ever had to deal with. Not only did they seem unable to apply themselves, but they didn't have much interest, either."

He shifted his position on the fence and faced me. The late

afternoon light emphasized the planes of his face and picked up highlights in his dark brown hair.

"After about a week of feeling like I was playing scout master to a bunch of juvenile delinquents, I sat them all down and gave them an ultimatum. They were either to shape up and at least pretend they were trying to learn something or we would pack up and go home. They would all fail the course."

My eyebrows hiked up my forehead. Yikes. Hard ass. His eyes softened at my reaction.

"I then made the mistake of telling them I needed to be out in the wilderness with a bunch of yahoos like I needed another hole in my head. For some reason, my little speech struck a chord. They laid down a challenge. If they found some fossils, and demonstrated they learned the proper skills for recovery, I would get another hole in my head. I figured it was a safe bet." He shook his head twice. "Inside of two weeks they hauled me to the local tattoo parlor to get this."

I caught myself on the verge of a laugh.

"They turned out to be a pretty good group, so I keep the earring to remind myself not to get too judgmental." He shrugged slightly, returning his gaze to the grazing horses, his profile to me. A pensive smile lingered at the corner of his mouth.

"Do you still see any of these students?" I asked.

He tipped his head, contemplating me for half a beat before he answered.

"Indeed I do. And they always check to make sure I'm still wearing the symbol of my misjudgment. They may have been a lot smarter than I was prepared to give them credit for, but they're still every bit as crazy."

"Where do you teach?" Now I was curious about this man who accepted his own fallibility with a touch of humor. It occurred to me I'd been waiting for him to embarrass himself. It wasn't going to happen.

"At the University of Washington in Seattle. I do a couple of courses at the extension campus in Bothell, too."

"Paleontology?"

"And geology."

He asked me what I did. As I finished a brief rundown of my accounting business and training with Uncle Henry, I remembered his initial comment about Blackie's name.

"Uncle Henry and I play a game or two of chess almost every Monday night. He's very good. Once or twice a year he lets me win. You obviously know the game. You should play him sometime."

"I have," he said.

Uncle Henry never mentioned anything to me. I wondered why.

"Did you lose?"

Paul straightened from his leaning position and stretched his back and neck.

"Nope." One corner or his mouth turned up in a small satisfied smile.

Now you know why Uncle Henry never said anything.

"Lucky," I said.

He laughed, soft and low, and walked back toward the apartment. I felt we had the beginnings of a connection, tentative and fragile, but it dissolved the farther he walked from me. The feeling was so ephemeral I could have imagined it, but the odd emptiness that replaced it lingered.

Paul joined us for a subdued dinner and excused himself soon after, claiming he had work to do. I watched for signs of his earlier openness. I admit I was eager for it, but there was nothing.

Worn out and feeling friendless, I wanted nothing more than to go to bed early. I helped Aunt Vi clean up after dinner, then took a quick shower. When I returned to the guest room the sheets had been turned down on the bed. The gesture, like a loving hug, lifted the depression that had been settling on me all evening. Silently thanking Aunt Vi, I slipped into bed and relaxed into the cool softness. I should have been asleep in minutes. But now that I was alone and undistracted my worries popped to the surface. Somewhere in Snohomish was a killer. And somehow I had to make sure the sheriff understood that. Blackie's life depended on it.

Chapter Seven

I opened my eyes to unfamiliar darkness and my heart rate tripled in the second and a half it took to remember I was in Aunt Vi's guestroom. I rolled over and groped for the bedside clock. Five seventeen. Too early for my aunt and uncle to be up, and little chance I'd fall back to sleep. I threw back the blankets and, shivering, dressed quickly then went to the barn. With Blackie here I'd share the horse-keeping work with Uncle Henry. Taking care of chores early was my self-imposed penance for upsetting them yesterday.

Breakfast for "the boys" was the first order of business. Eager nickers greeted me when I slid the barn door open, then subsided into noisy munching once I tossed each horse his hay. I made quick work of cleaning the stalls, then rolled up my sleeves, and scrubbed and refilled the water buckets. With hands numb from the cold, I closed up the barn and hurried back to the house.

Dawn made a weak showing through Snohomish's cloud layer, and the dampness in the air was a sure sign of rain to come. The warm glow that spilled across the yard from the kitchen window pulled me from a quick walk to a jog. With a well-timed jump honed by years of practice, I cleared the two steps to the back porch and landed on the dew-slick deck with a noisy scramble. Regaining my balance, I glanced through the window. Aunt Vi was busy pouring batter onto the waffle iron as if she hadn't noticed. I opened the door into the little vestibule off the kitchen and stepped out of my muck boots. The aroma of rich coffee and warm waffles with a hint of vanilla filled my lungs, and the familiar feeling of loving acceptance came at me with a rush. Uncle Henry sat at the table, already making progress on his waffles. He caught my eye and I steeled myself for any indication of yesterday's temper.

"Thank you for doing the chores," he said with his usual calm. "Watch your step on the porch. It's a bit slippery in the mornings."

"I noticed." I smiled and he winked.

Either our relationship was back to normal or he was doing a good job of pretending.

Pretending is okay, Thea. You do that yourself to keep the peace. Sometimes.

I washed my hands at the sink and snuck another glance at Uncle Henry, just to be sure. The anger he gave vent to yesterday was something I had no experience with, and guilt, deserved or not, still rode with me. He looked tired. I knew, without asking, he hadn't slept well.

After breakfast I packed up my overnight bag to go home. When I came back through the kitchen to say goodbye Aunt Vi held on to my hand.

"Why don't you stay?"

"I'd like to, but I have clients expecting me, and a ton of work to do. Besides, the sheriff's deputy demanded I go in to the office this morning and sign my statement."

"If you're sure." She frowned.

"Don't worry." I kissed her cheek. "Thanks for letting me stay last night. It helped."

"Well, come back tonight if you like." She pulled me back for a hug. "We don't like you being alone right now."

"I'm okay, really." I moved out of her embrace and edged

closer to the door. "I'll give you a call later, okay?"

"Come by after you've talked to the sheriff. We want to know what they have to say."

"I'll call."

"Why not stop by? I can fix you something nice to eat. We're not out of the way."

Outmaneuvered, Thea. Keep the peace.

"Okay. I'll stop by after I've talked to the sheriff."

"Bring your bag in case you want to stay."

"Let the girl go, Vi," Uncle Henry said. He smiled at me. "She'll be fine."

Once home, I fell into my habitual routine of showering and agonizing over what sporty pieces to wear for work on "casual Monday." Since I worked at home and rarely dressed up anymore, it was "casual Monday through Friday." The whole decision-making thing was a game I played to get into the right frame of mind for the day ahead. Today it played the additional role of comfort-by-familiarity. I settled on jeans, a long sleeved, pink t-shirt, and my pink, fuzzy bunny slippers. They were cute, and cheered me up -- though only the left one still had its little tongue sticking out and the right one's crooked eyes made it look concussed. I started the coffee, then went to my office-in-the-spare-room and prepared to download files. I'd do that task first to free up my telephone by the time my clients opened for business. Without a dual connection on my phone line, calls would route directly to voice mail.

You're so technologically behind the times, Thea. Maybe it's time to part with some cash and upgrade. Yeah, yeah, I know. But small businesses have failed spending too much too soon. Better to be smart. Besides, anyone desperate to get hold of me knew to call my cell phone.

I pulled the cell phone out of my purse and sat it on my desk. It beeped. Low battery. Again. *You need to spring for a new phone, too.* I ignored the urge to spend, turned the phone off and plugged it into the recharger. It would be fully charged by the time I left for the sheriff's office. Probably.

The doorbell rang, but it was the pounding on the solid wood door that alarmed me. I jumped up, zipped down the hallway, and yanked the front door open. Greg Marshall loomed in the doorway, fist raised, ready to pound again. I sprang back to avoid a blow. His appearance shocked me, too. Besides the fact that I had no idea he knew where I lived, his clothes were untidy and wrinkled -- a state I thought foreign to him. Dark smudges under red-rimmed eyes made him look ill -- or hung over. In place of his customary, handsome smile was an ugly twist. Anyone could see Valerie's death had hit him hard.

"Greg --"

"Where is he?"

The hostility in his tone checked my sympathy and sent me back another step. "Excuse me? Who?"

"That goddamn horse of yours. He's not at Copper Creek." His unblinking blue eyes bore down on me, igniting a cold fear in my chest.

Oh crap. I should have anticipated this. "Greg, I know you're upset, and I don't blame you, but you need to leave. You should go home and get some rest. We can talk later." The tremor in my voice belied my attempt at calm.

I started to close the door, but he stepped forward and pushed it forcefully out of my hand, sending it crashing into the wall. I flinched and backed away.

"I'm so sorry about Valerie," I said.

"Yeah, well, 'sorry' won't bring her back, will it BC?"

I turned, intending to make a dash for my office and the phone, but he was faster. He caught my upper arm and pulled me back, nearly lifting me off my feet.

"Greg, you're hurting me. Stop it!"

"Where is he?" He dragged me closer, forcing me to dance on my tiptoes to keep from falling.

"I don't know." I pried at his fingers and never saw the back-handed slap that connected with my cheek. My head snapped sideways and I cried out. He grabbed my jaw and jerked my face toward him. I tasted blood.

"We were going to be married. You've taken that away from me." He spat the words at me, his voice a growl. "Where is that animal? He deserves to die like Valerie did. You're hiding him."

"No. I'm not -- Greg, please, let me go, please. I don't know where he is. Only the sheriff -- please." My voice shattered around the last word as he shook my arm wrenching my shoulder.

"Bullshit. You know."

His nostrils flared with rapid breaths as he released my jaw and hauled his fist back. I threw my free arm up. The blow connected with my forearm and half spun me in his grip as if I were a toy.

"Greg no, please, no. Please."

Again he gripped my face and hauled me to within an inch of his.

God no. Make him stop.

"Now, you tell me where he is."

His breath sprayed my face. It was -- minty fresh? He'd remembered to brush his teeth? Surprise morphed to pissed-off. I struck at him with my fist and kicked at his legs. His fingers dug into my flesh, but the pain only fed my rage. I kicked and twisted.

"You squirmy little bitch --"

"Hey! What the hell's going on here!"

I staggered backward as Greg whirled toward the voice. Paul leapt the steps, and let fly. His fist connected with Greg's jaw and, before I could blink, Greg was flat on his back on my porch.

"Get out of here," Paul said, voice cold with authority, fists still clenched, still balanced on the balls of his feet.

Greg eyed him warily, one hand rubbing his jaw, as he struggled to get upright. Half way to his feet he paused. Paul coiled. Then Greg straightened, turned and strode down the steps. I held my breath until I heard his car door slam. The angry revving of the car's engine was followed by the squeal of tires on asphalt.

"Are you all right?" Paul's attention shifted to me.

"I -- I ...." My lip was wet. I dabbed at it with the back of my shaking hand and examined the red smear. Blood. Mine. I pressed my wrist against my lip.

"Here. Let me have a look."

His hand came toward my face and I reeled back. His eyes widened and his reach turned into a point.

"Ice. You need some ice on that."

I nodded, but as I headed for the kitchen my knees wobbled. Paul's hand on my elbow steadied me. He guided me inside to the sofa.

"Sit down. I'll get it."

I sat, listened to him rummage around in my kitchen, and swallowed down a wave of nausea as the "what ifs" began. What if Paul hadn't shown up? What if I'd broken and told Greg where Blackie was? What if he hadn't stopped beating on me? My chest constricted with emotion I couldn't contain. Tears washed down my cheeks.

A loud pounding on my front door nailed me to my seat renewing the terror. Paul strode from the kitchen at a quick walk and yanked open the front door. From where I sat I couldn't see who was there.

"Is Ms. Campbell at home?"

My heart pounded in my stomach and my teeth chattered. I clamped my hands over my mouth and listened. The man's belligerent tone and raspy twang sounded somewhat familiar, but no name or face came to me.

"She's not available. I can give her a message." Paul's cool tone didn't match the tension in his shoulders.

"You Fuentes?"

Paul made a slight shift to the balls of his feet. "No."

I stopped breathing. Oh lord, not again. My shoulders hunched against the shaking.

"You can tell Ms. Campbell that Randy Rucker stopped by. I'm on my way to pick up my wife right now, so I can't wait. But you tell her I will be having words with her."

Randy Rucker? I curled into myself, grateful Paul stood between me and him. Randy was a big man. I didn't think I was up to a second confrontation today.

Paul didn't answer him, but held his ground in the doorway until footsteps retreated across my porch. Cautiously, I shifted toward the back of the sofa and craned my neck for a peek out the window. Yeah. It was Randy, all right. Cowboy hat, broad shoulders, and swagger. The sight of him walking away from my home loosened the spring coiled inside me. A little.

Paul closed the door and clicked the dead bolt into place. He returned to the kitchen then came back to the living room a moment later with an ice pack and a tea towel. He handed me the ice. I murmured a thank you and eased the plastic bag against my bruised face.

"You heard?" he asked.

I cleared my throat twice. "Yes. Thank you for sending him away."

He frowned at me for a moment. "Is he a problem, too?"

Irritation at his tone forced some steadiness into my answer. "I can't imagine why he should be. I haven't seen him or talked to him since…a year ago, maybe. We had a brief discussion about me doing the books for his business."

"Don't worry about it then." He perched, facing me, on the coffee table, frowned, and focused on my mouth.

I watched him, shoulders drawn tight, and barely breathing. He raised the tea towel and I braced.

"May I?" His eyes left my mouth briefly, checking my eyes for the answer.

I nodded a fraction. He raised the towel to my chin and wiped lightly. The damp towel showed less red than I'd anticipated. He scrutinized my lip and dabbed a couple of times. I exhaled. A little.

"That's better." He refolded the towel, then brushed it across the tear-tracks on my cheeks.

"Thank you," I said between swallows.

"No problem." He stood, handed me the tea towel, and stepped around the coffee table.

I sagged in relief.

"It's pretty humbling to be on the receiving end." He smiled as if he knew. "Keep breathing."

I tried a small smile in return. It didn't hurt as much as I thought it would. I exhaled a little more. He sat in my coral, wing-back chair across the room, and leaned forward, elbows on his blue-jeaned knees, hands clasped. His dark blue tweed sports jacket sat well over his light blue, cotton Oxford shirt. Open collar, no tie. A nice look. Comfortable. Friendly. Safe.

"Why was Greg here?" he asked. "What was that all about?"

Oh. An explanation, of course. He'd want to know why he just got in a fight on my front porch. "Blackie. He thinks Blackie killed Valerie. He wanted me to tell him where he was. Greg wants to … he said … he wants to …." I couldn't continue. Tears ambushed me and I wiped at them with the towel.

"Oh, jeez." Paul squeezed his eyes shut. "I'm sorry. That's why I'm here."

The stabbing pain in my chest robbed my hands of strength. The ice pack slipped from my grip. I leapt up and raced to the phone in my office. In a fumbling few seconds I had Aunt Vi on the line.

"Blackie!" I shrieked. "What's --"

"Everything's fine now, he's fine. I'm sorry, duck. I didn't mean to alarm you."

"What happened? Is he hurt?"

"No, no, no. It all started after Henry left for the dentist. I didn't know what to do except send Paul over. I couldn't get through to you."

"What started? What happened? Are you sure he's okay?"

I clutched fistfuls of hair and paced.

"He's fine, he was just behaving so oddly."

"Why? What was he doing?"

"I don't know why. He was whinnying and running the fence line -- so unlike him. But he's quiet now -- gone right back to grazing with Duke."

"You're sure he's all right?" I wadded up my hair again.

"Thea, I've seen enough sick horses over the years to know when one isn't ill. Blackie's fine."

Of course she'd know. She'd been nursing horses for forever. My blood pressure plummeted back to normal. "Sorry. I'm sorry ... Aunt Vi?"

"Yes, love?"

"Greg's looking for Blackie. He'll hurt him if he finds him." My voice sounded small and scared even to my ears.

"You get to the sheriff's office like you planned and tell them. I'll have Eric come and stay here until Henry gets back. You come straight over here when you're done with your statement. I don't want Greg thinking you're standing in the way."

It was a little late for that, but he could come back. Suddenly, leaving my house for the rest of the day seemed like a good idea. "Okay. See you in a little while."

"Oh, and Thea, tell Paul 'thank you' for me. I hope I didn't make him late for work."

I disconnected and went back to the living room. Paul handed me the ice pack I'd dropped. His frown looked apologetic.

"I'm sorry. I didn't mean to upset you. Is Blackie okay?"

"Aunt Vi said he's fine. He settled down after you left." I placed the ice pack against my lip.

"That's good. He sure had himself a run up and down the fence line earlier."

I transferred the ice to my cheek. "Aunt Vi said he was whinnying, too."

"Yeah, he was. I saw him out the bedroom window. He'd

stop and look at the house, bellow like an elephant, then start running again. When I came out of the apartment I thought he was going to come through the fence at me. He slammed to a stop at the last second and screamed. That's one very loud horse."

I contemplated the air in front of my face, bit my lip, and winced. I'd forgotten. "Strange … doesn't sound like colic." I needed to check on him myself. I turned toward the front door. Paul's hand on my arm stopped me.

He shook his head once. "You should call the police."

"Why? The vet would make more sense."

Despite the lowered brows and twitch in his jaw, his voice was soft. "Greg attacked you, Thea."

I blinked. "Oh. Right. I'm going to the sheriff's office soon to sign my statement. I can make a report then."

"Do it now."

"I'll do it when I go there. It'll be more efficient. Eric's on his way to the farm, and I may be more able to convince the sheriff that Blackie needs protecting if he can't hang up on me."

Paul narrowed his eyes. I'd swear he was counting. He passed a hand over his mouth. The other hand went to his hip.

"You should stop at the Walk-In Clinic."

"I'm okay now, really."

"Thea." He pronounced my name with parental sternness, pushed his sports jacket open, and braced his hands on his hips. "Greg is as big a threat to you as he is to Blackie. I saw him beating on you, and I'm looking at what he's done to you. I know it was a shock, but for your own safety, don't retreat into denial."

What was it with men? Did they really have to be such --

His hands dropped to his sides. "I'm sorry. You don't need me bullying you, too. But it would be a good idea to stop at the clinic. You want to make sure you're okay. And tell the sheriff when you go in to sign your statement." He brushed at the hair I'd wadded in my fist when I'd talked to Aunt Vi before resting his hand on my shoulder. "Please."

My tension eased under his touch, my mind stopped buzzing, and my instincts told me to trust him. I had an ally with an intelligent plan. I could breathe.

"You're right, I know."

"Good." He squeezed my shoulder and slid his hand down my arm leaving a trail of warmth.

I looked into his eyes and a staggering, kick-you-in-the-knees incendiary flash rocketed up my neck and into my face, robbing me of intelligent speech.

"Aunt Vi, um, Aunt Vi said she was sorry...sorry if she made you late for, um, work."

He glanced at his watch and his eyebrows shot up. "Can I use your phone?"

I pointed toward my office. When he turned away, I staggered to the sofa and lowered myself to the edge. *Holy crap. Get a freaking grip, Thea.*

The call was too short.

"I need to run," he said coming out of my office. "Are you going to be all right?"

No. "Yes, I'll be fine. Thank you." I pronounced the words carefully.

He took a breath as if to say something. Instead, he looked at the floor and exhaled. His gaze shifted to my pink bunny slippers, and he smiled. "Lock the door."

Then closing the front door softly behind him, he was gone.

I got up, went to the door, and hesitated, listening, before I turned the dead bolt.

Dammit. I leaned my head against the door and closed my eyes. My opinion of Paul Hudson had changed. Just like that. Faster. I longed for him. I didn't want to. I didn't need this in my life right now. Dammit.

Chapter Eight

The doctor at the clinic was the suspicious sort. I was certain he didn't believe my story, although I told him the truth. And if his stern lecture was any indication, he didn't believe I was on my way to the sheriff's office either. Battered women, he told me, have a habit of keeping their mouths shut.

I had no intention of keeping silent.

I pulled into the parking lot at the Snohomish County Sheriff's Office just as a white Chevy pickup truck backed rapidly out of a parking place. I slammed on my breaks, narrowly avoiding a collision. The driver didn't even give me a courtesy shrug. How could she, unless she had eyes in the back of her head. She hadn't even bothered to look before throwing her truck into gear and didn't spare me a glance as she zipped past. But *I* saw *her*.

Melanie Rucker. Randy's wife. Alone.

"Ditsy woman," I growled.

Once inside, I checked in with a deputy at the sliding window, then looked around the sparsely furnished lobby. Just as I was about to lay claim on the solitary chair, an interior door flew open and crashed into the wall. I recoiled and tripped over the chair. Randy Rucker caught the door on its ricochet and shoved it again.

I turned to flee, tangled with the chair, and collided with the wall. It was all wasted effort. Randy galloped past me like one of his roping horses in pursuit of a frightened calf and flung open the exterior glass door before the interior one had time to slam. Miraculously, no glass shattered.

Randy hauled to a stop in the middle of the parking lot, snatched the cowboy hat off his head, slapped it against his thigh, and yelled, red-faced, before striding back into the building, flinging the door out of his way again. This time he made a bee-line for the sliding window, and pounded on the glass.

"Phone. I need a phone!"

The window slid open and one was set on the counter. Randy picked it up and hammered the buttons. He kept an eye on the door -- my escape route -- trying to pace, but the cord wouldn't let him.

"Hey," he said. "Get your goddamn ass in to the sheriff's office now ... I don't care what you got going on ... No, she was -- No she thought I might enjoy the walk. Yes, she left me here. What do you think? ... No, you moron, she's got the truck. We've got a car -- Christ Almighty, you're an idiot ... it probably is the one with the big H on it ... just get your ass in here!" Randy slammed the receiver back in the cradle.

That's when he caught sight of me. His eyes narrowed.

"You."

I gulped and backed against the wall. "Hi, Randy."

He took his time walking across the lobby, crushing and re-crushing the brim of his hat with one hand. "You," he repeated. "Are you happy now? Feel like you've gotten even?"

I froze, wide-eyed, gape-mouthed terrified. A little "eep" was all I had for an answer.

"Is there a problem here?" The deputy who'd been at the window was now halfway across the lobby.

Randy turned good-old-boy friendly. "None at all. Just having a neighborly chat." He smoothed the brim of his hat. "Isn't that right, Ms. Campbell?" His slow smile missed "neighborly" by a wide margin if the anger flashing in his eyes was any indication. He nodded to the deputy and ambled out the door.

I slid onto the chair I'd been standing next to.

"You okay?" the deputy asked.

I nodded.

"It'll just be a few more minutes before you can sign your statement."

I nodded again.

What the heck was going on? Although any fool could see Randy and Melanie weren't experiencing a moment of marital bliss, I couldn't imagine how it was my fault -- if indeed that's what Randy was so mad about. As alarming as his behavior was, it occurred to me (as my pulse returned to normal) that his tantrum wasn't too far out of character with the rough-around-the-edges, cowboy image he like to project. That image was probably one reason his stable in Marysville, where he trained reiners and cutting horses, was so successful. People thought they were getting the "real deal." Cowboys cuss and yell, right?

Melanie, despite her rapid departure from the parking lot, was the perfect foil for her husband. Her soft, Southern accent and genteel manners have the odd effect of lending a degree of romanticism to Randy. There had to be something noble somewhere beneath the crudeness if Melanie was attracted to him. Or so one would think.

A little over a year ago I had spoken with them, hoping to sign them on as clients for my accounting business. They decided they didn't need to pay someone for something Melanie could do for free -- in her spare time -- along with raising their daughter, cooking, cleaning and working a full-time job. Jeez.

After today I was glad they weren't my clients.

Ten minutes after Randy stressed the hinges on the inner door it opened again, this time with far more restraint. A portly, balding man stood in the doorway. Instead of a uniform, he wore a rumpled, light brown suit. Hardly a fashion statement, though I doubted he cared. The downward tug of the lines on his face made him look weary rather than angry. His eyes found mine.

"Theodora Campbell?" Hi lack of interest exceeded that of the preoccupied nurse who'd called me in to the doctor's exam room less than an hour ago.

"Here -- uh, yes." I jumped up. How was I supposed to act? I felt like a fifth grader being called in to the principal's office.

Mr. Could-Care-Less waved a file folder, motioning me toward the hallway, and introduced himself as Detective Thurman. He didn't return my tentative smile and he didn't bother to shake my hand. He did direct me to a small office and handed me the folder.

"Read this and make sure it's accurate before you sign it. You can sit there." He waved his hand in the direction of the only chair in the room besides the padded one he claimed.

I moved a couple of *Field & Stream* magazines off the molded, orange plastic seat before perching to read my typed statement.

Thurman didn't speak until I handed the signed paper back to him. "You know the guy who just blew out of here?"

"Only slightly. He's Randy Rucker. Trains western horses, so we don't really cross paths."

Thurman nodded. "Seems to know you. In fact, he said you were a 'lying little mother-of-a-dog' -- more or less -- and were 'just looking to cause trouble.' Also said I shouldn't believe anything you have to say about how he can afford the improvements on his property. But he wasn't that concise."

My mouth hung open. I snapped it shut and rubbed my forehead. Randy'd been talking to Detective Thurman about me? "What?"

"I take it you disagree with him." He watched me with cool, unblinking brown eyes.

Duh. "Detective, I haven't spoken with or seen the man in

over a year, and then it was only when he told me he and his wife didn't feel they needed to hire my accounting services. I haven't even driven past their place since them. I don't know what he's doing business-wise or anyway else."

"Apparently, I'm not supposed to believe that."

"I don't know what to say." Nothing that he'd believe, anyway.

Thurman shrugged and rolled a pen between his fingers. "Have you had any contact with either of them since then?"

"No. I told you."

Then he changed the subject with the same professional ease as every female member of my family. "That's quite a bruise on your jaw. Mind telling me how you got it?"

"Valerie's grieving boyfriend, excuse me, fiancé, was having a hard time distinguishing me from my horse this morning."

"Greg Marshall?" The detective's eyebrows rose slightly.

"Yes."

"What happened exactly?"

I gave him an accurate account of Greg's visit, including what he said to me, and finished with Paul's efficient handling of Greg's departure. "I expect I should tell someone official." I felt my face heat up, remembering Paul's insistence.

Thurman's mouth stretched into a long-suffering smile. "You just did."

Oh. Whoops.

"Do you want to file a complaint?"

"Because Greg went crazy for a while with grief? I don't think it's necessary. I just wanted to make sure you knew." I nodded quickly, my hands pressed together in my lap.

"Been to the doctor?"

"Yes, before I came here."

"Good. So, Greg Marshall was Miss Parsons's fiancé?"

"Yes."

He drummed his pen on the edge of his desk and studied me through narrowed eyes. I held my breath. Whatever was coming next wasn't going to be good.

The drumming stopped. "We determined your horse didn't kill Miss Parsons."

My exhale came like a sudden release of air from a balloon, and the knots in my shoulders untied.

"How do you know?"

"We got a partial autopsy report back." He pointed with his pen to a file in the basket on his desk.

"Isn't that kind of fast?" I didn't actually know, but I assumed it would take days.

He grimaced slightly, as though he'd tasted something disagreeable, and shrugged. "Money and power grease the skids, sometimes, and her father has plenty of both. Besides, I don't think the Medical Examiner has been too busy lately." Thurman tossed the pen onto his desk, shoved the pad to the side, and leaned back in his chair. It gave an alarming creak, but he took no notice. Instead, he continued to watch me, fingers laced over his belly. "You should be glad the autopsy report had extra incentive behind it."

Well, of course I was since it vindicated Blackie, but I had the uneasy feeling I wasn't going to like the reason. Maybe I'd be wrong again. I cleared my throat. "Why is that?"

He glanced at some paperwork on his desk before settling his gaze on me. "Seems the deceased's parents have been busy all morning trying to get a court order to destroy your horse."

A knee-weakening sick feeling dropped on me. Blackie had literally been snatched from under the executioner's blade. There would have been less time than I'd anticipated to protect him. I'd heard about Frederick Parsons, Valerie's father. Nothing official, of course. Not even close enough to official to print in the local gossip rag -- not without expecting the building that housed the newspaper's offices to have a tragic fire on some dark, moonless night. I'd never want to get on the man's bad side, and I'm not sure being on his good side was such a great idea, either. Off the radar entirely was best, but no longer an option. It hadn't occurred to me that her grief-stricken parents would be bent on revenge. Greg's temporary loss of control was nothing compared to the wreckage Valerie's family was capable of making of my life, if they so chose.

"Are you all right?"

"Yes, I'm just shocked they would go after my horse so aggressively, and relieved you finally agree with me."

"Agree with you?"

I waved toward the file folder containing my statement. "Agree that Blackie didn't kill her."

"You realize this means she was murdered, don't you?"

"Of course. I picked up on that a while ago."

"Do you have any idea who would have wanted to kill her?"

"Detective, I believe you will find that, among the people who considered Valerie their friend, she was more envied than liked." I straightened in my chair. "There were plenty of people who didn't like her, but I can't imagine why anyone would want to kill her." *You don't have to tell him how suicidal it would be if that person had any inkling who her father was. He probably knows, and doesn't have to know you do, too.*

"Even if, oh, I don't know, she stole someone's horse?"

"Delores said you'd think I had a motive, but I didn't kill her." And I'm not stupid. But his question was simply standard procedure. No need to take offense.

"Why did she take your horse?"

"I have no idea -- well, I know she wanted him. She offered to buy him several times, but *stealing* him? It makes no sense."

"Why not?"

"It'd destroy any hopes she had to ride in the Olympics, and it's dumb even if she didn't care about that. Steal a horse and put him in your own backyard? What was she going to do with him? Everyone knows he's mine, and besides, he's microchipped. It'd be simple to prove who he belonged to." One question niggled at me. "When was she killed?"

"That's something we're unsure of at the moment." Detective Thurman sat up and slid the yellow legal pad in front of him. "How about you tell me where you've been since, oh, Saturday morning."

"Saturday morning?"

He nodded, pen poised.

"Oh, well, um ... I rode my horse at Copper Creek."

"Witnesses?"

"Uncle Henry. That's Henry Fairchild. He came over and gave me a lesson at nine. Eric Fuentes and Delores Salatini were there. I talked to them both. I was home for lunch and Jonathan came by -- oh, Jonathan Woods, my, uh, boyfriend -- and he went over to my aunt and uncle's with me around one, but he didn't stay. We argued."

"What about?"

This was going to sound stupid. "What I was going to wear to dinner with his parents."

Amusement flickered across the detective's face. I sat a little taller.

"Witnesses?"

"To my argument with Jonathan? Well, Paul Hudson, and my aunt and uncle. Then I left for home a little after five. At seven I met Jonathan at Harvey Air Field and we flew to Seattle to dinner."

"Flew?"

"Yes." I knew what Thurman was thinking. Some people even said it out loud. I used my stock response without waiting for the inevitable. "Jonathan has his own plane, a small Cessna, and he uses any excuse he can to fly."

Thurman snorted. "Witnesses -- to your dinner, that is."

"Jonathan, his parents Walter and Marsha Woods, and everyone else in the damn restaurant. Then I went to McMurphy's about ten. I know. Greg Marshall and Paul Hudson both saw me there. Sarah Fuller, too, but she was sitting at a different table. Well, not at first. Greg was sitting with her when I arrived and I didn't want to bother them, so I sat at a different table across the room. Then he came over and sat with me. But Sarah didn't join us. I'm not sure she knew I was there. We didn't speak. We almost never do. She's kind of odd -- well, maybe just a little bit. Oh, and Paul got there about an hour later, because Aunt Vi asked him to pick me up, since ...." Thurman had stopped writing and was regarding me steadily from under droopy lids. I swallowed. Perhaps I needed to get to the point. What my sister had been doing wasn't important. "I got home about eleven thirty. Paul drove me from McMurphy's to the airport in Snohomish to pick up my car. Should I go on?"

"Yes, by all means."

"I went to bed. No witnesses." I gave him a hard look when he glanced up from his note taking. "And Sunday morning I was out at Copper Creek again by a little after eight when I discovered my horse was gone. Witnesses? Delores, Miguel, Maria, and Jorge. I saw Greg, too. He was looking for Valerie."

Thurman finished writing. "You're quite a busy young woman. If my daughter had as many men buzzing around her as you do, I'd be a little nervous."

That was unnecessary and rude. "I do not have men 'buzzing around' me."

He got up from his chair. "We would appreciate it if you wouldn't make any travel plans for the near future, Miss Campbell. Expect to hear from us again, soon."

My pulse rate jumped several notches. I stood, but made no move for the door. "You can't seriously think I'm a suspect."

Thurman smiled. Barely. "We prefer 'person of interest.' Good-bye for now."

"No, no, no. Now wait just a minute. How can you think I'm a 'person of interest'?" I made the little quotes with my fingers.

"What are you going to tell me, that you're just a tiny thing and couldn't possibly have the strength to have killed

Miss Parsons?" He shook his head as he stepped, casually, around his desk.

Sweat prickled in my arm pits. I set my jaw. "No, I'm going to wonder what kind of convoluted rationale you think I would have for doing such a thing. Sure I was mad when I found out she'd taken my horse, but I didn't even know he was gone until Sunday morning and from that point on there were people with me."

We squared off for a couple of beats before Thurman tapped his forehead like he'd just remembered something.

"Were you aware a 9-1-1 call was placed a few minutes prior to yours, also regarding Miss Parsons?"

"That doesn't make any sense."

"No?"

"No." I frowned at him. "Jorge and I were the only ones at the estate -- until you people came." Uh, oh. Had I just implicated Jorge?"

"Miss Campbell, we'll be in touch."

Yeah, I'll just bet you will. I shot him an annoyed glance on my way out the door, which he closed immediately behind me. I pulled my purse onto my shoulder, clamped my arm around it, and raised my chin. Even if he did consider me a "person of interest" at least Blackie was safe. Valerie's parents wouldn't come after me. They'd let the police do their job and find the real killer. Wouldn't they? I mean, sure, they'd be upset, but they wouldn't jump to conclusions. Because, if they did they could do far more damage to my business, family, and friends than Greg ever could. Just having the detective considering me a quasi-suspect was going to cause disruption in my family.

Somehow I'd made it through the lobby and into the parking lot without taking note of my surroundings. I stopped and looked around for my car, located it, and dug my keys out from the bottom of my purse.

Mother's going to have a stroke when she finds out what's going on.

I got in my car, slammed the door, and jammed the key into the ignition.

All I needed was for my parents to wade into the middle of this. I'd never hear the end of it. First, I walk out on Jonathan's proposal, and now I'm a "person of interest" in a murder investigation. I'll be dropped from the Christmas card list for sure.

I turned the key, but all I got was a sick "errrrr" sound. Damn. I'd been holding down the gas pedal and flooded the engine. I rubbed my forehead. I couldn't protect myself from my parent's wrath. How was I going to protect myself from Valerie's parents? Perhaps taking Delores's advice and getting myself an attorney was sound. But I couldn't call Jonathan like she'd suggested. He didn't practice criminal law. And this was the last thing I needed for him to hold over my head ... no, wait. Maybe this was just the ticket. I'd call and ask him to recommend an attorney. He'd be so scandalized he'd back out of his marriage proposal, and I wouldn't have to worry about him anymore. Sure it would be humiliating, but so what? He'd dump me and Mother would be sympathetic instead of critical of me for rejecting his proposal -- which she no doubt already heard about from Aunt Vi or Juliet.

I tried the ignition again. This time the engine turned over.

I needed to keep this quiet, though. I was not under the delusion the rest of my family would take such a sympathetic view of my involvement in a murder investigation, so it would be best if I didn't distress them with the "person of interest" news. I could handle this.

I stopped by Blackie's pasture to make sure he was fine before facing my aunt and uncle. He whinnied loudly and trotted over when I ducked through the fence, checked my pockets for treats, and sprayed me with a sneeze. Yeah, he was fine. I ruffled his forelock, then went to the house.

Aunt Vi clasped her hands to her face and peered in horror at mine. "Good Lord in Heaven, child! You never said a word about being injured."

Uncle Henry had been sitting at the kitchen table reading the paper. He was on his feet in an instant, the newspaper spilling onto the floor. A vein throbbed in his temple.

"Greg did this, didn't he?" His question sounded more like a statement.

I couldn't believe I'd forgotten about my bruises. Without warning, a tremor took the warmth from my skin and turned my lips icy. Aunt Vi supported my arm and guided me to the table.

"Did he ... did he ...." Uncle Henry was stammering.

That, in itself, shocked me, never mind the color had drained from his face. With a jolt I realized my uncle feared I'd been raped.

"No! No. Just this." I pointed to my face. "Paul came before ... before anything else ... happened." Now I was having difficulty getting words out.

"You poor duck. Henry, get the ice out." She hurried to the drawer with the tea towels. "My word, that lad's gone two stops beyond Barking."

Uncle Henry grabbed his jacket from the peg by the back door. He turned to us, one arm in the sleeve.

"I'm going to have a word with that boy."

Aunt Vi glanced in his direction, stopped, looked again and frowned. "Henry Fairchild, you put your jacket up this instant and fetch me some ice. You'll do none of us any good sitting in the clink 'cuz you've gone spare and whacked the boy senseless."

They eyed each other. Aunt Vi was right. Having Uncle Henry lose his temper wouldn't help any. I was about to say so when he pursed his lips and hung the jacket back up. He got a plastic bag from the cabinet and opened the freezer.

"Have you been to the doctor? The police?" he asked.

"Yes to both," I said. "It's just bruising. I'm okay. Uncle Henry, Detective Thurman told me Blackie didn't kill Valerie." The words rushed out, and I thought he looked a little relieved when he nodded in acknowledgement.

He cleared his throat and handed the bag of ice to Aunt Vi. "You'll be glad to know the vet stopped by. He gave Blackie a good going over. Couldn't find anything wrong. I'll keep an eye on him just the same." He turned his chair to face me, while Aunt Vi folded the ice in the towel. "What else did the detective have to say?"

"Just asked some general questions -- seemed to think I'd know something about the improvements Randy Rucker's making at his place. I thought that was pretty bizarre."

"I heard he was doing something up there," my uncle said. "Business has been a bit slow for him. Maybe he thinks he'll pull in more clients if he puts a new coat of paint on the barns."

Wow, that was catty coming from Uncle Henry, and news to me.

Aunt Vi snorted. "Well, I can tell you, he's needed to do something. The place is practically falling down around his ears. I've never seen such neglect." She handed me the ice pack. "Thea, you tell us everything that happened this morning. Don't be so economical with the truth. You said this would have been worse but for Paul."

I rested the ice pack against my jaw and gave a brief sketch of Paul's rescue to an attentive audience. Aunt Vi tipped her head. Her eyes and mouth formed little "Os." Of course I left out the emotional stuff and the Paul-thing after Greg decamped, although I gave Paul credit for his suggestions. Neither did I mention my encounters with Randy. That couldn't be important. No point in adding needless worry.

"Have you called your parents yet?" my aunt asked.

"Please don't tell Mother and Dad. I swear I'll tell them after the police solve this. There's nothing they can do. They'll only worry. Please?"

"They're your parents, love, they have a right to know what's going on."

"I know, but since I'm not involved anymore wouldn't it be better if we tell them after the sheriff solves this? Then they won't worry over nothing. Please, Aunt Vi?" I turned an imploring gaze on Uncle Henry. "Please? It's not like you're not right here."

He ran a hand over his face then studied me for a long moment.

"All right." He flicked a quick glance at Aunt Vi, who shook her head and turned her attention to preparing the tea. "On the condition that, should anything change and you become involved again, they'll be called immediately."

He meant if I were arrested. Good thing I'd left out how close I was to that. I slouched in my chair.

"Thanks. I promise."

Aunt Vi only harrumphed and intently arranged the porcelain tea pot and cups on the table. It was the Spode set with the red rosebuds I bought for her when Jonathan and I flew to Victoria for a weekend last January. If it hadn't been for the shopping and sightseeing, the trip would have been a colossal waste of time.

"It was Blackie's doing, you know," Aunt Vi said pouring the first cup. She handed it to me.

"What was Blackie's doing?" I asked. Talk about a non sequitur.

"At the end of the day, you'll see. He knew." She fixed a cup of tea with milk and handed it to Uncle Henry.

"Blackie knew?" Uncle Henry asked.

"Yes." She passed him the sugar bowl and stirred her tea.

My uncle and I looked at each other. He shrugged minutely. We'd obviously switched subjects, but I wasn't sure what the new subject was. "What did he know?"

Aunt Vi took a deep breath and pursed her lips on the long, slow exhale. Oh. I knew where this was headed but went for the wide-eyed sincere look, anyway.

"What?"

"He knew you were in trouble, of course. He tried to tell

us."

I knew it. She was creating a psychic connection out of a coincidence. I shifted around in my chair.

"You know how close you two are," she said. "Why, he always knows when you're on your way. I've seen him out there in the field stop all at once and gaze into the distance." She did a little impression of Blackie -- freezing as if on point, looking intently in the direction of my house, jaw slack. I had to smile. "See? Just like that. Then he whinnies and goes back to eating. Not five minutes later here you come rolling up the drive. I'm telling you, he knew you needed help today, Thea."

"Don't be ridiculous," I said, taking a swallow of tea. "The next thing you'll be telling me is Blackie can read your Tarot cards."

"You mark my words. I'm right." Up went her chin and a full dose of her we-are-not-amused glower cut off my unvoiced smart-ass remark and neutralized the accompanying smirk.

I cleared my throat, finished my tea with polite decorum, and got up from the table. "Thanks for the tea and everything. I need to get going. I've a ton of work to catch up on."

"If you must. Take that ice pack with you, too. In fact, why not come by for dinner?"

"I don't know if I can. Juliet is expecting me to help her practice her Tae Kwon Do this evening. She has a belt test coming up."

"I don't think that's a wise idea considering your injuries, do you?" Uncle Henry said.

"I'm fine. The doctor said it's just bruising, no blood --" I stopped abruptly. My mind had just made a brilliant connection. "No blood," I said. They looked confused. "There was no blood on the ground by Valerie's body."

"You're sure?" Uncle Henry asked.

"The ground was dry. It hasn't rained in a week. No puddles, and no mud. Surely, with a wound like her's she would have bled. In fact, there was a lot of blood in her hair.

She must have been killed somewhere else."

"Why would she have been in the pasture then?" Aunt Vi asked.

"To make it look like an accident," I said, feeling rather smart. "That's the only reason it could be. You'd think whoever put her there should have realized what a pussycat Blackie is." I pushed my chair in, took my cup and saucer to the sink, and tossed my napkin in the trash, aware of the unhappy looks on my aunt and uncle's faces. I should have kept my mouth shut.

"And just where do you think you're going?" Aunt Vi said, her words sharpened to a dictatorial edge.

Chapter Nine

I parked my car at the curb in front of my little gray-with-white-trim Craftsman cottage and gave the emergency brake a firm shove with my foot. I stalked past my well-planned flower beds on the verge of becoming colorful, climbed the steps to my porch, and headed straight to my kitchen for a glass of water. I took some ibuprofen and went to my office. I absolutely had to get some work done. I absolutely had to keep my flipping mouth shut. It'd taken some fast talking to get out of my aunt and uncle's house after all that thinking out loud.

I tried to focus on my work, but the more my columns of figures behaved in logical and predictable ways the more of a jumbled mess my life seemed. Part of my brain constantly made the comparison: tidy and neat versus messy and chaotic. I longed for order and needed to put right all that had upset my life lately. I loved my rut. It promised security, predictability, and no excitement or unexpected emotion to pump up my adrenalin. I thrived on serenity. In a moment of epiphany I understood why I'd stayed with Jonathan for so long, and why my need to stabilize my life right now made the idea of going back to him -- even accepting his proposal -- not so abhorrent.

The whirlpool effect Valerie's murder created was gaining momentum, and using Jonathan to try and save myself was foolish in the extreme. As irritating as she had been to me alive, she was downright upsetting dead.

Disgusted at my inability to concentrate, I gave up and shut down my computer. Tomorrow I would do what was necessary to enforce a routine on my life and bring back order. Right now I had unfinished business. I had to call Jonathan to get the name of an attorney, and I had to tell him I needed breathing room. I could only deal with one crisis at a time. Jonathan would have to wait to get dumped.

I balanced on the edge of my padded desk chair and dialed his office. His secretary told me he was in and available -- a disappointment, but better than leaving a message and having to field all of his reactions later.

"Thea." He sounded glad to hear me.

"Hi, Jonathan." I tried to sound casual.

"Have you --"

"No. I mean I haven't had time to think about last Saturday. Something's come up and I need information."

"Of course," he said in his professional tone, impressing me with how well he switched gears. "Is this about Valerie Parsons?"

"How did you know?" I was really impressed now.

"Connections," he explained, explaining nothing.

"This may take a couple of minutes. Do you have time?"

"Of course." Again in his best attorney mode.

As briefly as I could, I told him of finding Valerie dead in her own pasture Sunday morning, Greg's threat to Blackie, and my meeting with Detective Thurman.

"I know this isn't your area, and well, you'd probably rather not get involved, but can you recommend someone for me to call? You know, just in case?"

"Yes, of course. I'm always here for you. You should know that."

I heard him tapping on his keyboard, probably paging

through his address book. What I didn't hear were any horrified gasps or polite hints at ending our relationship. I knew I was going to have to be the one to end it.

"Jacob Green," he said.

I dutifully jotted down a Bellevue address and phone number.

"He's excellent, should be able to take care of all contingencies without a problem."

"Good. Thank you." I hoped that included Valerie's parents.

"You're welcome. I expect you'll be entering some horseshows, now that Valerie isn't around to take up all of Henry's time."

"No." My temper, previously nonexistent, shot perilously close to slamming-the-phone-down level. "Why would I do that?"

"Oh, uh, well," he spluttered. "Wasn't she the reason you wouldn't compete in horse shows? I mean, Henry's always wanted you to and...So, the guy who tossed Greg out of your house, Paul Hudson, isn't he the one who picked you up Saturday night from McMurphy's?"

It wasn't a question. I knew a question when I heard one. It was a deduction stated as fact and I was startled -- but only for a moment. He pulled his typical attorney trick on me, launching an offense as soon as he realized he'd made a mistake. I'd made a mistake, too. I'd told him too much.

"You followed me." I was on the edge of a shout. "I can't believe you followed me."

"Of course I did." He was equally irritated. "You don't think I was going to let you roam around downtown Seattle on a Saturday night by yourself, do you?"

"I'm a big girl, Jonathan. I can take care of myself."

"Ensuing circumstances might argue otherwise."

The insult had me on my feet. Damn his incessant parenting. I threw my anger into rapid pacing and explained again, with far more patience than I felt, how my sister called my aunt, who in turn asked Paul to drive into Seattle to fetch me. I repeated the events at the farm this morning and how my aunt's best option was to send Paul to my house when she couldn't reach me on the phone.

"What about Greg?" His question still telegraphed hostility. "It looked to me like you met him Saturday night."

This was getting ridiculous. Jonathan was far more jealous than I imagined. I just wanted to break up with him, not drag the rest of the population in as co-respondents.

"That was purely a chance meeting."

"He kissed you."

Jeez, and this morning he beat me up. That would demonstrate how much he cared for me. "I can't for the life of me explain why," I snapped. "He was drunk. He toasted Valerie, he toasted my sister's beguiling beauty, and he kissed me. You'll have to ask him why."

"Oh." He sounded like the starch had been taken out of his argument. "I thought you were toasting dumping me."

"Honestly, Jonathan, does that sound like something I would do?" I thumped into my chair. Wasn't it enough that the sheriff was considering me a person of interest? Did Jonathan have to chip in and assassinate every other aspect of my character?

"I don't know, Thea. I just don't know you any more."

There was no avoiding a discussion. I was going to have to toss another ball in the air and hope gravity didn't win. Not being argumentative would help. I took a deep breath and softened my tone.

"Why don't we have dinner someplace quiet and talk? Tomorrow, maybe?"

"Can't tomorrow. Wednesday will work."

I looked ceiling-ward for some kind of divine deliverance from Mr. Control-freak. None arrived. I gave up. "Fine. Where?"

"Bernard's in Snohomish. You like that place and it's decent. I'll pick you up at seven."

"Okay. See you then, and thank you for Mr. Green's name."

"Not a problem ... and Thea?"

"Yes?"

"I love you."

I grappled for a response that was true but not cruel. "I know you do." I immediately knew I'd missed the "not cruel" part.

Less than a minute later, as I rested my face in my hands and contemplated this character flaw, the phone rang. Now what did he want? On the third ring I picked up and sighed a "hello."

"Well, don't you sound down in the dumps." The brisk voice belonged to Andrea Anderson, my best friend since fifth grade.

Relief almost made me laugh. "I'm so glad you called."

"So," she said, slowly, as if testing the waters. "Rumors are flying. What's going on, and why haven't you called me?"

"About what?" So many things had gone on since I spoke with her a week ago I wasn't sure what she meant.

"Don't be cagey with me, now. Something's going on with Jonathan. Fess up. Am I the last to know he's been buying expensive jewelry?"

"Oh, that." I took a deep breath. "We went out to dinner with his parents Saturday night, he proposed, I failed to give him an answer, left and went home on my own."

"That's it? That's the condensed version. I want all the dirt."

"I don't know where to start. There's been so much going on."

"Jump in anywhere," she urged. "Obviously the rumor mill is woefully outdated."

So I did, and gave her a messy, disjointed tale of my recent misadventures, from Paul showing up at McMurphy's instead of Juliet, to finding Valerie's body, Paul dealing with Greg and again with Randy, and my fun time at the sheriff's office.

"Good golly, Miss Molly," she commented when I took a breath. "Are you all right?"

"Yes, I'm fine."

"You're sure? You're just saying that, I know you are. Be honest with me. Have you been to the doctor? How about the police? Tell me you've talked to the police about Greg, please. And a lawyer? I know some good ones."

Andrea is an attorney, and like Jonathan specializes in corporate law. I wish she'd find a guy, get married and have some kids so she'd quit practicing her mothering on me.

"Yes, yes, yes, and I've got a name."

"Who?"

"Jacob Green. Jonathan told me he was good."

"Jeez, Thea, I'd be traumatized into the next decade."

"I'm okay. Believe me, and stop worrying. Aunt Vi and Uncle Henry are fussing enough for everybody."

"Well, I can put a lid on the fussing, but I'm still worried. Is there anything I can do?"

"You're doing it."

"I can do more --"

"Andrea!"

"Okay, okay. You know, I can't believe the little witch got whacked. I wonder who she pushed over the sanity edge." Without waiting for my comment she made a quantum jump to her favorite recreational topic: men. "Who's this 'Paul' you keep referring to? Just how sexy is he?"

"Paul?" I said, slightly unnerved. "I mentioned him twice."

"Sorry to inform you, but I stopped counting at six."

"No," I attempted to argue with her.

"Yes," she interjected. "He sounds intriguing. Is he the one who turned your head from Jonathan?"

I closed my eyes in resignation and exhaled, covering the mouthpiece of the phone. This conversation needed a whole lot more time than the five minutes I could give it before I'd be late for dinner at my aunt and uncle's.

"I have an awful lot to tell you, Andrea, but I have to get going or Aunt Vi will be worrying about me again. Can we have dinner this week?"

"How about tomorrow. No, wait. Wednesday?"

"Can't. I'm having dinner with Jonathan."

"Oh, so you haven't actually broken up with him? Thea, Thea, Thea --"

"I've postponed the confrontation because of everything else that's going on." I could smell a lecture. I wasn't up to it.

"In all fairness, you shouldn't get involved --"

"I'm not getting 'involved' with anyone. *Period*. I'm just saying, with everything that's going on, dealing with Jonathan is too much. Besides, I know exactly how it's going to go. He'll bring out that ring again, tell me to just try it on, tell me we can have a long engagement so I don't feel pressured, then *poof*, we'll be married and I'll wonder how it happened." I wadded my hair up in my fist, released it, combed it back into place with my fingers, and took a deep breath.

"Be strong, Thea. You know what you want. Don't listen to his arguments or he'll have you convinced he's the best deal in town and he's doing you a huge favor."

"Don't I know. He could give telemarketers lessons." I leaned back in my chair and put my feet on my desk.

"All you've got to do is look at his hairline and imagine what he'll look like when that blond hair gets thinner and disappears. Should keep you from listening to a word he says."

A giggle escaped as a snort. I grinned. "That's a trick I hadn't thought of."

"Let's meet for dinner on Thursday then," she said. "And if he's talked you into something you don't want we'll have time to fix it."

I laughed and agreed. Why hadn't I talked to Andrea earlier?

"Ordinarily, Thea, I'd think it would be wonderful to have some guy be so attentive, but Jonathan? I don't know. He's so obsessive about you. Gives me the creeps. I'm sorry I introduced you to him."

"I don't think it's that bad." She tended to carry the over-protective thing a bit far.

"It is from where I sit. I'll bet I'm not the only one who thinks so, either. You're doing the right thing, and remember I'm here for you."

"Yes, Mother."

We made plans to meet at The Cheesecake Factory at the mall in Bellevue, two blocks from her office. We'd get dinner and retail therapy within steps of each other. I was feeling better already.

Right.

I should have known.

The doorbell rang as I put my last client file away. I wasn't expecting anyone, but then I had more than my usual share of unexpected visitors lately. I slid the metal drawer shut and went to the front door.

"Who is it?"

An unfamiliar male voice responded. "Mr. Frederick Parsons to see Miss Campbell."

Crap.

I sprinted into the living room and looked out my front window. A large black Mercedes sat idling at the curb.

Tell him you're not here. Tell him you're the maid, or the neighbor watering the house plants.

No. He'll come back. He has to know by now that Blackie is innocent. He can't know I'm a person of interest. Not yet. He won't hurt me. I pulled my cell phone out of my purse and stuck it in my pocket -- just in case. With my pulse rate pushing optimal work-out level, I opened the door and looked up at a Frankenstein-sized man in a black uniform and dark glasses. An extra twinge from some recess of my mind added to my tension. I pushed it down.

"Miss Thea Campbell?" The big guy did not smile.

"Yes?" I tried to.

"Mr. Frederick Parsons would like a word with you."

"Of course."

He turned toward the car and, as though through some pre-arranged signal, its back door opened. Out stepped a gray-haired man impeccably dressed in a well cut, steel gray suit. He moved with the square-shouldered confidence you expect of someone who is used to having people snap-to at his command.

He mounted the steps to my porch before he spoke. "Miss Campbell, good of you to see me."

"Not at all." I hoped my nervousness didn't show. "I'm so sorry for your loss, Mr. Parsons. Please, come in."

He walked in and glanced around. Although I'm sure my whole house could easily fit into his garage, he gave no indication he held any opinion of it. The big guy in the dark glasses did not come in, but closed the door leaving Mr. Parsons alone with me.

Up close, Valerie's father was not as old as I first thought. He had classic, handsome features, and oozed elegance. But a steel-like formality about him made it clear he was not a man to cuddle up to. I tried to picture him bouncing his little blond girl on his knee. Nope, not this man.

"Won't you sit down?" I asked.

"I don't want to take much of your time," he said, disregarding my invitation. "I came to talk to you about my daughter."

He looked squarely at me. His gaze flicked to the bruises on my face, then back to my eyes.

"I understand it was your horse in the pasture at her house."

"Yes," I said, and swallowed. Blackie seemed to be everyone's favorite topic of conversation lately.

"I also understand I was mistaken in believing my daughter's death was an accident involving your horse." The muscles in his face were so tense his lips barely moved when he spoke.

"That's correct."

"How did your horse come to be in that pasture?"

"Someone took him from Copper Creek Saturday evening."

"Someone? Was it my daughter?"

His expression didn't change and neither did the tone of his voice, but I felt a rush of compassion for him. He was grieving and worried about the kind of person his daughter actually was.

"Mr. Parsons, no one knows who was driving Valerie's rig. No one saw the driver. It could have been her, but quite honestly, that doesn't make sense to me." In half a heartbeat I'd announced my abandonment of the "Valerie-is-a-crook" stance -- again. Who could blame me? Maybe I'd believe it myself on one of these go-rounds.

"Nor does it make sense to me, Miss Campbell." The floor creaked as he walked across the hardwood of my entryway and into my living room. He looked around as if browsing in a gift shop. The photographs on the bookcase caught his eye and he strolled over to have a closer look. One picture was of Juliet. The other was of me on Blackie with Uncle Henry. Mr. Parsons picked up the one of Blackie and studied it, then did the same with Juliet's picture. "Your sister?"

"Yes." My face went cold, and my scalp seemed to shrink. I wanted to grab the photograph out of his hands. But before I made a move he returned it to its place on the bookshelf.

"Should you have any knowledge to share with me I would like to encourage you to do so. It would be prudent."

I locked eyes with him and set my jaw. "I'm afraid I'm as baffled as you, Mr. Parsons. More, perhaps."

"I intend to find out who killed my daughter and set her up to look like a common thief."

He held my gaze long enough for me to understand he considered me part of the equation. I did a quick reevaluation of my sympathy for him and discarded it. He nodded slightly, evidently satisfied I'd caught on.

"Thank you for your time," he said and left.

I closed the door softly behind him and slid the chain in place. It was a token gesture, to be sure. I watched from the living room window as the black car pulled away from the curb, then sat down to give my shaking knees a break.

Crap. How much worse could this get? An image popped into my mind of the little pig cowering in his straw house with the wolf at the door.

You're so pathetic, Thea.

No, now wait just one huffing minute. That story didn't end with the pig on a platter.

"Dammit, I've had enough," I said aloud to my empty living room. "I have absolutely, positively been terrorized for the last time. I will not continue to sit here and let people walk into my house and scare the hell out of me."

Chapter Ten

Considering how little time had passed since everyone seemed so concerned with my well-being, no one seemed to notice I was a bit late for pre-dinner cocktails. But, considering I was in self-sufficient mode that was fine with me. A quiet evening with no drama would go a long way toward getting me back to feeling in control. Juliet and Eric were in the living room with Uncle Henry and Aunt Vi. Their laughter -- mostly Juliet's -- made the scene seem almost normal.

"Blackie's doing fine," Uncle Henry said as I walked in. He handed me a glass of white wine.

"I just checked on him. Thanks. He certainly seems like his normal self."

"Did you find out what was wrong with Blackie?" Eric asked. I turned to answer him and he grimaced catching sight of my lovely bruises. "Ouch."

"Whoa, Thea! What happened to your face?" Juliet shoved her wine glass into Eric's hand and sprinted across the room to get a better look.

"Greg did that," Aunt Vi said, all lightness gone from her voice.

My sister and her boyfriend looked shocked.

"Why?" Juliet examined my face closely.

Aunt Vi jumped in before I could draw a breath. "Because he wanted to hurt Blackie and your sister wouldn't tell him where he was." She proceeded to relate the story, but with her own twist, saying that although she didn't know it at the time Blackie's odd behavior meant I was in trouble and needed help. The moment she sent Paul to me, my horse knew I'd be fine and settled down. Therefore, Blackie was the reason they weren't all visiting me in the hospital tonight.

"Wow," Juliet said. "I've heard of dogs having a psychic connection to their owners, but never a horse. How cool."

Eric caught my eye and raised an eyebrow. I studied the ceiling. The exchange didn't escape my aunt.

"All right for you, missy," she huffed in a proper British manner. "But I'll be the one saying I told you so."

I sipped my wine and laughed. "If we find out you're right, Aunt Vi, I'll buy you a new set of Tarot cards."

"Humph," she said, and disappeared into the kitchen, chin in the air.

Once we sat down to dinner the conversation returned to my encounter with Greg.

"So what happened? Greg knocked on your door and then what?" Juliet handed me the burden of the conversation along with the gravy boat. Unfortunately, the gravy boat was easier to pass along.

I related brief details, but they only seemed to intensify Juliet's interest, so I cleverly segued into Thurman's news clearing Blackie of fault in Valerie's death.

"You must have been sobbing with relief," she said.

"Well, no, not sobbing."

"Then dancing in the hall."

"No."

"Ha. I'll bet you threw your arms around that detective and kissed him."

"Hardly. Not when the next words out of his mouth were telling me I was a person of interest." Whoops.

Jaws dropped and eyes bugged around the table. Aunt Vi

found her voice first.

"Theodora! You said *nothing* of this earlier!"

I stammered an incoherent string of "uhs" and "buts."

"You?" Juliet burst out laughing and fell into Eric. Aunt Vi reached over and smacked her shoulder. "Ow!"

Uncle Henry jumped in. "Thea, why didn't you --"

"I got the name of an attorney from Jonathan," I spewed. "But I really don't think I'll need him."

"Let's hope you don't," he finished.

"I can't believe anyone could think my sister --"

"Why do they think you were involved? Because she took your horse?" Eric cut off a still-guffawing Juliet. He laid his arm across the back of my sister's chair and tapped her shoulder with his fingertips. She glanced at him and he shushed her.

"Just because Blackie was at her farm doesn't mean she was the one who took him," Uncle Henry said sharply.

Eric ignored my uncle's remark and squeezed Juliet's shoulder before picking up his knife and fork again. Evidently he thought she would keep her mouth shut. Foolish man.

"Are they going to arrest you?" Juliet asked, with a touch too much enthusiasm.

Eric's shoulders sagged.

"Is this attorney any good?" Aunt Vi's cheeks flushed pink with anxiety. "It's time to call your parents --"

"No, please --"

"You mean you haven't told Mother and Dad?" Juliet thumped Eric's arm and whooped.

"You should call your parents," Eric said, then shot an annoyed look at Juliet.

"No! I'm not calling them."

"Why didn't you mention this earlier?" Aunt Vi sounded hurt.

Guilt gave me a good slap.

"Well, after Andrea called and Valerie's father stopped by …." My excuse trailed off into silence. "I guess I neglected to mention I had a visit this afternoon from Valerie's father, too."

Everyone, including my sister, stared at me with identical, anxious expressions.

"I guess you did," Aunt Vi said, weakly. "What did he want?"

Uncle Henry and Eric exchanged quick glances. They both sat up straighter.

"Not much." I tried to downplay my blunder. "He asked me what I knew about Blackie being stolen."

"He probably wanted to size you up to see if you were capable of killing Valerie," Juliet said, then looked around the table. "What? I heard he's a scary guy. So," she turned to me with an eager spark in her eye. "What'd he say?"

I glossed over our brief conversation and didn't mention the big guy in the dark glasses.

"I hate to say it," Eric said, with a glance at my sister. "But Juliet's probably right."

"What do you mean, 'I hate to say it'?" Juliet snapped back.

"I mean," Eric said patiently, "sizing her up is probably what he was doing, and it makes me nervous." He added a smile.

"Oh," she said. "All he'd have to do is take one look at Thea to realize how harmless she is."

"I look harmless?" Her observation was a good ninety degrees out of line with the new me.

"Totally," she said. "You look like a strong breeze could knock you down."

"I do not."

"Do so. You've got this 'I'm so delicate' thing going on, with the cute little haircut and the big green eyes." She batted her gray eyes at me. "And you're short."

"I am not. Why does everyone think I'm short? I'm a good five-foot-two. And what's wrong with my haircut?"

"Well, excuse me, Xena, Warrior Princess, you're well off the national average. Besides, if Valerie's dad was checking you out, you'd better be frickin' glad you are minuscule, and so darned adorable." Her voice rose to the timbre one would use when talking to a baby, just before she reached over to pinch my cheek.

I batted her hand away and gave her a skinny-eyed look.

"Ohhh, aren't we fierce," she taunted.

"Juliet." Eric's voice held a warning, but my sister continued to smirk.

I decided to drop it since Uncle Henry and Aunt Vi still seemed a bit shell-shocked over Mr. Parsons's visit. Neither one had made any effort to staunch our sisterly bickering.

Eric assumed the mantle of peacekeeper and steered us back on topic. "I'm sure the sheriff has things well in hand. We're probably worried for no reason."

"You will remember to call this attorney fellow Jonathan told you about, won't you, Thea?" Uncle Henry asked. I knew it wasn't a request. More like a politely framed order.

"Yes, of course."

"First thing in the morning?"

"Yes."

"I expect he opens his office early."

"Yes, Uncle Henry. I'll call before I start work. I promise."

"See that you do." He didn't return my smile.

"So Eric," Aunt Vi said, clearing her throat. "How are your university classes going?"

Eric took up the hint to change the subject, and normal dinnertime conversation resumed. The subject of Valerie was dropped. However, as I gathered dishes from the table after dinner I caught Uncle Henry, deep in thought, standing in front of what Aunt Vi called their Rogues Gallery -- one wall in the living room covered with framed photographs of Uncle Henry's students and their horses. I didn't have to guess whose picture he looked at. I wanted to say something, but couldn't think of anything that wouldn't sound insincere.

I had plenty to say to Juliet, though, and saved it until we were left alone to do the dishes. Aunt Vi insists her good

Royal Doulton china and the silver be washed by hand, and she uses them for dinner every night. Makes for a lot of extra work, but long ago we quit making suggestions and just pitched in.

"When were you planning on telling me you were dating Eric?" I asked.

"I was going to get around to it."

"When? After you break up with him? He's not like the other guys you dated. He's a lot more mature, which means he's not going to play your games."

"I know that."

"I don't think you do." I put down the sponge and turned to her. "I think you didn't tell me because you didn't want a lecture."

"You mean like you're doing now?"

"I haven't even started. Juliet, you cannot play with Eric like you've played with every other guy. He's a mature man, not a commit-a-phobic adolescent."

"Oh listen to you. Ladies and gentlemen, please take note of the voice of experience standing to my immediate left."

"Correction: the voice of fricking compassion. Eric's a really good person. He deserves your respect and he deserves to be taken seriously." I ground my teeth and resumed washing up.

"I know that." She sounded defensive. My inconsiderate sibling cast a furtive glance over her shoulder then turned the water on full and leaned closer to me. "The reason I didn't say anything is because there've been problems."

"What kind of problems?" I handed her a delicate china plate I'd washed.

"It started about a month ago. Eric and I didn't want people gossiping about us, especially since we'd just started dating, so we tried to keep things quiet." She rinsed the plate and put it in the rack to drip dry. "Valerie found out, somehow, and she immediately went after him. She kept trying to get him alone. Stuff like that. He tried being polite, but she was getting on his nerves. Thea, you know how straight-laced Eric is -- he didn't do anything but kiss me until he was sure I was in love with him, too." She pushed a strand of hair out of her face. It fell back with soap bubbles attached. "He's so gorgeous women hunt him, and he hates it. Valerie is -- was -- a user. She might as well have worn a sign. He always avoided her, but she really turned up the heat. Well, I couldn't take it any more so I confronted her in the New Barn last week. I told the little slut to keep her hands off him."

"Juliet," I groaned.

"Well, she lit into me first, really, so what could I do but hand it back? It ended with Miguel hauling me out of the barn while Valerie and I screamed insults at each other. What a bitch. I'd have flattened her if she touched me. I told her that and she laughed."

"And that's why Delores was so mad at you."

"Yeah. I guess I deserved it. I'm lucky she didn't fire me. Eric probably said something to her, but he won't tell me. I caught hell from Maria, too."

"That wasn't a smart thing to do, Juliet."

"I know." She shrugged and sighed. Juliet doesn't sigh. Not like that. "Eric moved back into Miguel and Maria's house because Valerie kept knocking on his apartment door. Anyway, we decided to keep our relationship quiet. That's why I didn't say anything to you."

"I wouldn't have told anyone."

"But you would have lectured me about losing my temper with Valerie like you just did, even though you never liked her, either." She reached over and stirred the suds in the sink. "I'm glad she's dead." She didn't look at me. "I hated her and I hated the way she went after Eric. Well, he doesn't have to worry anymore and neither do I."

Now she looked, steady-eyed, at me, her jaw set. When I failed to say anything she took the dinner plate I'd been washing out of my hands. I scrubbed another plate while a knot grew in my stomach. Why was she justifying herself to me? Juliet never made excuses.

"So," she whispered, leaning closer. "Did you get some 'thank you' nookie?" Her sullenness evaporated and the sparkle came back in her eyes.

"Excuse me? I handed her the large platter to rinse. I wish people in this family would learn to put on their turn signals when they changed subject lanes.

"Oh, come on. This morning, after Paul tossed Greg out. A little gratitude smooching?"

"What?"

She took a salad plate from me and slumped, like she couldn't believe I was so dense. "You know, 'girl is in peril, guy rescues girl, girl is wowed by his masculine prowess, and offers herself up in gratitude for services rendered.'"

"No." I did my best to copy Aunt Vi's huffiness and dumped a fistful of silverware into Juliet's side of the sink for her to rinse.

"Right. You don't expect me to believe that, do you?" She reached over and flicked a small handful of soap subs at me, missing completely.

"Yes, I do."

"Ha. Guys love that. Makes them feel powerful, protecting the little woman."

"So why do you practice all this self-defense stuff?" Far better to dwell on her obvious incongruity.

"I'm no fool, sister dear. Besides, Eric's not my bodyguard. He has other body privileges that confirm his masculinity." She chuckled smugly.

"I'm glad you've been so thoughtful."

"Come on. A sexy guy like Paul, with those big, broad, muscular shoulders, and an adorable little ass, lands a right hook to Greg's jaw and sends him sprawling, and you don't turn into a puddle at his feet?" She sighed dramatically and slid a sideways glance at me. "You are made of ice, girl."

"And you are just plain --"

"What do you need ice for?" Aunt Vi interrupted. "Is your

bruise still bothering you, Thea?" Neither Juliet nor I had heard her walk in and we jumped simultaneously.

"No … nothing," we said together. I hoped I didn't look as guilty as Juliet.

Aunt Vi gave us both a narrow-eyed suspicious look and put two more wine goblets on the counter for us to wash. We were silent for the rest of the time it took to clean up.

I did my best to ignore Juliet's remarks about Valerie stalking Eric, but the way she nailed my reaction to Paul was insightful. Was my longing for him really only sexual attraction spurred by high emotion and danger? If so, anything between us was temporary and I needn't worry about my emotions flaring up the next time I saw him. I was back in control, and that's what I needed right now, control.

"Okay," she said, putting away the last dish. "Let's go."

"Go where?"

"You promised to help me practice for my Tae Kwon Do belt test. Remember?"

Disappointed she hadn't forgotten, I asked, "Why can't Eric help you?"

"He won't do it anymore."

"Why not?"

"He said it isn't right for a woman to practice beating up her boyfriend."

"He has a point." I gathered up the wet dish towels to take to the laundry room.

"He seems to think so."

"Are you sure you want to do this so soon after dinner?"

"Don't worry, it won't be that strenuous. Besides, you could use the practice." She eyed my bruised jaw. "You didn't remember a thing about the self-defense I taught you."

"You never taught me any self-defense."

"You obviously weren't paying attention, which is why you should help me tonight. Let's go up to the barn and practice in the aisle-way. Then we won't have to move furniture."

Juliet hollered to Eric where we'd be. I grabbed my jacket. The sun was going down and the temperature was dipping into the upper thirties. Juliet never seemed to need a coat.

The huge barn door slid easily in its track when I pushed it. I entered the dark aisle and flipped on the lights. The horses, still munching their hay, regarded us with momentary curiosity before going back to their evening meal. I love the sound of horses eating. There is a quiet, comforting rhythm to their chewing that lulls me into a sense that all is right with the world. I relaxed against Blackie's stall door, and clucked my tongue. He raised his head and stretched toward me until his nose touched the door's bars. I reached through and scratched his forehead. When he lowered his head for another mouthful of hay I left him alone and watched my sister warm up.

Juliet began by practicing her forms, a specific series of blocks, kicks, and punches that have a graceful, dance-like quality to them. Eric joined us and stood quietly next to me. I glanced at him. He was absorbed in watching Juliet, clearly proud of her ability -- or admiring her shapeliness.

The parts she wanted me to help her with were the self defense moves — specific "attacks" from the front and behind that she would counter with a combination of defenses. Fortunately for me, Juliet was more cognizant of pulling her punches this evening than she had been the last time I helped her practice.

At this point Aunt Vi and Uncle Henry joined Eric and audience participation became rather boisterous. Between the cheering and hollering, I "attacked" Juliet and she "defended" herself. I got into the spirit of the thing as well, feigning attacks and trying to catch her unawares.

After we'd executed every move and counter-move several times over, Juliet decided I should learn some of the defense moves, since I had a demonstrable need for them. She grabbed Eric's arm and dragged him to the center of the barn aisle, declaring him the assistant. His look of alarm prompted a laugh from all of us, even Uncle Henry.

"Please?" She batted her eyelashes at him and ran the tip of one finger slowly down his cheek in a deliberately provocative move. "We can do it in really slow motion."

The double entendre elicited hoots from us all. Eric blushed and laughed, and when he agreed, we cheered.

"Okay, Eric, do this. No, no, to me, so Thea can see." He took hold of her shirt. "Okay, I'm going to do this." She grabbed his wrist with one hand and brought her other hand up in a movement that would have hyper-extended his elbow. He released her and leapt back with a shocked expression. "Good. Right! Don't let me hurt you. Jump out of range so when I kick --" and she did, "I -- whoops. Sorry."

"It's okay." He grimaced, and passed a hand over his ribs.

"Now Thea, you try."

My first couple of attempts drew shrieks of laughter from our audience when Eric jumped nimbly away from me before I could begin the defensive move Juliet coached me through. At last he and I got the hang of it and pulled off an entire sequence of movements in acceptable form. Cheers went up from our audience, and even Blackie seemed to approve, giving us a half whinny and a toss of his dark head. Aunt Vi, standing in front of his stall, covered her ears.

"Okay now," Juliet said. "Let's finish off by seeing what you could have done to Greg this morning."

Although Juliet substituted for me, apprehension played havoc with my gut as I instructed Eric where to place his hands and what to do. Juliet deftly evaded him and delivered a couple of well-placed "punches." With a sigh of relief, I clapped and hollered with the others as the demonstration ended.

Then it was my turn. Eric was to be Greg, again. Juliet stood next to me so I could copy her moves. Several things happened simultaneously. As Eric put his hands where Greg's had been, I stared to shake. A loud rushing sound in my ears nearly obliterated all other noise, and everyone's movements took on a bizarre, distant, slow-motion quality. Beyond the roaring in my ears I made out Blackie's frantic whinnying and the crash of his hoof striking his stall door. As all attention turned away from me and in his direction I saw a hand close around Eric's forearm to remove his hand from my face. Normal perception returned with a suddenness that made me stagger.

A hand on my shoulder steadied me, and I heard Paul's voice. "I think her bruise is bothering her."

At that moment, Paul's presence surprised me enough that I didn't notice what I realized later -- no one had witnessed my panic but Paul.

And Blackie.

"Oops, sorry!" Eric said, and dropped his other arm. Blackie was immediately quiet. "Are you all right?"

"Yes, fine." I cleared my throat and gave him a weak smile.

"Your horse is weird," Juliet said. "Want to try again?"

"No, that's okay. I think I get the idea." I tried to sound matter of fact. I looked at Paul and flushed. *Please don't say anything.* His eyes softened and he gave me a tiny wink. *Just between you and me*, his expression seemed to say.

She relented. "As long as you think you learned something."

"Oh, absolutely. Thanks for the lesson."

"Sure." My sister gave no indication that she was aware of my distress. She had other things on her mind, apparent from the sly glance she shot at Paul and the eyebrow wiggling aimed at me. Paul didn't notice. In that moment he was looking at me.

"It's cold out here," Aunt Vi said, rubbing her arms. "Let's go indoors."

"Good idea," Uncle Henry said.

As our small group made its way to the house Paul hung back and placed a hand on my arm.

"Are you sure you're all right?" His voice was low.

"Yes. That was so strange." I shivered, slowed my pace and stopped.

"But not an unusual response to reliving a trauma."

"You seem well acquainted with trauma symptoms."

"I spent two years in the army. It's part of 'on the job' training."

My desire to linger near him conflicted with my determination to quit being so helpless. Once again he'd rescued me. Never mind that this time it was from myself. Evidently this "rescue-syndrome" Juliet had described so well was still at work, and I welcomed it with embarrassing enthusiasm. Standing close to Paul turned me into a hormonal train wreck. The muscles in my legs had the consistency of water and a hot flush spread rapidly up my neck to my cheeks. I mentally grabbed my self-control with both hands, and physically started toward the house. He matched my pace and stayed close enough to continue talking quietly, but not close enough to "accidentally" touch.

"When did you join our party in the barn?" I asked, pleased with my cool tone.

"A little before Juliet seduced Eric into cooperating." He chuckled. "She's good."

"The best." I watched her take Eric's hand. She pulled him close and whispered something in his ear. He gave her a one-armed hug and kissed the side of her head in response.

When we reach the kitchen I grabbed my purse off the counter.

"Goodnight, everyone," I said, and gave my aunt and uncle a quick kiss.

"Won't you stay another night?" Aunt Vi asked.

"No, I can't." I was tired and wanted to sleep in my own bed. The drama was over. "Thanks for dinner, it was great." I did a lightning scan of the kitchen for Paul while trying to appear casual. He was across the room, leaning against the counter. He met my gaze. "'Night," I said.

He gave me a small nod. "'Night."

I headed for my car only to be waylaid by my sister.

"Wait for us," she said, jogging up behind me. "We'll follow you home and make sure everything's okay."

"You don't need to," I protested.

"We don't mind."

"It's not necessary."

"I told Aunt Vi we would." She grinned at me, knowing she'd won.

So much for being a strong independent woman. I'd make sure to get the memo out first thing in the morning. I guess I was the only one who knew.

Chapter Eleven

The light that filled the room when my alarm rattled me awake could have only been produced by a cloudless day. It's amazing what sunshine can do for one's attitude. I jumped out of bed and threw back the curtains. Yup, I was right. It was a brilliant, turquoise and emerald day, the kind that makes half the population of the Northwest go out in shorts and t-shirts, even though it's still chilly enough in the shade to see your breath.

The narcissus had been blooming in my backyard for a couple of weeks, and the tulips looked promising. My little grape hyacinths still formed lonely little islands of blue, but I envisioned the tulips blooming and creating a spectacular effect. The only thing I could wish for would be a view of the mountains from my house. The Cascade Range had to be breathtaking on such a crystal day.

Since today was not my turn to muck out stalls at the farm, I ate a leisurely breakfast, showered, dressed as befitted a native, and got right to work. By ten o'clock I'd accomplished a gargantuan amount. The one bump in the road was a client who'd lost money on an investment -- or at least showed no return on it even though the time frame was longer than I'd have expected. To make sure there was no mistake, I dialed his number.

"This is an answering machine. You know what to do." An obnoxious beep! I was certain he'd manufactured himself followed the smart-ass instructions.

"It's Thea, Jim. I'm showing a fifteen-thousand-dollar loss from an investment last year. Call me back and let me know if it's accurate so I can submit your tax forms."

Taking a short break, I called Jacob Green, the attorney Jonathan recommended. His secretary told me he was with a client and would call me back around noon. Today seemed my morning for not connecting with people. I suspected I was encountering the usual excuses that crop up on a sunny day. Well, some of us had deadlines. I addressed myself to my work again, certain I would be able to get in a ride later if all went well.

True to his secretary's word, Mr. Green returned my call at twelve. I had just settled back at my desk after finishing my turkey sandwich.

His rich bass voice painted a vivid picture of a bear of a man with an efficient manner. He got right to the point.

"I understand you're a person of interest in the Valerie Parsons murder investigation."

"That's what they told me. I don't know what to do." I grabbed a pad and pen to take notes and explained my involvement in the events surrounding Valerie's death, including my conversation with Detective Thurman.

The lawyer listened patiently, then peppered me with questions, including asking directly if I'd killed her.

"No!" I was shocked he had to ask. "Of course I didn't kill her."

His tone was soothing as he responded. "I know some of these questions aren't easy, but they do need to be addressed. The police will be sure to ask them, and we need to be prepared. The more information I have, the more I can help you when, and if, it becomes necessary."

I reined in my indignation in the face of his logic and

continued to answer his remaining questions.

"I think that does it for now. Next time the sheriff wants an interview call my office and I'll arrange to be there with you. It's important that you not consent to any interviews without me present."

"Okay."

"I'll be talking to you before long, no doubt."

This was almost too simple. I gave myself a mental pat on the back, had a couple of chocolate chip cookies, and went back to work trying to ignore the uneasy feeling that accompanied Mr. Green's parting comment.

It was close to four o'clock when I applied the final touch to my last of my client files. I shut down my computer, changed into breeches and sneakers, and tossed my boots in the car. Time to go get Blackie's saddle, bridle, and other equipment from my locker at Copper Creek.

I stopped by the stable's office, out of habit, to say hello. My sister wasn't there but Delores was. She sat at her desk sorting the mail, glanced up, and greeted me as I walked in. I made myself comfortable in Juliet's vacant chair and rolled over to Delores's desk.

"I hear you've been pretty busy," she said, her gaze on my bruises.

"It was quite a day yesterday."

I gave her the short version of the events since Monday morning. She apparently had good connections because she was already aware of most of the drama.

"I'm not sure you need to worry about Valerie's father. He can be intimidating, but he's not a rash man."

Her take on Frederick Parsons differed from everyone else's. What did she know? As I finessed the question in my mind, she tossed a stack of mail into a basket on her desk and another stack into the waste can. Then she leaned back in her chair with her hands clasped behind her head and watched me for a moment.

"Your Detective Thurman's been a busy boy."

In the short sentence her opinion of Frederick Parsons no longer interested me. "How do you mean?"

"He's been interviewing everyone who'd ever come within fifty yards of Valerie."

"Like you?"

She nodded. "And Miguel and Maria."

"Really?"

Another nod. "Miguel took Jorge in on Monday, and came back with an invitation for me and Maria."

"So, how'd it go?"

She shrugged and sat forward. "Fine for us. I think it was a mixed bag for the detective, though."

"How so?"

"He walked Maria out to the lobby when they were done. She had him by the arm and was giving him advice on diet and exercise. She promised she'd call his wife, then gave him a little pat on the stomach."

"No." I grinned. It was like the home team scoring a point. "I wish I'd been there."

"On our way home Maria said she told him about the fight your sister and Valerie had over Eric. I expect by now you know all about their little set-to. Anyway, they went in for questioning, too -- Eric and Juliet. Juliet's there now. Thought you should have a heads up about that."

Within half a dozen accelerated heartbeats I couldn't form a single coherent thought. Delores reached across her desk and held my wrist firmly.

"They're both adults. They can handle this. You don't have to protect them."

"I -- yes, I know. It's just ... she's my little sister," I squeaked the last four words.

Delores patted my hand and gave me a reassuring smile. "It'll be okay. I didn't mean for you to worry -- just wanted you to know."

"Thanks. I do need to know and I'm not sure Juliet will tell me. Thanks." I swallowed, took a breath, and stood. "We'll just deal with things as they come up."

"That's all we can do."

"Right. Well, okay then. I guess I'll go collect my saddle and stuff."

"Good girl. By the way, I understand the funeral is on Wednesday."

"What? Oh. Thanks for letting me know." My knee-jerk thought was how I could avoid going. I caught Delores's small smile and shake of the head on my way out.

My locker offered little to pack up; saddle, bridle, pads, boots, brushes, some horse shampoo, a couple of blankets, buckets, and a few first aid supplies. After several trips, a little planning, and repacking, I got all of it to fit into my trunk and back seat. To be sure I didn't miss any of Blackie's toys, I decided to check his old stall, and walked back to the Big Barn along an alternate route through the New Barn.

A crash I recognized as a horse challenging his stall wall startled me out of my fretting over Juliet and Eric. I looked for the source of the equine temper tantrum and saw Nachtfeder, Valerie's horse, ears pinned and teeth bared, pushing his considerable bulk against the front of his stall. He clashed his teeth against the stall bars in an obvious effort to intimidate me. It worked well. I hurried past. Miguel poked his head out of the stall he was cleaning.

"Wow, that's one cranky horse," I said.

"He has always been difficult, but now every day he is worse."

"Maybe he misses Valerie."

He met my suggestion with a wry smile. "If he does, he would be the only one."

Except for Greg," I said, touching the still-sore bruise on my jaw.

"I think it's her money he misses." His eyes narrowed. "He do that?" He stroked his large bandito moustache with one hand. The smile that usually made the corners of his eyes crinkle was gone and without it he looked fierce.

"He stopped by my house yesterday morning pretty upset about Valerie. He tried to get me to tell him where Blackie was, but Paul came by and convinced him he should leave." I suspected he had heard some version of the story already.

"Paul, he is a good man." He gave an approving nod.

It was unnecessary and maybe even silly, but his opinion pleased me -- and, I couldn't help notice, further diverted me from the mood that Delores's news had provoked.

"I'll see you later," I said. "Thought I'd do one last check of Blackie's stall to be sure I got everything."

"Be careful," he said, looking pointedly at my bruises, and went back to work.

I continued to the Big Barn resolved to deal with Juliet later and wondering what Valerie's family would do with her horse. More accurately, how much they'd sell him for and if his crabby disposition would make it difficult to find a buyer.

"Hi, Thea," a woman's voice called from behind me.

I turned. Sarah Fuller, in the latest equestrian schooling couture, walked toward me as quickly as her boots allowed. Her waif-like appearance and lack of social skills always made me think of her as a child. But she was a professional financial planner and worked in Greg's office. Rumor had it the sole reason Sarah took riding lessons was to get Greg to notice her. Despite her big blue eyes, she should not have tried for such a direct comparison with Valerie.

She'd been doing some heavy-duty shopping since I'd seen her last. The tall black boots, so stiff and free of wear, had to be new. Likewise the quilted, impractical, white vest, shirt, and dark blue plaid breeches. By my calculations she'd plunked down close to a thousand dollars for an outfit she'd wear a couple of times a week in a dusty barn and arena. There was no chance she'd ridden already. She wouldn't be so spotless. Valerie was the only one I knew who could pull that trick off.

To say Sarah and I were acquaintances would be erring on the side of friendliness. Last time I saw her she wouldn't have anything to do with me. However, I had no solid reason to dislike her and always tried to be pleasant when I couldn't avoid her. This odd little reversal of behavior of her's had me curious.

"Hi, Sarah. Nice boot."

"I heard Valerie's dead," she said.

Oh, that's why we were having this little tête-à-tête. "Yes, she is."

"Somebody said you found her. Did you?"

Oh great. She was trying to pump me for information. Could I be rude and walk away from her? "Yeah, I'm afraid so." I turned to walk away.

"Was she, you know, awful to look at?"

The image of Valerie's dead face sprang into my mind and produced an involuntary shiver. For as peculiar as Sarah was, I'd never have pegged her for having a morbid curiosity. I guess I was wrong. I glared, chin lowered, and back rigid, before answering.

"Yes."

"I heard you found her in the pasture at her house and your horse was in the field with her. People are saying she stole him."

"Are they?" If she noticed my caustic tone, she gave no indication.

"But she was murdered, right? I mean it wasn't an accident or anything? Do they know who did it?" The corners of her lips twitched with a smile she couldn't quite suppress. I knew Sarah despised Valerie -- everyone knew -- but this barely concealed delight put her on a par with Bride of Chucky for creepiness.

"I wouldn't know." I stepped away.

She followed. "She sure was, like, brutal to a lot of people ... I've heard."

I halted my retreat. "Anyone in particular?"

"Yeah. You." She shifted on her feet under my angry stare. "So, what happened to your face?"

"I fell." I immediately regretted not coming up with a better story. The curl of her lip told me she recognized the lie.

"Yeah? Looks like it hurts."

"Not really." That at least was true. The ice had helped.

"A friend of mine got a bruise like that once."

"Oh? She must have had a bad fall, too."

"No, her boyfriend beat her up." She held my gaze for a beat.

"Sorry to hear it. I hope she broke up with him."

"He dumped her."

Something about the flat tone of her voice flipped on a mental light bulb. Sarah was referring to herself.

"Poor girl," I said, sincerely.

"Whatever. I need to get my horse for my lesson." And she left.

I watched her hurry away, overwhelmed with pity for her. I didn't understand the dynamics behind such relationships and prayed I never would. Violence and abuse did not belong in any relationship. What made her stay until she was discarded? Maybe I ought to be a tad less judgmental of her in the future. She didn't deserve my scorn.

A light, cool breeze wafted the enticing smells of hay, clean bedding, and horses to me as I entered the Big Barn. The aisle was swept clean, and was free of tack trunks and other clutter that people sometimes left outside their horses' stalls, making the interior of the barn look like a teenager's messy bedroom.

Blackie's stall was the fifth on the left. When he was here his wooden door often remained open with a nylon stall guard up so he could hang his head out and socialize. Now, with all the doors closed, I found that the sameness of the stall fronts required me to count to be accurate. A vision of Nachtfeder scraping his teeth on the stall bars reared up in my mind. I stopped, spun on my heels, and dashed out of the barn.

Miguel was busy cleaning a different stall in the New

Barn, and Delores stood in the aisle-way talking to him. I ran up, breathless, interrupting their conversation. From the concern painted on their faces, I'd alarmed them both.

"What if it wasn't Valerie who took Blackie?" I plunged right in to the middle of my epiphany.

"What do you mean?" Delores asked.

"I mean, Jorge didn't actually see the person who took Blackie, did he? What if it wasn't Valerie, but someone else? What if that person didn't know Valerie's horse by sight, but was told to come and get the dark bay horse in the fifth stall on the left?"

Delores cocked her head, eyes narrowed.

I held my hands out, stopping any possible comments from her. "If you walk into the New Barn from the front, Nachtfeder's stall is the fifth on the left. If you go into the Big Barn through the back door, which is where most people pull up with their trailers, the fifth stall on the left is Blackie's. I don't know why Valerie would send someone instead of coming herself, since the only people she trusted to handle her horse were Miguel and Uncle Henry, but it makes more sense that Nachtfeder should have been picked up." I sucked in a breath then continued. "Furthermore, Valerie had to have been alive when she arranged to send the rig over. I can imagine she would have been furious seeing Blackie walk out of the trailer instead of her horse. Maybe she was killed accidentally in an argument with the driver."

"Well," Delores said at a pace far slower than mine, "it would make more sense for Valerie to have her own horse picked up. But wouldn't that person, assuming it wasn't Valerie who took Blackie, have read the stall card to make sure they were getting the right animal?"

"They should have been able to do that," Miguel said, stroking his moustache. "The barns are not completely dark at night. We leave every third light on in the aisles so if there is an emergency we can see."

"What bothers me about your idea," Delores added, "is

Valerie always told me when she was taking Nachtfeder away from Copper Creek. I'd get phone calls and notes a week ahead of time. She'd usually have Miguel bathe him, and have the farrier out, as well. It was always a big production."

The holes in my theory deflated my enthusiasm, but I couldn't shake the feeling I was on to something.

"I need to think about this some more," I said. "It makes more sense to me than Valerie stealing my horse."

I gathered, from their serious expressions, that Delores and Miguel were not dismissing my ideas out of hand. I left for my uncle's with more unanswered questions than before. Delores suggested my theory was something Detective Thurman was considering.

In other words, I should butt out.

I wasn't so sure.

Chapter Twelve

My new theory niggled away at the back of my mind while I led Blackie in from the pasture. But, once I got him inside and pulled off his turnout sheet, my thoughts of Valerie receded. Two days without grooming had left my horse with a coat full of loose winter hair begging to be curried out. I stepped back and scrutinized the situation. Blackie turned his head as far as the cross ties would allow and swiveled his ears at me. Then he gave himself a good shake. A cloud of tiny hairs launched into the still air. He turned toward me again, this time lifting a big fore leg and pawing daintily. I laughed. Who says horses can't talk?

"Okay, buddy, I get it. A ride it is."

I flicked a brush over his coat, picked out his feet and tacked him up. Then I led him to the arena and used the tall step-stool to mount. Once we'd walked for a few minutes, I asked him for what dressage riders call a "long and low" frame. He complied, reaching down for the bit with a swinging back.

"Just a little stretching today, Blackie. Don't want you getting sore and crabby."

I reached forward and gave his muscular neck a solid pat then asked for a trot. He moved obediently forward with big, softly springing strides. His ears, bouncing gently like little airplane wings, told me he was relaxed and concentrating. Occasionally, one ear would flick back, acknowledging an aid from me. The gymnastic exercises I guided him through were less intense versions of our usual routine; large circles, loopy serpentines, leg-yields, shoulder-in. And they did their time-honored job, as Blackie became progressively better balanced and more responsive. There was no doubt he was happy to be back at work.

Transitions between the gaits came next, and I murmured, "Good boy," to my friend as he correctly answered my seat aids. I relaxed into the power of each stride and focused on the timing of my requests. Despite my being in "the zone" my uncle's quiet voice did not startle me when he interjected a comment into my concentration. That finesse is part of his genius as a trainer.

"Very nice, yes, very nice."

I glanced at him. He was in his coach's stance; feet slightly apart, arms folded, head cocked ever so slightly. Relief washed through me at seeing him here, in the arena. I hadn't realized how anxious I was to get back on a normal footing with him.

I straightened up a touch and made the mental adjustment into my familiar "student" mode. From years of working with him, I knew Uncle Henry would expect me to continue, independent of his direction, until he called me over. Several minutes passed before I heard the familiar, "Come to me and let's discuss one thing."

He noticed something I needed to fix, and I knew he would make me figure it out. I rode Blackie to him at an easy trot and halted.

"This is looking very, very good," he said, and stroked Blackie's neck. "But there is maybe one thing, just something small, you could do that would create a better harmony."

I waited, knowing he wouldn't expect an answer from me yet. He wasn't finished setting up the scene.

"When we ride the horse, and have in mind the perfect trot, or shoulders-in, or whatever it is we decide to do, when we are pleased with the result and think, 'yes, this is it, this is what I want,' it is exactly as if we have become one with the horse, as if what we have thought in our own minds has been created at the exact same time by the horse. We go forward from that point, keeping focused on what is coming up, and plan. Part of our mind has to keep in touch with what is happening right now to be certain our aids are being answered, but the plan has to be dominant." He paused and tapped his lip with his index finger, watching me.

"Oh," I said, after a moment's thought. "I'm waiting to see if Blackie keeps doing what I ask before I plan."

"Yes." Uncle Henry nodded with satisfaction. "Exactly. Even on days when there is less intensity in the workout, this is important. Otherwise, the next day's ride won't be as good as it could be. Remember, you are one creature with complementary functions when you sit on him. Always. He wants this as much as you do, but you are the one who must make the effort to look ahead. He is there waiting for you, ready to follow your plan. You must always have a plan. That is your role in the partnership." My uncle smiled as he watched me try and wrap my mind around the image. "This is what you must practice, being one, functioning as one," he continued. "You make the plan and communicate to him with your aids what it is you want. Perhaps it will help to think of it as starting first, but then you must trust him enough to let him perform what you have asked and keep your thoughts on what should happen next. With the flying changes at close intervals this is necessary. You must ride your plan and trust him enough to do his job of executing it. It's all up here." He tapped his temple. "The movements are almost beside the point. It will happen, but it takes practice and trust." He gave Blackie another pat. "Do you understand?"

"I think so." I felt like I had it by the tail. Barely.

The lesson was over. I knew he would leave me alone

now to practice. I gathered my reins and my focus. This was going to be more difficult than it sounded. I would have to catch my habit of waiting and watching, correct it each time it happened, and replace it with the elusive oneness that comes from complete trust in one's partner. It would require me to show more confidence. It was an evolution of our relationship and I knew I would try and fail at it many times before I succeeded. I began. I wanted this, and I would work until I achieved it.

When our ride was over and I'd given Blackie the thorough grooming he needed, I put him out in the pasture with Duke. They still had some quality grazing time left before Uncle Henry called them in for dinner. After unloading the remaining supplies from my car, I tidied the barn and dropped a bale of hay from the loft through the hatch in the feed room ceiling so Uncle Henry wouldn't have to do it later. On my drive home I contemplated my ride. I believed I had moments where I started to achieve the greater harmony Uncle Henry talked about, but it was a constant struggle to remind myself to be aware of the present while planning ahead, and not fall back into old habits.

I parked my car at the curb and strolled up the walk to my house. The place looked outrageously cheerful. Banks of tulips from pale peach to salmon were punctuated with white and peach narcissus. It seemed as if the plants all conspired to be rid of the winter blahs in the few short hours I'd been gone. As I climbed the steps to my porch the perfume of the purple hyacinths arrested my progress through the door, and I inhaled a lungful of the strong, sweet scent.

Inside, sun streamed through the windows of my living room, lending a warmth electric lights could never match. I walked from room to room gazing out the windows on the gardens. Thanks to the combined efforts of my sister, Aunt Vi and me last fall, I had more spring flowers in bloom than anyone else on my street.

Juliet was responsible for the thick wash of pinks and purples in the back. Last October she stood in front of the flower beds and threw handfuls of bulbs at the dirt. At the time I was horrified. Aunt Vi hustled me to the front yard and helped me plant my straight organized tows while Juliet buried her random casts. Now I was glad I left Juliet alone. The back yard was stunning. However, I prefer my organized method in the front yard.

It was dinner time, and I was ravenous. Taking a container of leftover lasagna from the freezer, I put a sizable square in the microwave to reheat, tossed a salad, then set my kitchen table. The moment I sat down to eat, the dead bolt on my front door clicked and the door creaked on its hinges. I jumped to my feet, pulse pounding.

"Yoo hoo, it's me!" Juliet called.

"You scared the living daylights out of me," I bellowed. "Is it beyond your intelligence to knock first? You know perfectly well what kind of bad news has been walking through that door lately. I was on the verge of hyperventilating myself into a coma. Have you no brains?"

"Oh, sorry, but I did holler when I came in." She breezed into the kitchen and looked out the window. "Hey, the flowers look great. I'll have to cut some for my apartment. I love fresh flowers. Hurry up and finish eating. Eric's got a soccer game tonight down at Pilchuck Park and we're going to go and cheer them on."

"No."

"Come on, what else have you got to do?"

"Well, I have yet to hear about your talk with Detective Thurman."

For half a second Juliet was speechless. "Oh yeah. I forgot about that."

"I'll bet." I crossed my arms and glared at her. She chewed her lip. "So?"

"It went fine."

"Is that right?"

"Yeah, it is. Now let's go. I'm going to be late. I don't want Eric to worry." She started toward the living room. I stepped in front of her.

"It's okay for me to worry, but not Eric?"

"Come down to the game. We can talk there."

"No."

"Oh, come on, it'll be fun," she said. "You need some fun in your life."

"I'd like to eat my dinner without getting indigestion. That would be fun."

"Then don't rush and come over after you eat. It's down the street."

"I know where the park is."

"Good. I'll see you in half an hour." She pushed past me and left.

Apparently, if I was going to get any information out of my sister, I'd have to do it at the soccer game. Nevertheless, I took my sweet time eating dinner, did the dishes, and cleaned the kitchen before I left. The park was a quarter mile from my house and I chose to walk. Despite my stalling, the game was still in full swing when I got there.

I had no trouble finding Juliet. She was the loudest of the assembled fans, shouting instructions to the players and whistling shrilly. The others watching the game appeared to be friends and family of the players, and seemed to be using the game as an excuse to visit. This was more a party than a sports event. Juliet couldn't have been more at home. An opportunity for a private conversation didn't look too promising. I could've stayed home, had a glass of wine to calm my nerves, and admired my garden. Well, she wasn't going to slip by me that easily. I'd get her later. I turned around and stared home.

"Thea! Theeeeaaa!"

I stopped, winced, and glanced over my shoulder. Juliet waved both arms like she was flagging down a search plane.

"Over here, I'm over here!"

I gave up.

I knew nothing about soccer. My acquaintance with spectator sports was limited to high school football and a little of the same of the college variety. I could tell there were two teams on the field because they wore different colored jerseys. Great.

"Is that all they do?" I asked Juliet. "Run relentlessly up and down the field trying to kick that ball into a net?"

"Pretty much. Except -- see that guy with the big mitt on his hand at the end of the field? No, that's the ref. Jeez, Thea, he doesn't have anything on his hands. The other guy in front of the net who's just standing around? Yeah, him. He tries to keep the ball out of the net."

"Oh. He doesn't get much exercise." About that time he launched himself through the air and the soccer ball slammed into his chest. I flinched. "I take that back. It all looks awfully intense."

It also looked exhausting. Adult males deliver a frightening amount of focused energy into their game -- more so than their younger counterparts. All the running, shouting, and grunting when bodies collide bears an unsettling resemblance to a battlefield. Occasionally, a referee blew his whistle and activity ebbed, then geared up again.

"Oh! Goal! Somebody made a goal!" I cheered and Juliet punched my shoulder.

"Wrong team. Jeez, Thea, pay attention."

"Oh, sorry."

"See number thirty-eight in the green jersey? That's Eric. Look at him run. Have you ever seen anything so beautiful?" She sighed and watched, her mouth partly opened. I stuck my elbow in her side nudging her back into speech. "Yeah ... see his shirt? 'Fuentes' is on the back, too, but it's kind of covered with dirt."

I tried to pay closer attention. A few players looked familiar, but they milled around too much for me to be sure. Besides, they all looked the same in their jerseys and shorts. I tried to follow Eric's progress throughout the remainder of the game. He seemed to be the team captain -- at least he was the one on his team yelling a stream of incomprehensible orders as he ran. He looked angry. That alarmed me. Eric was generally so laid back.

"Aren't things going well?" I asked Juliet in a whisper.

"No, they're good, why?" She answered me without taking her eyes off the action.

"Eric looks mad."

"Na, he's just into the game. The other team's pretty good. They're so into it. Raging testosterone -- OFFSIDES!"

Talk about being "into" the game. My ears rang from Juliet's shrieking. But when Eric made an assist that resulted in a goal for his team, I cheered as wildly as everyone else.

The game ended with Eric's team winning by one point. The elated players, soaked in sweat and decorated in grass stains and dirt, whooped and pounded each other with enthusiasm as they left the field. As they came in our direction I recognized a clerk from the 7-Eleven down the street and one of the young men who worked at the feed store. Eric walked off the field toward us with the player who had made the goal. With a lurch my heart rate shot into overdrive. The player was Paul.

Other team members walked or jogged by, slapping Paul or Eric on the back and saying something about the winning goal, which tended toward good if he was from their team, or a good-natured insult if he was from the losing team.

"Way to go, Doc." A lanky man gave Paul a resounding slap on the back. "Bend it like Beckham, eh?" The copious amount of blood covering the front of the man's jersey dragged my gaze away from Paul.

"You're such a wimp," Juliet said at my look of horror. "That guy ran his nose into some other guy's elbow right before you came."

"Hey, Thea." Mark Wong, my dentist, hailed me. "I didn't know you were a fan."

"I've been recruited," I said, meaning Juliet had taken it upon herself to expand my horizons. Mark glanced toward Paul.

"Oh." He smiled.

"I didn't know you played," I said.

"Three times a week," he said, and slapped his stomach. "Keeps the fat off." He raised a hand in farewell and continued toward his waiting family.

Eric and Paul reached us and Juliet threw her arms around her sweaty hero.

"Way to go, guys!" she said. "Killer game!"

Both men had the sated look of victors coming home from battle. Paul's gaze locked with mine and my heart rate geared up another few notches.

"Hi," he said, smiling.

"Hi." I smiled back. "Doc? You're a doctor?"

"PhD," he confirmed.

"I guess I should have realized, I mean, since you teach." The old grad school caste-system reared its Machiavellian head. I remembered it well, having only a lowly master's degree. Yet, here he was, communing with real people as if he was one of us.

Stop acting like a reverse snob, Thea. You know you're only doing it because he still makes you weak-kneed.

Neither of us looked away despite the lack of conversation.

From somewhere else Jorge strolled up and pounded Paul on the back. Paul blinked and looked at him.

"Hey man, good game ... for an old guy who cheats," he said and laughed.

"It's not too hard to beat a bunch of posers," Paul countered, grinning. "It might be worth your while to learn how to kick the ball."

Jorge feigned an affronted stance and took a wide swing that Paul easily ducked.

"How come you aren't on the same team as Eric?" I asked.

Jorge wore the opposing team's colors. "You do work together, after all."

"Our schedules are too different," Jorge responded. "We can't get to the same practices."

"Why don't you give Thea a ride home?" Juliet asked Eric. Still holding fast to his hand, she turned to me. "He's giving everyone else a ride. He can drop you off."

The prospect of getting into a small car with a bunch of sweaty men had no appeal, but I attempted a polite smile.

"Thanks, but I think I'll walk. It's not far."

Juliet rolled her eyes and Jorge laughed loudly.

"I don't think we smell very good," Eric said.

"You always smell good," Juliet purred.

Jeez.

Jorge punched Paul's shoulder. "Hey man, I almost had you on that last play. You must've felt me breathing down your neck."

The game-chatter started up again, drowning out Paul's comment to Jorge. All of them were still pumped, and it was obvious there'd be no getting Juliet away from Eric.

I wouldn't have minded talking to Paul longer, either, but with the post-game high still fueling their shared talk and laughter it didn't appear as though that was going to happen.

"Good game," I said, and gave a little wave. "It was fun. I'll have to come and watch you play again. Bye."

No one responded. I walked away, mentally chalking up a point to my sister. The creativity Juliet used to avoid a chat -- and have it appear as though circumstances intervened -- never ceased to amaze. I'd pin her down eventually. She couldn't put me off forever.

I hadn't gone twenty yards when I heard my name called. Glancing back, I saw Paul jogging toward me. He appeared younger, his soaked hair hanging over his forehead. His usual confident expression was absent.

"I need to go home and have a shower and change first, but I was wondering ... would you like to go out for a drink, or something?"

"Sure -- yes, I'd like that." The words fell out of my mouth.

His smile looked relieved. "Good. I'll pick you up in forty minutes?"

I nodded, feeling giddy. He turned and loped back to join the others. I hardly noticed the walk home.

Chapter Thirteen

I hurried into my bedroom, shedding my old, boring t-shirt and jeans, and brushed my teeth while I dug through my closet and bureau drawers. Three changes of mind later I had on my best, skinny jeans, ballet flats, and the red cashmere sweater Juliet wished she was petite enough to wear. Paul's knock on my front door coincided with my last swipe of mascara. After one last check in the hall mirror to be sure my hair wasn't behaving oddly, I pulled the door open.

His smile didn't look as nervous as I felt. When he said, "Your flower garden is really pretty -- so are you." he colored slightly.

I could've read him wrong.

"Thank you, you too -- uh, I mean nice, you look nice, too." My cheeks grew considerably warmer.

He did look good. The blue polo shirt matched the blue of his eyes, and his jeans fit … his jeans fit. I looked away quickly and reached for my purse.

He let my brainless remark pass. "I thought we might go to The River's Bend."

I smiled, too eager, and nodded, afraid to open my mouth and let something else idiotic fall out. We took Paul's car. Good thing it was such a short distance to the historical district where the bar was located because I couldn't think of a thing -- intelligent or otherwise -- to say. Amazing since I hadn't been able to shut up Saturday night. *First dates are always such a trial, Thea.* Omigod. This was a date. Why hadn't that occurred to me? Maybe it wasn't really a date. *You know it is. Don't be naïve. He asked, you said yes.*

I tucked my hair behind my ears, then untucked it. *Great, now you're fidgeting.* For a panicked moment I contemplated asking Paul to take me home. I'd made a mistake. No. That would be rude. It was just drinks. What could happen? I could as easily go out for drinks with my sister. Or anyone. Right?

Now would be a good time to start a conversation.

Frantically, I rummaged through my mental archives, but came up with nothing to interrupt the silence. I flashed Paul a tentative smile, and discarded the weather as too obvious and desperate. The thought that kept surfacing was the one reminding me I hadn't actually broken up with Jonathan yet.

But Paul knew all about what happened last Saturday night. *You told him. In detail. Minute detail, on the drive back to Snohomish.* Because he asked. Because I needed to talk to someone about what happened. *Someone? Right. Be honest. You didn't want him to think you were at McMurphy's with Greg.*

Certainly, to him, this was not a date. Undoubtedly, to him, he was simply having a drink with his landlord's niece. Just to keep the peace. Yup, that was it. I was overreacting because of this teeny little crush I seemed to have on him. Nothing I couldn't handle. Well, that was a relief.

Then why did I still feel ready to bolt?

"I meant to ask how your appointment at the sheriff's office went," Paul said as he pulled into a parking spot in front of The River's Bend.

Oh yes, *that* topic.

"But I didn't want to bring it up in front of your family."

"Thanks," I said, grateful for his perception. "Everyone's been a little reactive. Detective Thurman told me they determined Blackie didn't kill Valerie."

He turned off the ignition and we got out of the car. "What else?"

My mouth went dry.

His eyebrow arched, ever so slightly, and was followed a couple of beats later by the beginnings of a smile.

I meant to sanitize my response but it had a life of its own. "They, um, seem to think I'm a person of interest."

You blurted that right out. How did he know you left out information, and what's he smiling about? This is amusing?

"That means they don't have any leads. I'd worry more about Greg. Are you filing a complaint?"

"No." My tone meant to imply the subject was closed.

"I think you should consider it." He held the door of the tavern open for me, but I stopped and faced him.

"I don't see the point. He's grieving. He didn't know what he was doing. It won't happen again."

"Don't make excuses for him, Thea."

He was issuing an order? I bristled. "I'm not. I can't see how overreacting --" His frown stopped me. It wasn't anger. Something else. What did he know? "Unless you think ...."

But the expression on his face became neutral and he backed down. "Do what you think is best. I'm probably being too cautious." He broke eye contact.

Damn. I hadn't intended to sound so bossy. I chewed my lip and considered telling him about my visit from Frederick Parsons. No, bad idea. I didn't want to think about what he'd have to say if I brought that up. I'd handled it well enough, and I sure as heck didn't want a lecture.

"Mr. Rucker hasn't shown up again, has he?" he asked, motioning me through the door.

"No, but I saw him in the lobby at the sheriff's office."

Paul shot me a concerned look. "He talked to you?"

"Yeah. It was kind of one sided -- on his part. But he was already mad when he came flying out of the inner office."

"What did he say?" He stopped and looked around the tavern.

"Not much. He left in a hurry. I never did find out why he was there." I could handle Randy. I wasn't helpless.

"Huh." Paul slid me another brief look.

Damn. Had I said that out loud?

The waitress passed by and told Paul, with a flirty wink, to sit anywhere. He acknowledged her with a nod and threaded his way across the room to a table with a view. I followed a few steps behind, certain I'd put him off.

"Is this okay?" He indicated the table.

"Yes. Fine. Perfect." I sat in the chair he held for me. The smile I hoped was polite and friendly didn't seem to be earning me any points. He turned his attention out the large window to the Snohomish River that passes almost at the base of the building.

For lack of a better idea, I copied him, taking in the familiar scenery. The trees along the river bank were leafing out. They looked fresh and new against the river's dark, sinuous current. High clouds edged the last glow of the evening sky off to the west. Stars would soon be visible but, sadly, I knew it wouldn't last. It was a typical, nice, Northwest evening that announced rain was on its way.

"This is a great place to come in the summer," I said, too chipper. Paul, opposite me at the little table, looked in the direction I'd fluttered my hand. "They have a jazz band some evenings and it's a nice place to kick back and relax." Cripes. I not only sounded like a Chamber of Commerce ad, but as if I was planning future dates. "A little too cold to be out on the deck in April, though." *Oh, duh, Thea.*

He settled back in his chair, elbows on the arm rests, and regarded me in slightly amused silence.

Shoot me now.

I smiled at him. And swallowed.

He smiled back. His Adam's apple bobbed.

The waitress provided a welcomed distraction to what was rapidly becoming a disaster of a date. We ordered our drinks and passed on the appetizers. As I watched her walk away from the table, her white apron ties swinging across her very round butt, it occurred to me soccer might be a good topic. How much worse could I screw up? I plunged on, asking about his team.

"I joined a couple of weeks ago," he said, plucking a packet of sugar from the little dish on the table and examining it. "We had an informal league down at the U. Mostly grad students, a few of the staff. It's easier for me to play here since I moved."

He put the sugar back in its holder and picked up the salt shaker, turning the little glass container in his fingers. I watched, fascinated. He had a magician's hands. Strong and quick. Not a scholar's hands. I wanted to touch them. *Oh cripes, you've been staring at him!* I looked out the window and grappled for another topic.

"Do you do any sports, other than riding?" he asked.

"No, I'm afraid not." I tried not fixate on him. "Juliet is the one who dabbles in different activities. I tend to stick with one thing." I was so boring.

And I couldn't stop staring. I dragged my gaze to the visual refuge out the window once more. Quick find another category. *I'll take Mutual Acquaintances for five-hundred, Alex.* No question about it. I was losing it.

I cleared my throat. "Have you known Eric long?" I glanced at him, then found a tether for my disobedient eyes in the napkin holder. But he hadn't been looking at me, so I snuck another lingering peek at his face. Regular, masculine features—not handsome-pretty like Jonathan, but pleasing. Lean, but not sharp. I could detect his Italian heritage. Silky eyebrows ... they had to be soft. Deep-set blue eyes framed by black lashes, fastened on me -- oops.

Our drinks arrived, saving me. Paul shifted in his chair. "Yeah, a while. He took a class from me at the Bothell campus, which is when I found out he worked for my aunt at Copper Creek." This time he spoke to me instead of the inanimate objects on the table.

"Huh." I considered this. "I knew he took some classes. Is he working toward a degree?"

"He's been working on his B.S. for a while. He's majoring in computer science. I expect he'll graduate next year. He just got a bit of extra cash, so he can take classes more regularly now."

"Juliet never said anything." In fact, she told me precious little about her relationship with Eric. She used to tell me everything.

"I hope I haven't spoken out of turn." He drew a line through the condensation on his glass with his index finger then picked up his drink sipped and set it down a little further from him. "Maybe you'd best not mention anything yet. I'm not sure Delores knows. She depends on him, but he can't support a family on what he makes there -- not these days, anyway."

Whoa. That got my attention. "A family?"

"I'm guessing." He rubbed his jaw. "Eric hasn't said anything, but knowing him, I expect he's making plans."

"Juliet?"

He nodded. "Who else? He's had his eye on her for a long time."

"Ohhhh ...." Huh. Something else I didn't know.

Conversation turned slightly more personal. I asked him about his job, my next category of choice. He leaned back in his chair, an elbow on the armrest, and talked about teaching at the university and some of the projects he was involved with. And he smiled. A real smile that animated his eyes. It drew me in, nudging me forward in my chair, tickling my curiosity, rewarding the questions I asked as he talked. I watched his face, his hands, his posture, as he painted vivid images of the places he had been, digging fossils and discovering bits of creatures long dead, that no human had ever seen. His stories seduced me with the suspense of the hunt, transported me to windy mountain sides and dusty deserts, thrilled me when a stroke of luck revealed a dramatic discovery. How lucky his students were to have him for a teacher.

"I'm sorry." He cut himself off, eyebrows tilted in a worried manner. "I can get a little long winded. I didn't mean to lecture."

In the breath before answering, my heart took his picture -- his remarkable blue eyes, the strong line of his jaw, the way the edge of his sleeves molded to the muscles in his arms -- and I knew I'd have it forever.

"Don't apologize. I've enjoyed every moment. You make me want to rush home and pack for an expedition." The lines smoothed from his forehead. "Teaching is important to you, isn't it?"

His eyes softened, like a friend with a shared insight. "Yes, I suppose it is. Probably one of the more worthwhile occupations I've had in my life. What about you? Do you enjoy what you do?"

"Very much," I said without hesitation, but a little disappointed to rejoin the world that was not part of his stories. "I quit my corporate job a couple of years ago. It's not easy to get time off when you're your own boss, but it's a lot more rewarding. Not nearly as exciting as finding dinosaur bones in the wilderness, though."

A self-conscious chuckle escaped his lips and his gaze shifted to the table top. He rubbed his hand across his mouth.

I traced my fingertip around the lip of my glass. "The big advantage is having more time to ride since I don't have to deal with the commute anymore. And Uncle Henry finds it easier to fit me into his schedule." The memory of him touching my hair after Greg's attack surfaced, complete with a vivid flash of fantasy involving Paul's naked body. I felt myself flush, and looked away, making a small diversion out of sipping my drink.

"Henry's quite a man," Paul said. "Do you have any ambitions of following in his footsteps?"

"No, I'd never be able to do it. Two Olympic Games,

complete with medals, World championships, and countless international competitions. It's a grueling, demanding life."

"You don't compete?"

"No. Not any more." The moment the curt words left my lips I realized how unfair my tone was. He had no way of knowing.

But he seemed not to notice. "Dressage shows aren't like regular horse shows, right? There are individual tests and the horse is judged against a standard instead of against the other competitors? That what Henry told me, if I remember correctly."

I had to hand it to him, he must have paid attention. I picked up the conversation. He hadn't crossed any line. "Right. The tests are a series of patterns, done at the walk, trot, and canter, and they vary in difficulty depending on the level the horse and rider are working at."

"So one arrives at a competition and is handed patterns to memorize?"

"No, thankfully. The tests are published and available to anyone. They get changed once every four years -- the year before the Olympic Games."

"You mean a rider gets to practice the test, and ride it for four years before having to learn a new one? Kind of sounds like cheating."

I laughed, but he asked good questions. "You're equating a dressage test with the academic equivalent. This is a little different. The tests are used to help the horse progress through his training, not just evaluate his progress, and certainly not to trip him up by springing something new on him. And besides, over the course of four years the horse is bound to move up a level or two." It seemed he understood. At least his eyes weren't glazing over.

"If you know a lot about it, why don't you compete? It seems to me Henry would be top notch support."

My smile went rigid, and I straightened in my chair despite reminding myself that his sucker-punch was unintentional. I hedged my response. "I think he would like me to, and I might someday. It's more important to me to learn, though. I guess I got caught up in the education."

But I saw where this conversation was going and it depressed me. Any second now he'd smile in that condescending male-way they all did, tell me to cowboy up and not be so sensitive. After all, if I really loved dressage I'd take my reward from the doing of it, and other people's opinions wouldn't matter. I'd had this chat so many times before with Jonathan and others that I could have faxed it in.

"I can understand that." Paul sipped his drink and watched me for a moment. "It's easier to risk failure when you're not related to someone who's been remarkably successful at the same thing."

Okay, this was different. Maybe. I had the uneasy sense of being transparent until perception spoke loud enough to be heard over the grumbling of my good buddy, defensiveness.

"Sounds like the voice of experience." I tried to sound casual, but I was probing and not sure if I should.

"Yeah, I guess." He swirled the ice cubes around in his glass. "I became the family renegade and a teenager simultaneously. Made a big deal about not following my dad into medicine. Told my parents I wanted to do things my own way."

"Was that when you joined the Army? Right out of high school?"

"You could say. I joined the Army, then finished high school."

"You dropped out?" I never would have guessed, and couldn't help the amusement in my voice.

"Pretty funny, now, isn't it?" A corner of his mouth turned up and he met my gaze.

"I think it's admirable you've done so much." I sincerely meant it.

He shook his head, picked up the salt shaker, and moved it as if it were a chess piece. Still looking at it, he shifted in his seat, and what must have been his knee, brushed the inside of mine. A jolt sizzled up my thigh and collided with the base of my spine before sending its heat radiating into my belly. I gulped -- and waited for another touch. He shifted again, and I knew he'd moved his knee away.

"Mostly, I made things difficult for myself and everyone else. My folks are proud of what I do now even though I'm not a doctor like my dad and brother. Looking back, I think I was so scared I would fail I took a short cut to reduce the misery."

"But you didn't fail, you're doing something you love. And you did end up making your own decisions." Without thinking, I reached across the table and briefly touched the back of his hand.

His laugh was soft as his gaze met mine. "Not a waste of time in your book, then?"

"Hardly." His gentle humor made my heart flutter. He cared what I thought of him. "It's made you what you are. Nothing wrong with that."

It occurred to me, as our conversation drifted back to shared acquaintances, unique family members, and other subjects with varying in degrees of seriousness, that I could talk to him without being wary. I forgot my earlier discomfort. There was none of the judgmental posturing I was so used to, and so distrustful of, with Jonathan. Paul listened. *Why hadn't you noticed that on the drive home from Seattle Saturday night, Thea?* I knew the answer immediately. I had been too wrapped up in my own drama.

The waitress interrupted our sharing of grad school woes, clearing her throat at a decibel level we couldn't ignore. "More of the same?"

My glass had been empty for a while. I think she'd attempted to refill our drinks before and we ignored her. Whoops.

"Would you like another?" Paul asked.

"No, I'm good."

"Why don't we leave then? I haven't had a chance to look

around downtown yet. Are you up to playing tour guide?"

"Yeah," I said. "Sounds like fun."

Paul left a sizable tip. Maybe it was an apology.

We strolled down First Avenue, looking into the windows of the various merchants and abundant antique shops, now closed for the evening. Nearby bars and several restaurants were hopping. Parking would be at a premium for the remainder of the evening.

"I've never seen so many antique shops crammed into one place," Paul observed. "What's the history of this town?"

"Hmm...." I dug around in my inadequate memory and improvised a lengthy tale.

"So these buildings on First Street are original?"

"Yes. With a considerable amount of restoration and maintenance, as you can imagine."

"Do you know what any of them were?"

I pointed to a two-story wooden building on the river side of the street that housed a sandwich and pie shop. "I believe that was a tavern. And the one next to it a bordello."

Paul regarded both establishments briefly, then shook his head once. "You're making that up."

I looked up at him, wide-eyed, blinked, and fought to keep my mouth from turning up in a smile.

"Look at you -- you can't lie and keep a straight face!"

The laughter leaked out. "I am. But it sounds good."

He chuckled and took my hand as we crossed the street. Stepping onto the curb he released my hand, placing his on the small of my back as if to guide me. His touch was light, but lingered. I held my breath. Maybe he just liked the feel of my cashmere sweater. With my pulse flying, I imitated his gesture, barely touching him as I slid my arm around his waist. I could turn it into a "you first" kind of movement, if necessary.

Ah, no. Not necessary.

His arm settled across my back and his fingers cupped my waist with a brief, acknowledging pressure. A headiness surged through my veins. As I settled my hand more securely on his waist I tripped on a bump in the sidewalk. In an instant I grabbed at his body with one hand and his belt buckle with my other. He steadied my sprawl with a two-armed embrace.

"I'm okay." The words tumbled out of my mouth before I'd regained my balance.

"You sure?"

"Yes, sorry." I unhanded his belt and snatched my hand from his waist. "I, um … I just saw the perfect Christmas present for Aunt Vi." I took a hurried step to a shop window where a porcelain tea set was displayed, gulping down my embarrassment.

"You start early." Paul stepped beside me and looked in the window. Humor touched his voice.

"I try to keep an eye out." I kept my gaze glued to the shop's display.

We continued along the sidewalk, occupying our own individual space, conversation nonexistent, pretending interest in the other store's we passed. But I couldn't stay away from him. He was like a magnet. I brushed against him twice, three times as we walked. The last time the backs of our hands touched. He didn't seem to notice.

Crossing the next side street, I summoned my courage and reached for his hand. His response was immediate. He engulfed my hand in his. Without a word, we stopped to look in a storefront window. I glanced up at his reflection, meeting his eyes in the glass.

When he turned from our reflection to me, my pulse leapt, and time hung suspended. Gently, he brushed my cheek with the tips of his fingers, and the caress drew me in. His gaze swept my features. This time there was no confusion. His eyes and touch conveyed an unmistakable statement. He wanted me.

Thea, this isn't … I slammed the lid down on my inner voice with a lift of my chin.

I wanted to kiss him so badly my lips ached. He accepted

my invitation, kissing me with an electric, lingering, restraint that dismantled, down to the very foundations, any excuse that remained standing. With eyes closed, I drank in the exquisite, intoxicating tenderness of his soft lips, the delicious, warm, male scent of his skin. And when the kiss ended I opened my eyes and fell into his. He pulled my body into his, gentle at first, and led me into a kiss that fast became crazy with desperation to possess, consume. I didn't know where I stopped and he began and I didn't care. This was the kind of kiss I read about in trashy novels. The kind that can't be sated. The kind your mother never tells you about. The kind that makes the rest of the world disappear....

"I'm glad you found a way to occupy yourself this evening." The voice cracked through my consciousness like a shot.

Paul and I broke apart with an abruptness that made me reel.

"Jonathan," I said, gulping air. He didn't look very glad to see me.

"This must be Paul."

Should I introduce them? "Uh, yes. Paul, this is Jonathan."

"So I gather," Paul said. He sounded pretty unfriendly as well.

We were no longer attached to each other and were, in fact, standing several feet apart.

"What are you doing here?" I asked, still shocked and breathless.

"I came to talk to you, but you weren't home. I thought I'd walk around downtown a bit before I tried again. I can see there's no point in asking what *you're* doing." He was really angry. His nostrils flared. "I was planning on surprising you."

"I'm surprised."

"I meant surprising you in a pleasant way," he said, glowering.

He reached into his coat pocket and pulled out a little black box. My heart stopped, and not in a pleasant way. I glanced at Paul. His eyes were fixed on the awful thing. Jonathan flicked it open and three-quarters of Paul's annual salary leered back at us. Jonathan, the peacock in Armani, was strutting his enormous tail feathers like this was some kind of a courtship smackdown. I was beyond humiliated.

"I should go," Paul said. He wheeled and started to walk away.

"No -- Paul, wait!" I made a grab for his arm.

He jerked his arm out of my reach and gave me a look so cold I froze in shock.

"I am not accustomed to taking another man's girlfriend." His eyes were narrow with anger, but his tone was emotionless.

"I am not his girlfriend." My tone was emphatic. "I'm --"

"Thea! How can you say that?" Jonathan said, his jaw slack. The indecent display of his virility still lay exposed in his hand.

Paul glanced at Jonathan then turned on me, his voice low and even. "You led me to believe you broke up with him."

Guilt took aim and got me dead on. "No! I mean --"

"You can't have it both ways."

"Well, of course she hasn't broken up with me." Jonathan sneered the words at Paul, but Paul's critical gaze remained on me.

I didn't even glance at Jonathan. "Yes -- no. No. You don't understand. I --"

"I understand perfectly. You've been playing me ever since I drove you home last weekend."

"What? I've been what?" How did he come up with that notion? This was ridiculous. "How can you --? I don't 'play' with people!"

"Thea, explain yourself." Jonathan snapped the box shut and stuffed it back into his pocket. His hand closed on my arm, but I twisted out of his grip.

It took every ounce of self-control I had to block out Jonathan and maintain my focus on Paul, who was obviously suffering from a huge dose of egotistical misinformation. "You can't possibly believe --"

"I certainly can believe you've been maneuvering me ever since I met you," Paul accused, and nudged me right over the edge.

"You are out of your freaking mind." I leaned into the words. "The only thing I'm guilty of is being gullible. You've been playing Mr. Macho-rescue-the-poor-helpless-little-woman-I'll-bet-I-can-seduce-her-before-the-weekend-macho-guy, and I bought your whole sorry act!"

"All right. You want to discuss this now? How about you stop pretending --"

"*Pretending?*" I shrieked. My jaw went slack, then tightened to the point I could barely form words. "You, you, you -- I'll tell you what you can do with --"

"Now listen here --"Jonathan stabbed a finger at the air.

"Stay out of this," I roared at him. "You've caused enough trouble already!"

"Thea, control yourself," Jonathan snapped. "You owe me an explanation. You owe me."

"I think you owe an explanation to him *and* me," Paul said. *His* jaw was so tight I thought he'd break a bone.

"I do? The drinks, the walk, the, the, it was your idea."

"Yeah? My idea? That's not exactly --"

"This is all my fault, I suppose? I just led you along by the, the nose? Men! You can't get past your hormones, can you? Oh, it's so easy to stick someone else with the responsibility -- then you can do any *damn* thing you want!"

"Hey, I'm the offended party here!" Jonathan whined at high volume, darting left then right to get past Paul who somehow was able to keep his back to him.

"You want to talk lack of control, woman? You couldn't keep your hands off me!"

It was obvious Paul meant there to be no mistaking who was the target of his anger. Fine by me. I itched to hand back whatever he threw at me.

"You think you're so damn irresistible? Well I've got news for you, Paul Hudson. I don't have any problem resisting your sorry-ass passes."

His lips curled and he took half a step toward me. "Is that what you call what happened? Resisting?"

I rose up to my full five-feet two, panting with rage, and pushed my chin at him. Paul's eyes widened and he lowered his chin.

"Thea!" Jonathan yelped.

"Damn right," I snarled.

"Fine by me. I'm leaving." He stalked off toward his car.

"Not before I do!" I shouted to his back and swung a fist through the air. At least I had the presence of mind to stalk off in the opposite direction.

"Thea!" Jonathan called after me. "You can't leave! Not again! Not after all I've done for you!"

I rounded on him, beyond furious. "I can't ever recall you doing anything for me that wasn't specifically for your benefit."

His parting comment, to my back, had something to do with me having "no idea." Oh, I had an idea, all right. In fact, I had more than an idea. I had the whole concept, theory, and model down in a flash. He was a manipulating, selfish bastard who couldn't see beyond the end of his own nose. If I never saw him again, it would be too soon.

By the time I covered the scant mile to my home I'd walked off most of my anger and felt miserable. Miserable and ashamed of myself. I'd never had such a childish shouting match as this with anyone, except possibly my sister. I'd never been so humiliated. I dug my keys out of the bottom of my purse and let myself inside. My house, so calm and orderly, stood in stark contrast to my emotional state.

In my bedroom, the clothes I'd tried on and discarded earlier lay scattered on the bed. A missed omen of what a mess this evening would turn out to be. Sighing, I picked up each sweater, blouse, and pair of slacks. Slowly, deliberately, as if my actions could do the same for my jumbled feelings, I put them away. As I closed my bureau drawer I caught sight of my face in the mirror. I looked terrible. The purple bruises along my jaw stood out like neon lights against my pallor. Mascara smudged my face under my red, puffy eyes from where I'd rubbed tears away. My lipstick was long gone. My green irises glowed like beacons. I'd seen more attractive traffic lights.

I sat on the edge of my bed and contemplated the huge mess my life had become. But each time my eyes closed I tumbled into the memory of every touch, taste and scent that was Paul. I covered my ears, trying to block the sound of his voice, his breathing, his gentle moan in my mouth. He overwhelmed every sense in a way I never imagined possible. Pure, honest emotion propelled me into his arms tonight. I thought he was my friend. I wanted him for my lover. I believed he felt the same. How dare he turn that emotion into something I was so ashamed of?

Groaning, I collapsed across my bed, and stared at the ceiling. Damn him! He said unforgivable things to me. Wasn't he smart enough to see through Jonathan's posturing? How could he be so mean and insensitive? Jonathan, for all his pompousness, never said anything to me like Paul had tonight.

Be honest, Thea. He never had any call to. And you sure trumped him in the name-calling department.

But I knew Paul could be kind and thoughtful. In our conversations before ... well, before that horrible, very public scene, he talked to me in a way Jonathan never had. He shared his thoughts, was interested in what I had to say, and -- and his kisses, the way his body felt against mine, like I had at last reached home -- complete with the relief of being able to touch him, hold him -- oh, God. And then to lose it all.

What's wrong with you? You barely know him. Don't you jump on Juliet for the same thing? What happened to your resolve to be more self reliant, to stand on your own two feet? Thank goodness that's no longer an issue. You made damn sure of that.

Tears trickled out of the corners of my eyes and into my ears. I felt like a really bad Country Western song.

Chapter Fourteen

I was too steeped in my own misery to sleep. But I must have, because the last I remembered my room was dark. Now it wasn't.

I squeezed my eyes shut against the light and groaned. I was woozy, and someone was sticking a knife into my skull above my right eyebrow. That had to be it. Nothing else could hurt as bad. When I sat up it got worse. Dull knives pounded into my face below my eyes. I considered lying down again, but my stomach was awake and threatening. I went into the bathroom, leaned against the sink and waited for something to happen. While I waited I glared at myself in the mirror. I looked even worse than the night before. My eyelids were nearly swollen shut, and my face beyond colorless -- except for the bruises that had turned green and yellow on the edges, blacker toward the middle. My lips were swollen, too. I still wore my clothes.

Surely I suffered more than Paul. He hated me. I deserved it. And Jonathan hated me. Good cause there, too. I was the poster child for poor judgment and indiscretion. I was never going to recover from this. It would haunt me the rest of my life and for punishment I would probably live to be one hundred. I soaked a wash cloth in cold water and held it, dripping, over my face.

When I could stand upright without my head threatening to split down the middle I went to the kitchen and made coffee. Somewhere through my first cup, as I tortured myself with a mental picture of Paul entertaining a Valerie look-alike in his apartment and laughing over how stupidly I'd behaved, reality gave me a thump on the head. My turn to do stalls. I dashed to the phone and called Uncle Henry to apologize. Aunt Vi answered. I told her I'd overslept and wasn't feeling well, all true -- if incomplete.

"Don't worry, dear. Henry's taken care of them. It's no trouble," she said over my protest. Then with the accuracy of a laser guided Patriot missile she zeroed in on exactly what I hoped to hide. "You haven't seen Paul, have you? He didn't come home last night."

I choked up. In a small voice I said. "No." followed by a tiny sniff. That's all it took for Aunt Vi to confirm her hit.

"Oh, no." Did you two have a fight?"

"Yes," I squeaked.

"I'll be over straightaway. I'll make you a nice cup of tea and you can tell me what happened."

It should have taken her ten minutes to get to my house, but it seemed she knocked on my door almost before I had time to hang up the phone. Time flies when you're feeling sorry for yourself.

"Who's that in the fancy black car out front?" she asked when I opened the front door.

She took off her damp coat and folded it inside out over her arm. It was raining. Figures. I looked past her and saw Frederick Parsons's black Mercedes. The big guy with the dark glasses sat behind the wheel, looking intently at me. A picture flashed in my mind and for a moment the floor under me shifted. I caught my balance on the door jam. Holy crap. I wasn't sure if I'd just been diverted from my latest misery or added to it. Either way, there was no doubt. Frederick Parsons's chauffeur was the driver of the silver Honda I'd nearly flattened with Delores's truck on Carpenter Road. He must have made the first 9-1-1 call -- the one Thurman had mentioned. But why had he taken off?

"Never seen him before," I lied, shutting the door and locking it. "Aunt Vi --"

"Now you hush and come sit down." She propelled me toward the kitchen. "What you need is a nice cup of tea and a little something in your belly. Where're you slippers? You'll catch your death running around barefoot." She went to my bedroom and came back with the pink bunnies. Even the one that still had its tongue, whose crooked eyes made it appear demented, couldn't cheer me up.

After I downed two slices of toast and a cup of strong tea, she pried the previous evening's sorry tale out of me, piece by embarrassing piece. Then she spun it with her own perspective. It was not quite the flavor of sympathy I had in mind. I hoped for a good dose of men-are-scum (except for Uncle Henry and Dad), and a sample of you're better-off-without-the-Neanderthals. Instead I got something completely different.

"Give Paul time. He's unhappy right now and feeling a little foolish. It doesn't hurt a man to feel foolish every once in a while." She patted my hand and winked. "Keeps 'em humble. That's what my mum always used to say."

"He should feel foolish. He certainly acted that way. And I'm not interested in 'giving him time.' I made a huge mistake agreeing to go out with him, thinking it would just be a friendly little get-together instead of, of --" I waved my hands in the air.

"Well, your timing wasn't the best."

"My timing?"

She nodded and patted my hand. "Well, no help for that now, is there? Still some things have their own schedules and there's nothing you can do about it. Like Eric and your sis."

"I'm not Juliet. I don't jump into things. I take my time and evaluate." I shifted in my chair and sat up a little straighter.

Maybe I sounded righteous, but I was in real pain here.

"Oh, now, there was no jumping going on there with those two. I always thought they should have gotten together sooner. They've been friends for quite some time. Probably a good two years, and they've been dating for a good three months now."

"Huh. Three months? That's a record for her." And not quite what she told me. I sniffed. "Well, I need to be on my own, anyway ...."

"Thea, love, you've been on your own for a lot longer than most women your age."

"No I haven't. I've always depended on you and Uncle Henry, and Juliet and --"

"You've always made your own way. And what's wrong with having people around who love and support you? Do you think that makes you weak?"

"Well, no, but ...."

"It does open you up to pain, and it takes a strong person to risk being vulnerable." Without so much as a pause for breath, she adjusted her sights. "Don't push him away because the timing doesn't seem right."

"I didn't push him away. He left under his own steam."

"I know, dear."

"Well, it's true. You didn't see his face or hear what he said. He said hateful things."

More patting. "I know, dear."

"Then I said hateful things, too."

This time I got a shoulder squeeze. "I know, dear."

"He thinks I'm scheming and duplicitous. God," I groaned, covering my face with my hands, "I don't want to feel like this."

She sighed and poured me another cup of tea. "You know, your uncle and I have been together forty-six years."

"Great. I can't sustain even a date for two hours. I'm so far off the bell curve of success and failure in relationships I could be classified an anomaly."

She looked over the top of her glasses at me. I shut my mouth.

"As I was saying, forty-six years. Most people would think he and I have a perfectly compatible relationship."

I nodded. It was true. They seemed more content with each other than most couples I knew -- most of the time.

"Well, it hasn't always been like that, but we both knew it was possible. It was something each of us needed and wanted with our hearts and souls."

I thought about my grandmother, Aunt Vi's older sister, and remembered the stories she used to tell about the upheavals in their young lives. These had always sounded like adventures to me. Now I saw uncertainty and unhappiness -- more than two young girls deserved. How they must have longed for a life of predictability where the people you loved would always be there for you.

"The point is, Henry and I had to work at it. There were times when, despite two wonderful children of our own and the success Henry was achieving, I though one or the other of us would pack up and walk out."

That bit of history I would never have guessed.

"Thea, if you want something enough, you don't give up when things go wrong. If it's right and good, you have patience. Sometimes you have to trust, and not get so involved in the moment you forget there's a tomorrow that wants looking after."

"You sound like the riding lesson I had yesterday," I observed in a rueful flash of insight.

She held my gaze and nodded. "It's much the same, isn't it? People and horses. When they're good, you don't give up on them, even when there's a problem."

"It's too late. He's given up on me," I said, making a last stab at pathos.

She smiled gently. "You don't know what is or isn't in his heart right now. You have nothing to lose by biding your time, and maybe much to gain."

She was wrong, and though I was calmer than when she'd arrived I knew this was one horse that wasn't going to jump. Paul did not strike me as someone you could coerce or cajole without his permission. Sometimes you had to know when to walk away.

"You need to talk to Jonathan," she added after a few sips of tea.

"I know."

"He's basically a good man, but you're not right for each other. Neither of you brings out the best in the other. You both need something the other can't give, and you have to be the one to end things. He won't do it. The sooner the better."

"Yes, I know. I thought you liked him."

She smiled at me. "I like the man who makes you happy, and neither one of you has been happy for some time. He needs you to be someone you're not, and he constantly worries that you won't support him emotionally. You resent him for trying to change you. You need someone who thinks you're grand just the way you are, even if you're not a carbon copy of him. Even when you disagree."

I nodded and hugged her. Juliet had found someone -- obviously. Would I ever find my someone? It surely wasn't Paul. I clamped down on my lower lip to hide the tremble.

A deep breath later I asked, "How did you come to be so wise?"

She laughed and wiped a little tear from the corner of her eye. "If you're really, really lucky, life knocks it into you." She stood and gave me a hug. I was so lucky to have her. "Time for me to go and time for you to get to work." She smoothed her dress and picked up her coat and purse.

The phone rang and my warm, fuzzy feeling turned cold and clammy. She squeezed my hand.

"Remember what I said, and be strong."

She nearly reached the front door when I discovered my phone call was from one of the other men in my life, Detective Thurman.

I covered the mouthpiece and called to my aunt to wait. After listening to the detective's terse order, I hung up. "He wants me to come in today with my attorney."

"Better give Mr. Green a call right away."

Aunt Vi stayed until I completed the call.

"This afternoon at three," I told her. "His office will call and arrange it."

"You let Mr. Green do his job, dear. You have nothing to worry about."

But worry I did. And I had work to do. Masses of work. I went to my office and turned on the computer. Order and predictability were what I needed and I dug into the stack of client folders sitting on my desk.

I had no sooner opened the first file when I heard a loud knock on my front door. Reluctantly, I left my desk. My hand on the knob, I asked, "Who is it?"

"It's Sarah Fuller. I want to talk to you."

Sarah? What would she be doing here? I didn't know she knew where I lived. Then again, with the number of people who were showing up on my doorstep lately, there was probably a big green sign on the freeway with an arrow pointing to my house.

Cautiously, I opened the front door. It was Sarah, all right, and boy, was she not happy. Her face was splotched purple with rage. Her fine, blond hair, wet from the rain, stuck together in clumps, giving her the appearance of a very angry, soaked cat. Did every irate person in the county have me on their To-Do List? Her mouth worked for several seconds, making me wonder if she had dentures that weren't fitting quite right.

Then the recriminations erupted.

"You bitch!" she spat. "You sicced the cops on me! They goddamn came to my goddamn office to question me about goddamn Valerie! What'd you tell them? 'Get Sarah, she hated Valerie more than anyone else'? You damn near cost me my goddamn job! Greg's about to fire my goddamn ass and it's all your goddamn fault! I'm gonna sue your goddamn ass!"

I blinked at her, utterly dumbstruck. She raised both fists, and I jumped back out of reach.

"ARRGGH!" she yowled at me, did an abrupt about-face and fled from my front porch. I stood in the doorway and watched her car peel out down the street, feeling I'd just watched an anime cartoon in the original Japanese of a very noir Hello Kitty.

"Well, god damn. Wonder if the guy in the black Mercedes caught all that." I made my way, somewhat shaky, back to my office via the kitchen.

Two cups of coffee and six chocolate chip cookies later, I easily finished the files for three clients. A touch too easy? Maybe someone, somewhere, was taking pity on me and giving me a breather. As I congratulated myself on my near super-human ability to power accurately through stacks of paper, I came upon a stumbling block. Donna Orr-Block to be precise. Generally meticulous in her record keeping and conservative in her spending and investing, she had a rather large loss about mid year. Sure it must be a mistake, I poured myself another cup of coffee, grabbed another handful of cookies, and telephoned her to check. I expected to leave a message. Instead, Donna's life-partner Peggy answered, and I explained the problem to her. She was a client as well.

"Oh girlfriend, that's not a mistake," Peggy said.

"It's not?" I had the sinking feeling this was going to be complicated.

"Uh huh, and Donna's still mad about it. Darn good thing you got me instead of her. She'd still be on the phone with you tomorrow morning having herself a good rant about Valerie."

"Valerie? What happened?"

"Last year Donna and I had some, um, differences of opinion about how that roll-over from her retirement fund from her last job should be reinvested -- you remember? Greg made some suggestions, and while he was waiting for us to reach some kind of decision Valerie came along and just stuck herself right between us, know what I'm saying? Told Donna she shouldn't let me tell her how to invest her money, and ought to make the decision by herself. Only Valerie was right there with this supposed great idea. Some super high-yield investment. I said no, and she told Donna I didn't know what I was talking about, and I was going to cost her money." The laugh that reached my ear was not humorous. "That effin' bitch. You're not going to believe this, since you're familiar with how, uh, fiscally conservative our Donna is, but Valerie actually got her to go along with it. Probably because Donna and I were so mad at each other at the time. She threw the whole amount into that fund. And there's been no return on it. Nothing. Not one stinking penny. Just like I said in the first place."

"Oh, no. I had no idea. That's not good."

"Aren't you the queen of understatement. Donna keeps hoping to see some money come back, but personally, I know it's gone forever."

"I expect you're right."

"Damn straight. But I'm not going to keep shoving it in Donna's face. She feels like a first-class fool as it is. Valerie played her -- got between us and messed in something that was none of her business. It was deliberate. Both of us can see it now, and Donna still gets spitting mad about it."

From the tone of her voice it was apparent Peggy was not in a forgiving mood, either. "Isn't she kind of upset with Greg, too, because he let her make the investment?"

"Not really. It was Valerie's fault."

"But I'd think Greg would be looking out for his clients' best interest."

"Greg isn't aggressive, which is why Donna chose to do business with him in the first place. He didn't know Valerie was pitting us against each other, so when Donna insisted, I guess he figured he'd just do what she asked."

I didn't say what I was thinking -- that Greg was a financial advisor, and was supposed to be keeping his clients from making mistakes like throwing their entire retirement fund into something that was high risk. I made sympathetic noises and eased Peggy into taking about her plans to go back to school in the fall, and about Donna's softball team. She was her team's power hitter, and was getting ready for an away game in Mount Vernon the next evening. I told her I would finish their taxes and have them submitted electronically by the end of the day.

I sat back in my chair and closed my eyes. Valerie wasn't leaving me alone. She was interfering in my work and with my clients. The police were lining up a case against me, her father was poised to wreak his own special havoc, and I was getting visits at home from people who had an ax to grind. Valerie was more distressing to me dead than she'd been alive. To simply defend myself was no longer enough. That was getting me nowhere. Mr. Green suggested I sit back and wait. Wait for what?

I had far better ways to spend my time. I was in a position to look into a part of Valerie's life the police had no expertise in: the habits of a dressage rider. There was a chance I could unearth something to pass along to Thurman. This investigation needed to end. I shut down the computer and went to my bedroom to change out of yesterday's clothes.

I was certain Blackie had been horse-napped by mistake, despite the drive-through holes in my theory. If Valerie had been expecting Nachtfeder to be delivered to her farm, not Blackie, maybe something existed that would prove my hunch. But I couldn't, for the life of me, figure out why Valerie would move her own horse to her farm, much less Blackie. That would mean deliberately putting hoof prints in her perfect pastures, and I'd seen how she reacted to a dog trotting through the field at the dressage club's pasture-management meeting.

It was conceivable the police wouldn't know if the barn was ready to house her horse. But I would. I had plenty of time before my appointment with Detective Thurman. It would be easy to check out Valerie's barn. With luck I'd have something useful to tell him. I grabbed my purse and headed for my car.

I spent the fifteen minutes it took me to get to Carpenter Road to do some heavy thinking. Could she have gotten a last minute invitation to a clinic? Was there some event going on she had decided to attend? There might be information of that sort in the barn or in her house. The most useful course of action would be to look through her mail and e-mail to see if something had come up. Crap. That meant I'd have to search her house. I would probably find a house key in the tack room. Everyone kept a house key in their tack room. Everyone I knew, anyway.

I made my way up the long twisting driveway, past the big Victorian house, and parked at the barn. It wasn't pouring rain like it had been earlier, but it was cold and misting and unpleasant. At least I'd be inside. I hurried to the barn and slid the door open enough to walk through. After groping around I found the light switches and flipped them on. I was most definitely intruding, and the guilt made me cautious, even though no one else was there.

I'd never been inside Valerie's barn. Although the outside was fussy and silly for its purpose, I figured the interior would show more attention to functionality. I was wrong. The six oversized stalls, although nice, had expensive black enamel and brass grill-work on the doors and fronts. The aisle was set with cobblestone, like what you'd find in the driveways of some expensive homes. Pretty, but impractical unless you liked to spend your time sweeping and cleaning. Nachtfeder's name, in flowing script, was on a thick brass plate on a stall door. The stall should have been bedded if Valerie was expecting him, but except for the pristine stall mats, it was empty.

I checked the other stalls. Nothing. I could tell which one Blackie had occupied on Sunday, courtesy of Delores, because dirty hoof prints marred the surface of the otherwise unused black mats. I saw no buckets for grain or water in any of the stalls.

I tried the door knob on what I assumed was the tack room, although it was at the other end of the barn from the narrow grooming stall. The door swung open to an empty room. There were paneled walls, a slate floor, and a crystal chandelier, but not a single hook to hang a halter on, much less keys.

I shook my head in disgust at the décor. Maybe I'd have better luck in the feed room. There had to be supplies and special supplements Valerie used for her horse, like glucosamine and MSM. I recalled she used those and something with biotin in it, too, for Nachtfeder's feet. She wouldn't have skipped his supplements. She was too obsessive about them.

A smaller room across the aisle, although more practically finished, was similarly vacant. It contained no shelves, feed bins, or feed of any kind. There wasn't even a sign of mice. A ladder led up to the hay loft and I climbed up far enough to poke my head through the access door. I could see we had a theme going here. Not only was there no hay, but there never had been. In the loft everything looked as though the carpenters had just left.

Okay, I could safely say she was not expecting to house a horse in her barn. It wasn't necessary to have a horse inside when you had lush pastures. I went outside in the drizzle. I knew she had groundskeepers who regularly mowed the pastures. And because she had no resident livestock, the grass grew evenly throughout, including in front of the gates.

There were water troughs positioned near the gates in each of the three pastures, but none had water in them. I doubted they ever had. The plugs had been removed from the bottoms, standard practice to keep rainwater from collecting and creating a mosquito-friendly environment. The knowledge Blackie had spent an entire night and half the morning there without access to water angered me. He could have easily colicked. As particular as I knew Valerie was about her own horse, water was certainly not something she would have overlooked. She was famous, or at least supremely annoying, for her penchant of pitching a fit when her exact instructions weren't followed—and she always double checked.

I needed to look around some more. I'd whittled my mental list down to the bare essentials, and it wasn't looking good for any of the remaining items. If I found anything, no matter how small, I'd have to be careful how I got the information to Thurman so I didn't get myself into more trouble. Just thinking about it made my hands sweat.

I found the water spigots near the barn. There were no hoses attached. I went back to the feed room and rechecked. No buckets, no hoses. Unless Valerie stored her equipment elsewhere, she definitely had not been planning to house a horse here. What the hell was going on? I had to curb my impatience, take this one item at a time, gather information and then piece it together. But it didn't make the number of unanswered questions any less frustrating.

The mist turned to rain again, so I hurried to the other outbuildings (also built to complement the house, but not as elaborate as the barn) to avoid getting soaked. I had about as much luck with keeping dry as finding any horse-keeping supplies. One building held the tractor and mowing equipment as well as the horse trailer and truck. The other held miscellaneous gardening paraphernalia. With water dripping off my hair and into my eyes, I searched the garden shed. No horse stuff. Then, as I reached for the switch to turn off the lights a glint of metal caught my eye. A ring with a handful of keys hung on a nail in a recess by the door. One of them had to be for the house. I no longer had an excuse not to search there. Before I could talk myself out of it, I grabbed the whole set and jogged, head down, through the rain-turned-to-downpour to the back door of the three story Victorian.

Luckily for me the porch off the back door was covered.

The rain pelted on the roof like lead shot as I huddled, wet and shivering, over the wad of keys, trying to decide which might fit. The keys to the tractor and trailer were obvious, but the others, and there were quite a few, all looked as if they might belong to the house.

The third key I tried met with unexpected results -- a hand on my shoulder.

I screamed and spun. Frederick Parsons's driver loomed over me. He was dressed in black and, despite the rain, wore dark glasses on a face as expressionless as when I encountered him on my own front porch. I thought I was going to pass out.

"Keys." He held out his hand.

I swallowed a mouthful of dry nothing and dropped them into his upturned palm without a word.

"Why are you here?" It didn't sound like a question, but it must have been.

A gagging noise came out before any words. "Nothing, no reason. Just, uh, looking for clues."

He regarded me for a long moment from behind the dark glasses. I held my breath, waiting.

"There's nothing here," he said.

"Oh."

He stared at me. At least I think he was staring. He might have been napping for all I could tell. Only my own terrified reflection looked back at me from the shiny black lenses. Maybe I could leave.

"I think I'll go now." I edged past him and almost made it. He turned his head toward me and took hold of my arm. The blood fled from my face.

"I'm watching you," he said.

"Oh, uh, okay," I said in a small voice.

He released my arm abruptly. I scurried to my car, my heart rate at near stroke level, somehow got the key in the ignition, and took off not daring to look back.

By the time I got home I'd marshaled my wits and gotten a grip on my initial desire to continue driving until I reached my parents' house in San Francisco. I hustled up the walk to the porch but stopped, house key in hand, when I saw a page from a newspaper taped to my front door. Odd. The page was from the *Everett Times*. I removed it and glanced at both sides. Last week's edition. None of the articles looked even mildly interesting.

Then I saw the red circles. Someone had used red ink to mark individual words in different articles. Why? As I hung up my jacket, it hit me.

A message!

Duh.

I grabbed the paper and searched. Five words, or parts of words, were circled. I read, more or less left to right: "stop," "ing", "ions." "ask," "quest."

"Stoping ions ask quest? Doesn't make any sense. And "stoping" is spelled wrong."

I looked again and this time I read from top to bottom. "Stop asking questions."

Molar-grinding aggravation outmaneuvered my initial spike of fear. Dammit, I'd been assaulted, yelled at, interrogated and insulted--and that was the short list. Now some jerk was leaving me a stupid note right out of a bad movie. I had freaking had enough.

I locked the front door behind me and strode to the kitchen. Yanking open the freezer door, I pulled out a half gallon of triple chocolate fudge ice cream and grabbed a soup spoon from the silverware drawer. Cup of Aunt Vi's tea, my ass. I dug in.

Chapter Fifteen

At three o'clock I sat in a cold, hard chair, in a cold, hard conference room at the Snohomish County Sheriff's Office. Detective Thurman was late. My attorney, Jacob Green, held the newspaper message I'd handed him by a corner and read it while tapping an index finger against his thin lips. He exhaled abruptly and waved the paper like a flag.

"You said this was on your front door?"

"Yes."

"Any idea who left it?"

"No."

"Any idea what, specifically, the message is referring to?"

"No."

"Well, we'll let the good detective deal with it." He slid it into his briefcase and resumed the pacing I interrupted when I arrived.

Jacob Green was not what I expected, not even close to the image I formed from our first phone conversation. Rail thin, tall, and middle-aged, the attorney pacing a new track in the worn linoleum was straight out of Central Casting's supply of used-car salesmen. Right down to the ancient, ill-fitting suit and the I'd-rather-die-than-lie-to-you brown eyes.

He stopped pacing all at once and hit me with a narrow-eyed stare.

"You left out some information when I talked to you yesterday."

"I did?"

"I don't like hearing client information that my client should have told me from someone who is not my client."

"What do you mean?"

"Frederick Parsons. Stopped by for a little chat with you on Monday."

That startled me. "Oh. I thought it was irrelevant."

"It's not irrelevant unless I tell you it is. What did he say?"

"He called you?" Maybe I was naïve, but it struck me as out of line for the father of a murder victim to call the attorney of a person of interest.

"Yes. What did he say?"

"How did he know you were my attorney? Didn't he tell you what he said to me?"

"I want to hear it from you."

I related our conversation, verbatim, and mentioned the really big guy in the dark glasses -- just in case he wasn't irrelevant. Mr. Green grimaced, shook his head, and muttered something about not realizing Joey was out of prison. Then he resumed pacing.

Great. I was being watched by a felon -- or ex-felon. Maybe an escaped felon.

"I want to know how Frederick Parsons knew to call you," I said. When Green didn't answer, I persisted. "I didn't tell him the name of my attorney."

"Someone told him. I expect someone who heard it from you." Mr. Green's comment was off-hand, as if unimportant. "Now," he said, throwing on the brakes, "what about the phone call I dodged today? What was Parsons going to tell me that you should have?"

"Oh, uh, well, I kinda ran into Joey today out at Valerie's."

Mr. Green ran a hand across his comb-over and blew out a lungful of air.

"What were you doing out at Valerie Parsons's place?"

"Looking for clues."

He tugged an earlobe. "Did you find any?"

"Well, that's the funny thing. It's more what I didn't find. It looked like she wasn't expecting any horses at all at her place." Mr. Green gave me a long, silent look, adjusted his shirt cuffs with a quick jerk and set his feet into motion again. True, I was new at this, but why was he acting like my observation was unimportant? "Well, don't you think that's odd? I was thinking Valerie meant to have Nachtfeder picked up instead of Blackie -- that Blackie's theft was a mistake made by someone she hired. But now I don't know what to think. And, by the way, Joey is spending a lot of time parked outside my house."

"No. Is he really?"

I'm positive that was sarcastic.

The door swung open and Detective Thurman strode in, threw himself into the chair across from me, and slapped a file folder on the table. He pulled out a sheet of paper and slid it toward me. I reached for it, but Mr. Green snatched it up first. I scowled at him, but he didn't give any indication he noticed. He read it as he paced, then stopped abruptly to address Thurman.

"A word with my client, please."

The detective heaved himself out of his chair. "Two minutes," he said and left the room, closing the door behind him.

Mr. Green handed me the paper. I opened it, read it twice, and fought the urge to throw up.

"What is this, a joke?" Fury radiated to my fingertips.

"You don't recognize the bill of sale?"

"No, absolutely not."

"Is that your signature?" He paused long enough to point to the bottom of the page.

"No."

"You're sure?"

"Of course I'm sure." My answer was shrill. I pulled my wallet out of my purse and handed him my driver's license. He compared the two signatures and handed the license back to me.

"There isn't even an attempt at forgery," he said with a dismissive wave of his hand.

"I don't understand this," I said to his back. Dammit. I wanted to tie him to a chair.

"Neither do I. Shall we see if Detective Thurman can enlighten us?" He went to the door and opened it.

Detective Thurman wasted no time in returning. He, at least, sat down. Mr. Green pushed the paper back to him and made a flicking motion with his hand from my purse to Thurman. After a moment's confusion I understood it as a command for me to display my driver's license. Thurman compared the two signatures and flipped my license back to me.

"Is this your horse described here?" He tapped the paper.

"If it is, it's a poor description." I crossed my arms. "Wrong color. He's not black. The name's wrong, too."

"It's not," he read off the paper, "'The Black Bishop'?"

"No. His registered name is, 'The Black Queen's Bishop.'" I cringed and glanced at Mr. Green, realizing I'd probably said too much. Sweat prickled in my arm pits.

"Funny name for a horse, but aren't they all?"

I didn't comment.

"Is this Valerie Parsons's signature?" He showed me the paper again.

"I wouldn't know. I've never seen her handwriting, much less her signature. You must realize if this were a legitimate bill of sale my horse's breed, registration number, sire, dam, detailed description of height, markings, and other information would be included."

Detective Thurman scratched his nose, thinking. I glanced at my attorney. He stopped pacing and instead fidgeted with the change in his pants pocket.

I hated this silence.

"What's this all about? Where did you get this?" I tapped the table top near the folder harder than I'd intended.

"It was dropped off at our office this morning."

"By whom?" I leaned forward and our eyes locked. After a moment Thurman cocked his head.

"Is it important?"

"It might be." I tipped my head, imitating him. "Someone sure seems determined to drag me into this murder investigation."

"Why would someone want to do that?"

I sat back, staring at him in disbelief. "Gee, you're the detective. I would think you could figure that one out with one hand tied behind your back."

"What's your theory?" He acted like he hadn't heard the insult.

"Theory?" I squeaked. "Isn't it obvious? Someone is trying to frame me. If that fake bill of sale isn't enough, just look at this." I turned to Mr. Green and held my hand out. He picked up my hint, produced the folded sheet of newspaper, and slid it across the table to the detective.

"What's this?"

"My client found it taped to her front door this afternoon."

Thurman unfolded it, looked at both sides and frowned briefly. "'Stoping ions ask quest'? 'Stoping' is spelled wrong."

"Read it top to bottom, two words in each column," I said.

His eyes flicked back to the page then settle back on me. "So, someone wants you to stop asking questions. Why is that?"

"I don't know. I haven't even started asking questions."

"Is that right?"

"Yes. What are you going to do about this?" I pointed at the message.

Thurman appeared to mull over my question. "Throw it out?"

"It's evidence. In fact, it sounds like a threat."

He scrutinized it again, at such length I knew he was mocking me. "You think so?"

"Yes, I do." My voice trembled with frustration. I was surrounded by idiots. "I have some questions I would like the answers to."

"Ask away." Thurman leaned back and calmly folded his hands on his stomach. This particular chair didn't creak like the one in his office.

Mr. Green sat down and stared at me, steadily jiggling one leg.

I wanted to rub away the headache these two were giving me, but I didn't want to appear weak. Bad enough I had to clear my throat twice before any words would come out. "Are you looking into any 'persons of interest' other than me?"

"Like who?"

"Like whoever forged this bill of sale. Like any of the people who knew Valerie and might send me this?" I tapped the newspaper. "And do you always have to answer me with a question?"

Thurman raised an eyebrow but otherwise didn't budge. I sat up a little straighter and set my jaw. He was deliberately trying to make me nervous.

"'Yes' to your first question, 'no' to your second." One edge of his mouth rose.

"So, of those people, who would benefit from her death?"

"Benefit how?"

I gave him a hard look. "Financially, I have to assume, since she was wealthy."

Mr. Green coughed, but I ignored him. He stopped jiggling his leg.

Detective Thurman shrugged his answer.

"It seems to me you should be looking into these things," I said. "After all, isn't money often a motive for murder? And what about relationships she had? Aren't you curious to find out who was close to her? Maybe somebody close to her wanted her dead. There's some significant statistics that support that line of inquiry, you know."

He pursed his lips and nodded at me, looking for all the world like he'd never had the idea before. He was starting to irritate me. I looked at Mr. Green. I was already irritated with him. He looked at the table and rubbed his forehead. Well, hell. Was I the only one with any ideas?

"Oh, for crying out loud. Did you even think to look for jewelry on her? Maybe she was killed in a robbery attempt."

"It did occur to us, but nope, I don't think that was the motive."

"But she always wore big diamond stud earrings and a Rolex watch. If those were missing it could have been robbery."

"Expensive stuff to be wearing around every day."

I rolled my eyes. "Valerie had the best and most expensive of everything. She had to be better than everyone else, all the time. If Valerie saw that someone had something wonderful, then she had to have it. And if she wanted it, she got it.

"Except your horse."

"Except my horse."

"Why?"

"He's not for sale. He never will be."

"But didn't she want him?"

"Look, he's not the only nice horse in the world. I don't think she wanted him as much as she enjoyed pushing my buttons." *Crap. Thea, you're saying all the wrong things. What's wrong with you? Can't you think at all?* My heart pounded against my ribs and I dripped sweat. I was sure Detective Thurman would love to arrest me for being too stupid to keep from running off at the mouth and implicating myself. Mr. Green laid a warning hand on my shoulder. He had quit fidgeting.

"Is that right. Did she make you mad?" Thurman asked.

"No." I said, rigid with indignation. "She made me avoid her."

"I think the interview is over," Mr. Green said.

"One more question." The detective was still leaning back in his nonchalant pose, yet his intense scrutiny was as devastating as any dressage judge's.

"What's that?" Ask it already and let me go home.

"Where were you Saturday afternoon between three and six?"

"That's when she died, isn't it?"

He didn't respond to my question -- no doubt expecting me to answer his. But the king-sized monkey wrench he'd just tossed into the gears of my pet theory grappled for my attention. It was clear Valerie had nothing to do with Blackie's theft. Yet, despite the lack of proof, I knew Blackie's theft had to be connected to Valerie's murder. Thurman's bullet-like stare and Green's ominous silence reeled me back into the conversation.

"I was at my aunt and uncle's doing their taxes. I went there at a little after one and stayed until about five when I went home to get ready for dinner with Jonathan. I told you that already."

Thurman rose and leaned across the table, his weight on his hands. "It seems to me that this bill of sale makes a pretty decent motive for murder. Combine that with a witness who places you driving your car in the area at the approximate time of death and I think we've got a case against you, Miss Campbell."

My jaw dropped. "What?"

"Red Ford Escort. Woman driver with short dark hair." His smile belonged on a shark.

My mouth went dry. Was this where he pulled out the handcuffs and read me my rights?

"It seems to me," Mr. Green said with a calm I wouldn't have suspected he possessed, "that if you actually thought you had decent evidence, you would arrest my client." He was motionless.

The two of them had a brief staring contest, while I sat holding my breath and sweating. Detective Thurman blinked first. He straightened, walked to the door and stopped, but didn't turn around.

Did I dare hope he wasn't going to arrest me?

"Don't be planning any trips out of town, Miss Campbell."

I could have guessed he'd say that.

"What do I do now?" I asked my lawyer, as we walked to our cars. I still reverberated with the shock of the accusation and so-called evidence against me.

"Nothing," he said, tossing his keys into the air and catching them in rhythm with his stride.

"Nothing?" My voice hit an octave higher than usual. "They're on the edge of arresting me for a murder I did not commit and you're telling me I should do nothing?"

"Calm down, you're only a person of interest. You haven't been charged. Let them do their work and call me if they want to talk to you again. Oh, and in the future, don't try so hard to make yourself look guilty. You might want to refrain from cross-examining the detective, too." He got into his ancient blue and white Chevy and slammed the door. It didn't latch, so he gave it another mighty heave. "Gotta get this thing fixed," he said through a half-opened window I was fairly certain wouldn't close, either. Giving me a friendly wave, he drove off in a cloud of blue smoke.

Do nothing? Doing nothing was out of the question.

Chapter Sixteen

I got home shortly after four o'clock, took what remained of the chocolate ice cream out of the freezer, grabbed a spoon, and called Jonathan. I didn't even bother to think before I dialed. My life was a living hell. I might as well face everything I was avoiding. I needed to talk to him about ending our relationship, and ask him what the hell he was thinking when he gave me Jacob Green's phone number.

Jonathan's secretary put me through. He was less than friendly. His tone suggested strongly I change my confrontational attitude.

"Jonathan, can we talk?"

"I've got a meeting."

"Later?"

"I'll be in meetings the rest of the day."

I looked at the clock. Four-ten. Meetings. Right. "Can we get together for dinner tonight like we planned?"

"I don't think there's much to talk about."

"Please?" Guilt stabbed me repeatedly. "I'm so sorry about what happened."

"I'll consider your apology."

Now that was just plain childish. I pushed my temper down. It would get me nowhere. "I need to talk to you. Please?

You deserve an explanation. I really would like to see you. Please?" The man was making me beg. I probably deserved it.

"Seven o'clock. I'll meet you at Bernard's."

"Thank you," I said, but he'd hung up before I uttered the words.

I dipped into the carton for another spoonful of ice cream, but it was empty. Surprise. I had to stop eating like this.

You deserved that hang-up, Thea. He was a decent person and you betrayed him. You should change your name to Jezebel. And don't you ever criticize your sister again. At least she ended one relationship before she started another.

I tossed the empty ice cream container into the kitchen garbage and returned to my office.

Damn. I'd forgotten to ask him about Jacob Green. I wasn't going to call him back. Dinner was soon enough for that conversation.

At half past five my doorbell rang. I wasn't expecting anyone and approached it with my heart in my throat.

"Who is it?" I said to the door.

"It's me -- Delores. Glad you're taking some care answering your door. Now, let me in before someone sees me dressed like this."

I opened the door and did a double take.

"Wow," I said. "You look ... you look ...."

"Ridiculous?" she asked.

"No, stunning."

Gone was the usual blue jean and flannel shirt uniform. In its place, a heather gray, fitted suit, pale blue silk blouse and low pumps. Her short gray hair, usually barely combed, was styled. And she had makeup on. I didn't know she owned any. She had the willowy look of a senior fashion model. If it weren't for her vexed expression I wouldn't have recognized her.

"Are you going to stand there gaping at me or are you going to let me in?"

I let her in. She shouldered out of her jacket and tossed it on a chair.

"Just got back from Valerie's funeral," she said, taking her earrings off and dropping them in her purse.

My hands shot to my mouth. "I forgot. I suppose I should have been there."

"No. I don't think so." Delores dropped her purse on the floor next to the chair. "I would have reminded you if I thought it was a good idea, but under the circumstances I think it best you stayed away."

She had a good point.

"The place was packed," she continued, on her way to my kitchen. I followed. "Mostly friends of her parents, I think. Besides Henry and Vi, I didn't see too many horse people there. Greg was there, of course." She took a bottle of juice out of my fridge, poured herself a glass, and drank it down. "He was holding court, telling anyone who'd listen how upset he was he'd lost his fiancée. I heard him tell someone Valerie's parents were seriously considering giving him her farm since he was living there anyway. According to him, they consider him part of the family."

I sat down at the table, impressed with her eavesdropping skills, and aware I must have just missed Greg on my little jaunt to Valerie's estate.

"I went out to Valerie's earlier for a little look-see," I confessed.

"Damn lucky you didn't run into Greg."

"I didn't know he was living there. Otherwise I wouldn't have gone."

"Find anything?"

"No, nothing. Valerie was not expecting any horses to arrive. But then I kind of found out why when I talked to Detective Thurman."

"She was already dead when Blackie was taken, I expect."

"Yeah. How did you know?"

"Didn't. Guessed. Nothing else makes sense. So, what did Thurman want?" Delores pulled out a chair and sat.

I told her about the false bill of sale, and about the witness who claimed to have seen me near Valerie's at the time of her death. And how Thurman was on the edge of arresting me.

"What about your attorney? What did he say? Is he worried?"

"He said if they thought they had a case I wouldn't have been allowed to walk out the door."

"That makes sense." He jaw worked for a moment while her eyebrows met in a knot above her nose.

"I'm still worried, though," I said, hoping to prompt her into voicing her thoughts.

Delores straightened in her chair and patted my hand. The lines across her forehead relaxed. "I think it will work out fine. You've got a good attorney and a lot of friends to stand by you. You're not alone, you know."

"I'll be a little more alone after this evening," I said. She raised her eyebrows, questioning. "I'm meeting Jonathan for dinner at Bernard's, and I'm going to call it off."

"Good. You'll feel better. I understand you had a little excitement last night." She slid a casual look at me.

I groaned and covered my face with my hands. Who hadn't heard? I looked at her through my finger.

She smiled. "You look lower than a cross-rail for a pony. What'd my dumb-ass nephew do this time?"

"Jeez," I said, mortified. "It was my fault."

"You don't scream at people, normally. At least I've never seen it, and Valerie always tried her best to provoke you. What happened?" Her tone was matter of fact, but amusement touched the set of her mouth.

"We had a drink at The River's Bend, then went for a walk." How was I going to explain this to his aunt? "Jonathan was in town -- I didn't expect him -- and he saw Paul kiss me. He confronted us and we all yelled at each other. I walked home." That was it in fifty words or less.

"That dumb-ass," she repeated, but the smile was gone. "I told him he'd better leave you alone until you had your life sorted out, but does he listen? No. What does his old, uneducated aunt know? A sight more than a cocky thirty-five-year-old, over-educated bonehead with no self-control." She got up, poured herself another glass of juice, and sat again. "No wonder his last girlfriend kicked him out -- not that she was any prize. There are times that boy doesn't have two working brain cells to rub together. I ought to kick his butt from here to next Tuesday."

"It wasn't entirely his fault," I protested.

"Don't be stupid, girl, of course it was."

"I --"

"And don't you start defending him, either." She gave me a severe scowl.

I gulped. "Aunt Vi said he didn't come home last night."

"Oh, don't worry about him. He probably spent the night in his office. He always does that when he sulks and feels sorry for himself." Delores gave a dismissive flip of her hand.

I was going to ask if he did that often, but instead I said, "Oh."

She rose from her chair when she'd emptied her glass. "Look, Thea. Don't lose a minute of sleep over Paul. You young people spend way too much time making mountains out of molehills. You've got other fish to fry right now, so I'd best go, and leave you to it." She was lapsing into clichés. The funeral must have been an ordeal. "Take care of what you can and stop worrying." She walked to the living room, slung her jacket over her arm, took a couple of steps, and doubled back to pick up her purse. "Promise me that, child." She gave me a stern look. "Promise me you won't worry."

"I promise." I wanted to hug her, but I knew she wouldn't tolerate it.

"Good. I'll see you tomorrow when you come by for the receipts. By the way, what's Joey doing sitting out there in front of your house?"

"I don't know." But I wished he'd go away -- and how did she know Joey?

"Humph. I heard he fancied himself Valerie's boyfriend. Before he went to prison, anyway."

Oh, great. "Really?" I said.

"Well, that's neither here nor there. Don't worry. Everything'll work out."

She left, hurrying down the walk to her car.

No, I thought, don't *you* worry. I intended to do everything in my power to clear myself of suspicion of Valerie's murder, but first I will quit letting one person in particular walk all over me.

I took care dressing for dinner because Jonathan would better understand the finality of my decision if it came from my gender-neutral, slacks and jacket, "business woman" persona. I wanted a clean break. Well, as clean as possible at this point. That would mean keeping a lid on my temper, too. I knew Jonathan well enough to realize if I got testy with him he would take it as a sign I was indecisive and drag out our break-up forever. Besides, being rude wouldn't make me feel stronger. I made mistakes, including staying with him because it was easier than breaking up. And, I'd let Paul sweep me off my feet when I was vulnerable. "Vulnerable" was the polite term for "needy" and "sex-starved." It was past time to take control and set my own course. Past time to jettison the distractions. Past time to take care of myself.

I arrived at Bernard's at precisely seven o'clock. I loved this restaurant. The food was predictably excellent and the decor appealing. The walls were rough brick and mortar, and the tables and chairs, although plain dark wood, glowed with polish. On every table, fresh flowers in tall vases sat amid sparkling glassware. Antique schoolhouse lights hung from the ceiling, giving off a gentle glow.

At the back of the dining room was a magnificent bar. The huge antique had been barged down from Alaska in several pieces when the Gold Rush era saloon it had occupied was destroyed in the big 1964 earthquake. William and Connie, the owners of Bernard's, had lovingly restored it and could be encouraged, without much prodding, to tell the entire tale of this thirty-foot-long piece of history. This was my turf. I squared my shoulders and walked in.

Jonathan sat at a table near the front of the restaurant, waiting. He stood when I approached and held the chair out for me. Our greeting was awkward, and though I tried to catch his eye, he avoided mine. He must have come directly from his office because he wore his dark blue pin-striped Armani suit, blue striped tie, and a crisp white shirt. Gold cuff links flashed when he took the menu from William, who gave me a slight smile and a nod of greeting.

Jonathan glanced at the menu in silence. I did the same although I already knew what I was going to order. I put my menu down after a moment and looked out the window. Jonathan ordered the salmon for us both. He was right about my choice, and a small stab of anguish pricked me. I'd been unfair in thinking he didn't notice my preferences. Maybe I was wrong about him. Maybe I was trying to push too much blame onto him.

"Jonathan, I want to apologize --"

"I suppose I should --"

We spoke simultaneously and stopped. Apprehensive, I waited for him to continue.

"You first." He smiled stiffly.

"I wanted to say I'm sorry. I didn't mean or plan for anything to happen between me and Paul, and I don't believe he did either. It was a mistake, made worse by your witnessing it."

"Then you're not ...?"

"No."

His expression seemed, right away, less acrimonious. "I wanted to say that I'm sorry about Saturday evening. My mother was right. I should not have sprung my proposal on you like I did. I hope you'll forgive me."

"Of course." I smiled, feeling relieved. The tension evaporated. I could talk to him. He would listen and not overreact.

Connie brought our salads and gave me a small wink. She was one of Aunt Vi's weekly bunco card group. No doubt she knew why Jonathan and I were here. I had the distinct impression she was offering subtle support. I was touched, and smiled a thank you at her.

Jonathan started on his salad and missed the whole exchange. Just as well. He would have thought the familiarity improper. After only one bite he put his fork down and patted his lips with his napkin.

"I expect the sheriff will have everything cleared up by the end of the month."

"I hope so."

"So I made reservations for us at the Hilton in Tahoe --"

Relief evaporated and tension leapt back in. "Jonathan, no."

He pulled his chin in and frowned. "I thought --"

The shake of my head stopped him. "It won't work -- you and me."

"It is Paul, then." He flattened his hand on the table with enough force to rattle the glassware. It didn't take a genius to figure out he thought I'd lied to him. I was half tempted to run with it, but I couldn't.

"This has nothing to do with Paul. This is about us. Only us. I'm sorry, but I can't ever be what you want and need --"

"Thea, don't be foolish. You need me right now. And I know if you work at it a little you can be exactly the wife, uh, woman I need."

"No."

"There's some pretty frightening people keeping their eyes on you and you aren't being careful. You need me. This is no time to pretend you can handle things on your own. Thea ...." He reached across the table to touch my cheek, but I pulled back. His eyes widened slightly. "Your bruise -- it's not as bad as I thought it'd be."

Then he shrugged.

The gesture hit me like the idiot-slap that follows a revelation. My insides went icy and still. Never mind the fact he assumed I was his to boss around. Never mind the fact he just noticed my bruises and didn't seem bothered. Never mind he didn't seem to notice my shock.

I never mentioned my injuries to him.

Someone else had.

He barreled right along, self-important as ever. "You really are naïve. Let me handle things. Work at your little business, ride your horse, and stop ask -- stop asking for trouble. Valerie's not a problem you should worry about. I'm taking care of you now." His blink was slow and satisfied.

"You! It was you. You told Frederick Parsons who my attorney was. You discussed me with him."

"What difference does it make?"

"What difference?" People at nearby tables glanced in our direction. I lowered my voice. "Where were you Saturday afternoon after you left my aunt and uncle's place?"

"I went home, of course." His eyes tightened. "What are you implying, Thea?"

"Just answer me."

"I don't think I have to be accountable to that tone of voice."

"No, you don't have to be accountable to me at all. It's over between us, Jonathan. Finished."

"You don't mean that."

"How much more direct do I have to be? I don't want you in my life."

A muscle worked in his jaw, and the fingers that attempted to caress my face a moment before closed in a fist. "You're under pressure right now. I'm sure once you think about it you'll see I'm right."

"Once I think about it, I'll wonder why it took me so long to break up with you." I picked my purse up off the floor and stood. "And please, don't do me any more favors." I turned and bolted for the door, barely missing a collision with

William, who managed to dance out of my way without dropping the plates of food he carried. I spun toward him.

"That's my dinner, isn't it?" I snatched both plates from his hands before he could speak. "Jonathan will have them both." I marched back to where he remained frozen halfway out of his seat. "You can have my dinner too." I smiled sweetly and tipped the grilled salmon with hollandaise and asparagus down the front of his suit and into his lap, stacked the plates on top of his salad, and swept out of the restaurant, past a still stunned William.

Three women having dinner near the bar stood and applauded.

Once in my car, I sat and stared, unseeing, out the window. That bastard. How could I have been such an idiot? Well, no more.

Although I couldn't be certain he'd had anything to do with Valerie's death, I was positive he'd been talking to Frederick Parsons, maybe he was even involved with him and Joey. He certainly orchestrated some of what had been happening to me. Jonathan scared the hell out of me -- tried to scare the hell out of me so I'd run to him. Thank God I figured out what he was like before it was too late, before I caved in and married him. He'd manipulated me for the last time.

As I turned the key in the ignition, insight clocked me between the eyes for the second time. The indignation Jonathan provoked in me shed understanding on Paul's wrath. He thought I had manipulated him, and he'd probably played that game before. In fact, I was sure of it. I groaned and thumped my forehead against the steering wheel. Why else would he have rebelled so strongly as a teenager? No way would he ever trust me now. I was poison. The hope Aunt Vi had conjured vanished like the illusion it was, but the remaining hollowness was real.

Within the sadness of that truth was a seed of something important I'd gained: the knowledge of a potential for far more depth and passion to a relationship than what I'd experienced with Jonathan. Now that I'd glimpsed it, I wouldn't settle for less. I just wished it hadn't been necessary to be clubbed over the head with the lesson.

I took a couple of deep breaths, and my stomach complained. The grocery store was on my way home. I'd grab something for dinner, and replenish the supplies my sister had pilfered from my pantry.

As I stood in the checkout line chatting with one of my neighbors, Donna Orr-Block walked into the store. Instead of her usual business attire she had on sweat pants and her softball jersey. She must have just come from a game or practice. I waved. She wheeled her cart over and joined our conversation -- and lingered after I paid the cashier.

"I meant to give you a call," Donna said, her gaze darting to my bruised jaw for at least the fourth time.

"Horse accident," I said, knowing she wouldn't ask. She nodded. "Did I miss something on your taxes?"

"No, not at all. I wanted to thank you for being so alert and, um, I wanted to explain." She put her purse in her basket and straightened the hem of her shirt.

"That's okay." I watched her with interest, never having seen her stall for time to think.

She raised her chin. "It was such a stupid move on my part -- that whole investment -- I never should have agreed to it." She glanced around. No one was within earshot. "Now that Valerie's dead, well, I feel bad about some of the things I said. I'm sure Peggy told you."

"She told me a little." So, it was embarrassment that chased off her usual directness. "But you have nothing to apologize for. Valerie was pretty nasty to you."

She smiled, looking a bit less like she was facing the firing squad. "That's true. It was an unpleasant lesson to learn. It's myself I should have been angry with, not Valerie."

"Don't be so hard on yourself."

"Still, I'm the one with control over my finances. It was my decision. Valerie didn't steal from me." She nodded once, sharply, and anger etched lines in her face for a moment. "Speaking of Valerie ...." She leaned toward me, her voice low. "Melanie Rucker's got to be one happy woman right now."

"Melanie?" I copied her whisper. "Why would Melanie be happy?" I recalled her leaving the sheriff's office parking lot on Monday, and Randy's temper tantrum. She'd looked none too pleased then.

A young couple who lived near Juliet wheeled their cart past and said, "Hi."

"Don't tell me you don't know," she said, her eyebrows disappearing under her short brunette bangs. I shook my head. "Valerie had been carrying on with Randy for the last few months. All hell broke loose a couple of weekends ago when Melanie found out at a horse show."

"You're kidding! I hope Jacquelyn wasn't there to see it." Their teenaged daughter helped her dad on weekends with training and showing. "Besides, I thought Valerie and Greg were engaged."

"Engaged?" Donna made a half laugh, half snort, then glanced around again. "If they were, then they sure weren't exclusive. Greg's been fooling around with Jacquelyn, too."

"What?" My shriek drew a few glances. I lowered my voice. "But she's a kid!"

"She'll be graduating from high school in June. She's old enough, I guess -- old enough to exercise her own bad judgment, anyway."

I was floored. What a sordid little mess. Now I thought I knew why Melanie and Randy were at the sheriff's office on Monday. They'd undoubtedly been called in for questioning. That must have been interesting. But why had he been angry with me?

"How'd you find out about all of this?"

"Peggy, initially. You know she works at the *Everett Times* -- 'gossip central.' I think they get more news that's not fit to print than the other kind. Everyone on my softball team knows now, too, since a couple of them have kids with horses."

"Wow," I said, still absorbing the information.

"And to think it was a horse accident that killed her. I'd have thought -- well, it wouldn't have surprised me if someone deliberately went after her."

Annoyance that misinformation about Blackie's involvement in Valerie's death flared before the actual fact that she was misinformed sunk in. She should have known Valerie was murdered with such direct access to *gossip central*. "It wasn't an accident, Donna. Someone killed her."

The look of shock on her face seemed genuine.

Although our conversation ended on a different, less dramatic note, I revisited the gossip about Melanie and Randy as I wheeled my cart of bagged groceries out to the parking lot. The two red Ford Escorts parked next to each other swung my attention to a more immediate problem. I had to look at the license plates to tell which was mine. Good thing they didn't have interchangeable keys like I'd heard some older Saturns did.

I finished loading the groceries into my trunk and returned the cart to the queue. A quick glance in the window of the other Escort revealed softball equipment -- gloves, a couple of softballs, and bats. One of which was broken.

Donna's car.

I squashed my next thought before it was half-formed. I was imagining boogeymen under the bed.

I arrived home to find Juliet sitting on my front porch. She jumped up, dusted off the seat of her pants and met me at the curb as I parked my car.

"How'd it go?" she asked, looking worried.

"You knew I was meeting Jonathan?" I popped the trunk open.

"I think you might have told me. Did it go okay?"

I didn't remember telling her, but I didn't pursue it. Seems like everybody knew the details of my life right now.

"It went fine."

"Are you upset?"

"No, actually, I feel pretty good. Juliet --"

"Oh good." She put two fingers in her mouth and let loose a shrill whistle.

"Was that necessary?" My ears were ringing.

"I was letting Eric know he could come over."

A car door slammed. "You're calling him like a dog now?"

"It was his idea," she said defensively, taking the plastic bags I handed to her. "He didn't want to intrude if you were upset and wanted to talk to me alone."

Great. Another missed opportunity to talk to Juliet about her interview with Thurman. No offense to Eric, but I didn't want him in on the conversation.

Eric strolled over, said hello, and carried the remaining bags into the house. After helping me put the groceries away he pulled out a chair next to Juliet at the kitchen table, and stretched out his long blue-jeaned legs. Juliet gave him an appreciative once over. I put the kettle on for tea and brought mugs, tea bags, and biscotti to the table.

"Thea said everything ended okay with Jonathan," my sister informed him.

He took her hand lightly in his. "That's good."

She turned back to me. "No fireworks at all? Not even a little?"

"Not really."

Juliet chuckled. "Man, that's good, because after last night, with all that screaming and yelling you guys were doing downtown, and right after all that passionate making out— well, I figured you were going to have at it again tonight, 'cuz remember last week when I was bugging you about how boring your life was and you said you'd cut loose a little sometime soon? Oh, too, too funny. I thought you were trying to shut me up. But whoa, mama, don't you think you kinda overdid it a bit yesterday?"

My sister, once again, stunned me speechless.

"Juliet," Eric said, "I don't think you're being fair here."

"Oh, I don't know. My big sister is stirring up some good gossip in town, what with the mur --"

"Juliet," he said sternly. "Don't tease her."

She stopped abruptly, her previously lively expression changing to one of concern. "Oh, gee, I'm sorry, Thea. I didn't mean to upset you. I guess it must have been pretty bad for you to lose your temper like that at someone besides me." She looked at Eric and bit her lip. He smiled gently at her and squeezed her hand.

"It's okay," I said, even though it wasn't. It was my fault, not Juliet's. "It was pretty unpleasant, though. I feel bad about it." No point in denying it.

"I think Paul was pretty unhappy, too," Eric offered.

Regret swept over me. I looked at Eric, who suddenly displayed a great deal of interest in the biscotti. The tea kettle whistled. Juliet got up, took it off the range and poured boiling water into each mug.

"You've talked to him?" What horrible things had he said?

Eric submerged a tea bag in his mug with a spoon and stirred it with fascination. "Uh, no. He called and left a message telling me he was going to be busy and didn't think he'd be able to make practice this week."

"Oh." I tried not to sound as relieved as I felt. Then again, maybe Paul did say something and Eric was protecting my feelings. It would be like him to be kind. The silence in my kitchen felt desperate.

"We need to go," Eric said, without finishing his tea. "It's my turn to do the evening barn check."

He got up from his chair and stretched. Yeah, I saw why Juliet had a hard time keeping her eyes off him. A sudden yearning for Paul put an extra twist in my heart. My sister and Eric were lucky. They liked each other despite the physical attraction.

I walked with them to Eric's car. Frederick Parsons's black

Mercedes was parked down the street, but I didn't mention it. I was too exhausted to expend what little energy I had left on someone who could think of nothing better to do than keep tabs on me.

Chapter Seventeen

I burrowed deeper under the warm comforter the next morning and examined my mood. Not great, but also not awful. Best to put off thinking about it until I'd eaten and had coffee, just in case I was mistaken. While the coffee brewed, I padded down the hall to the living room and stole a look out the front window. The absence of the black Mercedes made me feel a little less tense, so I showered, washed my hair with a new shampoo that smelled like apples, and wondered about Randy and Melanie Rucker. Could either have killed Valerie? The motive was so classic it was a Hollywood staple. But however angry Melanie was, wouldn't she be going after Greg first? Wouldn't a mother's knee-jerk instinct be to protect her child? Still, it was a possibility. Perhaps she believed Greg cared for Jacquelyn. Perhaps Jacquelyn herself dissuaded her mother from taking her anger out on Greg. Of course, Melanie might have simply chosen the easier target.

After a bowl of instant oatmeal and a quick cup of coffee, I dressed in my old jeans and a t-shirt that said, "If this shirt is clean, my horse is still dirty," slid my feet back into the pink bunnies, and plugged in my hairdryer. As I looked in the mirror, comb to my short brown hair, I stopped. The notion that barely surfaced at the grocery store wouldn't be held back any longer.

Damn. I didn't want it to be Donna. She was a good person who cared about people, gave back to the community, and had been virtually robbed of her retirement.

No, definitely not Donna.

In five minutes my hair was dry, styled, and no longer smelled of apples. I went to the kitchen for another cup of coffee to go with my anxiety over my client and friend.

It was obvious I needed information if I was going to put my worry to rest. I needed to tap into the gossip mill. There were other factors, other people I hadn't considered. I knew of one reliable source who would talk to me, too. Someone who wouldn't assume Donna had a motive.

I turned on the computer and began downloading files from my clients. Time to multitask. I phoned Peggy, Donna's partner, hoping to catch her at home, confident I could learn something from her since she worked for the *Everett Times*. While the phone rang I peaked out the front window. Joey was back. Terrific. But before I had much opportunity to fret, Peggy answered. Being tactful required all my attention.

"Can't say I ever thought of you as interested in gossip," Peggy said, when I asked what she knew about Valerie.

"I'm not, normally." My face grew warmer, and I was glad she couldn't see. "This involves me, personally. Can this be 'off the record'? I mean, can what we say stay between us?"

"Thea," Peggy said, laughing. "I'm not a reporter. I'm a copy editor. I wouldn't give a reporter a lead on a story to save my grandmother. I doubt they'd listen to me anyway. They do their best not to on a daily basis. I'll tell you what I can, but I'm not sure I can be much help. What do you want to know?"

"I'm trying to find out who had reason to kill Valerie." I ran a damp palm down my blue-jeaned thigh.

"Huh. Doesn't exactly sound like a job for 'super-accountant.' Call me crazy, but I think this is where the cops come in." She sounded cautious.

"The police think I have a motive." My words rushed out like a confession.

"You? So you turned to the dark side, huh? Do you think they'll let you do our taxes from your jail cell? It's so hard to find a good accountant these days."

"Peggy, I'm serious!"

"Sorry, girlfriend, but I can't imagine why the police think you killed her."

"Me neither, but I'm afraid I look convenient to them. Donna told me about the Ruckers, but is there anyone else whose problems would have been solved with Valerie's death?" Had I worded that carefully enough to make it clear I wasn't asking about Donna?

"Let me see. Besides Melanie, who might have taken more of a giant leap out of her long-suffering wife role than a weeping meltdown at the horseshow, and gone totally LEO -- oh, that's Low Earth Orbit --"

"Huh?"

"Ballistic, insane, quantum anger. Keep up, girl. Anyway, the thing is, I don't know. Valerie always played on the edge. But besides thinking she was all that plus a family sized bag of chips, she was careful, or calculating enough not to cross any line that would mess with her ambitions of Olympic gold."

"Meaning?" Dirt, Peggy, give me dirt.

"She wasn't into drugs, to the best of my knowledge, or things that could get her arrested. Her father hushed up all the nasty stuff about her, too."

"What nasty stuff?"

"Gossip, affairs with married men, and at least a couple of miraculously dismissed civil law suits. You ever wonder how she happened to get that primo piece of real estate over on Carpenter Road? If that was totally above board, then I'm Tina Turner."

I jumped out of my chair and walked to the window with the cell phone pressed hard against my ear. Now we were getting somewhere. "How did he manage to silence all that?"

"He owns the paper. When he tells us to jump, we all say, 'yessir, how high?'"

'Oh, I didn't realize you worked for him. I thought he was in some kind of real estate development."

"Yeah, that too. He owns several business interests, and a few well-placed individuals."

"Do you know who? Do you think Valerie was caught up in any of his shadier deals and someone got carried away trying to get even?"

"Hard to say. Verifiable information like that is difficult to come by. I would think he'd keep his daughter out of those things, but we know she could get a little ambitious on her own."

"Hmm." I fisted my hand in my hair as I paced. I needed more.

"I got something to say to you, Thea. Donna didn't kill Valerie." Her words stopped my feet. My jaw sagged. "I don't want to find out you're trying to get out of something by pushing it off on her. You'll lose our business and anyone else's I can talk to. And you're going to have to deal with me."

"No, Peggy. That's not what I meant to imply --"

"I'm just saying." Her tone made me flinch.

Crap. I'd alienated a client and friend. "I'm really sor --"

"And something else you should know. Your sister was the one who tipped off Melanie about Randy and Valerie. She must have some serious grudge if she'd stoop that low."

That little piece of news all but knocked the air out of my lungs. "I didn't have any idea," I choked out.

"Thought you'd want to cover all your bases." Her voice held a hard edge.

I groveled, to excess. By the time I'd hung up, I'd mollified my client but wasn't sure about the friend. I slumped in my chair, feeling battered, spent, and humiliated. And clueless. However, I knew as insensitive and thoughtless as Juliet could be at times, there was no way she could have killed anyone or deliberately goaded someone else into it. How had Peggy gotten hold of that information about my sister? It had to be rumor. On the chance there was some truth to it, I'd make a point to chat with Juliet later about her lack of quality decision-making skills.

In the interest of "covering all my bases," I dragged my thoughts back to Frederick Parsons's less than legal inclinations. Unfortunately, it occurred to me if Valerie's death was connected in some way to her father's business dealings he would have figured that out by now, and in all likelihood acted decisively. The fact that he continued to have Joey watch me offered proof enough he was no closer than me to discovering who killed his daughter.

I sighed and turned back to my computer. There was work to do, and if I wanted to get away for dinner this evening with Andrea I needed to get to it or spend the weekend catching up.

But my own work was disappointing me as well. The second client I worked on showed the same lack of return on an investment. The situation was becoming too familiar. I was tired of seeing intelligent people make unintelligent mistakes.

This one included excess paperwork, as he always did, so I sifted through it to find out what had gone wrong. Sure enough, the prospectus was there. High yield investment described to make it sound like a slam-dunk. It was Greg's company, but it was Sarah Fuller's business card stapled to the inside of the cover.

Sarah's clients were losing money.

At least some of them were. It wasn't a crime for your clients to lose money or make bad investments unless you intentionally steered them in that direction. Could that be happening here? I was willing to bet that the client whose taxes I had done on Tuesday, and who also showed evidence of a loss, invested in the same fund. Why didn't people do their homework before handing over large amounts of money to a stranger? Sure, Snohomish is a small town, and people tended to be trusting -- a fact that could tempt nefarious individuals -- but people also tended to talk. Bad enough for any business to make mistakes, but to deliberately pursue what was not in one's client's best interest was idiotic. I needed to schedule some official chit-chat with the feds very soon. Jeez. More problems. Just what I needed.

With the weary feeling of déjà vu, I called my client, got his voice mail, and left a message that sounded, perhaps, a wee bit more like a lecture than necessary. I did promise to help him out, but really, he should know better. I returned, once again, to my computer and spreadsheets.

A knock at my front door diverted my concentration from taxes. Irritated, I pushed away from my desk, went to the hallway, and jerked the front door open.

Greg.

With speed born from shock, I flung myself into reverse, attempted to do the same to the door, and ran.

He caught the door with lightning reflexes. It rebounded off his hand and crashed into the wall.

"Wait, Thea! Sorry. Wait. Sorry."

I stopped in my office doorway, my heart crashing into my ribcage, and face him, hand on the knob, knowing I could slam my office door in his face and lock it before he even thought about putting a foot into my house.

"Please. Sorry. I only came by to apologize for my behavior on Monday."

I eyed him, not believing his words. But, he didn't look crazed. He looked like he'd come from his office. His well-cut dark gray suit and maroon silk tie would have made Jonathan envious. Still ….

"Apology accepted. You can go now."

"I don't suppose you'd invite me in?"

"You suppose right."

He scratched the back of his head and moved his gaze to the doormat he seemed rooted on. "I guess I deserved that."

I didn't answer.

"Listen." He looked at me again. "I also meant to ask if you wanted Blackie back."

"What?" I blinked.

"Blackie. I don't want him. Valerie's parents are letting me have a lot of her things because we were engaged, but I really don't want another horse."

"You -- what?" If he'd strung a bunch of random words together he would have made more sense.

"I'm willing to sell him back to you. Fifty thousand. It's half of what you got for him."

My jaw dropped. Now I understood, and I quaked with rage. "That bill of sale was fake, and you know it."

Greg shook his head. "No. It's quite real."

"You bastard, you son-of-a-bitch. You took that to the sheriff. You made it up and took it to the sheriff." The small amount of my remaining sanity kept me from running at him and beating him senseless.

He shook his head and tsked. And he smiled, cold and small. "Such language. Do the math. Count the beans. There are other people who'd pay four times that for him. You're getting a deal, BC."

"Fuck you. He's not yours."

"Watch your mouth, little lady."

The phone rang.

"Get out of my house."

"Think about it."

My fingers curled into a fist. The phone rang, again.

"I'm a patient man, but even I have my limits. You'll see it my way." His gaze held mine in an unmistakable threat.

"Out."

His lip curved in a mean twist and he gave me a little salute as the phone rang for the third time. Then he turned and strode off my porch. I dashed to the front door, slammed it shut, and locked it. I answered the phone with a shaky "hello" after the fourth ring, recognized Uncle Henry's voice, and burst into hiccupping sobs.

"Thea, what's wrong? What's happened?"

"Greg was here!"

"I'm on my way." Anger clipped his words. From the shuffling sounds coming over the line I knew he was putting on his coat.

"No, no, I'm fine. Greg's gone. It's Blackie." I continued to cry, barely able to choke out words, desperate to protect my horse. "Greg -- he thinks he owns him. He's trying to sell him to me. He might try and take him!"

"I'm coming to get you."

"No," I sniffed. "I'm okay. Keep Greg away from Blackie."

In the background a door slammed then Aunt Vi spoke. "He's calmed down now, Henry. Thea's safe, isn't she?"

"Blackie!" I yelped. "He's hurt Blackie --"

"No, no one's hurt your horse -- yes, Vi, she's fine." He addressed me again. "He was just acting a little strange and Vi was sure there was a problem --"

"Like last time?"

"Not quite. More whinnying than running. Are you quite sure you're okay?"

"Yes."

"All right then, don't worry about Blackie. We'll lock the gate and keep an eye out. Paul said he was going to be staying in Seattle through the weekend, so we'll know to be suspicious if we hear any vehicles. If I were you, though, I'd call Mr. Green. Can you do that?"

"Yes." I sniffed again.

"Good. I expect he'll tell you to call the sheriff, but you'd best talk to him first. I can come over if you want."

"No, don't. I'm okay now." I took a shaky breath. "I'll call Mr. Green and then I need to go over to Copper Creek."

"I don't care for this, Thea."

"Just protect Blackie. Please? I can take care of myself."

After fielding more protests from my uncle I called Mr. Green. As luck would have it, he'd just arrived at his office and was free. Back in command of myself, more or less, I explained what Greg had said about the bill of sale and his implied threat.

"I think it's time we took a restraining order out against Mr. Marshall," he said. "Don't worry about your horse. He'd have to prove the bill of sale is real and I doubt he can do that. I'm mostly concerned about his harassment of you. He seems to have it in for you for some reason. Were you two lovers or anything?"

"Absolutely not. You don't understand, we have to protect Blackie. You may not think he's at risk, but --"

"I'll take care of the restraining order. If you see Mr. Marshall around town, go the other way."

"Well, of course. But Blackie --"

"Oh, and if you see him around your house call the police. And tell your uncle to do the same if he shows up at his place."

"Okay." Finally, he understood.

It was nearly noon, so I made a quick sandwich and left for Copper Creek to pick up the weekly receipts. Juliet had gone out to eat with Eric, so Delores was alone in the office having lunch. I sat in Juliet's chair and gave her the news about Greg's latest visit while she wrote out the deposit slip.

"That moron," she said, picking up the cup of soup and spoon she'd set aside. "What does he want your horse for?"

Duh. "Money would be my guess."

"He must be dumber than I gave him credit for if he thinks you'd pay for your own horse. I think he's trying to torment you."

"What did I ever do to him?" I whined.

Delores put down her cup of soup and looked at me over the top of her glasses.

"He still seems to think you had something to do with Valerie's death. He was a wreck at the funeral."

"You'd think he'd want the real killer caught instead of going for the most convenient person. Did you hear about that mess with Melanie, Randy and Jacquelyn?"

"Oh, that's old news." She shrugged and began double

checking the deposit slip.

"Well, not that old. I didn't know about it until I talked to Donna."

Without looking up from her tally sheet she said, "Thea, you're the only person I know who can be unconscious and still have her eyes open."

I shot her a useless scowl. I noticed things. Lots of things. I pushed the "crime of passion" theory I'd formulated. "I think there's a chance the Rucker family is involved. If Greg had any brains, he'd think so, too."

"Oh pish. You think Greg would deliberately walk in front of a train? He'd give all his information to the police. Greg wouldn't take on Randy. I doubt he's got a death wish. Randy's what, six-four? He's easily two-hundred pounds of solid cowboy."

"Well, maybe there was such a blow-up after my sister broke the news that one of them lost what little sense they had left."

Delores pursed her lips and regarded me for a long moment before answering. "Found out about that, did you?"

"Yes."

"I don't think Juliet got that ball rolling, Thea, despite the yelling it reportedly started. This wouldn't be the first time he's been caught out, and I doubt he'd have felt too inconvenienced promising to give up Valerie. He wasn't wearing her like tight jeans because he couldn't find another pair. Melanie's full-time job is beating off the bitches in heat."

"She didn't manage to beat off Valerie. Or maybe she did."

"Let's get back to Greg and this bill of sale." She pushed the deposit slip and checks at me to double check. "I don't like all this business with Blackie. Let the police deal with who may have killed Valerie. You're the one I'm concerned with. You're getting dragged into something that should have nothing to do with you, and I don't know why. How about I have Jorge stay with you until things get sorted out?"

"I don't think he needs to. My house is pretty secure.

Besides, I don't have anywhere for him to sleep."

She grumbled something about me being overconfident while I finished reviewing the deposit slip. As usual she'd made no errors. Huh. Money. Barn. An idea popped to the surface of my mind. "Where do you suppose Randy got the money for the improvements on his place?"

"A bank."

"But would a bank lend him money if his business was going down hill and the buildings were falling apart? What if he went to Valerie for the money? Kind of convenient of her to die -- no one to pay back."

"Now just how would you go about proving that theory, Thea?"

"Well, I'd ask --"

"No, you wouldn't. The police will handle it. You're a small dog in tall weeds, girl. I'm going to send Jorge over tonight. He won't mind sleeping on the couch."

"No --" A knock on the door interrupted me.

Miguel came in without waiting for Delores's holler. "I need to talk to you. Both of you."

"What's up?" Delores asked.

"I have been thinking about this -- trying to decide if it is important. It might be. Last night, about ten, me and a couple of the chicos from Green Gate Farm went for a beer over at the tavern up from the Texaco station on Birch Street. You know the one I mean?"

Delores and I nodded.

"There was a man, a middle-aged white guy, waving bills around and buying drinks for everybody. He was pretty drunk and bragging about how he was getting rich driving a horse rig around." He looked at us meaningfully.

"You're thinking he was the one who drove Valerie's rig?" Delores asked.

Miguel nodded. "I think it is possible."

I could barely contain my excitement. "Do you think he'll be there tonight?"

"Maybe. I never saw him before, but I do not go to that bar too often. Maria does not approve."

I didn't imagine she did, since the bar he was referring to, The Broken Axle, had a reputation for hosting a rough crowd. The bar was a regular feature in the Police Blotter section of the local paper. I chewed my lip, thinking.

Delores looked at me suspiciously. "What are you planning?"

"I don't know. Maybe if we find out who hired the guy we might have an idea about who killed Valerie. They have to be connected."

"Interesting idea for the police to look into," Delores said.

Miguel frowned. "No. I cannot allow you to go, if that is what you are planning. It is too dangerous for a woman alone. You should tell the police."

"You should go with me," I said, ignoring his suggestion. The police would surely think his was flimsy evidence, at best. "Can you remember what the guy looked like?"

"Yes, I think I would recognize him again. And no, I will not take you."

I gave him my best wide-eyed innocent look.

"Oh no you don't, missy." Delores tipped her head at me.

I put my hand on Miguel's arm, disregarding Delores. "What if we go over about ten. Is that too late for you?"

"No, ten is not too late," he said, although his expression looked uncertain.

"It certainly is," Delores commented.

"Well, you're not going."

"You're obviously planning on going. Miguel obviously won't let you do this alone, and if I don't go there obviously will be trouble. Besides, Maria will have a fit. We'll go earlier."

"Can't. I'm meeting Andrea for dinner. Anyway, if he didn't show up until late last night I think our best bet would be the same time frame. He might have a job that keeps him busy until then. But you don't need to go."

Delores snorted. "Yes, I do."

I grinned at her. Miguel's moustache twitched and the corners of his dark eyes crinkled. Delores gave us both a resigned look. This felt right. I knew we were on to something.

I stopped at the bank to make Copper Creek's deposit before going home. Once back in my neighborhood I drove around the block twice, checking my rear-view mirror constantly and examining all parked cars. Satisfied neither Greg nor Joey were hanging around, I parked at the curb, waved to my neighbor, who'd been watching me from her living room window, and made a dash for my house. I lost my momentum on the last step to the porch. A light breeze lifted the single sheet of newsprint taped to my front door, then allowed it to settle back. I snatched the thing off my door and searched for the circled words. This time there were three. "You're not listening," it said. The name of one person came to mind. Sarah Fuller. The little twit. She didn't scare me, although she was starting to annoy me. Disgusted, I crumpled the paper into a ball and nearly tossed it into my yard before realizing I'd be the one picking it out of the bushes later. I unlocked the door and went inside.

Just to make sure Sarah wasn't planning something terribly Hollywood, like popping out of a closet with an ax in her hand, I checked the rest of my rooms. Convinced no one was there but me, I returned to my office. I had work to do. I would not waste my time with people who couldn't find more mature ways to express themselves than having temper tantrums and leaving stupid notes.

I worked steadily until five, then called my uncle to check on Blackie's well-being. At five-fifteen, satisfied my horse was safe and secure, I was in my car and headed for Bellevue and The Cheesecake Factory. I didn't bother to check for company. If Greg or Randy showed up I'd call the police. If Joey joined me, he could pay for dinner. And Sarah? Well, she could write me another note.

Chapter Eighteen

Despite heavy traffic, I arrived at the restaurant before Andrea. Never mind the eatery was right down the street from her office. Her tardiness occurred with such predictability I could have put money on it. This habit had nothing to do with the sporadic rain that had me constantly adjusting my windshield wipers, and everything to do with Andrea's tendency to squeeze in "just one more little thing before I go."

A waiter showed me to a table and brought me a glass of wine while I waited. Andrea strolled in before I had time to make a dent in it.

"Thea." She gave me a hug and kissed my cheek, enveloping me in an expensive blend of flowers and spice. "It's good to see you." Her perfect eyebrows descended abruptly. "Did Greg give you those bruises?"

I touched my jaw. "Oh! I tried to cover them. Are they obvious?"

She scrutinized one side of my face and then the other. "No -- a little worse on the right, but you did an okay job. People won't gasp and point." She slipped out of her stylish coat and draped it over the back of her chair. "Are you going after him for that?"

"No."

She frowned and drew a breath, but pressed her lips together instead of speaking.

"I just want him to leave me alone."

"And is he leaving you alone?" She settled into her chair.

"No."

"Oh, Thea, what happened? Tell me you're staying with Vi and Henry."

"I'm staying at home, but --"

"Jonathan is staying with you?" She cringed when she said it.

"I broke up with him yester --"

"Paul is staying with you. That's much better. You know he'll protect --"

"No, Andrea --"

"Thea --"

"I'm okay. It's Blackie I'm worried about."

"Why? He's at your uncle's, right?"

"Yes, but ... okay, I can see I need to fill you in on a few details."

"Would you, please? I seem to be confused."

But the waiter arrived to take our order, delaying my recitation of the "few details." I gave the menu a quick glance and ordered a chicken chipotle pasta. Andrea didn't bother to look. I think she had the menu memorized. She ordered the herb-crusted salmon salad, which reminded me of Jonathan — in a manner of speaking. I was beginning to feel bad about what I'd done. And concerned. I seemed to be making an effort to shock myself lately.

The waiter left and I related the week's incidents -- in chronological order. Andrea listened to every word. The only interruption was from the waiter bringing our dinners. When I told her about my dramatic exit from Bernard's the previous evening, she pressed both hands over her mouth, but laughed anyway. She sobered right up at Greg's impromptu visit and his offer to sell me my own horse.

"I'm glad you called Jake," she said. "I think that situation is under control. Everyone knows what he's up to now. If he so much as looks cross-eyed at you his ass is grass." She ate thoughtfully while I alternately picked through my pasta and sipped my wine. Then she laid down her fork, and leaned towards me. "Valerie's father concerns me, simply because I know what he's capable of. Believe me, you don't want to know," she added, heading off the question I was about to ask. "The upside is I think he's waiting for you to make a mistake, and since we know you didn't have anything to do with --" she glanced around, "with any of that, you're okay. He has a reputation for being a patient man, in that he doesn't act impulsively. That his employee isn't around all the time probably means you aren't at the top of his list of duties. Unless he's keeping an eye on any friends or family to use as leverage. But that's not likely." She gave an unconcerned wave of her hand and went back to her salmon.

The tension that had begun as an uncomfortable twinge when she mentioned Valerie's father had continued to build until I understood why. I reached across the table and grabbed her forearm as she raised her fork to her mouth. She raised a startled expression to me.

"Andrea," I whispered, afraid to speak louder. "Those are the words Greg used about himself -- he said he was 'a patient man.' Do you think Valerie's father is using Greg to get to me?"

She thought for a long moment. I barely took a breath. "I don't know. Frederick doesn't recruit from the amateur ranks, as far as I know. It's possible, however, since it involves his daughter. That hadn't occurred to me."

"Wouldn't that just be dandy." I released her arm, and picked up my fork, but Andrea was tapping her fingers on the table top, so I put it down again.

"I was going to comment how oddly connected all of this seems."

"What do you mean?"

"There's something we haven't recognized yet that's tying together Greg, Valerie, Blackie, Donna, Melanie and Randy. Oh, and let's not forget psycho-woman Sarah. There's some nexus. The thought won't leave me alone."

I sucked in a breath.

"Okay, it's a crazy idea." She stuck her fork into her salad.

"No, no it's not." I knocked my wine glass teetering, but caught it before it toppled. "This whole time I've assumed there was one thing, one person, a single event -- I should have realized. I can't believe I've been so blind. I've been looking at this all wrong." I was no longer hungry. I pushed my plate aside and pressed my fingers to my temples. "There's something else. Jeez, I feel like I've almost got it." I shook my head, disgusted. The answer was lurking in the shadows of my mind, and I could not entice it forward.

Twice, Andrea began to speak, and twice cut herself off. Then she pushed her plate away. "Okay, I'm done, too." She waved at a waiter. "Let's get out of here and employ some time-honored problem solving procedures."

"Which would be ...?"

"Retail diversion for purposes of clarification."

"Ah."

We paid for dinner and wandered out into Bellevue Square Mall, where Andrea kicked the conversation back into gear. We rehashed what we knew while wandering around Nordstrom looking at shoes on the first floor, then taking the escalator upstairs to the lingerie and Point of View departments.

"I know you think I'm obsessing," I said across a rack of Anne Klein Separates. "But I'm sure Paul knew Valerie. I mean really knew her well. You don't handle a guy the way she did when I saw them together at Copper Creek last week if you aren't more than slightly acquainted with him. Even Valerie wouldn't have done that."

"You might be right, or you might be underestimating Valerie's libido again, or you might be trying to turn Paul into a bad guy so you can convince yourself he wasn't worth all the hormones, since you're obviously not over him." She handed me a pale green silk blouse and a smug look. "Try this on. The color's great with your eyes."

I sneered at her and put the blouse over my arm with the other things I'd picked up to try, then moved to another rack and examined a sleeveless cocktail dress with wide straps. The tag said, "Petite." "I'm just trying to be thorough and consider all possibilities." I held the dress up for Andrea to see.

"Yeah, sure you are," She said, then looked the dress over. "Yummy. Try it."

"You don't think it looks too 'Juliet'?"

"No, too tame. Try it. Paul would like it."

I shook my head, refraining from commenting on her supposed knowledge of Paul's taste in women's clothing or her refusal to believe I wasn't holding out hope. Once in the dressing room I directed us back to a safer subject.

"I still don't understand why Blackie was taken. It had to have been a mistake, but on the other hand I can't get rid of this feeling that he's important in figuring this out."

"You know," Andrea said through the dressing room wall, "I wouldn't dismiss it." She paused, and a hanger rattled. "I think it's unlikely it was a coincidence, too. Tell me what you think of this."

I heard her door open and poked my head out of my dressing room.

"Nice, but not 'wow.'"

"Yeah." She scrunched her nose. "That's what I thought. What do you have on?" I opened the door wider and showed her the blouse. "Oh, get it! It's great. Let's see the dress."

I exchanged the blouse for the cocktail dress and stepped out. Andrea opened her door.

"Holy cow, cleavage! Who knew? You look so curvy. That little bit of ruching on the side is perfect, and I love the color on you. It's not actually gray -- kind of purplish. What do they call it?" She grabbed for the tag, read it and snorted.

"Blackberry? Huh. Not like any blackberries I've seen."

My bra peeked out at the bottom of the V. I tried, alternately, to push it down or pull the dress up. "You don't think it's too low cut?"

"No, I think you need new underwear. We can stop at Victoria's Secret."

"What I don't need is a cocktail dress."

"Au contraire, my dear. Since you have so cavalierly thrown Paul aside, you must have something to wear to the parties I'm going to take you to. Men will throw themselves at your feet, honey. Guaranteed. You'll discard so many you won't be able to remember their names."

"Gee, I can't wait," I said without an ounce of sincerity.

"Darned tootin'. I'll have you know I've found plenty of hotties with my method. Just haven't found one I want to keep, yet."

"What's your criteria for keeping one?"

"Not being able to forget his name, of course." She slid me a vampy look over her shoulder as she went back into her dressing room.

I laughed, glad she could be flip about something that caused her periodic angst, and took another look in the mirror. *Pretty form fitting and definitely sexy. Andrea's right, you look pretty hot.* I struck a pose and laughed again, then changed back into my own clothes.

"All right, I'll get it -- and not because what's-his-name might like it."

I took the items I wanted to the register to pay. Evidently it was a good shopping night. I ended up with the dress, two blouses, a pair of slacks, and a skirt that had a tasteful ruffle at the hem. Andrea thought it was sexy without being cheap. Hmm…all these pieces were the ones she liked. My shoulders sagged. Damn. She dressed me again, and used my distracted state to keep me from noticing one of her favorite habits. No wonder she was such a successful attorney.

The sales woman smiled the total at me and politely took

my debit card out of my hand. My consolation was seeing Andrea pay more for the blouse she liked than I had paid for my dress and skirt together.

We exited Nordstrom on the second floor, which put us on the upper level of the mall. As we strolled along looking in the shop windows, our conversation turned to Sarah and Greg. Andrea knew Sarah only because of what I said about her. She knew Greg because the nature of her job had her socializing from time to time with the very wealthy, though she'd not actually met him.

"If I were you I don't know if I'd be going home tonight."

"I'll be fine," I said, convinced I would be.

I looked over the walk-way railing to the shops on the first floor and toyed with other ways to spend money. Then I caught sight of a familiar figure and ricocheted sideways, nearly knocking Andrea down.

"It's Greg!" My voice was a frantic whisper. I grabbed Andrea as much to steady myself as her. "He's downstairs right outside of Tiffany's."

She glided to the railing and peered down, then dashed back to me.

"Oh shit," she whispered.

"What's he doing?"

She glided back over and watched again for a moment then came back to where I cowered in the doorway of a candle shop.

"He went inside." Her voice was barely audible. "What do you suppose he's going into a jewelry store for?"

I ventured a guess. "Jewelry?"

She gave me a skinny-eyed look.

I worried my bottom lip, straining to see over the railing. My feet refused to move any closer. "We should watch and find out where he goes when he comes out."

"Right. Wait. What if he sees you? I know." She glanced around. "Go sit over there by the coffee shop. I'll sit there on the bench where I can watch the store and pretend I'm on my cell phone."

I hurried to the bistro table and perched where I could see her. She arranged herself on the bench, crossing one long leg over the other, swinging her un-businesslike stiletto from her toes. She looked for all the world like she was enjoying a conversation with a friend. And if Greg saw her, her legs would keep him from looking in my direction.

At last Andrea stood and casually strolled toward me, still engrossed in her "phone call." She sat down at the table and put her phone away.

"He came out," she said, her eyes danced.

"He's not coming this way, is he?" I pulled my feet under me, ready to run.

"No." She waved her hand to her right. "He went toward the parking garage."

I let out a breath I didn't know I'd held.

"He had a little bag with him, took something out -- a box -- and what appeared to be a receipt and put them in his coat pocket. Then he threw the bag in a trash can. I think it's safe to go to Victoria's Secret now."

"Why would he buy jewelry ...? Come on." I pulled her to her feet. "The sexy underwear's going to have to wait."

"Hold on a sec. Where are we going?"

"To Tiffany's." With Greg safely gone, the excitement of the hunt put a grin on my face. "We're going to do some detective work."

"Oh no. In the movies this sort of thing always ends up in a car chase and shoot-out. Need I point out that we are not armed and with your car we'll have no hope of escaping?"

"Oh come on. I just want to get a little information." I headed off toward the stairs to the first floor without her. Andrea scurried to catch up, as I anticipated, and fell into a pouty silence. Also as I anticipated.

When we reached the store she grabbed my arm and stopped me. "What exactly are we going to do?"

"I need to find out what he bought. Follow my lead and

agree with everything I say."

"No problem." Her tone was as sour as her expression.

Only one clerk was present when we walked in, and I made a beeline for him.

"Welcome to Tiffany's. How may I help you?" He cocked his head attentively.

The well-dressed, pleasant-looking man was perhaps in his mid-fifties, with hair graying at the temples, neat hands, and a bird-like mien. I produced my most dazzling smile and set my Nordstrom shopping bags conspicuously on the counter, just to make sure we came across as Women With Money.

"I think my brother may have come in here a little while ago, and maybe bought a ring."

"We don't give out customer information," he said, no longer cocking his head.

I pretended I hadn't heard the comment. "He's thirty-two, six-foot, has on a gray suit and light tan trench coat." I wasn't sure what a "sisterly" description could get away with. But Andrea saved me. In my heart I knew she wouldn't be able to resist a bit of intrigue.

"She didn't mention how handsome he is. But then I guess sisters never think their brothers are good looking, do they?" She actually winked at the guy. "He's got dreamy eyes, perfect hair, and I'd kill for a manicure like that." She fluttered her eyelashes and sighed like she was describing a rock star.

"You don't look anything like him," Mr. Observant said to me. "You're a brunette. The gentleman I may have noticed had light brown hair with blond highlights, and like your friend said, a much better manicure." He cast a judgmental glance at my hands.

"I resemble our father's mother, although we do have the same color eyes." I crossed my arms, tucking my hands out of sight.

"No, I think his were more blue-gray. Yours are definitely green."

"Contact lenses."

"I see," he said.

I doubted it. I don't wear contacts.

"The point is," I continued, "Grandmother has a ring Grandfather gave her, and she wants Greg to have it for his fiancée. If he already bought her a ring I'm going to have to figure out some way to break it to Grandmother." I bit my lip and gave him an imploring, desperate, and worried gaze.

"Are you sure you're his sister?" he asked, looking at me sideways.

"Of course I'm sure," I said doing my best to sound offended.

"You're not his fiancée?"

"Oh, please!" Andrea rolled her eyes and leaned toward the man, as if to share a confidence. "Do you honestly think a guy that good looking would go for Miss Plain Jane here, even if she got her cuticles fixed and wore a little polish?"

"Oh, well, you have a point," he said, eyeing me in a peculiar avian manner.

I stared, openmouthed, at Andrea. She shrugged.

"Yes," he continued, finally buying my story. "I'm afraid you're too late. He was in a little while ago and returned an absolute stunner of a ring he bought last Saturday for a much simpler piece. It is lovely, though." I doubted he believed what he said. He looked like he'd just tasted something bitter—like a smaller commission. "A brilliant cut, white diamond solitaire, slightly under a carat, set in white gold."

"Oh dear," I sighed, trying for the right display of disappointment. "I suppose I'm going to have to break the news to Grandmother. Thank you for your help."

"Of course," Mr. Observant Bird said.

"'Miss Plain Jane'?" I huffed at Andrea when we left the store.

"Oh, come on, Thea. The guy was so gay he wouldn't know a good-looking woman if she bit him on the leg. Besides, you got the information you wanted, didn't you? I didn't know you were such an accomplished liar."

"I learned from the best." I shifted my shopping bags and patted her back.

"And that is why I am such a hot attorney," she replied, laughing. "So, who did Greg buy the ring for?"

"Well, I'm fairly certain the one he returned is the one he had with him Sunday morning at Copper Creek. But he's obviously gotten himself a new engagement ring. Do you think Melanie is forcing an issue with Jacquelyn?"

"Could be."

"Seems pretty cold, right on the heels of Valerie's funeral," I said.

"Maybe she's pregnant," she said softly, stopping to look in the window of a chic maternity shop.

Uh-oh. I needed to distract her from her biological clock. "Wouldn't that have pissed Valerie off."

"I don't think Valerie's in any condition to care." She'd rebounded into her attorney tone.

Phew.

"True. But that's still pretty heartless. I guess someone who plays around wouldn't have the decency to wait a respectable amount of time, even if the girl is pregnant. Lots of brides are pregnant these days. Some of them wait until after the baby is born to get married. And some don't get married at all." I steered our course toward the parking garage. It was late. I'd go look for a new bra some other time. "You know, Andrea, certain aspects of human behavior absolutely disgust me. Valerie is murdered and Greg rockets straight from grief to the altar. I wouldn't want someone who couldn't display even a drop of humanity. Melanie and Randy should show a little sensitivity, too, especially since their daughter's involved."

"I see stuff like this all the time, and worse, Thea. Someone dies and the family turns into a pack of hyenas."

"It's disgusting."

"But not uncommon."

"Do you suppose Greg's got something on Randy?"

"What do you mean?"

I told her about my "loan from Valerie" theory.

"Hmm ... hard to prove without access to bank records. For that, you'd need a search warrant." She patted my shoulder when I sighed. "Sorry. It's a worthy idea, though, and I expect the sheriff's looking into it. So what's next, Sherlock?"

"To The Broken Axle."

"What's that?"

"A biker bar in Snohomish."

"Eww." She scrunched her nose. "Do we have to? I really and truly don't like this idea."

"We don't have to, your majesty. However, I'm going."

"Not alone!"

"No, with my trusty sidekicks, Delores and Miguel. Miguel was there last night and he believes he spotted the guy who stole Blackie. We're going to see if he shows up again this evening. I think he's the key to finding out who killed Valerie."

"You're just not letting this go, are you?"

"Don't worry, I'll be well protected."

"Be careful. I mean it, Thea."

We reached my car and got in. I would drop her at her office, since she had walked over, then go home to change into something appropriate for beer with the bad boys.

"Call me," she said, when I pulled up next to her car. "Let me know you're all right and what's going on."

"One more thing, Andrea. What do you know about Jacob Green?'

"Your attorney? He's one of the best, why?"

"He's kind of weird."

Andrea laughed. "Jake is that."

"But does he know what he's doing? Am I going to land in jail because of some peculiar idea Jonathan has for revenge?"

"Thea, I told you, don't worry about Jake. He's excellent.

He'll take care of you. I wish you had called me for advice instead of Jonathan, but I can't fault him for sending you to Jake. Call me tomorrow."

We said goodnight and I waited while she started her car. It was time for me to rub elbows with the biker crowd.

Chapter Nineteen

Delores frowned at me when she opened her door to my knock. I grinned at her and her scowl deepened.

"Sit down. I'm not ready."

I sank into one of the overstuffed living room chairs and wished, as I always did when I sat there, that I had space in my living room for a chair like it.

"Are you sure you want to do this?" Her voice carried easily from the bedroom.

"Positive."

She walked into the living room in her stocking feet, sneakers in hand, and sat on the sofa to put them on. She wore her usual blue jeans and flannel shirt. There was no hint of the elegance I now knew she was capable of.

"You'll never guess who called me this evening." She tied the laces on the first shoe.

"Michelle Obama?"

She flicked an annoyed look at me. "Don't be a smart ass. It was Marjorie Fuller, Sarah's mother." She worked her other foot into its shoe.

"Sarah's mother? What'd she call for?"

"She canceled Sarah's riding lessons for the next month. Took the girl to the hospital. Said she had a nervous breakdown." She finished with her shoes and stood.

"Wow." I got up from my comfortable nest. "Did I tell you someone's been leaving me threatening notes taped to my front door? I'm certain Sarah's the one behind it."

"That child needs to spend some quality time with a therapist." Delores put on her down jacket. "And move out of her mother's house."

"Remember last summer when Marjorie helped with the schooling shows? What a disaster."

"Oh lord, how could I forget. If it hadn't been for your sister inventing that convoluted point system for year-end awards, and practically tying Marjorie to that old adding machine in the office, I would have lost all my volunteers." We stepped onto her front porch and she locked the door.

"Yeah. I never had anyone grab me by the collar before and hustle me out a door. The woman's a bully. Poor Sarah."

"I'm not sure I'd waste my sympathy," Delores said, as we walked to my car. "Sarah's an adult. She can make her own decisions. Anyway, dollars to doughnuts, we won't be seeing her back here."

We drove to the Copper Creek office to pick up Miguel, where he waited after doing the night barn check, then headed to the less picturesque side of town.

The Broken Axle, a single-story, concrete-block building with few windows, was painted a shade of blue usually seen on playground equipment. Neon signs, lined up under the eaves, proclaimed the brands of beer supposedly available within. The name of the bar was hand lettered across several sheets of plywood, affixed to the roof by an intricate structure of two-by-fours. A single spotlight illuminated the sign. The mist that hung earlier in the cold night air had turned to drizzle, making the seats of the numerous motorcycles parked near the door so reflective they appeared bright blue. Two men, not quite lost in shadow halfway along one of the building's walls, stood in close conversation. A quick exchange was made, a hand to pocket, then a glance in our direction. I looked away. Drugs, probably. Maybe one of them was an undercover cop. Maybe.

I stuffed my hands into my pockets, shrank into the collar of my parka, and stepped closer to Miguel and Delores. If I'd been alone I would have turned back.

Inside the bar was as crowded with bodies as the parking lot was with motorcycles. The din of laughter and shouts that passed for conversation surged around us like the acrid smoke-thick air. A basketball game blaring from the tiny TV over the bar, and the crack of billiard balls provided the only form of music in the place. Miguel led the way, winding past pool tables and around big men who, despite their inclination to study us with unconcealed interest, were disinclined to move. Every nerve in my body vibrated in a state of red alert. I stopped looking around and kept my gaze pinned on Miguel's broad back, only a foot in front of me.

He found an empty table and rounded up three chairs I touched the table top as I sat. Ick. Sticky. An ash tray directly in front of me overflowed with reeking cigarette butts. The stench, mixed with the odor of men who made scant use of deodorant or soap, stung my eyes and coated the insides of my nostrils. I couldn't remember the last time my senses had been so assaulted.

We'd barely sat when a young woman with blonde and hot pink, spiky hair, multiple facial piercings and an empty tray on her hip, slid between two customers and stood at our table regarding us with a bored expression.

"Beer?" she asked.

I was fairly certain we'd heard the entire selection.

"Three," Miguel said.

The girl pushed her way between the customers and disappeared. Miguel scanned the crowd. "I do not see him," he said, obviously referring to our quarry. "I will take a look around. Do not go anywhere." He looked directly at me.

I didn't think he needed to worry. Delores scooted her chair closer to me and glared at the backside of a guy who bumped her. I was hemmed in by similar blue-jean and leather-clad body parts. I wasn't going anywhere -- even if I wanted to.

Several long minutes later Miguel returned and gave a slight shake of his head. The waitress following in his wake kept me from asking him any questions. She held the tray with our three beers balanced on one hand at shoulder height. I put a twenty on the table and she snagged it with the first glass she banged down.

I seized the opportunity. "I wonder if you could tell me whether a friend of ours has been in tonight?"

"Who're you lookin' for?"

"Middle-aged white guy, brown hair, overweight," Miguel said.

"No kidding? He shouldn't be too hard to single out. Only half the guys in here look like that. Take your pick." Little Miss Sarcastic snapped her chewing gum and pocketed the twenty.

"He was here last night, dropped a lot of cash buying his buddies drinks," I added.

She gave me a suspicious once over. "He do somethin' wrong? You a cop?"

"No to both," I said. "We might want to hire him. I hear he drives trucks and sometimes hauls horse trailers."

"I'll let him know you been lookin' for him -- should I happen to see him." She shouldered her way back through the crowd with her empty tray.

"Keep the change," I muttered. We wouldn't see her again. I should have realized anyone here would treat us with distrust. We had no idea what we were doing.

"I think we should leave," Delores said.

I couldn't have agreed more. What a waste of time. Miguel took a couple of swallows from his glass before he got up, but Delores and I left ours untouched.

The moment I stood a strong grip engulfed my upper arm. My heart tried to break out of my rib cage, and my lips turned to ice as the blood left my face. A Sumo wrestler of a man, wearing yards of studded black leather, held me in place with his enormous paw. A dark blue tattoo covered the back of his hand and his forearm. The subject of the artwork was indiscernible, but then again, I wasn't studying it too closely.

"You gonna drink those?" He released my arm and pointed a sausage-like finger at our abandoned beer.

"No, be my guest," I squeaked, and edged away.

"Thanks." He plucked my glass off the table. "You lookin' for Lee?" He downed half the beer in one gulp and wiped his mouth on his tattoo.

I delayed my departure. "I guess so."

"He ain't here," my new friend said, then belched. "'Scuse me."

"So I've been told," I said, disappointed with the old news.

"Was here last night." He finished off the contents of my glass and exchanged it for Delores's. "Wouldn't buy me a drink, though."

"Really?" I tried for a non-committal tone, although I think I sounded sarcastic. He didn't seem to care. Why should he? We'd just provided him with three free beers.

"Yeah. Not like you nice folks. Had plenty of dough, too. He should've bought me a beer."

He was being chatty, so I took advantage. "I don't suppose you saw him here last Saturday night, did you?"

"Saturday night .... Nah, he wasn't here then."

Damn.

"Was here in the afternoon. Came in while I was playin' pool with Ripper. Didn't buy me a drink then neither. Neither did that prissy lookin' guy was with him."

I blinked. Had he just said what I thought he'd said? Could I be that lucky?

"He was here with someone?" I prompted. "Do you know who?"

"Uh uh." He took another big swallow from the glass.

Damn. Of course I couldn't be that lucky. Then again,

maybe Sumo Wrestler could describe the companion more clearly than "prissy." "What did Lee's friend look like?"

"Prissy. Like he didn't belong here," our clever friend said.

I narrowed my eyes at him, and he continued.

"Had a haircut, kinda blond, clean, good lookin', I guess, if you're the kinda woman who likes sissy men." He finished off Delores's beer and leered at me.

My instant recoil was not from the suggestive look. I cleared my throat. "Hey, thanks." I caught Delores's eye. She'd missed none of the conversation. Neither had Miguel. I hurriedly dug through my purse and handed my new buddy ten dollars. "What did you say your name was?"

"Didn't." He winked. "You can call me John, little mama."

Right. He probably had the same name as everyone else in this place. No matter. I'd recognize him easily if I had to find him again as a witness. Miguel stepped forward and took me by the arm, glowering at John from under heavy black eyebrows.

"Time to go home," he said, leading me away. His moustache looked particularly menacing.

"Sorry, man," John called after us over the din. "Didn't mean to move on your woman. Thanks for the drinks." He belched impressively again.

We walked to my car in silence. The earlier drizzle had become a heavy mist, wrapping its icy fingers around my wrists and neck. I shivered. I knew two men who fit the description of Lee's companion. I got in my car and glanced at Delores as I started the engine. She wore the same stony expression as when the vet has bad news. No one spoke for the few minutes it took us to get back to Copper Creek. No one needed to. We all knew. I pulled in front of Miguel's house and he patted me on the shoulder as he slid out of the back seat. He exchanged a quick look and a nod with Delores. She remained silent until we arrived at her house.

"Call the police first thing in the morning," she said. "It'll keep. I'll do it, if you prefer."

"No. It's better if I tell them."

She nodded.

I waited while she let herself into the house and turned on the lights. Then I headed home.

With my friends no longer present for support, I vibrated with barely controlled, irrational terror. Someone I knew well killed Valerie. He must know I knew. I wanted to run and hide.

Shaking as if I were hypothermic, I parked in front of my house, hurried through my front door, locked it, turned on every light, pulled all the curtains closed, and stared at the phone. No way did I want to be alone. I picked up the handset, listened to the dial tone, and hung up. It was past eleven-thirty. Uncle Henry and Aunt Vi would be in bed, asleep. I'd upset them if I called at this hour. Who could I call? Andrea? No, she was undoubtedly sound asleep. Nothing short of a fire would stir her until morning. I could call Juliet, but she probably wasn't alone. She'd simply turn around and call Uncle Henry and we'd have a repeat of last Saturday night when Paul rescued me. What would I say to him this time, anyway? "I've figured out who killed Valerie and I'm scared. Can I come stay with you?" Sounded like a sniveling child. I'd already done child-with-a-temper-tantrum this week. Besides, Uncle Henry said Paul was in Seattle through the weekend. Could I swallow my self-respect and call him? God no. I'd rather spend the night in my attic with the spiders. Besides, I had no assurance he'd be inclined to help me even if I knew how to reach him — which I didn't.

I was probably overreacting.

I was safe at home.

Pretty much.

I double checked the locks on the doors and windows, tossed my clothes in the washer, and stepped into the shower to rid myself of the smell and feel of the tavern. A loud thump sent me cowering to the corner of the tub, expecting to see the curtain ripped back and the flash of a butcher knife. The water pressure in the shower spray decreased abruptly. The washing machine. It'd shifted into the rinse cycle. Despite knowing the cause of the noise I rushed to finish rinsing, toweled off and pulled on my nightgown. With my heart still hammering against my ribs, I slid into bed.

Not five minutes passed before I got up, dressed in jeans and a sweatshirt, and lay down again.

Don't be such a weenie, Thea. You can do this.

I turned off the lights and stared, wide eyed, into the darkness, listening for any sounds.

At four o'clock I gave up pretending I would sleep, got up, and went into the kitchen to make coffee. The water gurgled as it heated and dripped into the carafe. It was so slow—and noisy. Why had I never noticed that before? I poured Cocoa Krispies into a bowl, ate, and tried to rehearse what I would tell Detective Thurman. When the coffee was ready, I filled a large travel mug, put on my sneakers and opened my front door, intending to leave.

Parked behind my car at the curb was an older Chevy I didn't recognize. Someone was inside, in the driver's seat.

Joey.

No, not Joey. My heart wedged itself into my throat and stopped. I well knew what Mr. Parsons's hired goon looked like sitting in a car, and this wasn't him.

Get back in the house, you idiot! No, wait. You'll be trapped. He hasn't moved. Maybe he didn't notice you. If you're careful you can still get to your car and the sheriff's office.

Cautiously, I took one step, and then another. Still no movement from inside the car. If he moved, I'd run. Drawing a breath, I continued to approach my vehicle on tip toe.

Still nothing.

I crept closer, watching. Once within mad-dash distance of my own car I recognized the lurking form.

My pulse plunged to normal. Jorge sat at the wheel, sound asleep. Miguel must have sent him over.

I walked over and tapped on the window. No reaction. I

tapped harder. Jorge sprang awake and looked around. I waved at him.

"Thea!" He rolled down the window.

"Go home, Jorge."

"I'm supposed to be protecting you."

"Thank you, but I'm going to the sheriff's office now." I made no comment on the quality of his protection.

"Oh, okay. I'll go home then." He yawned and dug her car keys out of his pants pocket. "I would have woke up if someone came by. I'm a very light sleeper."

"I'm sure you would have. I appreciate it," I added sincerely.

I smiled, got in my car, and started the engine. He put his car into gear only after I pulled away from the curb.

At a little after four-thirty the April sky in the Northwest is still dark. The cloud cover makes it even darker. The night officer at the Sheriff's Office made me wait while he verified my identification before letting me into the building. The entry was well lit, but there were nerve-wracking deep shadows beyond the floodlights.

"I need to talk to Detective Thurman about the murder case he's investigating," I said.

"Thurman won't be in before eight. You'll need to wait until then."

I sighed and checked my watch. I'd have a long wait in an uncomfortable chair, with no magazines for distraction. At least I had my coffee and I was safe.

"You don't need to wait here, you know," the officer said.

I brightened. "Should I wait in his office?" That would be better.

"You could go home."

"I don't want to go home."

"Are you here to confess?"

"No!" Oh my God, did cops I didn't know recognize me? Did everyone think I killed Valerie? I had to clear this up.

Now. "I have information for him. I think I know who murdered Valerie Parsons."

"Oh." He looked, without enthusiasm, at the clock. "It won't kill him to get out of bed. I'll give him a call."

He disappeared, and in less than a minute the sliding window from the office opened and he put a phone on the counter where I could reach it.

"Line one," he said.

I pressed the blinking button.

"Good God, woman, do you know what time it is?"

"I think I know who killed Valerie Parsons." I tripped over my words, inexplicably breathless.

"That's what Hausman said. You got your attorney there?"

"No. I can't imagine why I'd need him for this."

"Suit yourself. Okay, who's our killer?"

I told him, in detail, what happened, leaving out the parts irrelevant to the case.

"So, you decided the description of haircut, clean, kind of blond and 'good looking, I guess,' told to you by a sleaze bag who mooches drinks, that someone, who was with another guy named 'Lee,' might possibly have been the killer of Valerie Parsons, and maybe hired this Lee person to go to Copper Creek Equestrian Center, take her horse, and put him in the field where we'd later find Miss Parsons's body and think her death was an accident. But this Lee guy took your horse instead because the two horses look alike -- yeah, yeah, I know, same stall location, different barn -- which is why your horse was taken. How am I doing?"

"Uh, fine."

"And who is this mystery man who whacked the victim?"

"Jonathan Woods." I'd spoken his name at last. The silence in my ear went on for so long I thought the detective hung up. "Are you still there?"

"Yeah, I'm still here." Another lengthy period of silence ensued. "And what about this other evidence -- the bill of sale, the notes on your door, the witness who places you near the scene? How do those fit in?"

"They're separate issues, except for me being near the scene. That's an outright lie," I said, my confidence building.

"Have you mentioned your theory to anyone else?"

"No. I didn't say anything to Delores or Miguel either, because they were with me, heard what I heard, and I'm fairly certain they think the same thing I do."

"Well, at least no one will be filing a lawsuit for slander against you -- this morning, anyway."

"Excuse me?" Was he joking? I pressed my palm to my forehead, searching for another way to explain my evidence.

"Look, Miss Campbell." His words came out as a long sigh. "I appreciate the information, but it's highly speculative and circumstantial."

"I'm sure, but --"

"Miss Campbell," he said, cutting me off like an impatient parent. "You need to leave this to the experts. We do, after all, have a vague notion as to what we are doing."

"Well, of course you do, but --"

"Miss Campbell --"

"But --"

"Thea," he bellowed.

I winced. "I --"

"Okay, okay." He sounded exasperated. "I will take the information you've given me and have someone follow up on it. Will that do?"

"Yes."

"Okay. Now, I'm going back to bed, and I suggest you go home and do the same. Feel free to call me, during business hours, if you have any more ideas. Good night -- or morning."

I hung up feeling foolish, but only a little, and headed to the farm. As long as I was up, I might as well do stalls.

The kitchen light was on when I parked behind the house. Aunt Vi peered out the window and waved, probably recognizing my car's headlights. I tossed hay to Blackie and Duke, cleaned their stalls, then went down to the house. Aunt

Vi was still busy in the kitchen. I knocked softly so as not to alarm her, and let myself in. The comforting aromas of coffee and bacon cooking greeted me. Whole wheat toast, butter, and marmalade were set out on the table. With a deep breath, the tension holding me rigid since yesterday drained away. I was famished. After washing up, I gave Aunt Vi a kiss on the cheek and poured myself coffee. She put a plate of bacon on the table and called to Uncle Henry, then returned to the stove and began cracking eggs into a pan.

"You're up early," she said.

"I couldn't sleep." I picked up a piece of bacon and took a bite.

Uncle Henry padded in dressed in his robe and slippers, yawned a good morning and sat at the table.

"Why is that?" She asked.

I put bacon and toast on a plate and told them about my adventure with Andrea, then my excursion to The Broken Axle with Delores and Miguel. Aunt Vi's eyes went wide with distress as I told her of identifying Jonathan as Valerie's murderer. She made little consoling noises while stroking my arm.

"I'm glad you went to the sheriff this morning," Uncle Henry said when I concluded. The half shake of his head that he'd repeated throughout my narration told me he hadn't been too glad about my other field trip.

"Yeah, for all the good it did. They didn't believe me." I propped my elbow on the table and supported my heavy head on my hand. "I know the evidence is sketchy, but it makes sense when you consider how obsessed Jonathan has been trying to get me to marry him." I stifled a yawn. "He must have killed Valerie after he and I argued in the driveway on Saturday. He was probably thinking if he could get her to back off me I'd be grateful to him and say 'yes' when he proposed. He must have killed her accidentally, then panicked and hired this Lee person to move Nachtfeder, so it'd look like the horse's fault. But Lee got the wrong one." I took a piece of toast and buttered it, turning clues over in my mind. "We need to find Lee so we can be sure." Man, but I was sleepy. It was hard to hold on to individual thoughts as they popped into my head. I yawned. "It makes sense to me now. I'm pretty sure it does, anyway." I put my toast down uneaten. Chewing would take more energy than I had at the moment -- and small concerns from my conversation with Detective Thurman had begun to shift around like restless children. "Do you know for a while I thought Greg killed her? But he'd just come home from a business trip and walked into a tragedy. I still think he's scum, though." I shivered and stifled another yawn. "I don't ever want to see him again. I hope the Federal Trade Commission shuts him down and my clients get their money back. Serve him right."

Part of me knew I was babbling. That would have been the part that saw Uncle Henry and Aunt Vi exchange looks, and the part that noticed Uncle Henry helping me up out of my chair and Aunt Vi escorting me to the guest room.

"You need to rest. You've had a bad shaking," she said. "Why don't you lie down for a while? You went to the police. It's all over now." She sat me down on the bed.

"I'll rest for a minute," I said, easing my head onto the pillow. She covered me with the quilt. "Aunt Vi?" I curled up and pulled the quilt closer. Weights seemed tied to my eyelids.

"Yes, child?"

"Paul knew Valerie, I'm certain of it. I've been so afraid he had something to do with her death -- afraid because, you know, Delores would be upset."

Aunt Vi sat on the edge of the bed and stroked my hair. "He was here all Saturday afternoon and evening until Juliet phoned, except for an errand he ran for Henry. Don't bother yourself about that."

"But he didn't come here after he took me to my car at the airport when he dropped me off. I watched him go up Avenue D. He didn't turn."

I expect he went to the grocery store. That's where he was headed when I talked to him after Juliet called."

"Oh. Aunt Vi? Paul seems to have some connection with Greg, too."

"He'll have to tell you that, dear. All I know is there's no love lost between them."

She closed the drapes against the lightening of the sky and shut the door behind her as she left. I reviewed the things I knew, and tried to sort through the pieces, but my mind kept drifting. It didn't matter.

It was over.

I let go and drifted toward sleep.

Chapter Twenty

My first conscious thoughts puzzled over why I was at my aunt and uncle's, in bed, in my clothes, with daylight illuminating the drapes from behind. Not knowing what day it was also bothered me — along with some other vague worry I couldn't name.

I washed my face, went into the kitchen, and mumbled a greeting to Aunt Vi and Uncle Henry, who were finishing lunch. I sat, lump-like, in my usual spot at the kitchen table. Before I knew it a steaming cup of tea appeared in front of me. I inhaled the sweet perfume of the Earl Grey, and sipped it slowly.

"Did you get enough sleep?" Aunt Vi asked.

"I think so." I yawned. "What day is this?"

"Friday, love. Are you hungry?" I shook my head. "Juliet called a little while ago. She wanted to know where Delores is."

"I don't know." The events of the previous evening and early morning sorted themselves out in my mind. "She didn't tell me her plans for today. Juliet's sure she's not somewhere at Copper Creek?"

"Yes, she said she's been missing all morning."

"She's not in her house?"

"I think they checked. Everyone's worried."

I thought again, sipping more tea. Coffee would kick-start me faster. My head was still woolly. Perhaps she had gone to the sheriff's office. But she'd told me to go. I couldn't think of any possible explanation. I'd have to look for myself.

I left my aunt and uncle's, promising I would call them should I learn anything, and drove home. I brushed my teeth, changed clothes and drove to Copper Creek. Juliet watched my approach from the office window, her arms folded and a frown on her face.

"Have a nice nap, sleeping beauty?" she snapped as I walked in.

"Gee, I'm sorry, Juliet." I laid on the sarcasm. "I was up late and then at the Sheriff's Office at four this morning."

"Delores is missing, and no one knows where she is. You saw her last. Where is she?"

"Give me the key to her house."

She scowled, but went to her desk and got the ring of keys from the top drawer. "I already checked. She's not there." She threw them at me and missed.

"Well, I'm going to check anyway." I plucked the key ring off the floor.

Delores's home, a single-story modern rambler at the far edge of the Copper Creek property, was quiet and tidy. Someone had washed the breakfast dishes and lined them up to dry on the drain board -- most likely Delores. Mail was stacked neatly on the desk. I went into each of the two spare bedrooms and checked the closets -- why, I couldn't say. My mind offered numerous possibilities I didn't want to consider, even briefly. I found nothing there. I checked the bathroom, then went to Delores's bedroom. The bed was made, so I had no way of telling if it had been slept in or not. Just to say I had, I looked under it, found a pencil, but that was all. On the vanity in her bathroom stood several prescription bottles, a plastic pill case, and a small zippered kit of some sort. The pill case had fourteen little compartments, with the day of the week and AM or PM printed on each lid. The lid of the Friday morning compartment was up and it was empty, so she had taken this morning's dose of whatever. I peeked inside a closed compartment and counted six pills. I had no idea she took so much medication.

The zippered case contained a log book, and two small items, neither bigger than the palm of my hand. The wider of the two was equipped with an LED screen and a couple of buttons. I looked in the log book. It was filled in, but not copiously, with a range of numbers in the low one-hundreds. The column that caught my attention was the one titled, "Additional Blood Glucose." Evidently, Delores was diabetic. I never knew. From the number of other pills in her case, I guessed there were other health issues, too. The labels on her prescription bottles didn't tell me anything except the name of the drug, how much to take, and when. If I had any medical background I could have guessed what they were for. It distressed me that I'd always thought she was healthy. Why didn't I know? I left the house, locking the door behind me, and returned to Juliet.

"I didn't know Delores was diabetic," I said.

"Yeah. She has to eat regularly, and she takes a bunch of pills for that and other things."

"Why didn't you tell me?"

"What? You want a rundown on everybody's medical history?"

We glared at each other until I broke the standoff.

"It is not my fault she's missing. I'm trying to help. Where are the guys?"

Her expression didn't soften. "They're on the afternoon schedule."

The hardly informative answer meant they were anywhere on the property working on whatever projects Eric has assigned to them.

I tracked them down. They were worried, but had no clues. I talked to the instructors, something Juliet hadn't done.

Only Anne had seen Delores. She'd driven out close to nine o'clock. I went to Miguel and Maria's house, but only Miguel was there and I'd just talked to him.

"Maria went to the store," he said.

"Have her call me when she gets home."

There was nothing more I could do at Copper Creek, so I went home and called Detective Thurman.

"Delores is missing," I told him without preamble.

"Since what time?" he asked.

"A little before nine this morning. She was at the office early. One of the instructors saw her drive out."

"She hasn't been gone that long. She'll be back when she's finished running whatever errands she's got."

"This isn't like her to be gone so long and not let anyone know where she is. Besides, she's diabetic and has to eat regularly." I felt I had to make a point.

"There's nothing I can do right now, and I think she's old enough to get her own meals."

What did it take to get this guy off his butt? "She knows who killed Valerie, too." And I knew he didn't believe me. "What if something happened? I'm afraid for her."

"Look," he said, in a tone I was becoming all too familiar with. "Give her time. She'll turn up. If she's not back first thing tomorrow morning, we'll start looking."

That was all I would get out of him. I turned on my computer intending to get some work done, but turned it off before it fully booted up. This didn't feel right. Something was wrong. I'd have to find her myself.

By the time I drove back to Copper Creek, Maria had arrived home from the grocery store. The men were in the house for their afternoon break before evening chores, and Juliet was there as well. While Maria bustled around putting groceries away I told them about my conversation with Detective Thurman.

"She will be as mad as a wet rat when she comes back and finds out you called the police on her," Maria said.

"I wish someone would fill me in," Juliet said. "What do you guys know that you're not telling?"

Miguel and I looked at each other.

"Didn't you say anything?" I asked.

"No. I thought you would tell Juliet, she would tell Eric and he would tell Jorge."

"Oh."

Obvious communications breakdown. I guess I couldn't be too hard on Delores for the same lapse. So I told them about the three of us going to the Broken Axle. I knew Maria wouldn't be pleased, but I saw no way around it. Miguel would have to field this one himself. However, I never got a chance to tell them what we discovered. Maria came out of the kitchen like a mad bee on a mission and slapped Miguel soundly on the arm. He flinched.

"You lied to me! You know I do not like you going to those places!"

"But Maria, we did get some information."

"Ha! All you found was some drunk to buy beer for!" She planted her fists firmly on her hips. Her black eyes sparked fire.

"Well, actually, Thea paid for the beer."

"You let a woman buy your liquor?" She pulled at her hair. "¡Ay, Dios mio, Miguel!" She let loose with a stream of invective Spanish, none of which I understood, but whose meaning transcended linguistic barriers.

By the time she finished she had included Miguel, Jorge, and Eric in her diatribe. If appearance was anything to go by, each acted suitably humbled.

Then Maria turned on me. Shaking her finger and switching to English she told me less eloquently, but no less effectively, "You should not have gone to a place that has such a reputation as that one. Besides, it is not right for a woman to pay for things a man should pay for. You make yourself look like, like ...."

"A hussy?" Juliet offered.

I knew she'd get some mileage out of this.

"Yes, a hussy! You will never find yourself a husband. It is hard enough at your age, anyway. Why do you want to go and make yourself look like a hussy? No man will have you."

I was speechless. Juliet was finding it hard not to snicker. She poked Eric in the ribs with her elbow. Maria wasn't finished. She pinned Juliet with a stern look she'd undoubtedly learned from the nuns.

"You I must talk with in private the talk your own mother should have had with you."

Juliet opened her mouth but Maria's hand flashed up like a traffic cop.

"When the men leave we will talk about the cow and how she should not give milk away except to the farmer who owns her."

Maria must have thought she was being obscure enough for no one to catch her meaning. Juliet bit her lip and examined the carpet. Eric received her final rebuke.

"And you," she said, not bothering to switch to Spanish, "you will hear me about the dishonorable man who steals the milk."

She turned and marched to the kitchen, leaving Eric red with embarrassment and the rest of us afraid to speak. I heard cabinet doors slamming and pots rattling. A short moment later she reappeared in the kitchen doorway brandishing a long-handled pot like a war club. "All of you," she said, swinging the thing in a wide arc, "out of my house and back to work!"

We all moved toward the front door.

"Except you." She pointed the pot at Juliet.

Juliet cast a pleading look at me. I pretended not to see.

"All of this because Delores wanted to go look at a horse to buy." Maria marched back to the kitchen.

We looked at one another, shocked.

"Maria," Miguel called, "you mean Delores told you where she was going?"

"Yes, she told me." She reappeared in the doorway. "She was going to look at a horse to buy." Relief spread audibly through the room. "If any of you bothered to be where she could find you she would have told you, too." She returned to the kitchen.

As we filed out the front door, our moods greatly lightened, Maria yelled from the kitchen, "*¡Juliet! ¡Eric! ¡Aqui! ¡Ahora!*"

Chapter Twenty-One

It was time for life to return to normal, time to return to my beloved rut, and past time for me to call Andrea. There were three messages on my voice mail from her -- the last thirty minutes ago, at two thirty -- each sounding more agitated than the previous. The third time her message was brief.

"Damn it, Thea, where the hell are you?"

Swearing from Andrea -- a sure sign of near hysterics. I called her.

"Where the hell have you been? Why didn't you call me?"

"I'm sorry --"

"I've been worried sick about you!"

"I'm sorry, I --"

"Are you all right? You aren't in the hospital, are you?"

"No, I'm fine, I --"

"Well, for the love of --"

"*Andrea.*" Once able to insert a complete sentence, I told her about the results of our trip to the Broken Axle and my visit to the sheriff's office.

"Okay. I forgive you. You've been busy. But I'm telling you, Thea, I was ready to call the cops."

"I'm hoping they've got their hands full with Jonathan right now."

"Until you know he's in custody, you be careful. Understand?"

"Yes, mother."

Thus humored, she permitted me to get back to work, since I knew, even if Andrea didn't, that there was nothing more to worry about.

It was close to six when I wrapped up my accounting work. If I hurried, there'd be enough daylight left for me to ride my horse. Uncle Henry had lights for his arena, but they were expensive to run. I didn't like to use them if I could avoid it. I changed my clothes, put on my old sneakers, and grabbed my riding boots to change into later.

I opened the front door and the piece of newsprint taped to it flapped in my face. I snatched it off the door and read it. "So sad, too bad, BC."

My riding boots and purse fell from my hand as a sickening jolt of realization smacked me full in the gut. It was Greg, not Sarah, who'd left the notes. And he'd put this on my door while I worked in my office.

But that wasn't the worst of it.

Because of me, Thurman was going after the wrong man.

Frantic, I looked up and down my street. Nothing. Gone. But when? How long ago?

I ran, dodging through the hedge, to my neighbor's house and pounded on the door. Be home, please be home. I needed to know when he'd been here. A long moment passed and I raised my fist to knock again, but I heard footsteps and Mrs. Baron opened the door.

"Hello, Thea. Goodness, what's wrong, dear?"

"You didn't happen to see someone at my house in the last little while, did you?" Please, please, let this one-woman block-watch-program have seen something, I prayed to all available gods.

"I'm sorry, dear, but I've been watching TV. Oprah's on,

and she's doing one of those makeover programs. I hate to miss her show."

I shrugged off her next half dozen questions, trying not to appear anxious, then jogged back toward my house. I pushed through the hedge, and stopped. One of my riding boots lay in the middle of my walk. I hadn't left it there. I picked it up and raised my eyes to my porch. The front door stood opened. I knew I'd shut it.

I approached the house, eased up the three steps to the porch, and listened. Nothing. From where I stood I could look through the living room and down the hallway that led to my bedroom. My other riding boot stood in the middle of the hallway near my bedroom door. God damn it. The son-of-a-bitch was in my house. I ran through the door, down the hall, snagged my other boot, and skidded into my bedroom, boot raised above my head, ready to beat him senseless with it.

Empty.

Except for the note on my pillow. "You're going to be too late," was handwritten on a plain piece of paper.

The front door slammed. I spun and dashed into the hall.

Again, no one.

Nothing but the feel of cold air coming from the back of the house. I ran to the kitchen. The back door stood open. I was the only one in the room. The wind must have blown the front door shut when he went out the back.

Or he could still be in the house.

I closed and locked the kitchen door, then pulled a carving knife out of the knife storage block by the sink and eased toward the pantry.

No one.

I crept silently to my bathroom. That, too, was vacant. I checked under my bed, in my closet, my office. I rushed through the house, abandoning stealth.

I was alone.

Back in the kitchen I put the knife away, but my hand trembled so much I had trouble sliding it into its proper slot.

Damn him. What was he playing at? Then I knew -- Blackie! I dashed to the phone and dialed Uncle Henry's number. It rang once. "Pick up, come on," I pleaded. It rang again. "Come on, come on, pick up." It rang four more times. "Damn. Damn. Where are you?"

Okay, Thea, now think, think. It's Friday. What goes on Friday afternoons?

"Aunt Vi's hair appointment, and ...." I looked at the clock.

Uncle Henry has a lesson scheduled right now. That's why no one is answering the phone.

Okay, made sense. And my brain was working instead of reacting. I grabbed my cell phone, purse, and keys, locked the front door and headed to my car. Two steps off my porch, the obvious hit me.

Delores.

I flipped my phone open and punched Maria's number, praying someone was home. Maria answered. Silently I thanked her Dios.

"Maria, it's Thea. Do you know if Delores is back yet?"

"I do not see her car," she said. I could hear her walking around, probably looking out the windows.

"Listen, this is important. What exactly did she say to you this morning?"

"She said she was going to look at a horse a man was selling and should be back before too long."

I bit my lip and tried another tactic.

"Did she say she was going to see a man about a horse?" I held my breath.

"Yes, yes, that is exactly her words. How do you know?"

I flew to my car, phone pressed to my ear. "It's an expression. It doesn't have anything to do with horses." Although in this case it was close. "I'm pretty sure I know where Delores is. I'm going to get her."

I disconnected and punched the speed dial for Juliet's cell phone while I scrambled into the driver's seat and jammed the key into the ignition. Relief. The engine turned over on the first try. Things were going my way. I shoved the car into gear and peeled away from the curb. Juliet wasn't answering her phone. Damn. I need her to go to the farm to check on Uncle Henry and Blackie.

In quick succession I tried the Copper Creek office and her apartment, met with identical results, and ran a red light. I tried Eric. No answer. Where the hell was everyone? *Calm down. It's Detective Thurman you need.* Frantically, I punched his number while swerving through traffic. I hit the send key and my battery went dead.

"Son-of-a-bitch!" I jammed it into my purse.

There was no time to drive all the way to his office. I couldn't give Greg that much of a head start when Delores's life was on the line.

Greg's last note taunted, "Too late," "too late." My foot pressed into the accelerator.

I left forty-five behind in a twenty-five zone and hoped a cop would see me. No luck. Where were the speed traps when you wanted them?

It was after six o'clock. What kind of shape would Delores be in if she hadn't taken her meds on time or eaten a regular meal? That would have been the good news. Greg had killed Valerie. What would he do to Delores? *No, stop thinking like that.*

A pickup truck obeying the speed limit slowed me to a crawl. I pounded the steering wheel and honked repeatedly. He tapped his brakes at me.

"Move, dammit!" Use the pedal on the *right*!"

I passed him on a curve on a double yellow line and got a severe horn blasting for my heroics.

"Screw you," I muttered to my rear-view mirror, leaving him in a cloud of exhaust.

Once on Carpenter Road, I found an overgrown lane just past Valerie's property. I hoped it wasn't someone's private drive. Still, I'd rather risk that than pull up to the house and announce my presence to Greg. I wedged my car into the bushes then, not bothering to conceal myself, I ran as best I could up the long, steep driveway to the estate. I halted when I reached the top of the hill and bent double, my hands on my knees, sucking air into my lungs. The middle of the driveway was not a good place to recover from the dash. A small cedar tree stood a short distance to my left. I darted to it, and dropped into a crouch, hiding myself in its wide, aromatic branches.

As I caught my breath and the burning left my calves and thighs, I peered through the damp foliage. Before me lay an empty expanse of lawn, dotted with a few specimen plants and evergreens. The driveway angled to my right before it divided, one branch curving to the house, the other skirting around back to the barn.

The only car I could see from my hiding place was Valerie's BMW, and it hadn't moved since last weekend. I didn't see Greg's car or Delores's, but that didn't mean anything. She'd probably parked behind the house and gone to the kitchen door. Greg's car might be in the garage on the far side of the house.

Shouldn't you check for vehicles first before you look for Delores?

But what if he's gotten rid of her car? The absence of her car wouldn't mean anything.

Hey, the house is dark. It doesn't look like he's here.

Could I be so lucky?

Maybe. But there was no way to know without ringing the doorbell, so I waited and watched and listened, trying to pick out any sound beyond the tree frog cacophony, any movement through the darkened windows.

You should have been planning on the way over instead of driving like a mad woman. How are you going to find Delores? Come on, think.

Right. A systematic search was called for -- systematic but stealthy.

And for God's sake be smart. Don't do anything to draw Greg's attention -- if he's here.

The barn would be the quickest to search and my best bet for avoiding Greg. How was I going to cross that huge lawn without being seen?

Impatience and dread plucked at me, demanding a decision. I couldn't hesitate any longer so, good plan or not, I chose to circle to my left and come at the barn from the route that afforded the most opportunity for cover. I pulled off my light colored jacket and stashed it beneath the wet branches. My dark cotton shirt soaked up the dampness as I brushed against the foliage. I shivered. The cold went right through me.

I kept low and snuck from shrub to shrub, watching the house for any sign of Greg, until an open portion of the lawn was my remaining obstacle. Then I swallowed my fear, broke from my cover, and pelted toward the house. I reached the foundation plantings and fell to my knees, panting. As my breath steadied, I heard the soft sound of hurried footsteps on the grass. They were coming toward me. Terrified, I dove behind a bush and fell headlong into a window well. Instinct caused me to grab at anything within reach to arrest my descent, but I landed in a heap among the wet, rotting leaves anyway. Holding my breath and willing my heart to stop pounding so hard, I listened from my uncomfortable, contorted position.

Silence.

Except for ... tapping. What of? A faucet dripping into a sink?

I stopped breathing again.

The tapping didn't stop, but became louder and more insistent. I turned my head toward the basement window. A face, in deep shadow, peered at me through the dirty glass. Hair stuck out in all directions and the mouth opened and closed like a puppet. One hand made weird gestures. I drew a sharp breath, but before I could scream recognition hit me full force. It was Delores.

My exhale would have been a sob of relief, but the decomposing leaves I'd stirred up at the bottom of the window well provoked a sneeze. Delores had her finger to her lips. Yeah, yeah, quiet, I got that. The words she mouthed, however, were incomprehensible. I shook my head and she closed her eyes with an expression of labored patience and tried again, slower. This time I understood. Greg had been there, but she thought he wasn't there now. If she was right, he would come back soon. Considering I'd landed in the window well looking for a place to hide from pursing footsteps, chances were good he'd returned. I had to hurry and be very cautious.

Then she added something more. Her mouth seemed to form Sarah's name. Sarah was there, too? That couldn't be right. I shot her a quizzical look then sneezed again. She rolled her eyes. What she said next I understood: Be careful. Be quiet.

I heaved myself out of the well and crawled under the bushes, listening. Soft footsteps came rapidly toward me and I froze like a rabbit.

"Thea? Thea? I know you're here somewhere. It's me, Juliet." She whispered so loudly, she might as well have stood in the middle of the driveway with a bullhorn. I edged out of my hiding place, startling her.

"Oh, Thea, thank God!"

"Shh," I hissed and grabbed her arm, pulling her down next to me. "How did you know I was here?"

"I followed you." She picked dead leaves out of my hair. "Eww."

"What? Why?"

"I was worried about Delores and came to look for you." She brushed at my shoulder, her nose wrinkled in distaste.

"Stop that." I pushed her hand away.

"When I went to your house and you weren't home I thought you might be at the farm, so I went out that way and caught sight of you careening down the road. When you didn't turn to go to the farm I followed. I left my motorcycle by your car. I figured if you were being cautious I should be, too."

I had to give her credit for clear thinking. "Delores is here," I whispered.

"You found her!" She clapped her hands and bounced.

"Shhh!"

"How did you know?" She hugged me, then turned me loose, her nose wrinkled again.

"I'll explain later." Or not at all, to avoid looking like an idiot. "Do you have your cell phone?"

"No. It's at home, charging."

"Damn." I took a breath. "Okay, look, we have to hurry. Greg may be back soon."

"Greg?" She blinked in confusion, then her eyes widened. "Shit. You mean he's the one who killed Valerie?"

I nodded.

"Why didn't you say anything earlier?"

"Maria's harangue interrupted me." Fortunately.

"Why's Delores here?"

"I don't know. I'm guessing she came to talk to Greg. Maybe he called her. We'll ask her about it later. Right now we've got to get her out of here."

We ran to the back door of the house and cautiously tried the knob. Locked. We tried the front. Locked as well. Remembering the keys I'd found, I sprinted to the outbuilding with Juliet close behind. The key ring was back on its nail, but the only key remaining was to the tractor. In frustration, we went back to the window well and Delores.

"Does this window open?" I mouthed to her.

She looked at the frame and nodded. The latch was inside at the bottom of the small window, but she had difficulty with it, and used only her right hand. After a moment she disappeared from view. Sarah took her place. Juliet and I exchanged stunned looks

Sarah glanced at us before setting to work on the latch. If

the look on her face was any indication, she was straining hard. She stopped and looked over her shoulder then moved aside. Delores replaced her and grabbed the latch with her right hand and yanked. Her expression tightened as if she was in pain, but even so she managed what Sarah could not. With a screech of protest, the window opened. We all sighed with relief, but it was short lived.

"Take our hands, Delores. We'll pull you up," Juliet said.

"Can't," she panted, the pain obvious in her voice. "I think the bastard's broken my arm. It's swollen and hurts like hell when I try to move it."

"I can come up," Sarah said.

"Like hell you will," Delores snapped at her. Sarah shrunk back. "She'll run right to Greg."

"No! No, I won't!"

Delores rolled her eyes. "I've been listening to her bleat all afternoon. If it weren't for this arm she'd be trussed up and gagged."

"But he loves me," Sarah wailed and held up her left hand. Aha! That's where the other diamond ring ended up. "He asked me to marry him last night at the hospital. I snuck out and came here like he told me to. He loves me!"

"Don't even bother," Delores said to us. "She doesn't understand being tossed down here with me is not a sign of love."

"He does too love me," she said. "He wanted me to keep an eye on you while he was gone."

"You're dumber than a box of rocks," Delores said.

"He told me Valerie forced him into proposing to her and the whole other thing was her idea, too." Sarah directed her last comment to me, and I had no idea what she was talking about.

"We're wasting time," Delores said. "We need to get out of here."

Juliet grabbed my arm. "Why don't I go down through the window and help lift her through? After all, I'm taller than you. And stronger."

"Okay." I didn't think it was such a hot idea. We could hurt Delores more in the process, but there seemed no other way. Besides, Juliet was more than capable of trussing up Sarah, if need be.

I backed out of the bushes to give Juliet room to maneuver. She grunted as she squeezed through the awkward opening.

So intent was I on Juliet's efforts that I didn't notice the approaching footsteps. Before I had time to react a large hand clamped over my mouth and nose. A metallic click sounded dangerously close to my ear as I was dragged away from my sister and friend. Juliet's voice sounded a million miles away.

"Okay, I made it. Thea? Thea?"

Chapter Twenty-Two

It was Greg.

He dragged me away from Juliet and Delores. The hurried, backward movement and what was surely a gun against my head kept me from struggling. I was certain he intended to haul me to the pasture and shoot me at the spot where I'd found Valerie. Instead, he halted less than fifty feet from where he'd grabbed me.

His face rested lightly against my hair and he spoke in a calm, quiet voice. "I'm going to take my hand off your mouth. If you say one word or try to run I'll shoot you. Understand?"

Oh yes, I understood. I nodded quickly. Running was out of the question. The convulsive shaking of my legs made it almost impossible to stand. He bent down and retrieved something from the ground. I risked a glance. A rake? Gardening tools don't kill people, people kill people.

Shut up, Thea.

He gave me a push in the ribs with the business end of the gun, forcing me toward the house. I was amazed my legs obeyed and amazed we went right back to the bushes where he'd found me. His mouth was once again by my ear, but Juliet's impatient snarl cut him off.

"Thea, I said we're ready. Where are you?"

I pressed my lips hard together.

"Get down in the window well and shut the window," he whispered. "You even look like you're trying to get through it and I'll shoot you."

I nodded and stumbled through the bushes. Juliet looked up at me through the open window, her annoyance with me plain on her face. It was too dark to see Delores or Sarah.

"Thanks for showing up. I about killed myself getting in here."

The silent message I wanted so desperately for her to read on my face was going unacknowledged.

"Shut the window," Greg snapped.

I glanced in his direction. A metallic click prodded me into action. Using my foot, I slammed the window shut. Juliet banged her fist against the glass and pushed it open. Again I slammed it shut, shaking my head and mouthing, "No, please," as I held my foot against it. I had no trouble hearing her shout.

"What the hell are you doing? This is not funny, Thea."

The bushes rustled. "Take this." Greg thrust the rake at me. "Wedge it against the window, then get back up here. Don't forget about the gun. I doubt a rake is any match for a bullet."

I angled the rake between the window and the side of the window well, but it was a poor fit. Cussing with enthusiasm, Juliet tried to push the window open. I shook my head and mouthed, "sorry," with no effect, then I scrambled out of the hole and through the bushes to where Greg waited, praying I'd done a poor job of trapping my sister and friend. With luck Greg would take me far enough away so they could escape unobserved.

"Gardening tools come in so handy sometimes, don't they?" He spun me around and pushed me along in front of him. "You should pay more attention when you hold conferences in the bushes. It wasn't hard to figure out what you two were planning. I don't see a future for you in burglary -- don't see much of a future for you at all, actually." He chuckled.

We reached the back of the house and he shoved me at the porch steps. I tripped, broke my fall with my hands, then climbed up to the back door.

"Nice going, Grace." He laughed.

Maybe he'd amuse himself so much making fun of me he'd forget to shoot me.

Keys jingled. He reached around me, unlocked the door and pushed it opened. With the gun pressed firmly into my spine, he propelled me into the house and flipped on the lights.

We were in Valerie's remodeled kitchen with its granite countertops, tile floor, cherry cabinets, and awful smell of a toilet that hadn't been flushed for a long while.

"Now, shall we invite everyone up?" he asked.

He pushed me across the huge room. As we skirted the center island I caught sight of a pair of work boots sticking out from denim-clad legs. They were so out of place that my feet refused to continue until I'd made sense of it.

"Don't worry about Lee," Greg said, at my sudden stop. "We had a little disagreement about some money. He finally saw it my way." His high-pitched giggle plucked at my already taut nerves. He nudged me into another step and I saw the face of the man we'd been trying to locate at the bar. His skin was gray and his eyes stared, unblinking, at the ceiling. Blood -- what had to be blood -- pooled under his head and shoulder. The odor was not the same as the one that coated my nostrils and turned my stomach when I'd found Valerie. Of course. Lee was only recently dead. My knees buckled. Greg grabbed my collar and hustled me toward the basement door, then hauled me to a stop. With the muzzle of the gun against my ribs, he released the lock and swung the door open.

"Come on up, ladies," he called, as if inviting them in for

coffee.

I held my breath and strained to listen, hoping to hear silence, hoping they had escaped. Instead I heard brief scuffling and angry whispers.

"Come now," Greg called again. "You wouldn't want to leave your sister all alone with me, would you, Juliet? Why, she might not be able to resist my well-known charms."

He caressed my cheek and neck with his left hand, and I flinched at his touch. The stutter of his breath against my hair was undoubtedly amusement.

"Did you like my little love notes?" he asked, his mouth close to my ear. "You must have, since you seemed to want more. I had to improvise for the one on your pillow -- didn't have time for a newspaper note. Did I make you nervous?"

I clamped my lips together. His exhale came hot and long against my cheek. In one swift move he yanked on my shirt, dislodging several buttons, and jammed his hand inside my bra. My mouth turned sour and a whimper rose in my throat.

"How about now?" He dug his fingers into my breast. "Maybe I make you hot." His tongue flicked against my cheek and I jerked my head aside, my temple colliding with the gun. He laughed, short and ugly. I clamped down on my anger, but couldn't stop the tremor that shot through me. "Too bad I have to catch a plane. You and your sister together would be entertaining."

God, he was sick.

And there was no sound from downstairs.

He jabbed the gun barrel into the side of my face. "Invite them up."

He hadn't lost track of them, unfortunately. I prayed they were working on escaping, and stayed silent hoping to buy them more time.

"Do it. The other option is for us to go downstairs. If so, I will wound you so you live long enough to watch me shoot each of them. Your choice, but I'm getting sick of clearing bodies out of this damn kitchen myself and the smell is enough to make me gag. I could use some willing help. Then again, I might just set a match to the place. Hmm, maybe they should stay down there."

"Do what he says, Juliet." My voice shook so much I couldn't tell if it was loud enough for her to hear. I felt I'd signed our death warrants, even though I'd avoided his threat. Tears spilled down my face, but I was too frightened to sob.

After a moment there was more scuffling, then running footsteps on the stairs. Greg pulled me backwards several steps, his forearm tight at the base of my throat, choking me.

Sarah lurched through the doorway.

"Greg...?" She made a move toward us and he swung the gun at her.

"Stop right there, Sarah." She did, and her eyes popped with surprise.

More footsteps sounded on the stairs, but at a considerably slower rate. Juliet and Delores stopped at the doorway to the kitchen, behind Sarah. Juliet's eyes grew wide as she took in the scene. Delores's face, although expressionless, was ashen. She held her left arm carefully. Greg put the gun against my head again.

"Well, that's better. Now Delores, don't tell me you've gone and hurt yourself." His voice was saccharin with mock sympathy.

"You ought to know, you bastard," she growled. "You're the one who pushed me down the stairs."

"Not as spry as you used to be, huh?"

She held her silence, but her eyes narrowed.

"What am I going to do with you girls?" he said.

"Greg—"

"Shut up, Sarah."

She blinked as rapidly as the trembling of her chin.

An exasperated rumble vibrated in Greg's throat. "Looks like I've got more planning to do than I thought. You couldn't leave well enough alone, could you?" He pressed the gun to my head, again.

All eyes were on me, the obvious target of his question, but I was rigid with fear. I couldn't answer. I didn't want to die, not now, not like this. I didn't want anyone else to die, either.

"Now Lee," Greg gestured with the gun toward the legs on the floor. Delores and Juliet followed his motion and Juliet gasped. Greg laughed at her reaction. "He couldn't leave it alone, either. He screwed up, but the dumb shit thought I should give him more money. Now that's not fair. It's not my fault he drank the first five hundred. Why should I support his drinking habit?"

"Is he the guy who took Thea's horse?" Delores asked.

Sarah whimpered, and held her hand up like she was trying to stop Greg. He ignored her.

"Oh, how quickly we catch on. The idiot took the wrong horse, but I expect you figured that out already. Everything would have been perfect if that dickless moron had followed instructions."

Juliet slid a quick look at Sarah before addressing Greg. "Why did you kill Valerie?"

"I didn't kill Valerie."

Sarah jerked toward my sister. "See? I told you he didn't."

The sneer Juliet turned on her was as contemptuous as any I'd ever seen, but Greg jumped in, defending himself in a righteous tone.

"She was already dead when I got to her Saturday afternoon."

Liar.

Sarah waved her hands, again trying to stop him. "No, Greg! You weren't here! I picked you up at the airport. Thea did it -- caused all this trouble! You *told* me --" She stopped herself and cowered, watching Greg, worry and confusion stamped on her face.

He sighed. "Did you *see* me get off the plane?"

"No," was Sarah's whispered response.

"And you picked me up where?"

"At the curb outside of 'Arrivals.'" Again whispered. Tears dripped down her cheeks. "But --"

"How much of my business do you think would have survived if the police even questioned me about Valerie's murder? People would assume I did it if you ran at the mouth about how I found her. Then I'd never be able to get new investors to keep that deal going."

"I know you didn't kill her! I'd tell people that!"

"This is why I don't trust you, Sarah. You don't think, you just talk." He made a little gesture with the gun, smacking me on the forehead with the barrel.

I flinched.

Juliet caught my eye and I read her perfectly. I'd missed my chance to act while he was distracted. Disappointment sank through me.

"Oh, what's this?" Greg hadn't missed the look. "Secret signals?"

"No," Juliet said quickly. "I thought she was going to faint. She's so pale."

"Don't you worry about big sister." Greg squeezed my shoulders. "She's so little I can hold her up even after I shoot her." He laughed. "Oh, I almost forgot. It's going to be Sarah who shoots you all. Then, the poor thing, sick with remorse, will shoot herself."

"Greg!" Sarah wailed. "I love you! We're going to go away together. Remember? Last night? You told me you loved me -- you always loved me! You gave me this!" She held up her left hand. "You love me!"

"You're an anchor around my neck, you stupid cow."

He swung the gun toward her and she screamed. I let my knees collapse and dropped back against his chest. The moment he leaned into my weight I tipped forward, pulling him with me. With every ounce of strength I possessed I swung my arm down, slamming my fist into his groin. He yelped. I twisted and thrust my elbow hard into his ribs. His grip loosened and I pivoted, jamming the heel of my hand up into his nose. A sickening crunch erupted from his face under my hand, and blood gushed from his nostrils. Shrieking, Greg grabbed at his nose, flinging the gun across the room. It clattered to the tile floor and slid to a stop against Lee's leg.

Juliet leapt past me and smashed her fist into the side of Greg's head. He staggered and was tipping when she landed a round-house kick in the middle of his back.

It was a good bet he was already unconscious when he smacked, face down, onto the cold, hard, kitchen tile. He didn't even bounce.

Sarah screamed again, then sank to her knees and crawled across the floor to her would-be murderer, sobbing his name.

Juliet and I stared at him.

Delores stared at us.

"Did we kill him?" Juliet's question was almost indiscernible, since both of her hands covered her mouth.

"I don't think so," I said, surprised at how steady my own voice sounded. "We'd better find something to tie him up with before he comes to. He's going to be mad."

Juliet sprinted down the basement stairs and reappeared moments later with a roll of duct tape. We taped his ankles together, then pulled his arms behind his back and wrapped a large amount of tape around his wrists. Sarah tried desperately to undo the tape, but Juliet hauled her away by the collar of her shirt.

"Stop that." My sister plunked Sarah down against the dishwasher. "Now sit there and stop being so stupid. We just saved your sorry-ass life. You move and I'll tape you up, too." She looked at me and rolled her eyes.

Sarah curled into a ball and sobbed quietly.

I picked up the kitchen phone and dialed 9-1-1. As the operator answered, the exterior kitchen door swung open and Frederick Parsons strode in, impeccably dressed, gun drawn. We all stared, gap-mouthed, at him.

He looked down at Greg and shook his head. "Is he dead?"

Delores found her voice first. "No, he's not, Frederick. Put the gun away."

He didn't. Instead, he turned to me. The look in his eyes caused my insides to recoil.

"Are you calling 9-1-1?"

"Yes." The word was barely more than a squeak.

"Tell them you've made a mistake and hang up."

Delores and I exchanged a glance. She nodded once. I cleared my throat. Even still, my voice shook. "Sorry, operator, I've made a mistake. Sorry to bother you." I pushed a button on the handset.

Frederick Parsons waved his gun at me. "Over there, with your sister. Leave the phone."

I set it on the counter, and moved quickly to Juliet. Parsons scanned the room, shook his head slightly when he saw Lee's body and again as he took in Sarah weeping. He raised his gun and aimed at Greg. I sucked in a gasp. Juliet grabbed my arm.

"Frederick, no!" Delores shouted. "Let the police deal with him!"

"No!" Sarah screamed at the same time and threw herself across Greg's unconscious body. "He didn't kill her! He didn't kill your daughter!"

Parsons's shoulders sagged slightly and his eyes narrowed to slits. "Move."

"No. I won't let you kill him. He's innocent. You have to believe me! You'll have to shoot me too."

"I will," he said matter-of-factly. "But not with this gun." He moved toward Greg's gun, resting against Lee's leg, but the sound of footsteps on the porch drew our attention, including Parsons's.

Joey stepped through the doorway. Juliet's fingers dug into my arm and she whimpered. The gun he carried was bigger. Lots bigger.

"Ah, good," Parsons said. "Pick up that piece over there and dispatch these four, would you please?"

I clutched at Juliet and stopped breathing.

Joey raised his big pistol. The scream in my throat never formed. He wasn't aiming at us.

Parsons scowled and pointed at Greg's gun. "No. I said tha --"

There was a loud pop, like a beer being opened, but without the hiss. Parsons's eyes grew wide. He looked down at the red spreading rapidly on his crisp white shirt, then crumpled like so much dirty laundry.

Joey's expression never changed. He turned the gun around and laid it on the kitchen island. Then he raised both arms and put his hands behind his head, fingers laced together.

"Go ahead and call," he said, with a nod at the phone. "Don't touch the gun. Only my fingerprints should be on it."

Stunned and confused by the sudden turn of events, I obediently released Juliet and managed the few shaky steps to where the phone lay. "Are you still there?"

"Yes," the 9-1-1 operator said. "Are you safe?"

"Yes, thank you. We are now. But we still need the ambulance and sheriff." My words came out so slowly I thought I'd never finish the sentence.

"They should be arriving any moment. Stay on the line."

"Okay." I looked at Joey. "They're almost here."

He nodded. "We should go outside."

Delores, Juliet, Sarah (held firmly by the arm by my sister), and I followed Joey out the kitchen door. Once outside he knelt on the ground at attention, with his back to us, and his hands still at the back of his head. Even as my thinking began to clear, the entire scene remained more bizarre than I could have imagined. Not that I minded Joey's help -- which we obviously needed -- but I didn't understand what the hell was going on.

"Why did you kill him?" I asked.

The big man took a deep breath and exhaled before he answered. "I didn't have a choice. I'm the only one who knew he killed his daughter. He never would have been convicted, and I would have ended up as bear food on the side of some logging road before the trial ever started."

"But Greg --"

"Marshall never knew. We passed him when we left on Saturday, then turned around and followed him back here. Mr. Parsons's plan was to accuse him of killing Valerie, and have me hold a gun to the back of his head like I was going to kill him. It worked. Marshall was scared shitless. He cried, begged us to let him help find who killed Valerie when Mr. Parsons said the police would suspect him right away and we couldn't lie about finding him with her body."

"Why did he try to make it look like an accident? That was what he intended, right?"

"It was Marshall's idea, to give us more time. I think Mr. Parsons would have been okay with the accident idea, if it had stuck. But when it didn't, well, he had to put the blame on someone. He didn't much care if it was Marshall or you. He'd have ruined Marshall either way."

"Do you mean to tell me," Delores said, her voice cracking with fury, "Frederick intended to let Greg kill us all?"

Joey swallowed. "Yes, ma'am -- but I don't think he knew there'd be so many of you. He was going to shoot Greg after he killed Miss Campbell." He nodded toward me and my legs shook. Delores put her good arm protectively around my shoulders. "He planned to tell the sheriff it was self defense -- that Greg killed Miss Campbell and planned to kill him, too."

The first Snohomish County Sheriff's car rolled silently around the house and came to a stop. We all watched as the deputy, calm and business-like, exited the car with his gun drawn.

Joey continued. "I came into the house when I didn't hear a gunshot." His gaze held mine. "I'm glad you're all alive." Then he turned away, still on his knees.

"Glad" couldn't begin to describe my feelings. "Why did he kill his daughter?" I asked.

Joey took a shuddering breath then looked over his shoulder at me. Light reflected off the tears tracing paths down his face. "It was an accident. They argued about Greg and the investment scheme he dragged her into. Mr. Parsons lost his temper and hit her." He swallowed. More tears washed down his face. Another sheriff's cruiser pulled up. "He broke her neck." Joes faced front as two more sheriff's cars arrived and an ambulance.

"Everyone all right here?" Detective Thurman called, getting out of an unmarked car. His gun was drawn, too.

I cleared my throat. "They've arrived," I said into the phone. "Were you able to hear all that?"

"Yes, and thank you," the 9-1-1 operator said.

This time I actually did press the disconnect button. Then I addressed Thurman. "Yes. Mostly. I think Delores's arm is broken, though."

He nodded and motioned to the paramedics. Delores scowled.

"No backtalk, Delores," he said, then gave Joey a long look. "What am I arresting you for?"

"Murder."

"Whose?"

"Frederick Parsons."

Thurman's eyebrows shot up. He motioned to a deputy. "Cuff him and read him his rights." He turned his attention to me. "What am I going to find inside?"

"Two bodies. Frederick Parsons and Lee -- sorry, I don't know his last name. And Greg Marshall." Sarah sniffled loudly. I took a deep breath. "He's injured, maybe still unconscious, but we, um, secured him."

Thurman raised one eyebrow, then nodded at my hand. "You hurt?"

"No. It's Greg's blood."

His gaze shifted to my shirt. "Did he --"

"No." I yanked my shirt back together. "No. He was just trying to intimidate me."

"You want to talk to a woman officer?"

"No, thanks. I'm okay."

Another nod and a questioning look at my sister.

"You're doing all right?"

Juliet blushed. She blushed. "Yes, sir. I'm fine."

"Got things straightened out with your young man?"

"Yes, sir."

"No more weeping?"

Weeping?

"No, sir. I'm sorry about that."

"That's okay." He smiled and patted her arm.

Oh, did I have questions for my sister.

"And you, Miss Fuller ...." Thurman shook his head as Sarah blubbered, then he looked around. "Hausman!" The deputy I'd seen at the sheriff's office trotted over. "Take Miss Fuller to the office and get her statement. Hold her as a material witness, possible accessory."

Hausman led a wailing Sarah to a patrol car as another ambulance pulled in.

"You two," Thurman addressed Juliet and me. "Give your statements to the officers over there. Then go home. I'll talk to you both later."

I started to follow Juliet then stopped. "Detective?" Thurman looked a question at me. "Frederick Parsons killed his daughter. He was going to shoot all of us. Joey saved us."

Thurman shook his head and smiled. "Thea, you saved yourself and everyone else when you left the connection to the 9-1-1 operator opened. That was quick thinking. And pretty damn brave. You let us know just how and when to approach the situation." He winked and waved me off. "Go on. I expect you'd like to go home. We'll take it from here. I'll be in touch when we get this sorted out."

I smiled as I headed to the deputy who would take my statement. The backyard was now full of vehicles of all description, their strobe and flood lights illuminating the area that had been so empty and terrifying to me a short while ago.

I took a deep breath and caught the definite scent of spring, mixed in with diesel and other exhaust. It was not raining. In fact, the sky was bright with a nearly full moon.

A deputy approached and pulled a pen out of his pocket.

"You'll need more than one clipboard for this statement," I said.

Chapter Twenty-Three

When I was done dictating the evening's events I grabbed Juliet. She wasn't going to avoid talking to me again.

"Tell me about the weeping with Detective Thurman. And *do not* blow me off this time."

"Oh, I, uh --"

"Spill it," I said, through gritted teeth.

Juliet's flaming complexion was evident even in the poor light. She stuttered a bit more, then her shoulders dropped. "Oh, all right. When I went in to Detective Thurman's office to be interviewed I thought he was building a case against Eric."

I narrowed my eyes at her. I knew there was more.

"Okay, okay, I even thought Eric may have -- you know, by accident. Anyway, I had a story planned about how we spent the afternoon and evening together, but when I walked into that awful conference room I burst into tears. God, Thea, it was worse than you can ever imagine. I couldn't stop crying. Then I found out Eric thought *I* had done something stupid and was prepared to take the blame himself ... I must have gone through a box and a half of tissue." She cringed when she looked at me.

I skinny-eyed her. "Juliet, I can't believe --"

I stopped as a familiar gray Honda roared into view. I

nudged Juliet and she followed my gaze. Both the driver's and passenger's doors flew opened almost before the car stopped rolling. Paul and Eric jumped out and ran in our general direction, but before they had gotten far Paul stopped Eric, taking hold of his arm. He immediately jerked out of Paul's grip. They exchanged a few words before scanning the crowd.

"'Bout time the cavalry got her," she said, and laughed. "Oh, no wait! We're the cavalry! She laughed again.

Despite the hubbub of radio noise and people talking, Eric picked up the sound of Juliet's laughter. He slapped Paul's arm, pointed at us, and took off. Juliet grinned as she watched Eric run toward her. There were tears in her eyes. He swooped in and grabbed her in a crushing hug. Rapid Spanish spewed forth when he wasn't covering her face with kisses. I caught a few "*Dios mios*" and "*queridas*" but that was all.

Paul cleared his throat, drawing my attention. The truth is, I was afraid to look at him. My heart thudded as if Greg still held his gun to my head. All I could think of were our parting shots on Tuesday.

"You're okay?" he asked, eyebrows tilting up.

"Yes, fine." My smile wobbled.

We were saved from further conversation by the paramedics rolling a gurney past with a body bag. When the second gurney transporting the second body rolled past both Eric and Paul were visibly paler and identically slack-jawed. The third gurney, with a barely conscious Greg strapped to it, caused Eric to cross himself. Paul cleared his throat several times.

Greg, if anything, looked worse than before. Cotton wadding filled his nostrils and was held in place with tape. An IV bag hung from a pole and bounced along with them. Blood soaked the front of his shirt. Each time the gurney hit a bump, he moaned. It hit lots of bumps.

"Did you do that?" Eric asked Juliet.

She looked at me and grinned. "Actually, Thea did."

I held up my bloody hand and shrugged.

"Holy shit," Paul said.

"Juliet finished him, though." I smiled at my sister.

"Yeah, we make a pretty good team." We bumped fists.

"And the other two?" Eric asked.

"Not our work," Juliet said.

Eric looked relieved. Paul ran a hand over his mouth and studied the ground. Detective Thurman chose that moment to come by and give both Eric and Paul a professional once over. He scrutinized Paul an extra moment before turning to me.

"Is this the one you dumped the other evening?"

How he got wind of that I'll never know.

"No," I said, then pressed my courage into service once again and turned to Paul. "It was the other one."

Delores refused to ride in the ambulance to the hospital, so Paul drove her. Eric, after another lingering kiss from Juliet, took Delores's car back to Copper Creek.

Shortly after nine we all sat down at the dining room table in my aunt and uncle's house. It felt like midnight. Aunt Vi had a large tureen of soup on the table and hot bread just out of the oven.

"I knew Greg had to be involved all along," Delores asserted. Despite the cast on her arm, her appearance had improved considerably. So had mine, once I'd washed and put on fresh clothes.

"How could you have known that?" Aunt Vi asked, ladling another bowl of minestrone soup and passing it.

"It makes sense --"

"Ha." Juliet snorted.

"She must have pushed Frederick past his limit," Delores said. "When we got that description from the big fellow at the Broken Axle, I knew it was Greg and I really believed he killed Valerie." She turned her attention back to her soup.

"I think I was so stunned at how the description fit Jonathan that I didn't think it through." I wasn't particularly proud of my assumption, but there was no point denying it.

My blunder would come out sooner or later.

Paul stopped eating -- as if swallowing was suddenly an issue.

"What's the Broken Axle?" He asked, flicking at a bread crumb near his plate.

"The local biker bar," Juliet said.

"A biker bar," he repeated, and casually crushed the crumb. "You went to a biker bar. Why?"

"To follow up on Miguel's lead, of course," I said. Hadn't he been paying attention? Oh yeah -- the sulking in his office thing.

"A lead. At a biker bar." He nodded slightly to himself then turned to Delores. "You knew about this and just let her go?"

"I didn't see you here trying to stop her. Don't get your tail in a knot. Miguel and I went along." She tried to ladle more soup into her bowl. Uncle Henry got up and took over.

Paul's lips disappeared into a resolute line and his gaze moved slowly from his aunt to finally rest on me. I waited for a comment, but he just stared. I gave up and explained what we'd learned about Lee from the really big guy with tattoos who mooched our beer.

Paul and Eric looked at each other. "John," they both said with a kind of sign afterwards.

"You actually know that fellow?" Uncle Henry asked.

"Everyone knows John," Eric said.

Paul closed his eyes and pinched the bridge of his nose with his thumb and forefinger. "Why did you go to Valerie's this morning?"

"I went to talk to Greg," Delores said, taking a bite of bread. "I knew he'd be there, from what he said at the funeral, and I thought there was a good chance I could talk him into turning himself in."

Juliet laughed. "We can all see how well that turned out."

"It was worth a try," she said. "I was fairly certain it was an accident and he didn't know what to do. Unfortunately, I hadn't figured in the business angle. He started hollering about how it didn't matter if he killed Valerie or not, if he was connected with her death it would ruin him financially. Then he shoved me down the basement stairs."

"He was already ruined," I said. "I caught on to his Ponzi scheme. I just didn't connect it with Valerie. I was going to report him to the feds next week."

Paul leaned a forearm on the table and addressed Delores. "Why didn't you tell me what you were planning? I've known Greg for a long time. I could have told you your approach wouldn't work." Delores's frown didn't stop him -- he leaned back and tossed his napkin on the table. "When I got out of the Army and went to college, I kept running into him. He beat up a friend of mine over a couple of dollars the guy owed him and the school kicked him out, even though my buddy refused to press charges. Not only that, I was the one who broke up the fight, and Greg tried to tell them I started it. He's a liar and a cheat. Always has been."

"Thanks for the heads up," Delores said, trying to butter another piece of bread with one hand. "Maybe I could have been spared the broken arm."

"And you could have kept me informed as to what was going on, Delores. I hoped we were rid of him once the medical examiner determined Blackie didn't kill Valerie. I hoped that was the only reason he was being a problem."

"Was Lee dead when you arrived?" I asked Delores. My voice sounded high and a little frantic to my ears, but hey, somebody needed to break up the spitting and hissing contest the two of them seemed intent on. A half growl, half exhale came from Paul's direction. I didn't look.

"No," Delores said, and tossed a cool look at Paul. "He arrived midafternoon. I couldn't hear everything they said, but it sounded like Lee was trying to get more money out of Greg--"

"That would have pissed him off," Juliet interrupted, looking entertained.

Delores raised an eyebrow at her. "That's a pretty accurate assessment, since he shot him over the issue."

I stepped in again to deflect Delores's crankiness. "How did Sarah end up in the basement with you?"

"When Greg shot Lee, I heard her start screaming. I don't know if she actually saw him do it, but she told me she didn't. She said she was upstairs in a bedroom when it happened. Greg told her he had to leave and her job was to keep an eye on me."

"In the basement?" Juliet laughed. "What an idiot!"

"The poor girl was totally cowed," I said, hoping Juliet took it as a reprimand.

"If you'd spent the entire afternoon cooped up with that sniveling child I doubt you'd have a drop of sympathy left for her," Delores said. "Greg knew how unstable she was. I'm sure he figured the basement was his best bet to keep her under control."

"I expect he didn't count on you girls showing up looking for Delores," Aunt Vi interjected in a hurry. "Speaking of which, how did you boys know to go to Valerie's?"

"We didn't, we were out of options," Eric said, raising both hands. "When Juliet didn't show up at the soccer field tonight, Paul and I check places where she might be. We'd already been to Thea's house when you called and told us Blackie was going crazy, so we knew neither of them were there. We switched to trying to find Thea because of Blackie, but I had a feeling Juliet was with her. Valerie's was the last place we tried. We were getting pretty desperate at that point, what with you calling every five minutes."

"I'd like you to know," Aunt Vi said, "that the minute Thea was all right, Blackie settled down."

"You mean he stopped all his carrying on before we got there?" Eric asked.

"Precisely." Aunt Vi nodded, self-satisfied.

"I guess we should have followed the ambulance when we saw it," Paul said. "I'll know better next time." He looked pointedly at me.

"There won't be a next time," Aunt Vi said, copying Paul's stern expression

I should have laughed, but it wasn't happening.

"How are we going to test the 'psychic horse theory' then?" Juliet asked.

"We're not," Uncle Henry said, "I, for one, am unwilling to put that theory to the test any more. I'm quite happy to let it rest."

"It was a good thing I went looking for you this afternoon, Thea. You would have been in worse trouble without me. When Delores still didn't show up after all that time I knew something was wrong. I knew it wouldn't take her so long to decide whether to buy a horse or not. But I can honestly say, it never occurred to me my sister and my boss would start playing detective." She crossed her arms and sighed at the ceiling. "If you two hadn't gone mucking around in things —"

"Greg would be long gone and Frederick Parsons would have gotten away with murder," I finished.

"You don't know that for certain. The police would have caught him. Anyway. I'm surprised at my responsible, mature sister stirring up so much drama."

"*Me*? I was an innocent bystander"

"You're not. We only wanted you to break up with Jonathan. We didn't anticipate having to solve a murder, too."

"Nobody planned to solve --" The "break up with Jonathan" part hauled me to a stop. Particularly the "we" part. I couldn't be hearing that right, but each person at the table was looking somewhere else, except for Paul. He seemed to have lost the gist of the conversation entirely. What an idiot I'd been. I'd been suckered, set up, and manipulated. Juliet met my frown with defiance.

"Hey now, you have to admit you needed a little push. That break-up was a long time coming."

"A 'little push'?" I shrieked. "Is that what you call all the maneuvering that's been going on? 'Meddling' is a much better word."

"Oh, come on. We've been waiting for months for you to shake loose of Jonathan. All we did was make sure you and Paul met."

"Met? There wasn't one single 'meeting' you people didn't have a hand in, was there? I call that repeatedly throwing us at each other. Did you ever stop to think about what I might want? Or him?" I pointed diagonally across the table at Paul. "Well? Did you?" I turned on Aunt Vi. She leaned away from me. "That's what you meant the day Blackie was stolen when you said things weren't going the way you'd planned, isn't it?" I tried to stare down Uncle Henry, but he was rearranging his flatware. "Did you know about this?" I fired at Paul.

His eyes widened. "No." Then his brows slammed down as he turned to his aunt. "I should have known you were up to something."

She straightened and grumbled, but didn't meet his eyes.

"Now Paul, dear," Aunt Vi said. "Don't you be thinking we didn't have your happiness in mind, too. You've been a bit lonely. Anyone could see that."

I believe the comprehensiveness of the matchmaking conspiracy finally sank in for Paul. It certainly did for me. His narrow gaze took in each person seated at the table. Uncle Henry and Eric exchanged frantic, guilty looks. But Juliet, always confident, rolled her eyes.

"Oh come on," she said, sweeping us all with a disgusted look. "Mission accomplished."

I stared at her, slack-jawed.

"Well, you did give Jonathan the old heave-ho. All we did was a little arranging." She fielded Paul's glare with a sniff and tossed it back. "Step up to the plate, mister. I'm good, but I can only stack the kindling -- I can't start the fire. You guys did that yourselves. Don't go blaming us if you've got the hots for each other and don't know what to do next. I'm done holding your hands. Figure it out on your own."

I suddenly developed my own overwhelming interest in

the table cloth. Uncle Henry cleared his throat and valiantly changed the subject.

"Would anyone like more tea?" He was so British. I so loved him for it.

"No thank you" was murmured several times around the table and chairs pushed back.

"If you'll all excuse me," Delores said, "I'm going to hit the hay." She left for the guest room.

Eric and Juliet moved quickly, gathering plates from the table and taking them to the kitchen where both Aunt Vi and Uncle Henry were bustling around cleaning up.

Yes, I had unfinished business with Paul, but while I contemplated my apology he disappeared. I can't say I wasn't relieved. It would be awkward and embarrassing, and I was less than confident of the outcome. Tomorrow would probably be better. Or the next day.

Who was I trying to kid? I was afraid. He'd passed judgment on me and I was afraid to hear it. My friends and family all knew about what happened between us, they all had expectations, they were all watching and I was afraid…and this pattern was so familiar. And it was time to break it. I went into the kitchen.

"Uncle Henry?" He was putting dishes in the sink and glanced over his shoulder at me. "Uncle Henry, I'd like your help."

"Of course." He wiped his hands on a tea towel and came over to where I was rooted in place. "What do you need?"

I took a deep breath and bit my lip trying to figure out how to start. I met his eyes. He knew. He was smiling. How did he know?

"I want to enter Blackie in a dressage show," I said on a single exhale.

"I'll be more than happy to work with you." His smile broadened.

"I may be terrible at it, you know."

"It doesn't matter. What made you change your mind?"

I shrugged. "I think I understand you have to take a risk sometimes, do something that scares you because the regrets would be worse. Or maybe I've been waiting so long I forgot what I was waiting for."

"You'll do fine. You know I'll be there for you. It won't be all that bad."

"I know that now." I couldn't help grinning. It felt so good. "Besides, what's one more risk for an old veteran risk-taker like me?"

He laughed and hugged me. I hugged him back and over his shoulder I caught Aunt Vi's wink.

"We can take a look at the show schedule tomorrow and make plans. I think you'd best be going now, though." Uncle Henry loosened the grip I had on him. "I believe someone else wants a word."

I looked out the kitchen door in the direction he inclined his head. Paul stood by my car. With my heart thudding, I hugged Uncle Henry again, kissed Aunt Vi goodnight, and walked down the path at a pace considerably slower than the hammering in my chest. As I approached Paul held his hand up. I stopped and bit my lip, bracing for the indignant, and rightful, complaint that was surely coming. He cleared his throat then swallowed before he met my eyes.

"I owe you an apology," he said. "I am very sorry."

Oh. This wasn't what I was expecting, but, on the other hand, I could live with it. "Apology accepted," I said. "I owe you one, too."

He shook his head once. "I was hoping you might give me another chance."

And the surprises kept coming. "I could do that."

"Dinner? Next weekend?"

"Next weekend?"

"Yeah. If you don't have plans."

I shook my head a couple of times then glanced over my shoulder at the house. Although I couldn't see her I knew Aunt Vi was watching.

"I know a nice restaurant in Portland, short taxi-ride from the train station. Nice view of the river."

"Portland?"

He flinched ever so slightly and glanced at the house. "I don't think we'd run into anyone we know there."

I did a quick mental survey of this proposed date: At least a four hour trip each way, plus a couple hours for dinner … didn't sound like a day trip to me. More like an overnighter. I sucked in my lower lip to hold down a smile. It kind of worked. "That's a long trip, just for dinner."

One shoulder rose slightly and he had the grace to break eye contact.

"How about Bellingham?" I asked. His gaze jumped to mine and held. "It's only a two hour drive, and I don't know anybody in Bellingham. Do you?"

"A couple people. Wouldn't matter." His eyes smiled first, then his mouth. He opened my car door. "Maybe we can do Portland another time."

I pulled the car keys out of my purse and slid behind the wheel.

"Maybe we can," I said.

There was a small chance Aunt Vi wasn't able to see the way we were grinning at each other. He dipped through the open door, brushed a soft kiss across my mouth, then closed the door, lifting a hand in farewell. I missed the ignition twice with my key, and completely forgot about my seatbelt.

Aunt Vi would have had to have been blind to miss any of that.

SPECIAL BONUS SECTION

EXCERPTS FROM THE NEXT TWO

THEA CAMPBELL MYSTERIES

LEVELS OF DECEPTION

THE SECOND THEA CAMPBELL MYSTERY

Chapter One

Paul's e-mail said the craters left at the dig site in Montana had likely been made by big earth-moving equipment. They were literally deep enough to swallow a truck. Every last fossil Paul located last year was gone. With a scant two days before the start of his fieldwork class, he needed my help. Now. He was the professor in charge.

I shut down my computer, shoved my camera and the other assorted items he'd listed into a tote bag, and dressed at a rate that would have impressed Wonder Woman. He and I had been together for three blissful, intense months, and this was my first opportunity to show him I'd be there for him when he had a crisis. I flew out my front door and into the fickle Northwest summer sunshine, headed for Seattle and the Burke Museum. I was "girlfriend on a mission" doing everything she could to help the man she was crazy about.

In the short while it took to drive south from Snohomish, and the long while I spent bogged down in Seattle's frustrating rush-hour traffic near the University District, I mentally reviewed Paul's instructions and rehearsed the procedures: Find the parking garage, speed-walk to the museum's archives, locate and photograph each of the fifteen fossils he listed, in the manner he indicated, zip home and e-mail him the photographs. Piece of cake. I'd be a hero *and* have time to take a dressage lesson on my horse after a full day of work, exactly as I'd planned before reading Paul's e-mail.

However, the annoying delays I'd experienced negotiating the U District's narrow, clogged streets were nothing compared to what I found when I went through the big double doors to the museum's basement archives. My mission stood in danger of being aborted. I stood toe-to-desk with a guard-dragon masquerading as a severely coiffed, gray-haired receptionist. She would not let me pass and would not give me information. There was no negotiating with this woman. I wanted to smite her precious rules right off her thin, tight, policy-reciting lips.

"I'm sorry, Miss Campbell, I told you. I can't let you into the archives," Mrs. Mildred Peabody said, with a sanctimonious lift of her chin and a haughty flare of her nostrils.

Sorry my ass. I drew a breath to plead my case, but she cut me off.

"You're not a student or staff member. The regulations are clear. You missed your appointment time by an hour. General access to the archives must be limited to staff and students or research will suffer. Appointments are meant to be kept." She folded her hands on her aircraft carrier-sized desk. Her gaze did not budge, and her mouth formed an exact, upside-down U.

Freaking stubborn lizard-woman.

"I didn't have an appointment," I said, lowering my heavy bag to the floor and pulling out the printed e-mail. "My instructions arrived at eight this morning." I waved the print-out like a battle flag. "I drove in immediately. Thirty-four and a half miles from Snohomish. Dr. Hudson said," I cleared my throat, "'Go to the archives, find the specimens listed below, use your digital camera and take three views of each. Get them to me yesterday.'" For a long moment the dragon and I locked in a glare-off over the top of the paper. "Dr. Hudson made no mention of an appointment." He'd also failed to mention this potentially mission-foiling road block. I flipped the paper around and held it at arm's length for her to verify.

Her gaze skimmed along the e-mail over the top of her red-framed glasses, then flashed back to me as though she believed eye contact was all that held me in check. Clearly she had no intention of reading anything. Her rule was law. Any reasonable person would have recognized this as an emergency. Any reasonable person would have pitched in to help. Any reasonable person would have been, dammit, reasonable.

"I don't understand why you can't make an exception in an emergency." I crossed my arms. The e-mail still clutched in my hand now sported new creases thanks to my frustration.

"*This* is not an emergency." The little lines that led the way to her upper lip deepened into furrows.

"Yes, it is." I forced my jaw and mouth to relax so they wouldn't match hers.

Her eyes sparked. "If we make an exception for one person then it won't be long until we have a veritable stream of people wandering in off the street. That's what the museum upstairs is for. Those are the rules."

I'd be damned if I was leaving the museum's archives without the pictures. I opened my mouth, intending to defeat her with the calm, faultless logic that pointed out how a professor's emergency needs for his class pre-empted her trivial protocol, but my temper substituted words and turned up the volume of my voice.

"Then I guess you'll have to be the one to explain to Dr. Hudson why he can't get the material he needs for his fieldwork class, and why the robbery of his dig site isn't as important as your, your *rules*."

"Is there a problem here?" The man's voice came from behind me.

I spun, ready to defend my mission to the newest obstacle on the scene, but didn't get the chance. A girlish purr answered the very tall and angular middle-aged man first.

"Dr. Fogel."

I swiveled back to see who else had shown up. No one. No one new, that is. A glow bathed Mrs. Peabody's cheeks. She removed her glasses and delicately touched the edge of her crisp, white collar. The dragon had turned into the damsel, and she wasn't in distress. Astounding.

"This is Thea Campbell. She --"

"Oh, you're Thea," he said, his tone both surprised and pleased.

I made another quick pivot.

Dr. Fogel extended his hand. Pure reflex caused me to shake it. "Nice to meet you. I'm Andrew Fogel. Paul dropped me a note, said you'd be by sometime this morning. Helping him with some material he needs, eh?"

The unexpected courtesy caused me to stumble over my "Yes." I darted a sideways glance at Mrs. Peabody. Her gaze narrowed ever so slightly at me before focusing softly on Dr. Fogel.

"Dr. Fogel, Miss Campbell isn't a student or staff member." She seemed to be having trouble holding down a confident little smirk -- like she'd found the trump card necessary to boot me out.

I geared up to argue my case once more, but didn't get the chance.

He smiled thinly at Mrs. Peabody. "I guess you'll need to give her directions, then. I'm off to my meeting." He turned to me. "I'm sure Mrs. Peabody will give you all the assistance you need." With a minute nod, he was out the door. I hadn't had time to gather my wits and thank him.

"Through there." Mrs. Peabody pointed her glasses to a set

of double doors to the right, her expression a wintry shade of neutral. "Take the first right and second left. There will be a door on the right. The sign says 'Storage: Vertebrate Fossils'. The light switches are to the left, just inside the doors."

"Thank you," I said, shouldering my bag.

She ignored me, slid her glasses on and returned to her typing. If I pounded on my keyboard the way she did I'd break a finger. I walked away, shoulders braced against possible flying objects. None came.

When I rounded the first corner in the dank hallway I pranced an impromptu jig complete with a victory arm-pump. The dragon was conquered. I'd get Paul's errand done and save his class. His relief when he saw my pictures would light up the phone lines -- when he could get to a phone to call. Yes sir, we were a team, despite the hundreds of miles separating us.

I followed Mrs. Peabody's directions of a right turn then a left, separated by a couple of long hallways she didn't mention, until I reached the heavy metal doors with the sign "Storage: Vertebrate Fossils." I pushed through into darkness that smelled of frigid, dry dirt, and shivered. My skin shrank under my cotton tank top and summer-weight crop pants. My sockless ankles felt like they'd been splashed with ice water. A steady, low hum from an air-conditioning duct somewhere above virtually announced I wouldn't be warming up any time soon.

Feeling my way along the rough concrete wall, I located the bank of light switches, and flipped them all up. So far, so good -- until I turned around.

Row after row after row of industrial-heft racks stretched to the ceiling far above and marched away into the distance. Specimens crowded every shelf.

Like a little boat with a big hole, my mood sank, and with it my confidence in providing Paul the fast rescue he needed. Hope was lost before I'd begun. Hell, I was lost before I'd begun. If I moved away from the door I'd vanish, forgotten until my desiccated body was discovered years from now by some fledgling paleontologist who'd speculate over my remains, assign me a number, and shove me onto a shelf for possible future study.

Then my gaze settled on a scrap of salvation.

A paper scrap.

An index card taped to the end support of a unit.

I hurried over for a closer look. Hot damn. I'd been tossed a life preserver. On the card were handwritten numbers. Numbers with the same format as the ones on my list. A quick survey confirmed that there were cards affixed to each unit. My morbid musings dissolved. I was buoyant with hope once again.

I found the correct aisle, and located the first fossil. The dang dinosaur bone was heavier than it appeared. I wrapped both arms around it, hugged it to my chest, and staggered to the back of the storage room where Paul told me I would find work space. Sure enough, there was a large, sturdy table. I eased the fossil onto it and investigated the area. Lights, magnifying glasses and other tools that even an untrained person, namely me, could see were meant for examining specimens were stored neatly on open shelves or hanging on pegboard. A computer station was set up next to the table, a typed sheet of instructions taped to the desk top beside the keyboard -- coffee rings indicated its preferred use. I emptied my bag of the camera and other supplies, positioned the fossil on top of a large square of black felt, and arranged the lights. In no time, my makeshift photography studio was ready for business.

"At least three clear, shadow-free views of each specimen" were my instructions. I experimented with different orientations of the piece and took a number of shots, being careful to include a metric ruler to show size. Paul already had pictures of dinosaur bones, in situ, that he'd taken with him to Montana for the lecture and PowerPoint presentation that would start off his class. My guess was that the photographs I was taking were similar to what had been stolen, or what he expected to find at the new site. He probably wanted his students to see what the entire object would look like once recovered. Made sense. I'd sure need to see what I was supposed to be looking for.

A month or so ago I'd been leafing through one of his journals, looking at pictures of bones not yet removed from the ground where they were found. In most cases it was difficult for me to tell the difference between fossils and regular old rocks, even when someone was pointing to them.

"It takes practice to develop an 'eye'," my lover said. Delighted at my interest, he explained what to look for, pulling visual aids from his briefcase and dragging me out to the garden behind the house for a live comparison with actual rocks.

After that, every time I went out to the garden to weed I'd examine each rock for fossil potential. Every time he'd grin, kiss me, say, "Nope," and toss it into the blackberry bushes at the back of the yard.

After a week of that routine I uncovered a fist-sized, pulse-quickening treasure.

"Excellent example of *lepus silicis*." He hefted the smooth, gray, probable fossil, turning it with care.

Then he pitched it.

I jumped, too late, for his arm.

"Hey! That's a *lepus silicis*!" I restrained myself from smacking him with my gardening gloves. "Go get it out of the blackberries."

"You never took Latin, did you?" The edges of his eyes crinkled.

"No. I took Advanced Calculus to feel superior."

"*Lepus silicis*. Rabbit rock."

"What the hell's a rabbitrock?"

With solemn authority he laid a hand on my shoulder and looked me in the eye. "A rock you throw at rabbits."

I punched his arm. Laughing, he caught me before I could

hit him again, threw me over his shoulder, and carted me back to the house. Frickin' comedian.

An hour later, when we were both smiling contentedly, he enticed me to accompany him in July to Montana where he'd teach his six-week fieldwork class. But, there was no way I could leave my accounting business. The best I could arrange was two weeks. At the time it was barely May, and although he wouldn't be leaving until the end of June, a missing-him ache already surrounded my heart.

In hindsight, it turned out to be a good thing. My dedication to my clients made it possible to run these errands today.

I finished photographing the first fossil and admired the images on my camera. All twelve of them. I'd send them all. He'd be thrilled, and with the help I was giving him he'd still have time to scout out a new location for the students to explore and excavate. I was swimming in self-confidence.

After returning the first fossil to its proper shelf, I located the next one and repeated the process. As I was setting up the third specimen there was a whoosh and thump as the big storage room door opened then closed. I didn't expect to be the only one doing work but was a little surprised when the echo of footsteps came closer. A young man, probably a few years short of my twenty-nine, dressed in khakis and an almost white short-sleeve shirt, rounded the end of the stacks and approached. His aquiline nose found the perfect accompaniment in the unrestrained, enthusiastically curling brown hair that brushed his shoulders. However, an aggressive scowl trumped any potential friendliness his appearance might have produced.

"Hello," he said, and crossed his arms.

"Hi." I lowered my camera and smiled.

His gaze barely touched my setup before snapping back to me. "Taking pictures?"

Wow. What a masterful command of the obvious. In the pause before I answered, a flush crept up his neck and he shoved his hands into his pockets. Poor guy. He really didn't have a firm grip on "man-in-charge."

"Yes. Dr. Hudson asked me to take some photographs and e-mail them to him. I'm Thea Campbell, by the way." I held out my hand.

"Scott Loch." He extracted a hand from his pocket and gave mine a damp, cursory shake. "I'm surprised the web site photos aren't sufficient." His gaze went to the list of fossils sitting on the table. "Is this yours?" He picked up the e-mail printout.

"Yes. The web site shows only one view of each fossil." I was surprised he didn't know that. "Are you part of the Paleontology Department staff?"

Instead of replying, he took a long look at the e-mail with my name and Paul's in the heading. Call me crazy, but I was willing to bet he hadn't shown up out of curiosity. He was checking on me, and I suspected Mrs. Peabody had put him up to it. The woman wasn't going to give up. He put the paper down before he answered my question.

"More or less. I'm a grad student and Dr. Whitaker's secretary for the summer. Are you an undergrad?"

"Dr. Whitaker?"

"Department head."

"Oh, right. Actually," I said. "I'm a friend of Dr. Hudson's. I'm just running this errand for him."

A hank of his hair fell forward. Frowning, he pushed it back, briefly snagging his fingers. "He could have asked one of us. Why didn't he?"

"I'm sure I don't know." And as much as I hated to admit it, he had a point.

"Are you sure you're able to manage this?" He picked up the copy of Paul's e-mail again. This time he seemed to be reading the instructions. He kept glancing at my setup. "Pat should have gotten in touch with me."

"Pat?" I asked. The name wasn't familiar.

"She's Dr. Hudson's graduate assistant this summer."

My molars slammed together with enough force to send a sharp pain through my temples. Paul's graduate assistant out in the wilderness with him was a woman? Was there a reason he had not told me his assistant was female, had not corrected me when I'd commented on how pleased he seemed to be that he had gotten *him* for an assistant? This was phone call material. E-mail was too easy to evade. Not that I was jealous. Just cautious. And not stupid.

"The camera? Can I see it?" Scott's hand extended toward me and flapped in a give-it-to-me gesture. I guess I missed the first request.

Although I tried to think of one, I couldn't find a reason why he shouldn't see my photographs. Irritated, I passed the camera to him and waited for him to ask me how to operate it. He scanned the shots I had taken with the assurance of a techno-geek, then returned it to me.

"Don't let me keep you from your work," he said. "Nice to meet you."

Right.

Within two undisturbed hours I'd relegated Pat to the status where she belonged -- an academic necessity -- and photographed nearly all the fossils. There were four I couldn't locate, although I spent a good deal of time trying. Paul needed them. Maybe someone had checked them out, like library books. I rolled my shoulders and sighed. There was only one thing to do. Get help. I would have to go back to the dragon.

She wasn't there, but Dr. Fogel was. My jaw unlocked.

He stood, absorbed in some papers, and didn't notice me walk up.

"Excuse me," I said.

He paused in his reading, gave me a blank look, then a congenial nod.

"Miss Campbell, done already?" He pushed his glasses up his long thin nose.

"No, I'm afraid not. I ran into some problems and

wondered if you could help."

"I can try." Although the man was all straight lines and angles, his expression held soft humor.

"I'm having some trouble locating some fossils on my list." I handed it to him. "I circled the catalogue numbers of the ones I couldn't find."

All at once his edges and angles sharpened. "Ah yes, I see. How's everything going at the dig?"

He should know. Paul told him I was coming, he must have told him why as well. A zing of warning spiked up my spine. It was the same feeling I got whenever a horse I was riding telegraphed his tension when sensing a possible threat. Instinct kicked in; minimize my reaction, and divert attention. "He hasn't said much. So, the fossils I couldn't find -- I was wondering if someone might have checked them out."

Affable once again, his warm brown eyes regarded me with amusement over the top of his glasses. "No, all specimens remain in the archives. Although it's possible someone might have put them back on the wrong shelf. That happens sometimes." He perused the list, his eyebrows making journeys up and down his forehead as he read. "Well, let's go see what we can find."

He preceded me down the hallway at a brisk pace, my list fluttering in his grasp. I sprinted, catching the storage room door just before it closed behind him, slipping once again into the chilly, dry-earth-scented repository.

Dr. Fogel had already reached the first fossil location and was scanning the shelf above and below its assigned spot when I caught up. He made an about-face and examined the shelves on the opposite side of the aisle, just as I had done. He harrumphed, consulted the list, and hustled to another aisle. This he did twice more with the remaining specimens while I followed anxiously waiting for an exclamation of success that never came. With a shake of his head, he headed to the computer, pulled up a search screen, and typed in the catalogue numbers, his large hands moving with surprising dexterity over the keyboard. Then he repeated the search using the Latin name of each specimen, and again with other search criteria. With each effort his frown grew more pronounced, and the furrow between his eyebrows deeper. He consulted my list again, then headed for the stacks. Again. I listened to his rummaging as he moved from one area to another, checking areas of the storage room I hadn't. My worry grew right along with my irritation at being left uninformed. After several long minutes he returned.

"Let me check something else."

I chewed my lip and traipsed after him to the computer. He clicked on a couple of links, and stared at the screen, one hand resting on his hip and the other covering his mouth and chin. The blue and white screen cast an eerie reflection on the lenses of his glasses, making him appear eyeless.

"At least I can get the rest off to Paul." I tried to sound unworried.

"What? Oh, right, yes. Good idea." He lightly tapped his jaw.

"Maybe the photographs I have already will be enough."

He nodded as though he were responding to the sound of my voice rather than the words, then shut down the computer and walked away. He stopped and turned, his index finger touching his lips before pointing at me. "Perhaps the specimens you found will be sufficient."

"Thank you for your help," I said to his now-retreating back.

I combed my fingers through my hair and massaged the back of my neck, rolling my head. There was nothing to do but go home with what I had. The idea didn't make me happy. I should be able to do better than this. Giving up never sat well with me, whether riding my horse, working on my clients' books, or anything else. Paul was fast becoming the most important person in my life, yet I had to give up on something that was important to him. But, dammit, what else was I supposed to do?

I packed my camera and supplies in my bag and left. I'd found and photographed eleven of the items on Paul's list. I paced, distracted, down the now-familiar, long hallway flogging my memory for some clue, some approach I'd missed that would help me get the remaining four fossils.

Paul was efficient. Every photograph would have a specific purpose for his lecture, and he was missing better than a quarter of them. If I'd planned the presentation my list would ... include back-ups -- duplicates, or near duplicates, just in case there were problems.

I stopped. Why hadn't I thought of that earlier? That was it!

Had he thought of that -- to include back-ups?

My excitement sputtered. How was I going to find out? Why hadn't I asked Dr. Fogel before he left? The dragon was probably back at her desk. Now I'd have to ask her where I could find him. Damn.

I hiked my bag more securely on my shoulder. Okay, then. I'd faced her once. I could face her again. As I rounded a turn in the corridor Dr. Fogel's voice echoed softly ahead, coming toward me but still some ways away. Hope I could avoid Mrs. Peabody again quickened the pat-pat of my sneakered feet until Scott's angry, strident pitch cut off Andrew Fogel's quiet tone, halting my rush.

"If you don't do something I'll --"

"You'll do nothing. I'm certain he already suspects me. If you're found out it will --"

"I won't jeopardize our plan." Scott's tone was a sneer. "But I'm telling you we have to do something about her."

Her? Her who? Her me? What had I done? Crap. Their voices were getting closer.

There was nowhere to hide.

AN ERROR IN JUDGMENT

THE THIRD THEA CAMPBELL MYSTERY

Chapter One

Guilt tapped me on the shoulder for the hundredth time since my morning coffee --although plaguing me for another, more immediate, reason. Paul, my boyfriend of six months, stood directly in front of me, hand on his hip, tux jacket pushed back, and eyes narrowed to the point of hiding their luminous blue.

"Is there something you'd like to tell me? Something in particular you've been sitting on since, I don't know, all day?"

I shifted on my three-inch stilettos, clamped down on my lower lip, then turned it loose. I'd only chew off my lipstick. "It's Andrea, and ..." I trailed off. The excuse of our families and friends waiting for us to join them in one of the several huge banquet halls on the second level of the Seattle Convention Center seemed ... lame. Sure, the annual awards dinner for the Puget Sound Dressage Society would be starting soon. Because of my foot-dragging we were tardy. Now, because of Paul's insistence we talk, we'd be later still. The problem essentially came back to Andrea. I scanned the elegantly dressed people streaming past us in the massive glass, brass and granite foyer.

"Thea ..."

I returned my gaze to him and he circled my shoulders with an arm. At first I thought he intended to hug me. Instead, he gently steered me across the flow of pedestrian traffic to the protection of one of the numerous shoulder-high stone planters. Packed with large ferns and other greenery, they softened the cold, hard lines and gave the Convention Center's gleaming interior a Pacific Northwest feel. The main advantage -- and obviously Paul's intent -- was that the planter kept people from bumping into us. However, it did nothing to block the cold October breeze gusting in each time a door opened and raising goose bumps under the lightweight fabric of my long gown and tiny jacket. I should have worn a coat. What was I thinking? At least Paul's arm was warm.

"'It's Andrea and' what?" he asked, turning me loose and facing me. I shivered with the returning chill.

"And ... and we're going to be late, because I couldn't find my evening bag, ran over to Aunt Vi's to borrow one, messed up my hair and had to redo it, ripped a perfectly good pair of panty hose getting into this dress and had to go out again to buy more."

"That's all?"

"What? That's not enough?"

"So you're telling me all this stress has been about seeing Andrea?"

I swallowed and darted another look at the crowd. Not everyone was headed to our banquet, unless we had a bridal party joining us. I returned my attention to Paul. "Yes."

He closed his eyes briefly and ran a hand over his mouth before doing that hand-on-hip thing again. "Sweetheart, I told you it's not your fault. She's thirty years old, not --"

"*Almost* thirty."

"*Almost* thirty, not thirteen. Neglecting to sit up all night with her, eating gallons of chocolate ice cream and watching *Beaches* over and over when she broke up with

Jonathan did *not* drive her into the arms of this Svengali you keep talking about, much less affect her decision to marry him."

I snarled a look at him.

He held up both hands. "I'm using hyperbole to make a point."

"You're missing the point entirely. She needed me last summer. Paul, we've been over and over this. I want to see her, talk to her, but not with her husband around."

This time his hand went on my shoulder, and he caressed my neck with his thumb. I melted into his touch.

"You're missing the point," he continued softly. "You can't take care of everyone all the time. Don't worry. You two will have some time to catch up."

He was so sweet, and so wrong. "You don't know him. He -- "

A silver evening purse smacked Paul's arm, sending a shock wave through me and focusing every atom of my attention on the bag and the red-nailed feminine hand. And just as fast, suspicion leapt forward. The offending accessory looked exactly like the one I owned, down to the little jeweled loops where the strap should have been. Dammit, it *was* my purse.

And here it was in my younger sister Juliet's manicured, pilfering hand. I turned a tight-lipped glare on her.

She countered with an exaggerated huff that strained her blazing red, sequined gown. "Jeez, you guys, can't you save it 'til you're home?"

"That's my purse," I snapped. "I tore the house apart looking for it this afternoon. Thank God, Aunt Vi had one I could use."

Juliet poked a finger at me. "Do you have any idea how long I've been looking all over this freakin' place for you? I can't believe you're making out in the freakin' plants."

"We're not making out." To her, everything was about

sex.

Paul straightened and crossed his arms. Only his tight stare shifted toward her.

"You were going to," my sister said. "And you're hiding. Your dress almost blends right in."

I had an overwhelming urge to bean her. "We were having a private discussion, not seizing an opportunity."

She tapped my silver purse against her thigh. "Whatever. I'm not going anywhere without you two. Everyone else is at our table already. Your 'discussion' needs to wait. Let's go. Now. I don't want to miss dinner."

My original tension barged to the head of the line. I chewed my lip, remembered the lipstick and quit. It occurred to me that I stood a better chance of talking to Andrea alone after dinner and the awards than beforehand. Therefore, arriving late for dinner had merit. We'd be in time for Uncle Henry's speech and the awards. A number of my equestrian friends would be collecting ribbons and trophies for the scores they'd earned during this year's horse show season. I'd be there to applaud their accomplishments as well as my uncle, who'd already achieved, several times over, what many of them dreamed of: Olympic medals and international acclaim as a trainer.

Juliet put both hands around Paul's bicep and pulled. Nothing happened. "I mean it. I'm taking you with me." She tugged again with the same result, gave up and reached for me.

"We'll catch up," Paul growled.

Juliet waved my purse in the air. "And I flippin' *give* up." She strode toward the escalator leading to the second-floor ballroom, the hem of her clingy dress whipping left then right with each purposeful stride.

Unfortunately, this time guilt didn't tap my shoulder so much as sock me in the arm. I was wimping out. Paul understood how I felt -- well enough, anyway. And there were so many people at the banquet that it wouldn't be difficult to avoid Andrea until the right opportunity presented itself.

"We might as well go. We'll talk later. I promise." I reached up and ran an admiring fingertip down Paul's lapel. Just by putting on a tux he'd transformed into a dark-haired James Bond. Sure made it a lot easier to find my smile.

He cupped my face in a strong hand. "If you're sure."

"I'm sure."

Totally sure. All I needed was for Juliet to go back and report that we were here, but having a private talk. Then everyone would want to know what it was about, and if I didn't tell them they'd make something up. It wasn't like they didn't already know I was worried about Andrea, but Paul was the only one who knew how responsible I felt for her poor marriage decision. I didn't want them making my issues this evening's focus. I brightened my smile to reassure my lover.

The moment our eyes connected a familiar tug redirected my awareness. With a slow half-blink he bent toward me, delivering a soft kiss that lasted long enough to make my heart thump. As he drew back, my eyes fluttered and my gaze went to his mouth. I stood on my toes to claim another kiss -- just a thank-you kiss. Really. Maybe with a little body contact or a sly opportunity to run my fingers through his hair ....

"Stop that. You're going to get lipstick all over his face."

My sister had returned.

Progress into the ballroom was the usual stop and go of greeting friends and making introductions. People who usually dressed in breeches, serviceable jackets and dusty boots were almost unrecognizable in formal wear, including me. Double-takes prompted laughter and good-natured teasing. The banquet hall without decoration was impressive with its elegance, but our decorating committee had outdone themselves. Huge, banner-sized photographs of famous and not-so-famous horses and riders hung suspended from the ceiling, providing dramatic focal points throughout the room.

Tables with huge sprays of fresh flowers radiated out from a dance floor near the stage, already set up for the band that would be playing later. Around the perimeter of the room were tables displaying the door prizes donated by local tack shops and other businesses. Animated, mirthful conversation brought it all alive.

And I was doing a darned good job of acting like I wanted to be here.

We were a scant few minutes into our arrival tour when I halted. As if compelled by some unheard command, I scanned the crowd.

Andrea.

Every drop of the day's anxiety, every crumb of trepidation, descended into my stomach as an indigestible ball. Halfway across the room, she stood slightly behind her husband, intent on studying the floor. She hadn't seen me, I was sure. Other sensory input faded into the background like a classic Hollywood movie, and I studied her face, the slack expression, the pallor ...

My heart twisted. Something was wrong. More wrong than I'd thought.

For years -- since elementary school -- she and I had been best friends. Events this last summer had torn an almost insurmountable rift in our relationship. When I thought we were back on common ground, she'd disappeared from my life and not responded to any attempts I'd made to get in touch. At first, I assumed she was busy. After all, she was an attorney with a big Bellevue-area firm. I was busy, too, but not specifically with my accounting business.

The murder of one of Paul's colleagues, the theft of valuable fossils and the ensuing investigation had landed both Paul and me in the hospital on separate occasions -- and delivered emotional and relationship wounds we had to work at to mend. Even as life returned to the mundane, we were at the beck and continual call of the police. The cumulative stress was more than I was used to, and I freely admit to being self-involved.

In hindsight, too self-involved.

Rumors of Andrea's marriage in September broke my heart. It hurt to hear the information fourth-hand, but worse was learning who she'd married: Sig Paalmann, an exceedingly wealthy horseman. I knew him by his reputation as a dressage judge harshly critical of those who struggled with the sport. There were two habits of his that created the lion's share of responsibility for this reputation. The first was the demoralizing verbal commentary Sig fired at many a hapless competitor at the conclusion of their test, and the second was his custom to write additional, more callous edicts on the test sheet itself. Trainers and coaches carried packs of Kleenex to hand out to their unfortunate students who couldn't escape the arena soon enough at the conclusion of their ride, or who foolishly insisted on reading the scored test sheet at the end of the show.

Unfortunately, Sig's presence at the awards dinner was a given. Every local judge had been invited to this premier equestrian gala.

Andrea, of course, was with him.

I had to talk to her, no matter how painful. If I could find the courage. If I could get her alone.

After dinner was my best chance.

Pre-meal socializing was not going to work in my favor, if one could call the tense scene before me "socializing."

Lips drawn tight against his teeth, Paalmann spoke in a rapid burst to my great uncle, Henry Fairchild. In his mid-sixties, close to Sig's age, Uncle Henry had an unfailingly kind character that couldn't be more different from Sig's. But now, even from a distance, the flash of anger in my uncle's eyes was impossible to miss. Sig, punctuating his words with small chops of his hand, either didn't see or didn't care. He was engrossed in vehemently expressing an opinion my uncle found distasteful.

I doubted my uncle had said anything to provoke him.

I'd heard from show organizers and volunteers like my aunt that even when in a cooperative mood, Sig was unpleasant. The world revolved around his desires.

He'd obviously desired Andrea. Who could blame him? She was elegant, intelligent and generous. What had my friend seen in this sarcastic, egotistical bastard twice her age?

My sister prodded me with my purse, jerking my attention back to immediate company. "Andrea's put on weight since last time I saw her."

"She looks beautiful. Don't be so critical." But Juliet had a point. Although far from unattractive, Andrea wasn't her usual stylish self. Maybe the shapeless gray dress was to blame.

More likely it was her listless expression.

A horrible possibility crept into my mind. What if Sig had forbidden Andrea to contact any of her old friends ... like me?

An elbow gouged my ribcage. "Hey," Juliet snapped. "I said I'm not being critical. Besides, I hear everybody puts on weight after they get married." Juliet looked down, flicking a slender hand over the red-sequined curves every male had ogled on our way in. "Man, I hope it doesn't happen to me." She flashed Paul a wicked smile and reached across me to pat his stomach. "Aren't you kind of jumping the gun?"

Paul started, then stood up a little straighter. "I need to start running again," he muttered.

But he'd noticed Andrea, too, and I knew he was thinking. If he hadn't been, Juliet wouldn't have surprised him. This "thinking" of his concerned me. He'd chided me more than once for leaping to conclusions -- which I wasn't. He was wrong. And as surely as I knew how each and every Sunday would begin and end, I knew exactly what he was doing at this moment. He was sizing up an opportunity to prove to me that Andrea would be delighted to see me. My gut told me I needed to approach Andrea privately. Paul needed to be distracted.

I pressed against him, as close to face to face as I could manage while still holding his arm, and gazed up at him with as much ardor as I could self-consciously pull off in a crowd. Heat crept up my neck and scalded my cheeks.

"You look perfect," I purred, ignoring my embarrassment and praying I was subtle.

A corner of his mouth turned up. Tapping into his libido was a sure thing. Worked every time. I brushed against him and felt his long, slow intake of breath. His arm tightened, pressing my hand into his side.

"Gagging here, you two," Juliet groaned. So much for subtle.

"Let's go say hello to Andrea," he said, and took a step in her direction, spinning me on my too-high heel.

My heart slammed into my ribs while my "sure thing" dragged me toward the exact situation I wanted to avoid. Damn, damn, damn. What was wrong with him? Couldn't he take a hint? I hauled at his arm.

"No. I'll say 'hi' later." I said. "We should look for our table and Aunt Vi."

Paul urged me along. "Come on. They haven't even started serving the salad yet. She'll be happy to see you, and I know you want to talk to her."

"I do -- did -- do want to talk to her. But not right now. Later. When she's not with her husband."

"Why?" Juliet asked.

Great. I'd forgotten she was still with us. The short answer might save me from looking any more foolish. "Because he's a jerk."

"I thought he was a dressage judge. He's not nice?" Juliet said.

Paul's mouth twitched, but a small snort escaped anyway. However, the fear that Sig might be deliberately keeping Andrea from me scared off any levity I might have felt.

"'Nice' is not a prerequisite for a dressage judge," I said.

"Well, no duh." Juliet crossed her eyes, implying I'd been the one with the dumb remark. "Isn't he a friend of Uncle Henry's?"

"Passing acquaintance."

"Well, you must be wrong, Miss Know-It-All. Uncle Henry saves his stern lectures for friends and family, so the old guy next to Andrea who looks like he has a stick up his --"

"Juliet! And no, I'm not wrong. That's him, Sig Paalmann."

Paul tipped his head in interest, then looked again toward Andrea.

Juliet's brow furrowed. "He has to be as old as Uncle Henry. And the conversation seems pretty intense for a couple of guys who barely know each other."

"Oh, they know each other. They're just not friends. Uncle Henry has no patience for someone as deliberately nasty as Sig." At that exact moment my uncle shook his head once and walked away from Sig and Andrea. Not surprised, I continued. "And yes, Sig has to be around sixty."

She shivered. "Eww. Andrea's what -- thirty?"

"Next month."

"Sorry, but even if he was worth bazillions, it just doesn't make up for the ick factor."

"He is, in fact, worth bazillions," I said.

"Whoa. No shit. Well, I'd never let the flash of cash blind me, but looks like your BFF has." She wiggled her fingers, palm up.

I scowled at Juliet's insult. Could my friend really have changed that much? The Andrea I'd known since grade school wasn't a money-grubber. She regularly worked more *pro bono* cases than anyone else in her firm, and championed the Great American Small, Struggling Business. Unfortunately, her track record with men hit the "also ran" lists -- due to her tendency to get doe-eyed over a handsome face and ignore the warning signs of a man-looking-for-a-sugar-mama. She had made consistently bad choices and ended up getting used. Sig, while distinguished, was not her usual well-built, testosterone-dripping, needy fare. To the best of my knowledge he did not require any rescuing and was, by reputation, an emotional deep freeze.

My heart lurched. Had she thought she was breaking her old pattern with him, only to overlook warning signs more dire? A cold certainty made me shiver. Andrea's cocoon of silence since her hasty September wedding had not been of her own making.

Juliet narrowed her eyes as she continued to study my friend and her husband. "Sig Paalmann ...." She tapped a long red fingernail on her chin. "Isn't he Paal Toys?"

I nodded. "Makes those cute dolls. You know the ones."

"Apple Cheek Babies? Wow. Who'd have thought the guy who makes the doll on 'every little girl's Christmas list,'" she had deepened her voice to a good approximation of the TV announcer's, "would look so opposite of Santa Claus? Well, except for the gray hair."

Paul tipped his head again, first at Juliet, then me. "Wait a minute. Did you say Sig *Paalmann*?" He pronounced his last name differently than Juliet and I. "That's who Andrea married? *The* Sig Paalmann?"

I eyed him. "I suppose so. How many of them could there be?"

"He's got one of the most extensive private collections of dinosaur fossils in the world -- that's public knowledge, anyway. Not that any of my colleagues have had any more opportunity to view them than I have."

Juliet rocked her head side to side. The conversation had veered to the uninteresting -- for her. If there wasn't loud music and louder laughter, she'd find something else to do. However, the increased animation in Paul's voice alarmed me. I had to keep him talking or this time he'd succeed in dragging me to them.

"I know he owns an impressive art collection and antique cars, but I'd never heard about the fossils."

"The rumor is he limits access. To a paranoid degree. Most paleontologists would give their left -- um, would really like to be invited to inspect the collection."

"Including you?"

"Yeah. But I draw the line at giving over body parts I use." He grinned. "So, let's go say hi. I'll lay you odds he'll be so busy bragging to me about how much he knows about my area of expertise that you and Andrea can do some catching up."

Damn. No way was this going to work out well. "No, really. I don't think ...."

"Come on." He patted my hand, which was still clutching his arm.

I'd encountered that man-on-a-mission spark in his eye before. Short of throwing myself on the ground and shrieking, my chances of turning him aside were zero. I'd have to ditch Plan A and go with Plan B -- whatever that was.

"Have at it, you guys," Juliet said, peering through the crowd in another direction. "I'd love to tag along and find out what Andrea sees in the old fart, but I need to protect my sweetie from all the dressage queens. They lust after that god-of-a-man. Can't say I blame them. Eric dressed up is almost as delicious as Eric naked." Her voice dropped to a sultry timbre with the last sentence, and she flapped her lashes at Paul.

He reared back.

Her mouth curved, cat-like. "I must go remind them all they don't stand a chance. You know how I hate waving this ring, and other things, under people's noses." She held her hand out, examined the modest diamond, and gave it a quick polish on her sleeve. "Sometimes one must sacrifice." She flitted off, left hand pressed delicately to her bosom.

"I could have lived my life happily never hearing any of that," Paul said, grimace still in place.

I'd wanted to chuckle, but my throat constricted the moment Paul moved off in Andrea's direction. I hoped she, in realizing the attraction of the fossil collection for Paul, would introduce him as Dr. Hudson, professor of paleontology at the University of Washington. Then, while the men talked shop, the two of us would shift around making inane, self-conscious chit-chat and I'd figure out how to arrange to meet with her later.

Perhaps Sig would show a kind side. Perhaps Andrea would be glad to see me. Perhaps she'd understand I was still her friend, if I could untie my tongue enough to explain how the murder investigation and nearly losing Paul was a wound too private to share at the time, even with her.

And perhaps Paul would luck out and Sig would invite us to view the famous private collection.

Then again, sometimes you never get a chance to find out.

FROM THE PUBLISHER

All Thea Campbell Mysteries are available in both e-book and print formats. Check with your favorite retailer. Remember, if you don't see what you want, ask!

About the Author

Susan Schreyer lives in the great state of Washington with her husband, two children, a couple of playful kittens and the ghosts of other, much-loved, pets. The horse lives within easy driving distance. When not writing stories about people in the next town being murdered, articles for worthy publications, or blogging, Susan trains horses and teaches people how to ride them. She is a member of the Guppies Chapter of Sisters in Crime and is co-president of the Puget Sound Chapter of SinC. <u>Death By A Dark Horse</u> is her debut mystery.

Susan would love to hear from you. She can be contacted through her website:

http://www.susanschreyer.com

Or either of her blogs:

Writing Horses
http://writinghorses.blogspot.com

Things I Learned From My Horse
http://thingsilearnedfrommyhorse.blogspot.com

25092141R00180

Made in the USA
Charleston, SC
18 December 2013